P9-CEM-996

MATTERS OF THE BLOOD

"Dark, seductive, and bitingly humorous. . . ."

—Heartstring

"Fast paced, take-no-prisoners action . . . grabs you by the throat from the go and doesn't release its grip until you're done."

—Preternatural Reviews (4 stars)

"An absolutely spectacular addition to the paranormal landscape. . . . A classy, teasing tale riddled with intrigue and paranormal bliss."

—BookFetish

"A complex plot with the requisite twists and turns of a mystery, the passion of a paranormal romance, and the unearthly elements of urban fantasy."

—SF Site

"A brilliant tale of supernatural power, revenge, and the excitement of newfound love."

—Darque Reviews

"Refreshing. . . . I loved the story's vividly drawn rural-Texas setting."

—FantasyLiterature (4 stars)

"A superb paranormal whodunit with a touch of romance and with plenty of interwoven subplots . . . but the center holding this superb tale together is the likable Keira, who makes the abnormal seem so normal."

—Alternative Worlds

Blood Sacrifice and all of the Blood Lines series
are also available as eBooks

Don't miss the four previous adventures in the Blood Lines series by Maria Lima!

"Another top-notch paranormal thriller. . . . A complex plot, superb world building, and phenomenal characters spin *Blood Kin* into a dark and sexy urban fantasy. Maria Lima is a great addition to the paranormal genre."

—Romance Junkies

BLOOD BARGAIN

"Maria Lima captures the essence of urban fantasy, mystery, and romantic elements in *Blood Bargain*."

—SF Site

"A real pager-turner. . . . Ms. Lima has created a wonderful blend of paranormal, mystery, and romance. She has a real knack for building characters you get to know and care about, and the setting she paints seems so real. She is also darn good at building suspense and keeping you guessing."

—Bitten By Books (5 stars)

"Urban fantasy fans are going to love this—especially the Kelly clan, an extended family of supernaturals living within human society. . . . A strong tale that fans of Kelly Armstrong and Kim Harrison will want to read."

—Worlds of Wonder

"I couldn't put it down. Maria Lima's second Blood Lines novel is even better than the first, a fun and sometimes poignant paranormal treat."

—Fantasy Literature

"Grabs you from the start and keeps you turning pages until you solve the mystery. . . . I certainly will be watching for more books by Maria Lima."

—Fresh Fiction

"Ms. Lima spins a suspenseful tale and packs it with paranormal elements that will hold the reader's attention to the end . . . fast-moving."

—Darque Reviews

BLOOD
SACRIFICE

BOOK FIVE OF THE BLOOD LINES SERIES

MARIA LIMA

POCKET BOOKS
New York London Toronto Sydney

Pocket Books
A Division of Simon & Schuster, Inc.
1230 Avenue of the Americas
New York, NY 10020

This book is a work of fiction. Names, characters, places, and incidents either are products of the author's imagination or are used fictitiously. Any resemblance to actual events or locales or persons, living or dead, is entirely coincidental.

Copyright © 2011 by Maria Lima

All rights reserved, including the right to reproduce this book or portions thereof in any form whatsoever. For information address Pocket Books Subsidiary Rights Department, 1230 Avenue of the Americas, New York, NY 10020

First Juno Books/Pocket Books paperback edition September 2011

JUNO BOOKS and colophon are trademarks of Wildside Press LLC used under license by Simon & Schuster, Inc., the publisher of this work.

POCKET and colophon are registered trademarks of Simon & Schuster, Inc.

For information about special discounts for bulk purchases, please contact Simon & Schuster Special Sales at 1-866-506-1949 or business@simonandschuster.com.

The Simon & Schuster Speakers Bureau can bring authors to your live event. For more information or to book an event contact the Simon & Schuster Speakers Bureau at 1-866-248-3049 or visit our website at www.simonspeakers.com.

Cover design by Laywan Kwan
Front cover photo by shutterstock

Manufactured in the United States of America

10 9 8 7 6 5 4 3 2 1

ISBN 978-1-4516-1269-1
ISBN 978-1-4516-1271-4 (ebook)

For Queue
You help keep me sane.
A fo ysgawn galon, ef a gân.
The lighthearted will sing.

ACKNOWLEDGMENTS

To Tanya Kennedy-Luminati, for her l33t and mad beta skilz. You are awesome, chica!

To Janna Marks, whose patience is legendary as I prattled on and on about writing and plotting and just stuff.

To David & Keith of Literature & Latte, because getting Scrivener 2.0 out made the final bits of the writing MUCH easier.

To my mother, Yolanda Bodine, for encouragement, faith, and help in Spanish translations.

And of course, to all my readers, without whom these stories would just be living in my head. . . .

Thank you
Muchisimas gracias
Mille mercis
Diolch yn fawr

We cross our bridges when we come to them and burn them behind us, with nothing to show for our progress except a memory of the smell of smoke, and a presumption that once our eyes watered.

—Tom Stoppard

CHAPTER ONE

"How you expect to run with the wolves come night when you spend all day sparring with the puppies?"
—*Omar Little,* The Wire

For a breath, for a moment suspended in disbelief of what I faced, I seriously and without a doubt, considered matricide. Homicide of all sorts, really, except for the premeditated kind, raced through my stunned brain.

I don't do guns, but right now, what I wouldn't give to have a Kalashnikov rifle or, at the very least, a couple of Browning 9mm semi-autos just to see how fast I could re-create the final scene from that episode of that old TV series *Dynasty*. This wasn't a wedding, but it was damned well close enough—a blood-bonding: Adam and me; my brothers with Liz; Tucker and Niko; all of the aforementioned to Adam and me as our Protectors. Not exactly a typical Alamo Heights wedding party; in my world, it was practically the same thing. We'd received our guests, one at a time, representatives from all over the Southwest—wer and sprite, brownie, hamadryads, every manner of fey and Other acknowledging our leadership, pledging their fealty in return for our support. Only there was a Balrog in this woodpile. My former lover, my cousin, Adam's half-brother, Gideon, arrived, representing the Unseelie Court, with a pregnant wife in tow; herself heir to the High Queen Angharad, the Seelie Queen. It didn't take the formal declaration of Challenge to see how things stood. Gideon, also heir to the Kelly clan, as was I, was throwing down. I guess he didn't much care for having his status as heir ignored by our matriarch.

My muscles tensed, hands immediately forming fists, ready to throw down, to toss fire, fury and lightning. I was *very* good at the lightning—and mage fire, the kind that burns forever until its fuel is no more than ash. My great-great-granny and her minions had taught me well.

A cool palm against my forearm slowed me down. I didn't have to look to know it was Adam—his saner head prevailing.

"What does this mean?" He wasn't addressing me. I knew that. I settled a bit, my ruffled feathers smoothing as I listened to his voice—deceptively calm and quiet. Underneath, his true anger seethed.

He'd gone allover vampire, outward expression blank as a bare concrete wall and as emotional as a porcelain doll—and just about that creepy. Didn't bother me though. I'd seen it, was used to it. The fact that he'd stopped me irked a bit. Though, in reality, I knew I couldn't actually let loose. We had a reception hall full of people who'd just sworn oaths to me, as Kelly clan heir and to Adam as my Consort and ruler in his own right as vampire king and heir to the High King of the Unseelie Court. Shit. Almost incestuous if you looked at the myriad ways we were all connected. Those connections were exactly what my scheming clan chieftain had intended. Minerva freaking Kelly, great-great-grandmother and matriarch of the Kelly clan and my mentor.

On the other side of the family equation: my mother, Branwen ferch Arianrhod, whom I damned to whatever levels of hell I could imagine. She was the one who'd triggered this beauty of a dilemma by handing me a rolled up parchment. Innocuous in itself, but chock-full-o'nuts—if nuts were a traditional Sidhe Challenge. Exactly what it entailed, I still didn't know, but it couldn't be good. They never were. At my mother's side, Gideon, once a person I'd loved, until he'd shown me his darker nature—and no doubt the actual instigator of said Challenge. Adam's father, Drystan ap Tallwch, High King of the Unseelie Court, also father to Gideon—unknown quantity. Did he side with his younger son or his heir? Gideon's new wife, the very pregnant Aoife ferch Angharad, daughter and heir to Angharad, High Queen of the Seelie Court—safe to bet she'd support her husband. A smattering of courtiers, most of them nameless, but all from my mother's court. People I vaguely recognized.

All about us stood our guests, assorted fey from all over the Southwest: ariels and hellhounds, werewolves and sprites. Even Old Joe, a changeling I'd run across recently who'd been returned to his fey family. Most of them just watched us, a few smug expressions acknowledging the absolute deliciousness of this standoff. Others mingled around the ales, wines, and other spirits freely given and shared. Fucking politics. A pox on all our bloody houses for this . . . this whatever this was.

I remained silent, staring. Adam removed his hand from my arm as I relaxed a bit. None of us spoke. None of us moved. Niko and Tucker's tension felt like high-tension wires strumming a song of violence, just waiting to be released.

My mother took a step back, her outstretched hand wavered a smidge as she realized I wasn't planning to take the parchment from her hand.

I smirked as I did a quick mental calculation. Three of them against whom? All of us? But wait, perhaps others would side with them. Would Drystan side with Gideon? With Adam? Would he remain neutral?

"Father?" Adam seemed to read my mind as he prompted Drystan in the continued silence of my mother's renewed haughty glare. Part of me was a little relieved to see it, to see what I'd so long recalled. I'd hated her my entire life, then visions I'd had this past spring seemed to indicate that perhaps she hadn't been as evil or uncaring as I'd remembered. Was she who I thought she was? Who I'd remembered? Or was she truly sorry to have given me up?

Tonight's actions so far seemed to indicate my long-held perception had been correct. She'd walked into our Reception alongside Gideon and claimed Challenge on behalf of my former lover and Adam's half-brother. By doing so, she'd declared for him, had picked sides. Was this truly her stand or something required of her by her queen and cousin, ruler of the Seelie Sidhe court and the very person who'd sentenced me to a life Above—away from half of my heritage?

Drystan, tall, dark, and just as handsome as both his sons, stepped forward, pushing past my mother with a grimace on his face. "I knew nothing of this, my son." He bowed, low to the ground, a gesture from one subservient to his superior. I nearly laughed aloud—not in joy but at the absurdity of his charade. Bows and scrapes galore like dogs baring their bellies to the acknowledged alpha? No, not so much. In this subset of the crowd, we were *all* Alphas—all rulers of some sort or another, or the designated Protectors of such. Oh wait, except for Gideon, who was only related by blood to us all. Okay, wow. Not even *Dynasty* got this twisted, did it? This was more Jerry Springer material.

"No, he most certainly did not." Gideon, still pompous, crossed his arms, a petulant pout on his face. "I don't need our father, *Brother*," he sneered at Adam. "Nor do I need the Unseelie Court. My wife and our child—"

"*Your* child?" Drystan straightened out of his bow, his posture stiff. "She's near eight months gone with child, Gideon. You've been Changed a scant four of those months. You expect us to accept—"

"Accept what you will." My mother broke her own silence. "My cousin, the Queen acknowledges this child as his father's blood and her daughter's husband's seed."

"This kid is going to be her *heir*?" I made an attempt to step forward, once again stopped by a slight pressure from Adam's hand, which had returned to my arm. "Lady, you've let your mother pass you over?" I directly addressed the beautiful woman who stood silent next to Gideon. In principle, a protocol faux pas as we'd not yet exchanged formal greeting, but whatever. My Kelly cranky trumped Sidhe politicking any day.

"Accepted? I requested it," Aoife said, her voice bored as her expression denoted. "I wish no part of Sidhe politics."

"And how's that working out for you?" I muttered under my breath. My brother Tucker chuckled, his hearing too good not to catch my not-so-quiet asides. "You really think you can avoid it?" I rephrased my question and spoke louder. "Gideon as your husband, your child heir to the Seelie Sidhe throne? I've no doubt you're already hip deep in politics and intrigue."

Aoife raised a languid hand and made a slow waving motion, as if dismissing the very idea. "My husband may play Court to his heart's desire," she answered. "I shall retire with my ladies and spend my life away, secluded. I prefer a simpler life."

Away? What the hell? She came to *Texas* to get away from her *mother*? Seriously not what I'd expected her to say, but hey, I could relate. I began to ask about the Challenge, hoping for some explanation, but Adam preempted me.

"Then why challenge us, lady?" he asked gently. "A simple request would not have gone unheard."

Gideon took a step toward us. I did what I could to hang on to my raging emotions, trying not to give in to my instinctive urge to just beat the ever-living shit out of him. How *dare* he come here and do this? Simple jealousy? That didn't make any sense.

His words echoed my thoughts. "Brother, do you truly believe that if I'd come here with my bride, my child about to be born, that our cousin, our *lover* would have allowed you to grant us access to the caves? To our lands Below this ground?" With a sweep of a hand, he knelt, his posture formal. "I beg of you, allow us this Challenge, so this may be settled within our traditions."

I gritted my teeth against the outburst I felt trying to force its way from my lips. "Our lover," indeed. "Challenge is a long way from a simple request, *Cousin*," I said. "There are many territories within the Americas if you felt the need to be on this continent. Why this one?" *Why my turf?* is what I was truly asking. This just didn't make sense outside of some twisted need for Gideon to best me. I don't think he'd yet realized how little I cared what he did as long as he left me out of it.

"We wish to establish our base here," my mother said. "Because the door to Faery in this location has been closed too long. We shall reopen it, revitalize it. Make our way in the new world."

"The 'new world' isn't all that new anymore, Branwen," I said. "Modern humans populated this land centuries ago."

"A held breath and time for a few thoughts. Nothing more." My mother eyed me up and down. "You are still young, Keira, and despite your ties to the Kelly clan, you are still half Sidhe. Half Seelie. You belong with us as much as you belong with them."

"I belong wherever the bloody hell I wish to belong," I spat, trembling in my anger. "And that is as far from you and yours as I can physically go. You want this? Well, then—" I swallowed a yelp as Adam's grip tightened.

"We shall review your terms of Challenge and respond as per protocol," he said. "In the meantime, we declare Truce." He nodded and Niko stepped forward to take the parchment from my mother's hand.

Terms of Challenge? Shit. I had no idea what Adam meant. Frankly, I was totally bluffing all of this. I'd heard of Challenge, but only in a learning-about-history way, something vague and well in the past. Sidhe traditions weren't taught in much detail in Kelly-land, other than in passing and as something that happened to other people. Adam should know, though. He had

to. After all, he was the firstborn son and heir of the
king of the Unseelie Court. Despite Gideon's Change
and the revelation that he was Drystan's son by a Kelly
woman, just as I was Branwen's daughter sired by Huw
Kelly, Adam remained his father's heir, though a Sidhe-
turned-vampire prince was far beyond tradition.

Adam bowed to Gideon, a short obeisance, courtesy
only. "Truce, my brother?"

Gideon remained still, gaze fixed on us both, face
tight with some emotion or another. I used to could
to read him, but no longer. As I waited for his answer,
I suddenly remembered we had a room full of guests.
Guests that seemed weirdly silent. I glanced to my right.
Couples danced to music I couldn't hear, small groups
mingled, exchanging silent conversation. It was if I'd
pushed the mute button on a TV remote. Why weren't
we still surrounded by avid eavesdroppers anxious for
a breath of scandal that they'd then take back to their
own people? Rumor and gossip were like pure cold water in a Texas drought to most supernatural clans. We
all tended to live longer than most humans, leading to
ennui and the need for fresh information, new data. But
not a one of them appeared to even notice us. Even the
group that had been standing near us watching had dis-
persed.

"We accept Truce," Gideon finally said, returning
Adam's bow. Gideon's gesture was just short of rude, if
you cared about picking nits. I'd drilled for ages on the
variations on a Courtly bow—how to do it, how long,
and how deep were skills taught to every Kelly child,
practiced until we knew every iota of this unspoken vi-
sual language, every subtle cue. I'd never cared about
it, but I knew how to read bows. Gideon had stopped

short of a "fuck you." I bristled, about to respond, my surroundings once again forgotten.

"Until we meet again, brother." Gideon stepped back and took his bride's arm.

"Until Lughnasa," Adam countered with a nod of acknowledgment. Five weeks from now. The next holiday and, perhaps not coincidentally, my birthday. I'd turn thirty-eight that day, after one hell of a year. Guess after what we'd all been through the past eight or nine months, I should've expected that I couldn't start my rule peacefully.

If I had to guess from his smug expression, Gideon had *expected* Adam to ask for Truce—which I knew was a formal declaration that a Challenge get tabled until the next high holiday. Why? Was he not ready for this Challenge, either? Of course the answer to that depended on the actual words and rules set forth. Everything I knew about Sidhe formal Challenges could fit into less than half a thimble—confused tales mixed up with Disney and the Little Golden Books of my childhood.

Adam gestured outward. "Now that we've settled, please go eat, drink, be merry."

"For tomorrow, we fight," I muttered.

CHAPTER TWO

"Life's challenges are not supposed to paralyze you, they're supposed to help you discover who you are."
—*Bernice Johnson Reagon*

With an audible pop, the noise and chatter of the crowd intruded on our little bubble. I belatedly realized that we'd been inside some sort of privacy pocket. Had I unconsciously isolated us? Or was it someone else's doing?

Just before turning away to accompany Aoife, my mother nodded to me, a weird roll of her head seeming to indicate that she'd been the one to produce the silence bubble. I returned her nod with one of my own. A silent acknowledgment tinged with grudging thanks. I should've realized it myself. I was glad, though, that we hadn't aired our dirty political linen to those who'd sworn fealty to us. No need to undermine our position. Not that we had any intent to play rulers in the traditional sense. Neither Adam nor I had any taste whatsoever for that kind of life. We'd be there for them. We'd help when necessary, but for all intents and purposes, each clan could do its own thing. Only if they intruded on us would we intervene.

Adam squeezed my hand and led me away, motioning to Tucker and Niko to follow. Gideon and his cronies had melted into the crowd. I caught a glimpse of Old Joe, former trash man, who'd recently discovered his true heritage as a Changeling fey child thanks to me. Joe nodded and smiled at me, then turned back to his conversation with a cute dark-skinned woman dressed in moss greens and browns. A hamadryad, I thought. One of many representatives we'd met tonight. All of them ours, oathsworn and bonded. Our people. Sobering thought, that.

"So what are these Challenge rules?" Tucker piped up as soon as we'd maneuvered our way past the majority of the crowd and to the back of the room.

Niko handed the rolled parchment to him. "Would you care to do the honors, love?"

"Wait." The voice came from behind me.

I turned to see my mother approaching us. I gritted my teeth. Really? Did she have no couth at all? I hadn't exactly hidden my antagonism toward her. Surely she'd not forgotten that in the past five minutes—or thirty years.

"I just wished to . . ." She stopped at a safe distance— safe being well outside my physical reach. "Keira, you are my daughter. I never meant . . ."

"What? You never meant to ignore me? Toss me away like last week's inane diversion?" I closed my eyes for a moment, trying to rein in my temper. Count to ten, Keira, I reminded myself. No, count to a thousand and ten.

"Branwen." Adam gave her a short nod, ruler to lesser queen. "Was there something you needed?"

"No, Adam, wait." I placed my hand on his arm. "I want to speak with her."

"As you wish." He began to retreat, but I tightened my grip. "No. Stay." I took a deep breath. "Branwen, some months ago, before I Changed, I had a vision of a time when I was still Below, still with you. I was maybe just turned seven. You were arguing with Daffyd's father Geraint about letting me stay with you. You said I was worth something, to give me a chance. You fought for me then. Why this now?"

A slight start, then my mother's expression returned to stoic. "You know Daffyd?"

Did I know my Sidhe cousin? The cousin who'd been holed up in a pocket of Faery located on Wild Moon property for decades, watching me? Did she not know we'd not only met but traveled together? He'd accompanied us to Vancouver, where I'd flown in great haste after hearing that Gideon was dying. Part of me wished he'd done so. Instead, we'd learned that Gideon had also Changed and that he was Adam's half-brother. Afterward, Daffyd had returned to Faery using the faery door at Victory Square. Or so he'd said he would. He was part of my mother's Court, supposedly. His father definitely kowtowed to Branwen. Had Daffyd not returned to the Sidhe?

"You could say that," I answered my mother's surprised question, trying to be cautious. Did she not know anything that had transpired? What had Gideon told her—or conned her into most likely?

"Very well. I would speak privately." My mother motioned to a corridor that led back from the main reception hall. "Is there a room there we could use?"

"No. Speak here and now. This is my family, my blood. We have no secrets." I crossed my arms over my chest. The formal reception hall had once been a house, renovated inside and out, and decorated by my great-great-granny as part of her contribution to my new status. Most of the inside walls of the one-storied building had been removed to create one large room, but there were still a couple of small rooms in the back that had been set up as private parlors. The entire basement of the house was my very well-appointed physical and magickal training facility. There was no way I wanted Branwen in anything resembling family areas.

"None?" She looked me over with cool appraisal, then did the same to Adam, to Tucker, to Niko. A faint sneer appeared and swiftly vanished as she regained control. "I say there are many secrets within this family of yours. Secrets about your heritage—"

"About Gi— Minerva's genetics experiments? None of that's a secret. We know."

"You know that your leader's motive was to bring all the clans, tribes, fair folk under Kelly rule?"

I considered Gigi's past actions. Manipulating genetics by "encouraging" pairings to try for multiple Kelly heirs? Summit type meetings with leaders of the supernatural world? Well, yes, of course she was trying to unite the tribes. Frankly, we *had* to unite, to work together. I had no doubt that Gigi saw herself as a sort of committee chair or council leader, but planning to take over the world herself? What purpose would that serve? She was always ruthless and ambitious, but why the hell would she want to be the one queen of the known universe? Then again, why in all the hells would Gigi plan or do anything? I'd never expected her to have played god—effectively creating me, Gideon, my late cousin Marty, in some sort of twisted cross-breeding experiment, trying to force more than the usual single heir.

Heirs were special to our clan: instead of having one primary Talent at adulthood, we could use all the Kelly powers. As far as I knew, this was the first time in all known history that there were two of us.

"Maybe she is. Maybe she isn't," I said. "Regardless of Gigi's ambitions, this Challenge is still ridiculous."

A tinkle of a laugh. "How very charming that you still use a childhood name for your clan chieftain."

"Your point being?" I suppressed my instinctive eye roll. Childish, whatever. I hadn't been able to say "Minerva" when I was brought to her as a child, speaking only Welsh and scared out of my skinny self's wits. Rescued from Below, from the Welsh seat of Sidhe power and brought to my father's people, I'd glomped onto my brother Tucker and learned to call my great-great-grandmother "Gigi," for the two "greats." I'd only begun to refer to her by her official first name after my Change earlier this year.

"No point." My mother just smiled her enigmatic smile. Typical of the Seelie Sidhe, I thought. Say something to just say it, to perhaps dig to see if they were pushing a button or ten.

"Then answer my question. Why did you seem to want me, but then let me go?"

"I knew you had the potential for magicks, as do all of Kelly blood. When you did not demonstrate our own people's magick, then I knew there was only one solution."

"To treat me—"

"Do not impugn that which you know nothing of."

"Then enlighten us." Adam took my hand. "Enlighten us all. If you knew Keira was more Kelly than Sidhe, why did you not simply arrange for her to be raised with her father sooner?"

"It was not that simple." She sighed and brushed a hand over her face. An affectation? Perhaps. I'd not known Sidhe to allow themselves to seem tired or less than perfect, especially those of Seelie origin. "I waited until I knew that her Kelly strain was stronger than the Sidhe strain. I knew there was another, being raised Above, by his mother. Son of the Unseelie King. Geraint wanted to bring the boy to us, and I argued against it. If we brought the boy to us, we tempted the wrath of his father. Instead, we chose to have your father raise you. You, we could monitor Above. Geraint's son, Daffyd, volunteered to be your guardian. We'd hoped to pair you with your counterpart—"

"Gideon? You knew about him and were matchmaking?" I'd expected some sort of lame explanation but this took the cake. "You were the ones who set Daffyd on me? Did you close the door to Faery, too? Lock him in there?"

"A miscalculation."

"Some miscalculation," I growled. "This entire thing is ridiculous. All of you people plotting to match me up with Gideon for what? To control the supernatural world through us?" I threw up my hands, every muscle wanting to incant spells, to cause bodily harm. "Did you ever consider that I would not be your puppet to control?"

Branwen seemed to dismiss my comment. "Ridiculous or not, we are here and a legitimate Challenge has been issued within the strictures of our kind."

"So instead of marrying us off, you marry Gideon to Aoife, instead. What do you think that will get you? Closer to your sister's throne?" She said nothing for a moment, as if choosing her words. Had I struck a chord? My mother was queen in her own right, but a lesser one. She was not in line to rule the Seelie Court.

"If you accept it, then we continue and the magicks will decide." Branwen's voice remained chill.

"If we don't?" Adam asked, his voice calm, but I could feel his fury beneath, barely contained. I knew he was as angry as I was, though he was better at hiding it.

"Then it's war," Gideon interrupted, appearing from my left. He smirked as the words left his mouth, as if he were anticipating just that. A war. A bloody battle.

"War? So that's what you want? I'm game if you are." I clenched my hands back into the fists that had become second nature over the past half hour or so. "No need to issue Challenge, Cousin. I'm here right now and willing."

Another smirk slid into a smug grin. "You will fight me?"

"Anytime."

"Keira." Adam took my hand again. "No fight until we understand the Challenge. If you will excuse us."

I swallowed my anger and let Adam lead me away.

CHAPTER THREE

"Accept the challenges so that you may feel the exhilaration of victory."

—*George S. Patton*

"Technically, we're not required to actually battle," Tucker said, his eyes scanning the parchment, which he'd unrolled across the top of Adam's desk. It wasn't overlarge, but it seemed to take up the entire desktop.

After Gideon's snarky comments, Adam had forced us to do some official mingling with the rest of our guests long enough for propriety's sake. We'd then left the Hall to seclude ourselves in Adam's office over at the main inn. No one was there, thanks to the Reception. Most nights, the entire Wild Moon bustled, coming alive from dusk until dawn, sanctuary for vampires and Kelly alike. Tonight, nearly everyone was still at the party. Our day manager, John, and his family were, no doubt, cozy and snug in their own small home for the night. He'd be up at daybreak, tending to the property while we all slept. Adam had built this resort as a hangout for his small tribe of bloodsuckers, most of whom disliked preying on humans and wanted to explore alternative sources of nutrition. He'd bought this particular property in the Texas Hill Country to be near me.

I sat in one of the side chairs across from Adam's desk, attempting to remove the fripperies from my hair with Adam's help, as Tucker studied the document my mother had handed over. "What is it then if not a fight to the finish? Don't most of these things mean a real fight—like spells, weapons, and so on?" I tugged at something tangled in my hair. Adam pushed my hand aside.

"Let me," he said. "I have a better angle."

I dropped my hands and pushed the long flowing sleeves from my dress to my elbows. What I wouldn't give to be dressed in my usual jeans and tank top.

Tucker tapped with his index finger. "In legend, yes. But, this doesn't seem to say anything about war or a battle specifically. I'm not a hundred percent sure, but . . . Adam, would you mind taking a look at this phrase?"

"Ouch!" I yelped. "Watch the hair, please." A piece of my hair had re-tangled in one of the beads that dangled from the intricate headpiece I'd worn for the Reception. A pretty thing, but really a pain to remove.

"Apologies, love," Adam said and quickly freed me. "Niko, could you take over here whilst I read with Tucker?"

"Certainly." Niko left his post at the door where he'd been standing guard. "Adam, if you don't mind?" Niko motioned to the now empty doorway.

I closed my eyes. Men. No matter what bloody species. With a quick mutter and hand wave, I cast a do-not-disturb ward. Nothing complicated, but just enough to give us fair warning if anyone approached. "There. It's not as if you need to physically guard the door, guys," I said. "I trust that all of us can move fast enough in case of an attack. Besides, he gave us Truce. Unless he's got something else up his evil sleeve, he's not breaking that. There are consequences, right?"

"There are." Adam crossed the room to join Tucker at the desk. They bent over the elaborately illuminated scroll, muttering to themselves as they studied the calligraphy.

Niko took up where Adam left off, his hands gentle and fingers nimble in my hair.

"You're good at this," I said in a quiet voice.

Niko gave a grunt of assent and kept unweaving my hair from the ornate decoration, placing all the bits and bobs of jewelry onto the table next to me. "I've done it before," he said. "Back when . . ."

"Yes, back when." I closed my eyes and let him work his magic. His hands soothed the tightness out of my scalp. I was so unused to hairstyles fancier than a braid but had succumbed to dressing up to suit the occasion. As he worked, I wondered about the details of his "back when," as a lonely child born in the first Elizabeth's era, purchased by some court noble as a plaything. Niko never spoke much about this part of his background. I could empathize with the loneliness, but couldn't even imagine being someone's toy, someone's property.

"Tucker's right." Adam straightened and turned to me.

Niko patted the top of my head. "Done," he whispered.

I shook my hair free and ran my fingers through it. It felt so good to be loose of that crap. "Right about what?" I began twisting a braid as I spoke.

"They are not asking to fight us. It seems to be a challenge of proof."

"Proof? Sorry, I don't follow." A part of me was disappointed. Actual physical battle against Gideon? Oh yeah. I could do that. Niko handed me a hair tie as I finished braiding. "Thanks."

"Background or short version?" Tucker asked.

"Short version first."

"We need to prove that we belong here. That the land is tied to us."

I stood, sweeping my gown out of the way. I couldn't wait until I could go home and change into something less heavy. It was still bloody hot outside and the a/c in here, though doing its job, couldn't overcome stifling layers of fancy gear. "Okay, let's try for something a bit more explanatory and less cryptic," I said as I strode over to the desk.

The parchment gleamed in the soft overhead light, its colorful illuminations as complex and grand as any manuscript painstakingly hand-drawn by medieval monks. Only this was fresh off the pen . . . or spell. I could feel magick tied into the complex symbols and imagery. Unicorns, wyverns, dragons, and other fantastical creatures entwined in some sort of mystical dance, while runes and knots embellished the sides of the parchment. Perhaps they were only protective spells, keeping the information from being read by anyone other than us. Perhaps not.

"Did you feel the magick?" I asked.

Adam nodded. "It is part of the material itself."

I looked at him in surprise. "And you didn't think to not touch this without checking with me? What if—"

"It's mostly harmless," he said, without apology.

"And you can tell this how?" I crossed my arms and glared at him. He may be his father's son, but when he became vampire, the Sidhe part of him died, replaced by the magick of the Nightwalker.

"I'm not sure," he said. "But I know." He smiled. "Give me a little credit, Keira. I may no longer have my magick, but I can feel it."

"Hmph." I stepped closer, but avoided touching the document. "I'll take your word on that for now. What language is this? I sort of recognize the symbols, Ogham runes, right?"

"*Beith-Luis-Nin,* yes." Tucker ran a hand down the side of the sheet. "They used the script to write in the Old Tongue, grandfather to modern Celtic languages. See this word?" He pointed to a set of runes. "*Arigeacht.* It means 'fealty.'" His brow furrowed as he translated. "Here, '*Gideon Branogeni Mucoi Kelly.*'" That's 'Gideon, born of Raven of the tribe Kelly.' It goes on with various phrases of ownership? I'm not positive. I can recognize the runes, as they're similar to my own early learnings, but the language is old, not something I'm well versed in."

"'Born of Raven?' That's precious." I growled. "His mother wasn't named Raven, but that was a name she took after Change."

"Is that significant of something in particular?" Adam asked. "I know that in some cultures, children take a new name upon adulthood, but I'd never thought you did so."

"Not typically," Tucker answered. "Alys, Gideon's mother, fell very much into the sixties counterculture. She ran off to the Haight in sixty-five, came back a few years later and Changed somewhere around the early seventies. Then she seemed to fall back in with the family and got pregnant with Gideon."

I stared at my brother. "You're not joking?"

"No, why would I be?" He seemed puzzled at my question.

"So Gideon is the product of some airhead former druggie hippie—and the Faery King?" I began to laugh. Oh, the irony. "No wonder he's so fucked up. I never knew that about his mother. He didn't talk about her much."

"I never said she was a druggie," Tucker said. "Though you aren't off the mark. She really enjoyed the sixties."

I couldn't control my mirth. "This is priceless."

Adam shook his head, smiling at me. *You amuse me,* he said with a look. I could only wipe my eyes and shake my head. It was too funny not to laugh. Despite the Challenge and the silly pomp-and-circumstance of the Reception, I couldn't help but think life had become something out of a bad Syfy Channel fantasy movie. What next? CGI dragons? Mega Shark meets megalomania?

Adam's hand brushed the center portion of the scroll, ignoring my chuckles. "Much of this primary text is in the old language. Part of this is slightly more modern, not using Ogham. It's a mix. The Ogham speaks of *dair* and *muin*—oak and vine—or oak and neck to be more precise. Old-fashioned way to describe property, land. Here, *ymarddelw.*"

"That word I know," I said. "That's Welsh. 'Setting up a challenge.'" I peered between the two men. "Here, *ymhòni,* that's more a claim, a challenge for one's self."

"He seems to be claiming the land if we cannot show our own claim is valid."

"So, I'm guessing this doesn't simply mean showing them your deed to the ranch?" Not that I actually thought it would be that easy. It couldn't be, otherwise Gideon would have never tried this on. He may be another Kelly heir, but if my heirship was anything to go by, I didn't lose my own natural instincts. Gideon had *never* done anything that required real work. He tended to look for the easy way—thus his walks on the dark side. Short cuts came naturally to him. Short cuts and lack of forward thinking—*"consequences"* wasn't a word Gideon thought much about.

A grin flashed across Tucker's face at my sarcastic statement, an expression endemic to him but that I'd seen little of tonight. "Remember what I told you about this land being on ley lines?"

"Yes, you said something about that when we met the werewolves' Fenrir last week. That I'm tied to the land because I'd bled here. I bonded here and I Changed here."

He tapped the scroll again. "This basically challenges us—as a group—to prove our ties and to prove the land responds to us and accepts us as its caretakers. If we can't, then Gideon can claim the right of *perchenodelb,* of ownership."

"Okay, then maybe I do need the long parts version," I said. "How the hell are we supposed to do that?"

"Keira, Gideon states that the land is failing here under our care. That the long drought is a direct result of it rejecting us."

"Is that possible?" This was so far out of my knowledge base, I couldn't begin to understand the entirety of it. I'd been trained to fight, trained in some court protocols, a little healing magick. Nothing about land and ties and whatever. I didn't suppose that Gigi thought I'd need it—or at least need it quite just yet.

Adam shrugged. "Perhaps. There has been much chaos since I came."

I snorted. "You think?"

Tucker rolled up the scroll and tied the ribbon around it again. "I think it has less to do with the fact that we've experienced upheavals," he said. "I don't think that really matters so much."

"But then what does?"

My brother's voice turned solemn, almost sorrowful. "Land usually responds to life, fertility, growth."

"Well, yes." Where was he going with this? Basic agricultural information notwithstanding, what he was saying seemed obvious enough. Land prospered with rain, nurturing, and care. The last few weeks here had been hellacious and still were—a record heat wave and subsequent drought. But this kind of weather wasn't uncommon to the Hill Country. So the weather records were being smashed. It's not the first time and hey, climate change, right? Other parts of the nation had record snowfalls, flooding. It was just our turn here. It wasn't the first drought season, nor would it be the last. We were doing everything we could to help—limiting our water use, making sure all the livestock watering holes were okay. Adam kept a herd of rescued exotics on the ranch, alongside the usual whitetails, a few head of cattle—nothing out of the ordinary. This was part of living in South Central Texas, in the Hill Country.

"Keira, I think what Tucker is trying to say to us is that we brought death, not life," Adam said in a gentle tone.

My brow furrowed. "Death. Well, yes, but people die—"

"Not people, *us,*" Niko spat. "I get it."

The clue shoe finally dropped on my head as Adam's meaning sank in. "Well, fuck. Death. As in the living dead."

I sank onto the edge of the desk, my skirts knocking the parchment to the floor.

The four of us watched it roll itself up, bounce and rattle against the polished hardwood as it rolled and stopped at my feet. I could almost see the magick within it quivering. I looked away.

"So the land is dying because you are vampires and not strictly living."

"And we are infertile," Adam reminded me. Right. Dead men can't make babies—a phrase I'd snapped at my aunt Jane when she'd tried to convince me to return to Canada, to leave Adam. Of course, that conversation had happened before everything changed . . . including me.

"Which means . . ." I didn't even bother to finish my own sentence. I knew what it meant. In the traditional "king must die" sense, the old king, when no longer fertile, sacrificed himself so the new, young king could take his place, impregnate his queen and continue the line, satisfying the land. Persephone, eat your bloody heart out. I was living with Hades—and his sidekicks. "I do hope no one's considering what I think they're considering," I warned. No way was I about to allow anyone of my family to commit suicide so we could keep *real estate*.

Three heads shook in the negative.

"Then what do we do?" I asked. "Do we let Gideon take it?"

"First, before we do anything, we need to leave," Adam said.

"Leave?"

"That would be part two of the Challenge." Tucker bent down and picked up the scroll, tapping it on his palm. "This says that if we choose Truce, during the challenge period and through the final day, no one may live on the land in question."

I rubbed my forehead. "This whole thing is giving me a headache."

"It should do," Adam said. "I believe that part of the interwoven spells is to cause consternation and confusion."

"Lovely. Because you know, my life so far has been so full of bunnies and fluffy kittens that I needed something like this to take my mind off the sheer boredom." I stood. "I need to get out of this gear and into something more me," I said. "Let's table this for now, regroup after some sleep?"

"I'm afraid we can't." Adam stepped closer and took my hand. "It is fairly specific. We can either leave now and continue the Challenge, allowing ourselves until Lughnasa to provide our proof, to have the land accept us, or we pay a price."

Fan-bloody-tastic. So we evacuate the only true home I'd known in a long time, uprooting an entire group of vampires who were innocent of anything more than being Adam's people. They didn't deserve this. *We* didn't deserve this. "Does that thing explain what the 'price' is?" I asked. "Or does it just leave it up to us to figure out?"

"It's rather vague," Adam said. "Just that there will be consequences."

"Multiple and varied," Tucker supplied, almost in humor.

I couldn't really blame him. In one respect, this entire thing was beyond ridiculous. I mean, who the devil presented Challenge anymore? This wasn't the old days, the old ways. We were in twenty-first century America, with cell phones and digital entertainment and space flight. Yes, Faery still existed, but they kept Underhill, out of sight. I knew that my Sidhe cousin Daffyd had been hungry to get out, to come Above, but he'd been trapped in the pocket of Faery, not free to return to his home. This entire situation could only come from some sort of misguided jealousy. Right?

"You're not helping," I said to Tucker.

"What Tucker means, love, is that the Challenge, though specific in what we must do, isn't quite as forthcoming in what exactly happens if we ignore it. Only that the payments will be numerous and of great consequence."

Every muscle tensed as fury flashed through me. Great consequence? Knowing the bloody Sidhe, this could be anything from petty annoyances up to and including death. When they spoke of payment, they didn't mean money. Sidhe had no need for currency— they only traded in lives and life force. All I wanted to do right now was to find my former lover and pound him into the ground with my fists. No magick, just pure unadulterated physical joy of beating him into a pulp. Adam grabbed hold of my wrists and pulled me to him, his eyes flashing. For a moment, I wasn't sure if he was aroused or disturbed—or both. He held my wrists tightly to his chest, kissed each of my tightly closed hands and then looked me deep in the eye.

"We *will* get through this. We will do it together."

"All of us," Niko said. "As a family."

I let my head sink onto Adam's shoulder. "All of us." That's the only way I could do this. My new family, my brothers/Protectors, blood-bonded and sworn to me and Adam. I wasn't alone anymore. Didn't have to fight Gideon on my own. Didn't have to run from my mother's icy indifference.

After a few moments of silence, during which I attempted to collect myself, my brother spoke.

"So what'll it be? Door number one?"

What indeed? The lady or the tiger? Problem was, the lady was often more vicious than the hungry beast.

CHAPTER FOUR

"It is a wise father that knows his own child."
—*William Shakespeare,*
The Merchant of Venice, Act 2, Scene 2

A knock on the door interrupted my thoughts.

Niko looked to us, a question on his face. I nodded, as did Adam.

"See who it is. The wards didn't ping, so it's someone neutral." As all three men looked at me quizzically, I shrugged. "What? I'm perfectly capable of spelling up a few warning wards," I said. "Early detection system. Easy peasy."

A laugh, and Niko opened the office door, Tucker right beside him, both men creating a block with their bodies, just in case. I chuckled at their actions.

"I came to see my son and daughter." Drystan's calm voice didn't betray anything. It was as if he'd stopped by for afternoon tea.

"Let him through," Adam said.

"Aeddan," Drystan nodded in acknowledgment as he stepped into the room. "My daughter."

"Drystan." I echoed his greeting.

"What brings you here, Father?" Adam asked.

"I could not help but believe that I may be of some assistance."

"Against your only other son?" Adam's sarcasm nearly equaled my own usual tone. "I find that difficult to believe."

Drystan raised both hands in a gesture of peace. "I come to help, Aeddan. I find that I dislike this division."

I snorted. "You didn't seem much fazed by it a few months ago," I said. "When we first met and you'd taken to Gideon as if he were the prodigal son returned. Only that's really Adam, isn't it?"

"Prodigal son?" Drystan sounded confused. "I do not understand your reference, Daughter, but yes, I must admit that then I was not so knowledgeable about my second son's . . . shall we say, proclivities?"

"Since when do Unseelie shy away from the dark side?" I retorted. "Unless you mean Gideon's lack of anything that resembles leadership skills."

Drystan laughed and stepped closer. "My dear child, you are a fit match for my only heir. May I?" He gestured to a chair next to me.

"Please. Sit." I said the words with as much grace as I could. I didn't dislike Adam's father, per se, but I didn't trust him, either. When we'd gone to Faery in the spring, right after I'd Changed, he'd been all "hail fellow, well met" to Gideon, though I had to admit he'd shown the same cheery welcome to us, too. At least the Unseelie tended to stab you as they faced you. They didn't hide much, unlike my mother's relatives who often fed you sugar as the dagger entered your back.

"Your brother," Drystan said to Adam, "is not the kind of person I'd wish as my heir."

"So he did ask you," Adam said. It wasn't a question.

"Yes, and I quickly disabused him of the notion."

"Was that before or after he tried to kill me?" I asked.

Drystan sighed. "My apologies, my dear. I did not intend for any of this to happen. Not then, and not now."

"Answer the question, Father."

Both Niko and Tucker moved just a little closer. They'd both fallen back into guard mode as soon as Drystan had entered.

"Before. I swear it." Drystan caught my gaze, his expression open and guileless. "I had hoped to have your cousin, my son, as companion. A son at Court again," he explained. "When he came to me. I only wanted . . ."

"A son to replace the one you sacrificed?" I stood, needing to *move*. "Tell me, Drystan, do you regret it?" I stepped closer and closer, forcing myself into his personal space, my eyes sparking.

"Keira, no," Adam said. "It's not—"

"What? It's not relevant? Maybe just not polite? Oh, no, definitely not." I stepped even closer, letting my anger show, letting some of my shielding down. The vibrating tension of my energy surrounded me.

Drystan cringed visibly, but recovered in a moment. He straightened, haughty once more. "I did what was necessary, Daughter. You could not begin to understand."

"No, you're right about that one. I have no idea—"

Adam's hand clamped down on my arm. "Keira, this is neither the time nor the place." He turned to his father as I stepped back, heeding Adam again—but only for now. I had every intention of pursuing this later.

"Father, why did you come here? You said you wished to help."

A quick nod from Drystan. "I do."

"Can you help us read the Challenge?" Tucker asked. "You surely must have experience."

"I can try," he said. "But my only knowledge of these Challenges comes from lore. There have been no Challenges in my time."

"Wait, you either?" I pulled away from Adam and joined Drystan. "How can that be? Didn't the Tuatha Dé Danann fight the Fir Bolg? There had to be a Challenge issued then."

"My dear child," he began.

"Seriously, Drystan, stop calling me that. My name is Keira. Your endearments aren't helping."

"Very well. Keira, then. The Morrigan and her battles are but ancient history to me. I was born less than two millennia ago during the time of the *Rhufeinig*."

"The Romans?" Tucker's brow furrowed. "Then you and my clan chief are of an age."

"We are."

I glared at Tucker. How was that important? "Fine, whatever. Read this. I unrolled the parchment and handed it to Drystan. "See what you can tell us that we don't already know."

He nodded and complied. I returned to my chair, Adam sat next to me, a parody of our side-by-side throne-type chairs in the Hall. Even Tucker and Niko had unconsciously (or consciously) completed the picture, each of them standing at our sides, ready to fight bear—or Sidhe kings, as the case may be. As I waited for Drystan to finish reading, I mentally explored my pissiness. Adam's father hadn't done anything really, other than stay out of the fray when we'd confronted Gideon earlier. In Faery, when we'd discovered Gideon's bloodline and his heir status, Drystan had done little but observe. So like the Sidhe, sit back and watch the others fight, then scoop up the spoils. Only . . . Adam was full-blooded Sidhe, plus vampire. *He* wasn't the type to sit back. Had he learned this from his vampire teachers? Or was I missing some key component of Drystan's nature?

"This parchment is heavily warded," Drystan said after ten long minutes. "I can but read a few words, primarily those along the sides. They seem to be spells of concealment."

"How so?" I asked, suddenly more interested. "I'd not picked up on that."

"Some of the runes," he said. "When taken separately, they are nothing more than words—oak, vine, Gideon's lineage." Drystan chuckled. "Though him referring to himself as the son of his mother amuses me."

"Yes, well, go on," I prompted. "Unless that's relevant."

"Only in that he has ceased to align himself with me," Drystan replied. "It seems he expects nothing from me. From my people."

"Given up, has he?" I muttered. "Well, then."

"The runespells?" Adam asked. "Could you explain more?"

Drystan pointed to a few places on the parchment. "There and there," he said. "Come look."

Adam and I joined him. He pointed to a couple of illuminated runes, plain words surrounded by inked pictures of leaves, curlicues. "I guess it's not just for pretty?"

"No. It's a spell," Drystan explained. "This and this here." Two runes tied together with what looked like thorns. "Alone, that would mean 'Kelly' and 'blood,' but with the thorn vine . . ." He straightened and turned, addressing all four of us. "This Challenge is spelled not only directly to you and Adam, but to be readable only to those who share Kelly blood."

Adam's eyebrow raised. "I can read it because Keira and I share blood," he said. "But you cannot read it?"

"Precisely," Drystan agreed. "I can read some of the spells, but not the primary text of the Challenge."

"Then we need Gigi," I said. "None of the rest of us can decipher all of this."

"One word, Dau—I mean Keira," Drystan said. "When I say 'share' Kelly blood, I expect the spell is quite literal."

"I don't understand."

Adam frowned and looked at the parchment. "Bloody hell." He slapped the desk. "He's right. He means '*share*,' as in not a full-blood Kelly."

"But Tucker—" I began.

"Tucker is pure Kelly, but he shares blood with us both and with Niko," Adam said. "He is no longer precisely full-blood Kelly as the blood of others runs in his veins. He is bound to us. I share blood with you, therefore I share Kelly blood, as does Niko due to his bond with you and with Tucker."

"Damnation," I exclaimed. "That bloody good-for-nothing weasel. Gigi's not going to be of much help."

"I am truly sorry," Drystan said. "I do wish to assist."

Adam nodded. "I understand, Father. Perhaps you could help another way."

"I am willing." Drystan gave Adam a short bow, this one from peer to peer. "What did you have in mind?"

"If my brother is dead set on staying in the so-called new world," Adam said, "perhaps he could be persuaded to choose elsewhere."

"Yes," I said, excited to have an option. "Drystan, there are hundreds of caves in the Southwest if Gideon's dead set on this general area. New Mexico, Colorado, Arizona is full of them as are other places. You can create a door to Faery, can't you? You are high king, after all."

"I can." Drystan looked thoughtful. "Though, I dislike this place, this new world of yours. These lands are too raw, too rough. However, I could create a new door if I must. I would perhaps be amenable to creating a place for Gideon and his family if that is his wish and if this will assist you."

I'd begun to speak when without warning, Drystan turned and threw out his hands, a spark of angry energy flung away from him, splashing against the back wall of the office, tearing a slice of paint and drywall away, exposing the stud. "Centuries, for century upon century I have lived in a fair peace—at least a truce—alongside my Seelie counterparts within a country small enough to fit many times into this Texas of yours. And now, an errant son of mine chooses to begin what must surely end in war." He stomped over to the wall and with a gesture repaired the rip he'd created. "Whatever Gideon wishes to accomplish by issuing Challenge, I cannot believe he is the instigator. This reeks of manipulation and collaboration. He is far too young to be this subtle."

And far too unlearned, I mused. Gideon was many things, but a work this convoluted meant he'd had help.

My mother, surely. Someone else? I wish I knew more about the Seelie players, the courtiers who'd fluttered around Branwen, whispering, flattering. Not important enough to sit above the salt at the high queen's table, some of them did rank in my mother's own Court.

Drystan continued. "I had thought wars to be things long past, a diversion no longer craved by us Sidhe royals. The modern world is too big, land too available for these kinds of disputes. Though many still prefer the old country that is by our choice, not set by any restrictive boundaries. In fact, one can almost say that our Courts live harmoniously—as unfriendly neighbors."

"You mean the kind that nod their heads politely in passing, but no one you'd invite to tea?" I said.

"Unless forced to." Drystan grinned. In a flash, I could see Adam in him. That handsome face, slightly different, broader and less sharp, but still, definitely Adam's sire.

"Then why do this? Why would Angharad allow this Challenge? Could she be unaware of it?" Adam eyed his father. "Could you ask her?"

Drystan met Adam's gaze with aplomb. "I could and I shall. From one monarch to another. If my son is indeed Challenging without the approval of his Queen—"

"*His* queen?" What did he mean by that? "Has he pledged fealty to her?"

"I can see other explanation," he said. "He got her daughter with child. These are her direct heirs. Angharad may be a scheming bitch, but she would never allow her pups to stray far from her."

"Wait, but you accused Gideon of lying about the baby," I reminded him.

"I did, and I stand by it. Aoife is too far gone with

child. Despite that, if Angharad claims the child as heir, as her own daughter stated, then there is only one explanation. Gideon swore allegiance to the Seelie Queen. In return, she gave him her daughter and the child to call his own. By extrapolation, Gideon is also an heir—at least until the child comes of age and if Aoife does intend to step aside. It is not the way of my Court," he said, "but Angharad never leaves the heirship in the hands of a mere child. When her daughter was young, your own mother was heir until Aoife grew to her majority. If what they said at the Reception is true, then my son, your cousin is now acting heir to the Seelie Court."

"Hell of a gift," I said. "Angharad in the habit of handing these kinds of things out?"

"A gift that will keep on giving," Drystan chuckled, a twinkle of humor in his eye. "And no, she is not, but Gideon's Change may have been the catalyst. My counterpart enjoys her power."

"Oh, *now* you know popular cultural references," I said.

He laughed. "Indeed. I have not ignored the world above entirely, my dear. On occasion, I find myself intrigued by its entertainment."

I shook my head in wonderment. What next? Disco dancing at Court? "So you'll speak with her?"

"First, I believe I shall attempt to speak with my son," Drystan said. "And with his wife. If I can allow him to see the futility of this . . ."

"Revenge?" I supplied.

He nodded. "Yes, that, I suppose. From the little I know of him, Gideon is not above seeking to win over his brother. He tried me first, and I gave him nothing but an enjoyable life. He could have remained with me,

Below, in my corner of Faery. It would not have been an onus."

"No, but then he wouldn't have been able to lord it over us—over me," I said.

"Yes, well. You are correct. Perhaps persuading him will be fruitless, but I shall attempt to do so. If I cannot, I will venture back to Faery and request an audience with Angharad. While I am there, you all must abide by the Truce. You must act as if nothing can be done to stop the Challenge." He faced me, his eyes dark and dangerous. "Keira, do not take this lightly. Challenges come with a great price, both from the one receiving as well as the one issuing."

"How so?"

"Gideon had to tie this Challenge with blood and promise. I do not know what particular rituals he chose, as I cannot read the words, but the runespells alone taste of darkness. This is no idle threat, nor foolish endeavor. The consequences to him may be as serious as those to you."

I fell back into the chair I'd so recently vacated, a shiver running through all my bones. Gideon *meant* this. This wasn't some sort of childish revenge fantasy of his. Not when he'd had to tie something equally precious to the Challenge. What in all the bloody hells had he begun?

CHAPTER FIVE

"Honor isn't about making the right choices. It's about dealing with the consequences."
— *Midori Koto "The Samurai"*
(Highlander: The Series)

"All we've got here is bad choice after bad choice," I muttered as once again, I tried to reread the parchment. Damn Gideon and his obscene timing. Drystan had left nearly an hour before, hoping to track down his wayward offspring and get some answers. Not that I held much hope in that. After Drystan had refused Gideon's blatant ploy a few months ago and had reconfirmed Adam as heir, I was sure that my cousin wouldn't give Drystan any information.

We were back to square one—leave or pay the consequences. No other wise words had revealed themselves in our further perusal. I'd tried a few spells I knew, even some I hadn't really studied (with the help of Tucker). Still, the words remained as slippery as Gideon's underlying motives.

You think Odysseus had it bad with Scylla and Charybdis? I was flailing between dumb and dumber in my own options. "So if we leave, we're golden, but then we have to send away our vampires, the people we've sworn to protect. If we stay, we're breaking nine million stupid Faery rules that will quickly bite us in our respective asses. But we don't know exactly what those bites will consist of. Nor are we sure what we have to do to get to come back."

Adam nodded, a solemn look on his face. "Basically."

I threw up my hands. "Just . . . ugh." What in all the hells were we supposed to do? Frankly, the land didn't mean that much to me in and of itself. I'd be happy anywhere as long as I had my family with me—and that meant Adam, Tucker, Niko, and the rest, including the vampire tribe. The only problem was ceding this place to *Gideon*. If he'd been anyone else, *any* other person, I'd be tempted. Hell, if Drystan had been on board with Gideon, I'd say take it and relocate, and then trust to Drystan to keep his son in check. Except there'd be no holding of Gideon's reins on Drystan's part now. Just how had my former lover conned my mother into jumping on his personal bandwagon and waving the "Gideon Rocks" flag?

"Retreat, regroup, rethink." Tucker stepped closer and put a hand on my arm. "Keira, it's only smart to take advantage of this truce period. We've got five weeks. Let's take the opportunity to figure out how we can succeed."

Adam agreed. "There is no point in making a final decision now. You know I'd willingly hand over the ranch to Gideon if it would make him happy. This land means little to me as such."

I smiled at him as he echoed my earlier thought. "Nor

me," I agreed. "But with Gideon, it's never straightforward. Never just what's on the surface . . . especially if my mother and her aunt are involved, but I'm willing to ride this out until it's done. You?"

Adam nodded. "Whatever you wish, my queen."

I smacked him lightly. "Quit that crap. We're going to get enough of the formal ritual bullshit with this Challenge."

He threw me a smile. "As you wish." Turning to Niko, he continued. "We can send the tribe back to the UK, get Andrea on the phone and make arrangements. Sooner the better."

"On it." Niko turned on a heel and exited the room.

"To the UK?" I asked. "What if we need them closer? It's a good ten, eleven-hour flight from London back to Austin, then another hour here."

"A good point," Adam said. "But I feel that they will be safer at my estate. This fight is not theirs."

I nodded. "True . . . yet, still . . ."

"I know. Having our entire backup force gone from here is worrisome to me, as well. That said, should it come to a war, as my father fears, vampires versus Faery? Fangs against magick is not something I wish to see. It would be slaughter."

I shuddered as I envisioned the bloodletting. He was right. I turned to my brother. "Tucker, would you call Bea and Dixxi for me? I think they need to know what's going on. Tell Bea I'll call her in the morning." I glanced over at the clock on Adam's desk. "Shit, it's well past the wee hours," I said. "Closing on three. Better yet, don't wake them up, Tucker. Send a text or email and I'll make sure to call them later."

"Will do," he said as he left.

I let myself sag back down into a chair, my mind whirling with random what-ifs and how-comes. "You think we're doing the right thing, Adam? I hate the idea of going through with the Challenge, but frankly, I'm scared shitless about the true reasoning behind it."

Adam drew closer, putting his arms around me. I shut my eyes, just letting myself absorb the comfort he offered.

"We're in a tough situation, Keira," he whispered. "As I said, the land itself means little to me. You know I bought it so I could be near you. I've accomplished what I needed to." A quick peck on the lips then he continued. "I realize it is different for you. You grew up here. These are your people, your realm, so to speak. Leaving permanently, ceding the Challenge now would be foolish. Until we know the consequences . . ." He let his voice trail off and pulled his head back, catching my gaze. "You have good instincts, my love. We stay nearby, figure out the Challenge and do our best to win."

"And if we don't?" I voiced my deepest fear. "Losing to Gideon . . . will it mean our lives?"

"Possibly," Adam said. "The Challenge in and of itself seems far too vague on its surface. I need to know specifics. I've not had to decipher the Old Tongue in too many centuries and don't wish to make a guess. My initial supposition would be that Gideon wishes to have the land and the door to Faery. However, merely wanting to call this place theirs is too stupid, too transparent a reason for all of this. My half-brother is ambitious, greedy. He wants something dark, something he doesn't wish to expose now . . . not even to his bride, I'll wager."

"You think?" I was being facetious, but Adam took the words at face value.

"I do. I have no knowledge of why Angharad wed her daughter and heir to Gideon, since I am still our father's heir. Gideon has no claim to the Unseelie Court. Nor do I know why Aoife would so easily give up her claim to the throne. If the Seelie queen were looking to unite Faery, to gain influence over my father's Court, this seems a rather awkward way to do it."

"And awkward is the last thing the Seelie Sidhe are. Devious, yes, but awkward, never." I kissed Adam's cheek. He stood and leaned against the front of his desk, the very pose I remember so clearly from months ago, when I'd first entered this office. Now, instead of wondering what this amazing person wanted of me, I wondered how I'd ever made it this far without him—and how very lucky I was that we were together. Sure, I'd bet all the barbecue sauce in the entire state that if I weren't married to Adam, weren't blood-bonded to him, that Gideon wouldn't have come up with this insane idea. At the same time, I wouldn't give Adam up for the world.

"Where do we go?" I asked. "You started to say something earlier about a place you knew?"

"A small inn, near downtown San Antonio. It's quite old. The proprietor specializes in our kind."

"Huh, that's different," I said. "Hadn't heard of any place like that. A vampire inn?"

"Not precisely. More of a place where those of us who are Other can stay, no questions asked. The owners are human, but part fey. There have been several seers in their family."

"That'll work, I suppose. You, me, Niko, Tucker?"

Adam stood. "Yes, I think just the four of us. Liz and the twins should return to the Kelly enclave in Canada. Be safer there."

"They'll not like it," I said, knowing my brothers. Rhys and Ianto may be less knowledgeable about Faery, but they'd met Daffyd, spent a little time in his company. "I think it's going to be tough selling this to them."

"You think they should stay?"

I nodded. "I'd rather they did. Only . . ." A thought crossed my mind. "I have an idea, instead of them coming with us to the inn, they can stay at one of those rental condos across the lake, rent a powerboat for transport. I'd rather have someone local, close by—at least closer than a nearly three-hour drive." We'd be too far away in San Antonio to deal with any problems immediately. Normally, I wouldn't give three dead rats' tails about this, but we'd just held a Reception and taken fealty oaths from numerous groups, many of whom lived in and around the lake. We were their liege lord and lady, and had sworn to keep them safe, to be there when they needed us, just as much as they'd all sworn to us. San Antonio wasn't far in Texas terms, but I wasn't comfortable not having someone on the spot—or as close to the spot as we could. "Will that satisfy the Challenge rules?"

"It should," Adam said. "The land in question is the land I claimed for my own, not—"

"Adam . . ." My voice shook as I processed those words. "You do realize that what we've claimed is the entirety of Texas and the southwest? Not just the Wild Moon acres."

Adam stood upright, for once his face displaying the emotional blow. Usually, when confronted by a problem, he'd go all neutral vampire, wiping all trace of expression off his face. Now, it was as if he'd been slapped by the very audacious extent of Gideon's arrogance. "How?"

"Did he word it specifically like that?" I pressed. "The land you *claimed,* we claimed? Not the land you own?"

"He did." Adam whirled, scrabbling through papers on his desk. "At least, that's how I decipher it."

"Tucker took the scroll with him, love. If that's what you're looking for."

He shook his head. "Not that, this." He held up a mobile phone. Not the one he normally carried. He pressed a number key and the key to dial.

"Who?" I mouthed as I listened to a woman's voice answer the call on the other end.

"Get her," he said into the phone. The woman said nothing, but the sound went silent. "Keira, could you grab Niko? I just remembered. I'd arranged for two scientists to fly over today—to set up that genetics lab. We need to try to catch them before they leave. See if Niko's still on the phone with Andrea?"

"Fuck." I ran out the door and down the hall, calling out Niko's name, hoping I'd catch him in time. The last thing we needed was to have these guys show up unaware and trigger some sort of Faery trap.

Niko poked his head out of his office, his mobile to his ear and a puzzled look on his face.

"Andrea?" I asked.

He nodded, but said nothing. I could hear her voice on the other end, saying something about planes and freight. When she paused, I held out my hand for the phone.

"Hold on a moment, Andrea," he said and handed it to me.

"Andrea, hi, it's Keira," I said. "Long time no talk." Niko watched quietly as I spoke. I loved this part about being in charge. As one of my Protectors, blood-bonded to me and to Adam, a lot of things didn't need explaining. He knew that my asking for the phone wasn't just a whim, but something important.

"Hello." Andrea's voice, smooth and silky even over the crappy digital phone connection didn't betray any trace of emotion—not wondering why I was talking to her, nothing. She'd been in charge of security at the ranch when I'd first come here to the Wild Moon, but then she'd left to run security ops at Adam's estate in England. This was the first time I'd spoken to her since.

"Sorry for barging in on the conversation, Andrea, but Adam and I totally spaced on the two scientists. I believe they were scheduled to fly over today?"

"Yes. I'm texting them now to stop preparations," she said. "Thank you for the reminder." Again, no inflection. I got the feeling she'd already been on top of this and was just humoring me. Oh well. As long as it was handled. When this all settled down, when we retained our rights to the land, to the ranch, then we could worry about setting up the lab. In the meantime, Adam's pet geneticists could stay and work right where they still were. I'd have to hook Dixxi up with them, maybe via Skype, so she could video conference. Despite all the insanity, I still needed to make sure Bea's pregnancy went smoothly and that Dixxi had everything she needed. Dixxi Ahskarian and her gene studies were part of Bea's chance to have a healthy baby—considering the father was an Armenian werewolf whose family was prone to Tay-Sachs and other genetic diseases. Bea's pregnancy had been my biggest concern before the current mega-crisis.

"Thanks, Andrea," I said. "Could you and Niko work out details for video conferencing and such for Dixxi? I want to make sure she gets whatever equipment she needs."

"I will."

I handed Niko the phone back. "Sorry for the interruption."

He smiled. "No problem," he said, and went back into his office to continue his call. Behind him, Tucker sat at Niko's desk, feet up, the phone receiver for the landline tucked in between his ear and shoulder as he typed furiously on the computer. I couldn't see the screen, since it faced away from me, but I knew he was probably messaging Dixxi and Bea while conversing with someone else. We really needed to get Bea an up-to-date computer and Internet service. The last thing I wanted was to be out of touch again. After I'd Changed, after I'd sentenced Bea's attacker to death by Sidhe, Bea had withdrawn, hadn't spoken to me. Then events had forced me to leave. For a long three months, my best friend, the only person outside my blood family who'd stood by me for thirty years, wouldn't speak to me. When I'd returned, we reconnected and I wasn't letting that estrangement happen again. Who knew what kind of mess I was in now? I wanted Bea to know that I'd never abandon her, no matter what.

"Tell her I'll call her around ten or eleven," I mouthed to Tucker, who nodded and waved a hand in acknowledgment.

Good, all set.

Adam came out of his office, talking on his mobile. "Hold for a moment." He motioned to me and I stepped closer. "Have Niko go to John, wake him if necessary. He needs to take care of coordinating shutdown for the ranch and the Inn—getting the utilities and all taken care of, and whatever else. You get her set?"

I assumed he meant Andrea. "Yeah, Andrea's on the ball. Who are you on the phone with?"

"Minerva."

CHAPTER SIX

"What we wish, we readily believe, and what we ourselves think, we imagine others think also."

—*Julius Caesar*

"Why the—?" I stopped talking as I heard my great-great-grandmother's voice on the other end of the call. Handy thing having enhanced hearing and being able to hear both sides of the conversation at once.

"I suppose this is an emergency." Her dry tones conveyed nothing more than a busy leader torn away from something vitally important. Considering how late it was, past midnight her time, she was likely in bed . . . alone or with company. I really didn't want to know.

Adam quickly filled her in on the situation. "If we can't stay in Texas or the U.S., we may need to come to you or go to my estate in England."

"Don't be hasty, boy," Gigi admonished. "Faery challenges can be tricky things to interpret. How much experience have you?"

"None," Adam admitted. "I know of no official

Challenges in my lifetime, neither made nor given to us."

"Very well then. Have you spoken with your father?"

"He is equally as ignorant."

"Gigi," I said, butting in. "This parchment is spelled against reading by anyone who doesn't share Kelly blood. Drystan wasn't of much help there, but he's going to try to see Angharad. He agrees with us that in no way did Gideon conjure this up by himself. My cousin is shite at languages."

"Angharad? A possibility," Gigi agreed. "Though, how exactly did you consult with Drystan?"

"He's here," I said. "He came for our Reception." *And you didn't,* I silently accused. I knew she hadn't planned to. That she'd wanted Adam and me to establish ourselves without her presence, without needing her influence, but still, it rankled just a wee bit.

"Ah. Well then, I understand. He came with Gideon."

"He did," Adam said.

"Drystan volunteered to help." I explained Drystan's plan to seek out Gideon first, to try to persuade his recalcitrant son of his folly in issuing Challenge.

"That makes a certain sort of sense, Keira," Gigi said. "I'm proud of you, girl, for thinking things through and not flying off the handle."

I snorted. "Yeah, well, three months in your illustrious company had to result in something." How had she known? Maybe because I hadn't immediately rushed to call her first? Whatever.

Her laugh tinkled through the phone line. "Indeed."

"Minerva, my gut instinct is for us four to come to you," Adam said. "I'd intended for us to sequester ourselves in San Antonio, but since we are not sure of the interpretation, perhaps bringing you the scroll is a better idea. Even though it's bespelled, we can perhaps transliterate as best we can and maybe you can assist?"

"You think my Kelly blood will more easily help than your father's Sidhe blood? A good thought. However, that's wasting time. Scan the thing and email me the images. I'm not sure spells will stand up to electronics. Old language and old spells never took into account modern ways of copying."

Adam and I both looked at each other with the same expression. How had we not thought of that? The spells were woven into the scroll's parchment. If Gigi wasn't in the same physical space as the actual parchment, perhaps that would void the runespells since the images were not the thing itself. Hell, it was worth a try.

"No need to." Tucker announced as he strode through the door. "I've taken several photos of it and texted them to you."

"Well, you're on the ball, Brother," I said. "What made you think of that?"

"Because every time I looked at the damned thing, I interpreted it a bit differently," he said. "Then the same thought occurred to me. If we emailed it, it wasn't the actual parchment, therefore the spells embedded in it might not pertain. I was just coming down to tell you that I'd sent Minerva the files, but then I heard you were speaking with her."

Again, handy thing our preternatural hearing. Saved us a lot of time and fuss.

"I've received the files," Gigi said. "Give me a few moments to look at this."

We all stood there, silent, waiting. A few "hmms" and "ahs" came over the phone. I half expected to hear a rustle of paper, imagining Gigi bent over an ancient manuscript with a magnifying glass, instead of viewing an electronic file on her computer.

"Just as I suspected. I can read most of it, but it's not clear. It's subtle and very, very tricksy. Your first instinct was correct, Aeddan," she said, calling Adam by his formal name. "It's similar to the Kellys' own twenty-four hour rule. We require those of supernatural bent to report in, as it were, if they come within one hundred miles of Kelly land. With this, it seems that as long as no one of your blood is within one hundred miles of the boundaries of the property—not your claimed rule, but the property you call your home, the heart of your land, you will fall within the strictures of the Challenge. This is old traditional language, a formula set in the days when the lands one held weren't quite so . . ."

"Global?" I supplied with relief. Leaving to go stay in San Antonio wasn't my first choice of events, but leaving the country entirely perturbed me beyond simple worry. Sure, easy enough to clear out and head north to Canada, but the farther we were from this property, the easier it would be for Gideon to win . . . or so it appeared to me.

A tinkle of laughter resounded through the room. Even via the phone speakers, Gigi's power resounded. "You are my heir, Keira," she said, her tone sobering. "I have begun procedures to ritually sever Gideon's ties to the Kelly clan."

I nearly fell to the floor at her announcement. Adam's eyes widened, but otherwise his face revealed nothing more. Tucker beamed, while Niko only shook his head, his gaze on the floor. I couldn't tell if he was laughing, though I suspected he was.

"What, no reaction?"

"Words fail me, Minerva," I said. "After everything, I never thought—"

"No, I suppose not," she replied. "It was not my intention to limit ourselves. I had hoped the boy would step up, forget this foolish ambition of his and be content, happy with sharing the heirship."

I snorted, then tried to turn it into a cough.

"Be still, Daughter," Gigi said. "Though you may be amused by this, I most certainly am not. This scuttles many of my plans. I shall have to regroup, rethink. In the meantime, you must move everyone."

Was I supposed to ask her about her plans? Adam, as if anticipating my question, shook his head. "Not now," he mouthed. I nodded. We had plenty to think about. I could talk to her later. After we'd settled this.

"Everyone?" Adam asked her. "We *must* move them all?" He sagged a little. "I had hoped . . ."

"Yes, everyone."

Adam whirled, fists gripping the phone. "Minerva, this is a commercial concern. It's not as if it's just for show. My vampires are here because they are mine. Not to mention the fact that we provide a sanctuary for rescued exotic game. I'd planned to leave my human day manager on site to keep things in shape, to keep an eye on the place, maybe even hire some temporary human staff to take care of the exotic livestock. I suppose I'd assumed that the language meant everyone of supernatural blood."

"I see no problem with you arranging for humans

not sworn to you to care for the animals, but otherwise, I don't think Faery tradition bothers to take into account our modern ways." The answering tone was as dry as the outside air. Gigi didn't need to state the *No shit, Sherlock* that automatically loaded itself into my brain—a childish retort that I'd once learned to use to perfection in junior high. I hadn't even thought of the livestock; they paled in importance to my own family. My instinct was to keep *us* safe, keep *us* from harm. The livestock would surely be fine in our absence.

"Damnation." Adam held my gaze, then Tucker's, then deliberately punched in the code to mute the phone's speaker. Before he could say anything, I spoke.

"Adam, when we first met up again," I said gently, "just last year, you told me you'd bought this ranch for me. To be close to me. To be able to be near me and woo me. You reiterated that fact again tonight. Is that still true?" Yeah, well, okay, there was still a small part of me that was insecure, even after our blood-bonding. He'd said a lot of things then, a great many things . . . like the fact that he was vampire—something that he'd been able to effectively hide from me for more than eight years when we were both residents of the UK. But he'd not told me of the other part of the story. That he was not only a Nightwalker, but also Unseelie Sidhe and the heir to the throne. That gem hadn't been revealed until we'd gotten ourselves into a pickle in Vancouver, just after I'd Changed and learned I was the Kelly heir. So, sue me if I thought that there still might be something not yet said.

"I did, and it was," Adam replied, truth evident in his gaze. "I've never lied—"

I laughed, short, bitter and oh so angry. Not at him, really. It wasn't his fault that the fucking fickle fingers of Lady Fate had been messing about in our particular bloody pie. Adam had been as ignorant of the Machiavellian machinations of Minerva Kelly as I had been. Neither of us had known then that my former lover, Gideon Kelly, was in fact, half Sidhe, like myself, only from Adam's side of that fence . . . and Adam's half-brother. Now, all this ridiculous political and genetic manipulation was coming back to bite the Kellys in the proverbial ass. And I was the ass it was biting . . . hard. "Truth," I snorted. "Such a slippery concept with the Sidhe, is it not?"

He flinched, a slight grimace crossing his face. I waved a dismissive hand at him. "No, not you, love," I said. "Never you. You did what you had to, to try to keep things in place until it was the right time. It's my bloody cousin's fault, this is. I'm afraid he got way too much of Gigi's ambition and drive and not enough of her practical sense."

"That's more than evident." Adam set the phone on the desk and walked toward me. "I am beyond glad that despite everything, we still found each other."

I had to smile at him. From the look on his face, I could tell he still held some insecurity, too. Sure, we'd blood-bonded just a few hours ago, or was it only minutes? I had no real idea of the time. The entire night so far had passed in a ridiculous tornado of insanity . . . kind of like my life for the past, oh, eight months or so. But hey, who was counting? Oh yeah, I was. All I could think about right now was that I wanted to leave with Adam, go back to his house and lock ourselves away for at least a week. No phones. No email. No interruptions. In fact, that had been the plan. After the formal foofaraw was over, we were going to stay home and shut out the world for a bit. Let other people run the ranch while we just existed. Only, whatever god or goddess of luck I'd pissed off somewhere down the line had other ideas.

CHAPTER SEVEN

"The fox changes his fur but not his habits."

—*Proverb*

After a moment, Adam nodded and thumbed the phone back to normal operation. "Our thanks, Minerva," Adam said. "We will evacuate tonight."

"Your vampires?"

"Will go to my estate in Wiltshire. I have a pilot on his way now. Niko's made the arrangement."

"They could come to me instead. It's far closer."

"An offer quite appreciated, Minerva," Adam said. "Though sending them to the Kelly enclave sounds logical, there's a part of me that wishes them to be gone entirely from this continent. It is not their fight."

"Nor is it," Gigi agreed. "You must do what you think best, Adam. Though, your plane can't get to your estate until well past morning."

"Understood," Adam said. "I'd planned for them to make a stop in Dallas. They can be there by dawn. I have someone there who can house everyone safely until nightfall."

"If I remember correctly, your plane seats only a dozen or so."

"True. However, my hired pilot has a larger plane we can use."

"Pish-tosh." I could imagine Gigi's well-coiffed head shaking. "There is no need to involve others. I've a plane that will suit. It can transport everyone in safety directly from the ranch airstrip." For a moment, I wondered how she knew our airstrip could support a larger plane, then I remembered. She was the one who had the bloody thing built. No doubt it could handle the entire Kelly fleet—including, evidently, a vampire-ready jet.

"The plane has blackout windows?" I asked.

"Yes, and will be freshly stocked with blood. Seats up to eighty-five. The plane will be there in three hours. Have them ready."

"Thank you, Minerva," Adam said. "This will be extremely helpful."

"Gather your vampires. Have Ianto, Rhys, and Liz go with them."

"But—" I began to protest, but Gigi cut me off.

"No, child, I know they've blood-bonded to you, but you need to be lean and agile now. They will best serve you guarding the rest of your people. The four of you will have more than enough to worry about. Let them help where they're needed most."

I couldn't argue, even though I wanted them here. They were mine, damn it. But she was right. As much as I could use the support, tying Rhys, Ianto, and Liz here would accomplish what exactly? Waiting and pondering in some lakeside condo somewhere? They'd be just as reachable via phone if they were in the UK. Hell, for that matter, we could set up several computers with Skype and do video conferencing if we needed to. "Gigi, what else can you tell us about the Challenge? What do we need to do?"

Dead silence for a moment stretched into more, then finally, "I wish I knew, Keira," she said. I heard something in her voice that I'd never heard before—defeat. She'd no more been able to interpret the rest of the Challenge than we had. "You already know much of the basic information. The Challenge seems to suggest that you need to tie the land to you. There are many ways to do this in lore. You've already established residence. You've given blood and sweat and tears. You've consummated your joining and have pledged to care for your people. They've pledged fealty to you in return. This, however, this puzzles me. The only thing left is true sacrifice. At least, in my own interpretation of such things."

I did not like the way this was going. Though my knowledge of Faery lore was less than expert, I still knew many of the basic tales and too damned many of them required sacrifice—of an actual person. Yes, oftentimes in modern days, that sacrifice had evolved to something more symbolic, but I'd read that parchment and the language was about as modern as Atlantis—the actual city, not any movie or TV show. "I'm not letting anyone here—"

"Of course not," Gigi interrupted. "That's insanity. Gideon may be a fox, but he's not a lunatic. He knows you'd not go that far. He's counting on it, more than likely. Though, that said, I doubt he'd be willing to stick his own neck out quite that far. In most Challenges, what is required of one party is required of the other."

"Then no, you're right. He's probably counting on us reneging." I'd finally clicked into the overall picture. Yeah, well, I was a little slow, mostly because I wasn't sure why. If Gideon gained the Wild Moon, gained permanent access to our door to Faery, I had absolutely no doubt that his first act would be to banish us. But with him being riven from the Kelly clan and disinherited from the Unseelie, effectively unblooded, I wasn't sure what him gaining the land would mean. Gods and goddesses, I hated Sidhe politics. It was always like this, hidden, mysterious, double-edged, and triple-tongued. Nothing was straightforward—oh yeah, kind of like my own fucking family. I had accepted my role as Kelly heir, if not gladly, with practicality. I mean, what else could I do?

After we'd learned that Gideon, too, had Changed, had become heir, something that was supposedly impossible, Minerva had granted me, with Adam as my consort, the rule/oversight of the lands in Texas and the Southwest. A trial, of sorts, and a learning experience. She had no plans to abdicate anytime in the near future, which for her, could mean centuries. In the meantime, Adam and I could set up camp, set up our own small fiefdom and learn how to rule without being my great-great-granny. Gideon, spawn of fucking Satan (if that particular construct really existed outside of fiction and bad films) had been relegated to his blood father, Adam's father, high king of the Unseelie Court. We now knew how well *that* worked out . . . as in not at all.

"I would not go so far as to presume that taking your land, your rule, is his only intent." My clan leader's voice clanged like a warning bell, emphasizing my own fears. Yeah, I was no idiot. I may have once thought myself in love with Gideon, but events then and events now had proven my instincts right. He was trouble with a capital fuck-me-for-being-so-stupid.

"Well, I did figure he's got something more in mind than just living on a ranch in the middle of nowhere Texas," I said. "Ruling here, ousting us sounds like it could be an end result, but not the only one. I wouldn't put anything past him."

Tucker stifled a sound that sounded suspiciously like a "duh" snort. I put my hand on my hip and shot him a "shut up" look. I was damned tired of all the stupid spanners getting tossed into the gears of my life. I truly was bloody well near to saying Gideon can just have the damned ranch and damn the consequences. We could all leave along with the vampires. I'd not ever seen Adam's estate in England. I'm sure I'd love it. After all, I didn't really care where we lived. But reality and a nagging sense of guilt kept bopping me on the head. What would happen to the human residents of Rio Seco if I absconded? I couldn't trust to Gideon's good intentions. He'd never had any.

Adam shifted his stance, something I'd never once seen him do. Was he nervous? Was he interpreting her words differently, catching a nuance I couldn't? Had he come to a different conclusion, perhaps? I jerked my head, trying to signify that he should speak to Gigi. He shook his head and mouthed "later."

"Keira, all of you, take care. I'm going to do a little follow-up of my own here," Gigi said. "I have a few ideas."

"Any help would be greatly appreciated, Minerva," Adam said. "We'll phone you if we come up with anything at this end. I'll text you where we'll be staying and will keep this phone with me at all times."

"You do that."

With that, my great-great-granny, clan chief, matriarch of the Kelly clan, and Machiavelli's clone, severed the phone connection.

Adam placed the phone on the desk, avoiding my glance.

"You mind telling me what's going on?" By this time, I had both hands on my hips. I was sure I looked like some sort of harridan, hair going all over the place, dressed in finery fit only for a formal traditional supernatural Reception, eyes flashing and face flushed. I did not want to look into a mirror and frighten myself. "Is that the Batphone or something?"

"More or less." Adam crossed his arms. Niko and Tucker just stood in their now-accustomed bodyguard places and grinned. "Minerva gave this to me before we left Vancouver. It's got one number programmed into it and she will always be available if I use this phone to call."

"More like a lifeline than a Batphone, I'd say," Tucker piped up.

"Shut it," I growled. "Were you planning on telling me?"

Adam gave me a small smile. "Honestly, I'd utterly forgotten about it," he said. "You came back and well . . ."

"We dropped right into the middle of a series of hate crimes. Yeah, yeah, all right." I had to concede the point. "So we're to go to this inn, then."

"It seems so."

"She'd damned well better be right about the boundary thing," I muttered. "Last thing we need is for Sidhe magick to disrupt us while we're trying to figure out what to do."

"Point. Now, let me get to work and coordinate with Lance and Jessica. We'll need to get our residents notified and packed up so they can get on the plane when it arrives."

Thank goodness for our vampire assistants. They'd be sure to corral everyone and everything that was needed. "I think I'll go back to the house and pack, unless you think there's anything else I need to do?"

"No, that's fine," Adam said. "Pack for the both of us if you don't mind? Niko and I will need to go to the inn as soon as possible since our hours are limited. We'll take one of the ranch vans. You and Tucker can come along first thing in the morning. I'd like you to make sure John and his family get off all right."

Tucker nodded. "We'll do that. Where are they going to?"

"I'd like him to make sure the Wild Moon is closed up behind us. Then he and his family can drive to Austin and catch a commercial flight to London tomorrow," Adam replied.

"That'll work."

Part of me was ecstatic that we were doing *something,* anything that seemed like action, like forward motion. The other part was trying to freak out that this was happening so fast. I stuffed down the gibbering part of my brain with a ruthless mental "later" command. I'd break down later. This wasn't anything big, just a temporary relocation. I refused to think of anything else right now but getting my stuff packed. No problem. I traveled light. San Antonio is a big city. If I needed anything, I could just go to a store. Right?

Adam pecked me on the cheek. "See you later, love."

"I'll come with you, sis," Tucker said. *"Cariad."* He kissed Niko. "I'll pack for us as well. You two get out of here quickly, okay? It's three hours to San Antonio from here. You need to go within the hour to beat full sun. Everyone else will be fine. I'll help make sure they get on the plane and get out of here."

Niko laid a hand on Tucker's face. "I'll get him out of here. Why don't we take your van? You and Keira can come in her car after."

The four of us stood in silence for a moment, regarding each other. This was huge. Huger than huge. We were about to abandon the one place that I'd felt safe, loved, cherished since my family had left more than two years ago. The place where I'd found love. I knew that my ties here were strictly emotional, but damn it, I didn't want Gideon to take this—and there was no way I was letting him rule in my stead. I'd been dealt this heirship hand and I was going to play it out, as long as I had Adam next to me and my blood-bonded family supporting us.

The mood broke as John, the day manager, bustled in with a clipboard and a long printout of something or another and gave us each a quick greeting. From his cheery demeanor, I couldn't tell that he'd probably been wakened from a sound sleep and hurriedly brought up to speed on the situation.

As Tucker and I left, I could hear Adam, Niko, and John organizing and coordinating things I'd never have thought of—such as suspending deliveries, clearing out perishables in the restaurant refrigerator, hiring someone to drop by and check the water tanks for the livestock. I felt as if we were preparing for a long haul, some sort of mental and physical entrenchment for Armageddon. I hoped I was wrong.

CHAPTER EIGHT

"Time is a great healer, but a poor beautician."
—*Lucille S. Harper*

"**O**h, *hells* to the no. You expect me to stay *here*?" I looked at the place one more time, hoping that I was hallucinating. Nope. Still the same—a clapboard house, two stories and a porch that looked like the second cousin of the Bates Motel—the cousin that only got hand-me-downs third hand. Normally, I'd be okay with just about anything, despite my brothers' teasing that I was only used to four- and five-star hotels, but this place? The house leaned dangerously to the right, the porch leaned the other way, every single step broken and worn in multiple places. What was left of the once-white paint on the wooden clapboards was now a dingy dirty gray, decorated with clods of dried mud, smears of I don't know what, even smashed bits of insects. A lone shutter hung precariously by one hinge on one of the upstairs windows. None of the other windows even had shutters. The entire place looked abandoned, broken, unclean. A decrepit wooden sign hung from the edge of the porch roof, the only thing about the place that wasn't falling apart.

A line drawing of a flower—meant to be a rose, I thought—graced the sign, just to the left of the worn words "Rose Inn." Shabby, like the building, the sign swayed gently in the quiet breeze. A sense of decay, genteel, but decay nonetheless hovered around the building. Cracks in the paint shimmered in the heat. The requisite wooden swing hung from beams to the left of the double front doors, both open. A pair of shredded screen doors were the only thing holding back the outside from inside. A scraggly gray tomcat wandered into view from the right of the house. He stopped, fur rising, hackles drawing up. With a hiss and spit, he arched his back, tail stuck straight up at least three times bushier than at first sight. Tucker bared his teeth and let out a low growl. The cat hissed once more for good measure before disappearing back the way he'd come. Great. Feral cats plus a run-down piece of shit building. What had Adam gotten us into?

"Seriously, we're staying here?" I repeated. He couldn't mean it. This place was beyond a dump.

"Yes." My brother didn't sound as if he were joking.

"Tucker, really? Why not the Menger or Emily Morgan? Nice, clean hotels. Or if you insist on low budget—not that I have any idea why—we can always find a Days Inn or something. I mean, for goodness sake, this place looks like the bastard child of the *Psycho* house crossed with the Liberty Bar."

"And how do you plan on housing our two vampires in a Days Inn?" Tucker asked. "It's not as if we have many choices in sunny San Antonio. This place has all the amenities we need. Adam and Niko will be safe here."

"This is a choice?" I muttered.

"They know us, remember?" Tucker replied. "The proprietors are used to the unusual. Besides, Adam and Niko are already here. It's this, or move out even farther. It's vampire friendly," Tucker explained. "Plus there's a hell of a lot more to it than at first glance."

"Damn well better be," I muttered. "Bad enough I had to leave my home because my bloody cousin can't keep his dick in his trousers."

"It wasn't his penis that dictated his ridiculous actions," Tucker said. "I blame your mother."

I shook my head as I scooped my backpack from the floor of the Rover. "Not me, as much as I'd like to. This has the stamp of Gideon all over it. Branwen may be deep into this, hell, she probably encouraged it, but I've no doubt Gideon instigated every bit of this charade. I still don't know what he promised her, nor how he figured doing this, but it was him."

"You've got a point, but I doubt Gideon knows any more about Sidhe Challenges than we did. If the High King of the Unseelie hadn't seen one in his long lifetime, then I don't know how Gideon got this stupid idea."

"Is Angharad older than Drystan?" I asked. "She could well be the instigator, or at least the enabler."

Tucker shrugged. "I don't know for sure, but Adam might. Though I do think she may be about the same age as Adam's father. We can hope that Drystan gets through to her."

"Yeah, because we both know that him trying to persuade Gideon to give this up is about as likely as an above-freezing day in Antarctica."

I hadn't shared my fears with anyone yet—that we were about to become a party to a modern-day war worse than any technology could provide. Magick and power thousands of times more deadly than the worst nuclear bomb could be released. Or, we could just be fighting a battle of wits and words. We had no idea and very little guidance. Gigi had emailed back her interpretation of the text, but with a very strong *caveat lector* attached. She'd been able to give us the gist, but none of the nitpicky details that still fretted me. We still had no bloody clues other than a tangled knot of words written in a mélange of languages, one of which was dead even to its own people. Most Sidhe spoke modern-day Welsh these days, at least the Sidhe I'd known.

"Soon as we get settled, Keira. I'll try Gigi again," Tucker said as he hauled our bags from the back of my Land Rover.

"She's not home yet," I said. "I called while you were getting gas. Aunt Jane told me Gigi wasn't expected back until tomorrow or the next day at earliest."

"She certainly took off in a hurry," Tucker said. "I'm not giving up on her answering her messages, though. She does check her cell phone. She's the clan chief."

"A clan chief who pronounces she needs to handle something, isn't specific, then takes off without so much as a 'hey, I'll be in touch,'" I retorted. "Granted, after finding out about the official Truce, she probably figured we'd be fine for a few weeks." We should be, though frankly, her leaving like this was a bit odd. Her message to me delivered via text had been curt: *Off for a bit. Don't worry. Will be in touch soonest.* "Do you think she's—"

"She's fine, Keira," Tucker said. "I'm sure she's gone to do her own version of research as she said. To help us out."

"I kind of expected she'd send her minions," I replied. "Not that she'd go haring off herself."

"This is research that will affect her now one-and-only heir. I doubt she'd entrust this to her minions. Besides, she never goes anywhere without her Protectors."

He was right. All I could do now was wait and work with Adam, Tucker, and Niko to help decipher the bones of the Challenge. I was sure Gigi would let us know as soon as she found something relevant.

As I stepped closer to the disgusting building, I felt a shimmer of energy sliding just below normal sensory feel. "Warded? By a Kelly?" No mistaking that energy. Someone in my family had set pretty heavy-duty protection around this miserable dump. So heavy-duty, in fact, they'd even been hidden from me until I'd actually stepped into it.

"Gigi."

"Oh, really?" I answered as my great-great-granny's signature made itself known. "Did she come here, then?" Not that I expected it, but yeah, she could've made it via one of her other private jets. Three or so hour flight from the enclave directly to the private terminal at San Antonio Airport or even to Stinson Field? That wasn't outside the realm of possibility. After Adam and Niko had left last night, Tucker and I packed, made sure all the vampires got off safely. After a flying visit and breakfast at Bea's Place—thank goodness she opened at six—we'd driven here. Bea hadn't like the idea of us leaving, but understood. I'd promised her I'd call once we got settled.

"I doubt she's here," Tucker said. "Gigi set these up some time ago. It's a—"

"Bolt hole. I get it. She created a bolt hole." Of course she did.

Tucker nodded. "No group in its right mind would

leave itself without a place to escape to. It's on the list of Kelly properties."

"The list I've not yet read?" I asked with a heavy dose of sarcasm. One more thing I hadn't yet done in my heirly duties. I'd come back home from three months training in British Columbia to discover a series of hate crimes against a newly arrived werewolf pack—one of whom had knocked up my best friend, Bea. I'd barely had time to get fitted for my dress for the Reception and to learn the basic protocols, much less do the boring business reading. Adam had promised to go over it all with me—our holdings in Texas, in various parts of the Southwest states. The Kelly clan reached far, across the globe, in fact, and our small portion of property was centered here. A test, no doubt, to see if we could co-rule peacefully and carry out the Kelly agenda—whatever the hell that was. I still had plenty of time to learn. Gigi didn't plan on stepping down anytime soon.

Tucker chuckled. "Well, yes. We don't own this place outright, but we invest in it."

"You knew of this place, too?"

"Nah, not really. I looked it up after Adam told me the address. It rang a bell—albeit a vague one."

As we stepped closer to the run-down porch, the air shimmered and shook, the wards recognizing us as kin. I felt the magick purr, energy surrounded my skin, sliding up and down as if wanting to be petted. Weird, but not unexpected. As the Kelly heir, any wards set to keep out non-Kellys would welcome me.

One more step and the image of the run-down inn wavered, changed and steadied, its boards now shining white in the morning sun, scrubbed clean of all its filth, no longer a derelict building. It welcomed me, encouraged me to open the door, go inside. "Okay, wow, this is different." I stood for a moment admiring the view. "It's rather pretty," I said.

Before I could continue, the screen door opened to reveal a tall woman standing just inside.

"A glamour," she said in a low voice. She stood at least six feet, slender to the point of model anorexic. Her gray hair fell in a blunt cut to her shoulders and she wore a bright pink cotton Mexican dress and huaraches, along with a beautiful cloisonné rose necklace. A silky pashmina scarf was draped over her shoulders. No wedding ring, nor sign of one on her hands. A couple of silver bracelets dangled from her wrist, moonstone earrings in both ears. She looked black Irish with a wee hint of something else—not Kelly, not necessarily inhuman, but something I couldn't define. Adam had said the owners were part fey and I had absolutely no doubt this was so.

"Greetings, Keira Kelly. We welcome you and yours to our dwelling. In peace and plenty, we welcome you."

She opened the door wide and we stepped across the porch to meet her. Turning, the woman picked up a platter that sat on a small table just inside the door. The plate was loaded with slices of home-baked bread topped with thin slivers of meat and a dollop of a sweet jam.

Tucker bowed slightly. "We accept your hospitality." He reached for a slice of bread and ate it, then took another one and presented it to me. I followed his example, recognizing the ritual. By eating her food, we accepted her welcome. By this offering, she was swearing she would abide by host truce.

A thought struck me. Gideon had violated *our* trust,

our hospitality. The same host truce rules applied to the Reception as to here, at this modest inn. We'd all been in such a state, such an insane hurry to leave and not be forsworn that we'd missed this angle. He'd submitted the Challenge during our Reception—a traditionally neutral gathering. He was *Guest,* in all that implied— the rules of hospitality should have been in force. Just as Macbeth violated hospitality by murdering Duncan, could Gideon be held to a similar standard as formal Guest violating the rules of neutrality? I tabled the thought for later discussion, not knowing if this was something we could use against Gideon or just another example of my former lover's ambition and greed. After all, no one was dead . . . yet.

"Please enter," the woman said. "I am Grace Rose, proprietor of the Rose Inn."

We stepped across the threshold and another ward parted for us.

Immediately inside was a sort of sitting room or lounge, with couches and chairs in conversation groupings. White plaster walls were lined with bookcases and the requisite fluffy cat sprawled across a divan. The furniture was old, heavy and wooden, yet fit perfectly in the quiet room. No fancy decorations marred the simplicity of the decor.

A second woman approached us from the back of the house. Like Grace, she was tall, thin as a stick, but unlike Grace, her skin was as pale as any vampire's— though she was definitely alive. I could hear her heart beat, slow, steady. Her hair was more silver than gray, long and braided back from her face in a soft style. She wore a silvery dress that almost matched her hair color, her feet bare, no jewelry. "Verena Rose," she said, her voice the whispery softness of someone very old, though she seemed not much older than Grace. I squinted in the dark hallway, my night vision didn't seem to be kicking in. Maybe the sudden contrast from the brightness outside? She seemed blurry somehow, as if seen through a smeared glass window. I couldn't pinpoint her age at all. Sixties? Seventies? One hundred? Human ages were starting to mean nothing to me after spending so many months with my vampires and my family. I'd grown up around them, used to be able to tell, but over the past few months, I'd been so sequestered, I'd started thinking along the lines of decades and centuries—not next week or next year.

I held out a hand, but Verena ignored it, simply watching me from unblinking eyes.

"She's a seer," Grace said. "She won't touch you unless she's reading for you."

"Ah." I nodded, acknowledging Grace's remark. Both of them fey, then. No pure-blooded human had powers, despite rumors to the contrary. Unlike the Kellys, whose biology wasn't compatible with that of humans, lesser fey had interbred for centuries. Some bloodlines had only a tiny percentage left, some won (or lost) the genetic lotto game and recessives reinforced recessives until fey characteristics began to emerge more strongly. Now that Grace had told me, I could blink the blur out of my eyes, as if the knowing in and of itself cleared the glamour around Verena. Her sister, I supposed.

"Yes," Grace answered. "Our great-great-grandfather was fey. Sylph, born from a baby's laugh, he once said."

Great. Was she serious or was she just quoting J. M. Barrie? Verena looked me up and down, finally moving a bit closer. A long hand went out, not to shake, but as if she were touching my aura—which she very well may have been. I grimaced and held onto my protective mind-shields tighter. No way was I allowing this woman through. A soft caress and then it was gone.

"You have many miles ahead of you, Keira Kelly," Verena said. "Miles and wiles." Her eyes glazed a bit. "Be careful. Not all is as it seems." With a tilt of her head, she smiled then, her eyes now clear. "I do believe it will all work out." With that, she faded back into the shadowy hallway, her feet nearly silent against the Saltillo tile of the floor.

I stared after her. What had she meant? I made as if to follow her, but Tucker touched my hand and brought my attention back to our hostess.

"Do you know what she meant?" I asked.

"My sister's words are often vague," Grace murmured. "She Sees, but cannot often interpret." She motioned forward. "Your rooms are up the main stairs," she said. "Up a flight and to your left. Ms. Kelly, you are in room eight. Mr. Kelly, room six across the hall. Your partners arrived safely, just before dawn and are now sleeping. We have no other guests and will have none while you are here."

"Our thanks, Madame Rose," Tucker said. "Keira, shall we?"

I nodded to Grace and followed my brother in silence. I needed time to rest, to think.

A Sidhe Challenge we still had to decipher. A part-fey hostess who could See me. An inn shadowed and glamoured by Kelly, though known only to Adam. What next?

CHAPTER NINE

"The more enlightened our houses are, the more their walls ooze ghosts."

—*Italo Calvino*

I should have known. The sheer age of the place should have been a sign. Sure, it was welcoming on the outside, but inside was a whole other matter. The initial disgust I'd felt when viewing the glamoured building returned, only now, it was because of something not seen, but most definitely sensed.

I beefed up my already strong shields as I ventured farther into the building. Though the interior decor was as pretty and picturesque as the actual exterior—all done up in faux Victoriana with lace doilies everywhere—the atmosphere inside was distinctly less than cozy. Death oozed out of every minuscule crack in the masonry, between every single seam of the wallpaper. Pinholes barely visible to even my eyes pulsed with sadness and grief. Crap. I'd not felt this in the entryway, but now I couldn't ignore it. Even without the disguise, I could tell this house was at least two centuries old. Plenty of time for spirits to conglomerate, though not perhaps in this thick concentration. Since we meant to stay here for the next several weeks, I was going to have to do some serious retooling of my default personal shields. Around the ranch, I mostly used lighter shielding. There hadn't been much of a need. Among humans, I had a default setting that let me remain in their company and didn't allow for their own energies to bother mine. This, though, was more than I'd consider normal.

I'd meant to go straight up to bed, to join Adam, do not pass "Go," do not stop for anyone or anything. Only . . . not so much. Halfway up the main staircase, I'd begun to falter under the oppressive feel. I stumbled and grabbed at the wall, then recoiled. Ugh, slimy. Only—not physical. The whitewashed wall had no actual moisture on it when I peered at it closely. Only a psychic slime then. Gross.

"Hey, are you all right?" Tucker reached to grab hold of me, but I waved him away as I regained my balance. We were at the first landing and I couldn't go on. Not yet.

"Jesus H. Freaking—this place reeks of death, Tucker. Don't you feel it?" I shut my eyes and tried to focus. Being sensitive to death aided me once upon a time—when I was a child—at least in Clan reckoning. I'd learned to escort my family members to their final end when they'd chosen to go. Now, with the addition of the myriad of Kelly Talents, my sensitivity seemed to be turned up to eleven. I had to struggle to keep it together. I could feel Adam and Niko's separate energies pulsating above us, slightly left of where we stood, a quiet sensation that let me know they were both deeply asleep. The darker, muddier energy surrounding me was old, settled into the pores of the plaster walls, embedded in the wallpaper, into the very molecules of the air, like pet odor or something equally as nasty, a psychic stink that I couldn't seem to shut out completely.

"'Fraid not, sis," Tucker said. "It is kind of an odd place, but you know, been around for a long time."

"More than *long,* I'll wager. It's like this place was party central for death and all its minions. Didn't really start feeling it until we got farther up the stairs. Was this place always an inn?"

"I don't know. I think so. Anything I can do?" Tucker looked concerned.

"Not really. Could be that I'm just way overtired," I said. "I need to concentrate a bit, get a handle on my shields and close them tighter. Why don't you go on and get settled? I'm not going to be able to sleep until I get this taken care of."

"You sure?" He took my backpack from me. "At least let me carry this."

"Yeah, thanks. If you'll put it in my room, I'll go find Grace—"

"I'm right here." Grace's soft voice startled me. She stood right behind me, one step below, her arms clutching the pashmina around her as if she were cold— though by my reckoning it was at least eighty degrees in here. Better than outside, but still stuffy.

Tucker frowned but after a nod and a wave from me, kept walking up the rest of the staircase and turned left, disappearing into what I assumed was a hallway. He may be one of my Protectors, but frankly, I was pretty sure I could deal with Grace by myself.

"What the . . . ?" I waved my hands around and broke our stare. "I'm figuring you know what I'm talking about?"

Grace gave me an enigmatic smile. "There are many of them, aren't there? So many should have passed over long ago, but yet, they linger . . . some less dead than others."

"Less dead?"

"There are two men sleeping in my guest rooms that some would consider dead."

My brow furrowed and I bit my tongue on the sarcastic words. This wasn't my brother or one of my own family who knew me and my style of communicating. I needed to be more formal here. Grace was our Host. I was a Guest, though technically, since she and her sister were both fey, I was their liege.

"Does this place have some sort of history I don't know about?" I finally asked. "From the presences I can feel, either every single guest died in their room over the last say—hundred years or so—or we're dealing with something else."

"Something else," Grace said. "This house was first a funeral home for many decades." She motioned upward. "Would you care to follow me? We could go to my sitting room to chat."

I studied her calm serenity. Why did I need to go with her to chat? Call me crazy—or maybe just cautious—but I didn't know her from . . . well, anyone who wasn't Adam, Niko, or Tucker. "Thanks for the offer, but I think I'd rather just talk right here," I said. "No offense meant."

She nodded. "None taken." She ran a hand along the flocked wallpaper, fingered the brass of a sconce now shining with electric light, no doubt retrofitted some decades ago. "My grandfather was an odd one," Grace said, utterly without irony. I blinked. Odder than

Grace and her sister? Well, perhaps. My own relatives weren't exactly card-carrying middle-of-the-roaders. Though, we had our nature to thank for that. None of us were human. Then again, she'd said her great-great grandpa had been a Sylph, an air spirit.

"This being the part-fey grandfather?"

"Yes."

Her thin hands continued to move, the silky fabric of the shawl floating in the air as she followed the whorls of the wallpaper pattern, stroked the brass of the sconce again as if she couldn't just be still.

My headache, such as it was, vanished with a pop as the final mental locks of my shields snapped into place. I heaved a sigh of relief. It was going to be work to keep them at this kind of level—practically worthy of Homeland Security. Could I stand to stay here until my birthday? I wasn't so sure. Two months was a long time to withstand this kind of psychic intrusion.

"Better?" Grace asked, flashing me a broad and somewhat coquettish smile. I couldn't help but smile back.

"Yes, thank you."

She leaned against the wall and studied me for a moment. "You have much to learn," she said softly. "Things you know little about." Her voice began fading out, growing fuzzy as she closed her eyes.

I started as she spoke again, this time, in a louder, more determined tone, her voice deeper, less vague. "Seek help from someone outside, Keira Kelly. Someone who straddles both worlds. Study. Learn. Someone will save you." With a shiver, Grace opened her eyes and stared directly at me. Another odd smile crept across her face. "I think Father liked Minerva."

I stood, my nerves tingling, muscles taut with unease. "Grace . . . are you okay?" If that hadn't been a classic example of channeling another entity, I didn't know what was. Only . . . what the heck did I do now? The seers in my family were kept away from the rest of the family, more for their own sakes, since triggering a Seeing could be rather detrimental to someone who wasn't prepared. This woman wasn't at all of our family . . . part fey, like her sister, no doubt.

Grace laughed, seemingly unaffected by whatever had just happened. "I'm splendid, my dear, just splendid. It's been years since one of your ilk stayed here." A short beep sounded and she leaped up, scrabbling at a digital pocket watch clipped at her waist. I hadn't noticed it there before. "My apologies, I can get so longwinded. I need to see to supper. You'll be joining us. You and your brother." It wasn't a question. "We dine at five. I know it's early, but we like to keep working hours."

I shook my head, feeling as if I'd fallen into an episode of *Carnivàle* or some other similarly odd TV show. It was as if some television or movie scriptwriter had come up with spooky Victorian house with eccentric sisters, added in the fact that this was a former mortuary and tossed in a bit of haunting. Only this wasn't a TV show and I was smack in the middle of something more bizarre. Figures. Out of the proverbial frying pan into the loony bin. Story of my life thus far. Why should today be any different?

Grace practically floated down the steps, silk fluttering around her, as if she were some sort of overgrown demented butterfly. "We'll see you then, dear," she called back to me. Without further ado, she reached the ground floor, turned left and vanished out of my sight.

I fell back against the stair rail. This was going to be one hell of a something—were we really going to stay here for weeks? There had to be somewhere else in the area that could accommodate a couple of Kellys and their vampire lovers, right?

CHAPTER TEN

"Who is the leader of these vandals? I will tell you. They are encouraged by Evandalists!"
—*Sally Brown,* Peanuts (by Charles Schultz)

I found my room down the left hallway, just as Grace had said. No sign of Tucker or Niko, but the *Do Not Disturb* sign was hanging from their doorknob. Chuckling, I entered my room to find Adam deep asleep, curled up on his side on the left of the rather large king-size sleigh bed. The clock on the top of the tallboy said it was just half past one—still early. I could try to sleep, in the soporific heat, but even with the ceiling fan going at full blast the room was far from cool. The small window unit was doing its best, but it couldn't overcome the weather. The disgusting heat wave still blanketed most of central and south Texas with little relief in sight. Was this horrific weather part of this curse? We'd had no rain in weeks, according to Tucker, and no chance of rain forecast in the near future. Had we brought this by our arrogance, by thinking that this land, so long under Kelly purview, would survive the Clan leaving and being replaced by yours truly and the vampire tribe?

No, I couldn't think about this now, couldn't focus on something I had about as much chance of proving as a Millennium Prize Problem being proved by someone who didn't understand higher mathematics. Maybe I should just lie down and try to relax. Adam and I could talk about this later . . . tackle that damned parchment again and perhaps make some progress in figuring out what we had to do.

I quickly tossed my sweaty T-shirt and jeans into the hamper and wandered into the bathroom. A cool shower then a lie down would make things seem better, or at least, not worse. Adam stirred a moment, his eyelids fluttering.

"Keira?" He sounded groggy.

I quickly crossed the room and gave him a peck on the forehead. "Shh, love, I'm here. Going to shower first."

"Mm, 'kay." He fell back asleep in less time than it took me to cross the room.

A small window in the bath overlooked the back of the property. I pushed the curtains aside and peered out, curious as to what the inn backed up on. Nothing much out there but more dry land, some wilting shrubbery and a sad patch of what was probably once a fairly nice bit of lawn. A concrete pad extended below, about ten feet by twenty, just enough for some patio chairs and a couple of small tables—only there weren't any. Odd thing. Most small inns had at the very least some picnic tables and the standard Texas limestone barbecue grill or even one of those oil drum grills. This looked unfinished, as if no guest ever ventured outdoors. Then again, I thought, if all the Rose Inn's guests were supernatural—an educated guess on my part—perhaps the usual amenities weren't needed.

About fifty yards or so past the patio, a small stand of live oaks seemed to act as a dividing line. What was that back there, anyway? Small stone markers sunk into the ground at regular intervals, brown grass, trimmed to perfection, a small shed off to the right—wait—was that a cemetery? Huh. That was certainly different. Sure, we had an old graveyard on the Wild Moon property, but it had fallen out of use decades ago. Not uncommon to have older cemeteries on ranch properties, but we were in town here, though, admittedly a fairly old part of the city. San Antonio was established in the late seventeenth century, and this area was one of the first settled by whites. This certainly didn't look like a modern cemetery. The stones seemed worn and some were broken—at least, from what I could see at this distance. The grounds looked fairly well tended. Perhaps I should go check it out.

The sun glinted off something and I started and stepped back as a man appeared from inside the shed. He carried a hoe, its metal gleaming in the brightness of the afternoon. His movements were those of someone in pain, old and infirm. I couldn't see his features from the window, as he wore a floppy straw hat. He was clad in loose-fitting chinos and a long-sleeved cotton shirt, worn sneakers on his feet. Probably the gardener. Oh well, time for my shower. I could explore a bit later, after the sun went down.

After a nice long cool shower, I joined Adam in the huge bed. I'd barely fallen asleep when a pounding on the door woke us both.

"Keira, Adam, wake up." Tucker sounded upset. I rolled out of bed and scrambled to put on a robe.

"What is it?" I asked as I flung the door open. Tucker's

hair was loose, flowing wild around his shoulders. He wore only a pair of boxers.

"Carlton just phoned," he said as he handed me my mobile. "Sorry, I think I put your phone back in my stuff by mistake."

"What is it, what's wrong?" Adam joined us. He'd pulled on a loose bathrobe, his bare feet silent on the wooden floor.

"Tucker says Carlton phoned," I said.

"I was half asleep when I answered," Tucker explained. "Something about the old cemetery. I told him we'd call back."

"The what?" I rubbed my eyes and yawned. "The one out back?"

"What one out back?" Tucker asked.

"The cemetery behind this place," I said. "I saw it through the bathroom window. Some old man was out there hoeing."

"I was not aware of a cemetery here," said Adam. "Though admittedly, I've not been here in a long time."

"Well, from what I could see, that graveyard out there is at least a century old." I motioned Tucker inside our room and shut the door.

"I doubt Carlton cares about this cemetery," Tucker said as he planted himself in an armchair. "He was talking about the one at the Wild Moon."

I shrugged, and hit the speed dial number for the sheriff's office in Rio Seco. Yes, I still had it programmed into my phone. Not for Carlton, former boyfriend and now just friend, but as the local law. At the rate things kept happening in Rio Seco, it made sense.

"Sheriff's office." A woman answered.

"Daisy, it's Keira Kelly," I said. "Carlton asked me to call?"

"Sure thing."

"Keira?" The smooth voice of my former lover came on the line. "Where the hell are you?"

Tucker rolled his eyes at Carlton's question.

"In San Antonio, why?"

"I wondered. Is your . . . is Walker with you?"

"Yes, Adam's here. So's Tucker. What's going on, Carlton?" I sat on the bed. Adam joined me.

"Last night, I got a report of someone three-wheeling or something up near the old crossroads, up there at the far end of the Wild Moon property. I figured it was some kids going on the conservatory land, so I didn't think much of it. Sent Rudy out after lunch to take a look in case they'd torn down any fences or anything." He paused a moment. "You're not going to like this."

"I'm already not liking this," I said, my crankiness coming to the fore. "Look, Carlton, I've had very little sleep and it's hot as hell so could you just get on with it?"

"Someone's defaced the cemetery."

A chill ran through me. "Defaced how?"

"Gravestones unseated, garbage all over the place, tags—you name it."

I handed the phone to Adam and closed my eyes. "Deal," I said. I couldn't. Not this time. I'd spent ages as a kid, keeping the place tidy, clean. Learning respect for the human dead, learning what it meant to not be human, to be a Kelly. I'd tidied, scrubbed, kept it up. Then a few months back, before I'd Changed, I'd found my cousin Daffyd there, living in a pocket of Faery closed off from the rest of his people. He'd been watching out for me, keeping an eye on me.

"Larsen," Adam said, his voice neutral. "How bad is the damage?"

I could almost see Carlton scratching his head, his brown hair cut regulation short. We'd been lovers for a while, when I was much younger and more naïve, thinking I could enjoy caring about a human. He'd wanted to get married. We'd fought and both of us left Rio Seco—him to San Antonio and the police department, me to London and the bosom of the European branch of the family. I'd met Gideon there. Met Adam. Perhaps it had all been meant. Who knew? In any case, this confluence of my former lovers and my current lover/husband/consort was getting far too insane for me.

"Bad." Carlton's voice sounded bitter. "I haven't done anything more than snap photos and try to cordon off the place as best I could. I've stationed a deputy there for now. I think you all need to come take a look."

"Tell him we'll be . . ." I stopped before I could say we'd be there soon because, no, we wouldn't—we couldn't.

"Thank you for the information," Adam said. "Could you perhaps email Keira the photos? We'll see what we can do. Do you have any leads?"

"Not really. I'm guessing kids getting high, maybe gangs because of the tagging, but none of us here could recognize the tags. Hang on a sec." I heard him fumbling with something and a beep or two from the phone on his end. "Texting you the pictures."

A moment, then there they were. Tucker and I

crowded around Adam on the bed, so we could see the small screen.

"We received the photos," Adam said into the receiver. "I thank you for calling." With that, he disconnected the call and the three of us sat silent as Adam thumbed through the photos.

Two gravestones toppled onto the dry ground, one broken in two jagged pieces. A pile of something at the base of another stone. What was that? "Is that bones?" I asked. "There, at the base of that marker."

"I think so," Tucker said. "Looks like fur and bones, of some small animal."

"Yes." Adam's thumb slid across the phone screen, another photo, more vandalized gravestones. Filth smeared across most of them, a few behind the first with some sort of symbol.

"That is no street gang tag," Adam said, tone solemn. He pointed to a small symbol. "That's a Sidhe spell, a warespell of some sort."

"Warespell?"

"It's meant to be a channel, a way for Sidhe to see and hear what is happening in a place. Sometimes we—they—use bespelled stones or other objects. This marking turned that whole grave marker into a warestone."

"Then did the damage come because of the Sidhe?" Tucker sounded as confused as I felt. "I guess I don't understand the logic behind this."

"Nor do I," Adam said. "Someone spelled the marker, but I do not know if this was done before the vandalism or as part of it."

"Could've been a red herring," I said. Both men gave me a questioning look. "You know, like when someone fakes a robbery to hide something else they've done."

"Only a real vandalism to hide what?" Tucker asked.

"Spells, as in plural spells." Adam stood abruptly and tossed the phone on the bed. "Get Niko up," he commanded. "We need to talk."

CHAPTER ELEVEN

/

"Renew. Regroup. Rethink."

—*Motivational Poster*

Tucker wasted no time in exiting our room. I shivered despite the heat, my body reacting to what I knew now was danger with a capital Magick and Mayhem. "This isn't good."

Adam shook his head and began to dress, pulling on a pair of lightweight cotton slacks. "Far from it." He rummaged around in the tallboy and pulled out a folded T-shirt. Black, just like the trousers. "Get dressed. We can discuss this downstairs."

"What, in the full glare of the afternoon sun?"

A pair of bike shorts landed on my lap along with a tank top. "I am fully aware that it's still day, Keira," Adam said.

I threw off my robe and dressed. "I know that, Adam. Sorry for the snark, but . . ."

"There's a basement room," he said. "We can get there down the back staircase. No windows."

"You do know this place well."

"I do."

I followed him out the door and to the left as he headed for the other end of the hallway, opposite the stairs we'd come up earlier. Servants' stairs? Must be. "So, if you know this place so well," I continued. "How come you didn't know there's a cemetery out back?"

Adam started down the first step then turned. "I've used this as a place to sleep, nothing more. I've never seen the grounds."

"Oh." With that, there really wasn't much more to say. Why was I getting so sarcastic and stupid? What Adam had done before we were together meant little to me. I mean, I knew he and Niko were paired for centuries, lovers for a long time, and family even longer. I didn't care about that. Maybe it was just this place, so full of whispers of the past, of restless spirits.

We descended the stairs in silence, past the opening to the kitchen, past the sounds of the women chattering, down another flight into gloom. A carved wooden door stood at the bottom, stained dark with age, its carvings intricate and very obviously done by hand. A weak lightbulb illuminated the landing. I peered at the carvings. "Angels?"

"Yes, angels, devils, saints, and sinners," Adam said as he pulled open the door. "This used to be the chapel."

He stepped through the silent doorway into the darkness beyond. I followed.

The cool of the room came as a blessed relief. Inside were several benches of some sort, up front, a table? Adam reached the front of the room and flipped a hidden switch. A few dim overhead lights sprang to life, illuminating wooden pews and an altar. Well then. "I take it 'used to be' is a heck of a lot more recent than I thought," I said.

"Yes." Adam ran a hand down the edge of the wooden altar, its rounded edge smooth and shiny. No fancy embroidered cloth covered it as it sat naked on the slightly raised dais. "I believe the sisters still use it regularly."

"It's not consecrated?" No duh, I thought. Or else Adam wouldn't have been able to enter the room.

"Sacred, but not consecrated," he said. "No cross, no trappings of man-made religion. It was once blessed, but no longer."

"Just a quiet place to pray." Niko's voice came from behind us. "I'd forgotten this was here." He smiled a little and, like Adam, ran a hand down a pew, as if re- membering, savoring thought and memory by touch. "It's a good place."

"Where's Tucker?" I asked.

"Charming the ladies," Niko chuckled. "Your brother thought it would be good to get food. I don't think you two have eaten in a while, have we?"

"Good idea," Adam said. "We may be here for quite a bit." I had to agree, it was a good idea. I hadn't no- ticed until now, but I was famished. I think the last actual meal I'd had was sometime yesterday evening, before I'd dolled up for our Reception. I'd grabbed a protein bar this morning while organizing the final exo- dus with John, but that was about it. I knew that Adam hadn't fed properly, either. We'd been too wound up with preparations and the little blood shared as part of the ceremony hadn't been for nutrition but only sym- bolic. He'd fed a little before he left, but not enough to satisfy. I doubted that either Niko or Tucker had done any better.

"Tucker filled you in?" I asked Niko, who'd pulled a

pew to one side and positioned a folding table in front of it.

"Yes," he answered. "Here, help me, would you?" He motioned to another pew. "Could you bring that one over here, too? That way we can sit around the table."

I did as he asked. Adam stood silent, facing the altar. Was he praying? Thinking? Probably not the former, as he, unlike Niko, had never been human, never followed a religion. Perhaps just contemplating our limited options.

My first instinct had been to rush to the ranch as soon as it was dark, only we couldn't. That damnable Challenge forbade it.

"So, food's on," announced Tucker as he entered, bearing at least two laden trays, with a couple of jugs of water dangling from each hand. "Shall we eat and contemplate our imminent demise?"

I laughed, unable to help myself. Only my brother. "Let's shall," I said. "Eat, drink, and be merry, for tonight . . ."

"Tonight," echoed Adam. "We may die."

Food. Drink. Comfort, right? Only not today. Not this afternoon. The sandwich went into my belly like lead. The water sloshed down my gullet, chilling me. We ate in silence, the vampires drinking water and sipping on some blood wine that Tucker had packed. Better than nothing, but I knew that both Adam and Niko would have to feed—which meant Tucker and I had to eat as heartily as possible. I managed to chew through a hefty roast beef on ciabatta with a side of crudités. I knew I needed the nutrition, but I could've been eating week-old plastic-wrapped vending machine food for all I tasted.

"This totally sucks," I finally said, tossing the last bit of crust onto the tray. "What fucking choice do we have?"

Adam looked up from some scribbling he was doing on a piece of parchment that had lined the serving tray. "At this point? Nothing."

"They've desecrated our land, Adam," I began, my voice rising.

"And we shall deal with it," he responded. "I'm trying to figure out these symbols." He pointed to the paper. "See this?"

It was a squiggle topped by a slanted line and a few more lines bisecting it. "What language is that in? I recognize the Ogham runes, but . . ."

"Ogham runes spelling out . . . hmm . . . seems to be some Latin words perhaps. Could be the Old Language, possibly a shortcut spell symbol."

"Possibly? Could you be a bit less vague?"

"Hmm." Adam murmured something I couldn't make out, then bent back over his scribblings. "Can't really," he finally said, after retracing a symbol or two. "The photos the sheriff sent weren't clear enough. He concentrated on the destruction, not the symbols. Probably thought they were just scribbles."

"Or gang tags," I said.

"We're going to have to go there, aren't we?" Tucker asked.

"If we wish to decipher these spell markers, yes."

Niko's eyes widened. "But the Challenge restrictions—"

"Yes, well, there's the rub." Adam pushed aside his

paper and tossed the pen back onto the food tray. "This is useless. Other than the one warespell I recognized, without seeing them in person, I can do nothing."

"But if we go . . ." Repeating Niko's statement wasn't likely to get me a different answer, but I had to.

"Yes, exactly." Adam leaned back in his chair and rubbed his face. "It has been a very long time since I felt this caught between options," he said.

"What if we leave this alone?" Tucker pulled the paper off the tray and studied it. "I can recognize variations on a theme, but as you said, there's no way to tell if you're right. In my opinion, this is one of Gideon's tricks—hire someone to vandalize the cemetery, scribble fake spell marks on various gravestones and lure us back."

"What in all the hells did he hope to accomplish with that?" I stood and paced across the floor. "I'm angry, yes, but frankly, this isn't a 'must do now' situation. Carlton's keeping an eye on things, so we can let it lie for now."

"Maybe." Adam tossed me the phone. "Look at the second photo. The stone that is to the right and partially obscured by the broken one."

I caught it and checked the photos. A shot from the entrance gate, one gravestone broken in two, the bottom still stuck in the ground, the top fallen in front. Just behind and a little to the side, another stone, this one intact, but with blue paint marks. I could make out part of a loop, two slanted lines and what could be a second loop at the bottom. "What am I supposed to see?"

"That mark could be one of several symbols," Adam said. "The most innocent of them is nothing more than a mild digestive curse. These aren't fake spells."

Brilliant, just bloody brilliant. "Okay, well, what would set it off?"

"Anyone walking in the vicinity," Adam replied. "At best, your police friends won't be able to stay on the job long, due to bellyaches and loose bowels."

"At worst?"

"Death."

I sank to the floor, staring at the photo. "You weren't kidding." I wasn't asking.

"No. Without seeing these in person, I cannot even begin to figure out how we can neutralize the spells."

"What if the symbols were just painted on by someone human?" Niko asked. "According to the Challenge rules, no one beholden to us or part of Gideon's people are allowed on the property during the Truce period. If he hired some locals . . ."

Adam nodded. "A possibility. If they were painted on by non-magick folk, then they are just symbols."

"But do we want to take that chance?" I said. "I can think of several scenarios where Gideon conned or persuaded someone who is not of his crew, nor ours but yet still Sidhe to set the magicks." I sighed. "We're back to square one, aren't we?"

No one had to answer me. We were. Damned if we did, and possibly damned if we didn't. Could I take the risk of those spells being true spells, being anything from discomfort to death? Was that even an option?

"Adam, is there any way to contact your father?" Tucker asked.

"If he's already gone Below, then we can try to Call him," Adam said. "It's not a Summoning, but more like a request. Keira would need to do so, since I no longer have Sidhe magicks."

"What's your angle, Tucker?" I asked. "Not that I'm not willing to try, but what can Drystan do?"

"Well, to be precise, he's neither beholden to you, nor is he part of Gideon's retinue."

"But he is our father," Adam said. "He is bound by blood to us both."

"Damn it." I pulled my knees up and hugged them. "So what do we do?"

"I don't think it's a bad idea to contact my father," Adam continued. "He may not be able to go to the land without violating the sanctions, but he might have some other suggestions. I have been vampire much longer than I was Sidhe."

I sprang up. There that was more like it. Action. That I could do. "What do I need to do?"

"We'll need blood and a candle."

"On it," Tucker said. "I can get us the candle and matches from the kitchen."

"The blood?" I asked. "Mine?"

"Mine," Adam answered. "There are a couple of sigils you'll need to draw on the floor or the wall whilst concentrating on my father. I'll draw them out so you can follow. They're not complex."

"I'm game," I said. "What is this calling going to accomplish?"

"We should be able to speak to him."

I laughed. "So our version of a floo call?"

Niko frowned. "Floo?"

"Harry Potter books," I said. Niko still looked confused. "Never mind, Niko. After this is over, I'll lend you my copies."

Adam shook his head as he drew on the reverse side of the paper. "Yes, like a floo call," he said, "but without the special effects. This is pure old-school, voice only."

"As long as it works." I watched over his shoulder. The marks seemed fairly easy. A circle, bisected by a squiggly line with some loops and curls. Pretty. "So if he wants to come through, physically that is, can he use that?"

"No, this is simply a Calling. A Summoning would require more focus than we have here."

"When we were in Vancouver, I Summoned you from Below," I said.

Adam finished the drawing and handed it to me. "That you did. The difference is that there, we had the Portal to Faery handy. Here we do not."

Damn it. The only door to Faery I was aware of anywhere in our region was the one situated in the very cemetery that had been vandalized—the one potentially full of booby traps and on the land none of us could set foot on without breaking the restrictions of the Challenge. Damn it times a thousand.

"I'm for trying Gigi again," I said. "She can't access the cemetery, but she can bloody well fly here and help. This mess is partially her doing."

Quizzical looks from all three men made me rephrase. "Yes, I blame her for part of this. I know it's Gideon and his never-ending quest for whatever makes him hard—power, prestige, revenge—"

"All of the above," Niko inserted with a wry smile. "From what I've experienced of your cousin, he's not in this for anything more than him being on top of the mountain."

"We can natter on about this as much as we like, but we're still getting nowhere." Tucker stood. "I'm taking the trays back to the kitchen. You call Gigi and see if she's got any brilliant ideas."

"If she's unwilling, I will then try to Call my father," Adam said.

"Or both," I said as I pushed the speed dial button on my phone. "Wouldn't hurt to have both of them here."

CHAPTER TWELVE

"If you don't know where you are going, any road will get you there."

—*Lewis Carroll,* Alice in Wonderland

"**W**hat do you mean she's still not back?" I practically yelled into the phone. "Jane, we need her. Gideon's on some sort of power trip. We're banned from our own land and things are so far from peachy and keen that we can't think straight."

"Keira, I'm sorry." My aunt Jane's soothing voice did nothing to calm me. "Minerva's not been back, nor is she answering our calls to her."

"Where in all the hells did she go?" Adam placed a hand on my arm. I shook it off. "Get Dad for me, would you?"

Jane huffed into the speaker then the on-hold music came up.

"She's not happy with me," I said.

Adam frowned. "I don't think that's all of it. She doesn't sound happy with the entire situation. Has Minerva ever done this?"

"Disappeared incommunicado? Not as far as I know,

but Tucker might." My brother and Niko had gone
back to their room. I'd let them, knowing that having
them there wasn't doing anything to help. They might
as well get some more rest, because I wasn't about to.
My nerves sang with tension, my energy-aura or whatever you wanted to call it shimmered so brightly that I
could almost see it even without focusing. I knew Adam
felt it, his soothing strokes along my arm, my back
meant to relax me. But the fury of a Kelly trumped his
attempt. I might not be redheaded, like my brother, nor
have ever been a Viking Berserker, but I felt on the verge
of a true rampage right now. How dare Gigi disappear
like this? She'd said she was going to do some research,
but I needed her. "Damn it." I slapped a hand against
the solid wall. "I hate being kept waiting on hold. I hate
this whole fucked-up situation."

Adam, wise enough to know not to say anything,
just nodded and kept stroking my back.

Two long minutes later, my dad's perplexed voice
greeted me. "Hello, honey. Fire up the face chat thing,
would you?"

I did as he asked. Convenient this new face-to-face
chat app. Made it a lot easier.

"Dad, we're in a jam," I said, reverting to daughter
mode. "Gigi's gone and scarpered and we're in a bit of
a mess. You have any ideas?"

His calm expression didn't change, but he shook his
head in a slow negative. "I'm sorry, Keira, but she left
without saying much. Just that she needed to see someone about something important."

"She's our bloody matriarch, our clan leader. How
can she just walk off the premises without leaving some
sort of way to contact her?" I rubbed my jaw, which was

starting to hurt from the tension. "Dad, what's going on? This seems really odd to me. Don't you think?"

"Well, yes, somewhat." He paused a moment. "She's never really done this to my knowledge, Keira." Dead silence.

I closed my eyes against the worry that began to cross his face. This wasn't normal. For my entire life with him, he never lost his cool, never seemed to lose the innate calm that permeated his body. I'd not ever doubted that my dad could handle anything. He'd been born to a small branch of the clan in what later became northern Scotland and had seen his share of true battle—the kind fought with hand weapons, as well as magick. Very little fazed him. Only now, I could feel his anxiety almost as clearly as I felt my own.

"Dad?" I said. Adam had stopped stroking me, his hand frozen in place on my back. He'd felt it, too.

My father gave a huge sigh and rubbed his face. "Keira, Gigi told me about the Challenge. It's not good."

"Did she show you the photos of the parchment?"

"Yes."

"Just 'yes'? Nothing else?" I prodded.

"She gave it to some of our more linguistically able scholars," he said. "Gigi set this task on them before she left."

"It's really that difficult?" I asked. "I mean, I understand that perhaps Tucker and I don't have the requisite knowledge of the language. After all, it's not exactly modern Welsh."

"I only caught a glimpse, but it's not Pictish, nor anything I'm familiar with. And Adam?"

"He's right here, Dad. Behind me. Can you see him?"

"No, I mean how did he fare in the translation?"

"Huw, it's extremely odd construction," Adam said, as he leaned forward so the phone camera lens could capture him. "Seems a blending of many variations of the Old Tongue. The repercussions of mistranslation could mean our losing the Challenge."

Dad grimaced. "I was afraid of that."

"It's the tiny discrepancies that can make all the difference," Adam continued. "Like the arguments of Bible scholars translating Aramaic—was it 'maiden' or 'young woman'—that's what we're facing here."

I gaped at Adam as all of a sudden, I truly understood the precariousness of our position. I'd assumed that eventually, we'd figure this out. After all, it was language and language could be translated. But now I got it. Nuances could mean everything. That Bible thing, I'd read about it some time ago, where some scholars said the original work meant Mary, mother of Jesus, was referred to as a young woman, not a virgin. Needless to say, that upset the traditionalist religions, considering how much of their faith and beliefs were tied up in the whole virgin birth thing. If that kind of subtlety is what we were dealing with, our chances could be even worse than I thought.

"I don't know what to tell you, Son," Dad said. "You're about as right as you can be. We're doing our best here, but it's been pretty tough going. Three or four of the scholars will agree on a phrase and just as many will argue against it. We're getting nowhere. I'll go back to help as much as I can, but language translations just isn't my strong suit."

"What I don't get," I began, as the implications sank in. "How did Gideon, my own contemporary, manage this? He's no scholar of dead languages."

"He's not?" Adam seemed taken aback. "I'd assumed . . ." His words trailed off. "That makes little sense."

"Exactly," Dad agreed, nodding enthusiastically. "That's part of the overall puzzle. Gideon's always been a bit of a dilettante, studying whatever suited him or took his fancy. He's never been good with completion."

I handed the phone over to Adam so I could pace. Did it help? Not really, but standing there hunched over a phone screen wasn't doing much to relieve my tight muscles. Pacing could at least work out some of the energy. "He had help, obviously."

"I'd assumed as much," Adam replied, "but whom? Aoife seemed less than interested in this entire situation, insofar as the Challenge itself. Your mother?"

I shrugged as I fiddled with a piece of tile that I'd found on the ground. "Maybe? I know so little about her."

Dad snorted. "Branwen? She was as much of a pawn as I was," he said. "We did our duty by our respective families, that was all. She was no scholar, either."

"But then why is she here?" I insisted. "Why is she helping Gideon?"

"She's what?" Dad's mouth dropped open. His image wavered, blinked out and then came back. "Sorry," he said. "A wee burst of unintentional magick."

"You didn't know my mother is here?"

"No. Though it doesn't change my evaluation of her ability to write this Challenge," he said. "This is the work of someone old, someone craftier than your mother."

"My father might have been able to do it with help," Adam ventured. "But it's not like him."

I pushed one of the chairs we'd sat on earlier under the small table. "He did sell you to the vampires," I reminded him. "Though he has seemed to be helpful now."

"'Sell' is a bit harsh, Keira," my father chided. "Back in the day, in those days, rather, kings made these sorts of arrangements all the time. Marriages for power and money, fostering children. You're young. Grew up in the modern world and amongst humans. I'm not sure the latter was as good of an idea as it sounded at the time. I think you missed out on being raised within clan."

"It's not as if you all weren't with me," I protested. "I had the same childhood lessons as the rest of the clan kids."

"Only then it was you and Marty, no one else." Dad's face grew sad. "Sometimes I wish I could just go back and undo some things."

"It wasn't your fault," I said. "Whatever you think I missed out on or didn't get to do, you were the one who came back for me. You rescued me from Below, from living a life as an outcast child." I started to sniffle, tears welling up into my eyes. How had this turned from a discussion about where my great-great-granny had gone to my father blaming himself for not raising me properly? How could he even feel that way? There was nothing I'd not do for him or any one of my brothers, my clan. They'd raised me from perdition—from hell, really, if you can think of the Christian hell as a place of abuse and torture. I'd been ignored, abandoned and mocked. Yes, and abused physically sometimes, a harsh word turned into a slap. Lack of proper warm clothing. Lack of proper food. Seven years of this hell, knowing only that I was unwanted and a freakish child. I had no magicks, or so they'd thought. I was worthless.

"Huw, we'll phone back later," Adam said. "See what you can do to find Minerva."

"Will do," my dad said. "Keira, honey, I love you. We'll help you get out of this, I promise."

I nodded, even though he couldn't see me from where I was standing. "Thanks, Dad." I managed to get the words out.

Before I could take another breath, Adam was there, holding me. "I can't stand this," I said. "Breaking down like this. There's not time—"

"There is always time," Adam said. "You've had a lot to deal with over the past few days. You've not had a chance to relax, to just be."

"No, not so much," I chuckled through a few tears. "Stupid life and stupid, stupid genetic heritage." I wiped my face. "I thought I'd had this down, you know. After those three training months at the enclave. I really had accepted being heir, being part of the political machine. I could do this. But now . . ." I sighed and looked Adam in the face. "If it weren't for you," I said, I might have chosen to run."

"Away from Minerva?" Adam smiled gently. "I can understand that."

"From a lot of things, I think. I don't like being this angry, this anxious. Anger on behalf of someone else, yeah, I can do that. That's part of the gig. Having to be angry because someone's decided to not let me exist peacefully in my own house, on my own land? Makes me insane with it. I just want to fight, to bring it to the table and let it all out. One big knock-down, drag-out fight to the finish. Don't you ever feel that way?"

"Constantly."

"Really?" Was he just humoring me? "You're usually

so . . ." I gestured to him. "Like now, you seem to be taking this in stride."

"I'm not going to play the age card," Adam said. "When I was a young vampire, even though many years older than the rest of the others in true age, I knew that the only way to survive was to temper my instincts and emotions. It's not that I don't get angry. I'd just rather get even." White teeth flashed, fangs and all. "Don't underestimate my emotion."

"No, I can't do that," I said. "When you needed to, you got us to Niko in time . . . even though I don't know how, exactly."

"Nor do I," he confessed. "But I had to do something."

I nodded. Niko had been captured, taken by a group of nasty white supremacist types who'd stumbled across a local werewolf pack. Through some sort of magick—his or mine—Adam, Tucker, and I had bent through space and arrived at the place Niko was being held. Suffice it to say that there wasn't anyone left alive after we got through with them. It was the first time I'd seen my brother go Berserk—the old-fashioned Viking way. Adam, though, he'd coolly dispatched the others.

"We will prevail, Keira," Adam said. "This situation will not break us. I have every faith."

"In whom?" I wondered aloud. "You're Unseelie Sidhe and a vampire, faith seems to be the province of humans raised in a religion."

"In us, of course."

Us. I knew him to mean all of us, not just him and me. Our family. Our blood-bonded Protectors. We weren't your typical couple with two point four kids, but then what other family included the heir to the Unseelie Court and a large vampire clan, heir to the most powerful supernatural clan in the world, vampires, shapeshifters, necromancers, and the like? Oh yeah. Pretty much just us. Then "us" would have to do.

CHAPTER THIRTEEN

*"Strategy without tactics is the slowest route to victory.
Tactics without strategy is the noise before defeat."*
—*Sun Tzu*

Four hours later, Tucker and I came back loaded for bear—or at least research. We'd hit every bookstore and library within a ten-mile radius and then some. There'd been no point in the four of us remaining in the chapel room to hem, haw, and stay frustrated with our lack of resources, so we'd decided that it was time to put up or shut up. Since it was still daylight, Mohammed couldn't go to the mountain, so Tucker and I took on the task of bringing the mountain to Mohammed.

"Help me with this?" Tucker asked as he attempted to juggle three boxes of books. Niko leaped up to help while Adam took a couple of the laptop boxes from my own pile of treasure.

"Did you buy out the entire Apple store?" he joked. "Four laptops and what else?"

"A couple of those portable Wi-Fi routers, some stuff to set up a network." I shrugged. "I'm not sure what half of this is, but Tucker knows."

"I figured we could set up this room as a sort of HQ," Tucker said. "Get some more furniture. At least something more comfortable. Set ourselves up with wireless Internet service and a local network so we can share information as needed. There's a huge hard drive there to set up as kind of a central file drop point to save stuff."

"We bought all the books we could find on Faery lore," I said as I stacked boxes along one wall. "Tucker managed to charm his way into a couple of university libraries and I glamoured us out of there."

"Why the libraries?" Adam asked as he began to search through one of the book boxes I'd placed on the table. "We can buy whatever we like."

"Only not," Tucker said. "Here, feast your eyes." He dumped a box on the floor in front of Adam, who immediately squatted and opened it.

"How?" Adam reached in, his hand nearly trembling. "These are fifteenth-century manuscripts," he whispered.

"Exactly." Tucker beamed. "I raided four or five different special collections."

Niko's eyes grew wide. "You stole from libraries?"

I put a hand up. "I know, I know, it sucks, but you know what sucks more? Us being killed or whatever if we can't figure out this damned Challenge. We will put them back." Or at least leave them somewhere and file an anonymous tip, I thought. "I hate the thought as much as you do, but what choice did we have?"

Niko subsided. "I suppose you are right." He joined Adam, who was gingerly lifting what looked like a rolled scroll encased in leather onto the table.

"Ack, do not put that there," I yelled. "That table is

filthy with crumbs and such from lunch. Here wait, let's get this place cleaned up a bit more before we settle, okay?"

Adam placed the scroll back in the box with a careful nod. "Agreed."

Tucker looked around the room. "Don't suppose we can rustle up some brownies?"

"I take it you don't mean the chocolate kind."

"Those, I bought. I meant the other kind—and not Girl Scouts."

"Really," I drawled. "Geez, bro, you allergic to housework all of a sudden?" After relishing in his sheepish look, I laughed. "Stand back. I'll take care of this." With a few well-placed spells, the room brightened considerably. The years-old paint and dirt on the walls now scrubbed clean, the floor spotless. I tossed in a few light balls in the upper corners to give us more to work with. Despite my efforts, the place was still rather barren, but at least it was more than clean.

The men all laughed and set to moving about the chairs, table, and boxes to best figure out a setup for the computers and the rest of the electronics. Niko squatted in front of the mini-fridge, which was now plugged in and humming happily. He began to shelve food, his moves efficient and neat.

"What? No thanks?" I mock pouted.

"You never say thanks to a brownie," said Niko, all too amused.

I smacked the back of his head as I joined Adam in opening the boxes from the libraries. "That's for being cheeky," I said. "Brownie, indeed. Why don't you and Tucker go back up, find Grace, and get us some comfy furniture. These pew benches are murder."

"Will do," Tucker said and dragged Niko up the stairs with him.

"I think I'll just move these pews back against the wall," I said. "You're better than I am to sort those old books out."

I shoved one pew up against the right-hand wall, hoping to leave the left side of the chapel for our work room. The stairs emptied out onto this side, and frankly, I would be a lot happier with some sort of barricade while we were all four in the room. Paranoid, much? Well, just because I could be paranoid didn't mean there wasn't anyone out to get us. We knew there was.

Instead of immediately digging into the books, I could see Adam walking slowly to my left, as if measuring the walls.

"What's up?" I asked.

"I've been here a few times, as I said before, but never really paid much attention to the layout," he said. "I believe there's a door behind that one tapestry." Adam nodded toward a small alcove to the right of the altar. "I think it leads to the sacristy."

"The what?" I grunted the word as I shoved a third pew against the first two. Damn it. They weren't going to fit together as easily as I'd hoped. I wanted to Tetris them together, one atop another and some next to them, making one fairly solid barrier wall, easy to shove up against the stairwell door if needed. It wasn't going to work. At best, I would have a tottering tower of wooden pews, too easy to shove over.

"Where the priests got their groove on," Tucker responded as he and Niko strode down the staircase.

"That's where they store the vestments and all the

sacred vessels and such, you sacrilegious man," Niko answered. "I'll help you move the pews, Keira."

I straightened and wiped my hands on the back of my jeans. "Didn't take you guys very long."

"Nope. Didn't have to go far to find things, evidently."

Tucker strode over to where Adam said the door was, removed the tapestry by unhooking it from some hidden upholstery tack-like fasteners. The wall was some sort of plastered over adobe type material and the fasteners looked like parts of iron nails. Sure enough, there was a door there. Hung on ornate iron hinges, it was made of wooden beams fastened by iron nails and iron bands of some sort. Reminded me of barrel staves.

"This door is really old." I touched the worn wood above the latch. "Centuries, I'd guess from the handmade hardware."

"Two centuries or more," Verena's voice floated down from the staircase. "It was part of the original chapel." She reached the floor and crossed to where we all stood. "Go on in. There are several pieces of furniture in the sacristy. We stored them there some time ago."

The door opened onto another large room, this one lined with cupboards and shelves. A couple of wardrobes stood against the left wall next to a fairly large sofa, covered by some sort of sheeting. Quite a few cushions and pillows were stacked on it. A few armchairs blocked one of the back cupboards, covered in what looked like bedsheets.

"To avoid dust," Verena said. "Grace and I covered it all and moved it here when one of the studies got water damage a few years ago. Feel free to use any of it." She came down to the floor level and wafted over to the doorway. "There's a couple of camp beds in here, too," she said. "Linens and bedding, too. In the cupboards."

"We're sleeping in here, too?" I asked.

"If you like," Verena said. "Tucker said you wanted to set up a war room. I only figured . . ."

"Thanks, Verena," Tucker said. "You've been very helpful."

She turned then and looked straight at me. "They won't come down here. You might be more comfortable."

I stared back into her watery eyes. Old eyes. Older than she looked. "It's no longer consecrated," I said.

She blinked once, her expression remaining the same neutral emptiness it had been since she'd first appeared in the front hallway. "But it is sacred."

I shivered as her words echoed my earlier conversation with Adam. Had she been listening to us?

Without another word she turned and disappeared up the staircase.

CHAPTER FOURTEEN

"The only people without problems are those in cemeteries."
—*Anthony Robbins*

Two hours later and I was beat. We'd hauled in furniture, even a few area rugs, all rich, plush, and in excellent condition. The chapel now looked like some sort of eclectic hippie hideaway, if said hippies were in their mid-forties with money to throw around. At least one of the carpets we'd uncovered in the sacristy was an Aubusson, somewhat faded, but still glorious in its reds and bronzes, and woven in the style of the Bayeux Tapestry. We used that one as our centerpiece. Other smaller rugs lined the cold stone floor.

We'd set up one long plush couch along the left wall, with two wide armchairs flanking it, one on each side. A hand-carved wooden table had been holding up a stack of moldy cloth. I'd rescued the table and banished the cloth to an empty trunk. To the right of the grouping and up against the back wall left of the door, Tucker set up one camp bed, piled high with clean sheets and blankets. He'd done the same at the opposite end. Both bedding areas had lamps and small side tables.

I wiped my brow. A layer of grimy dust came off on my tank top. Gross. My head was pounding and my sinuses felt full of gunk. "Guys, I'm going to step out for a bit. I need some air." I escaped up the staircase. Yeah, I lived with a vampire and spent a lot of time in his underground bedroom, but you know, this seemed different. Maybe it was the underlying oppressive feeling that kept seeping in, despite my shields, or maybe it was just my own self, weirding out. Before I committed to spending hours in the chapel, head buried in a book or online doing research, I needed to get outside for a bit. Take a walk under the stars. Was it even full night yet? I extended a feeler. Yup, thank goodness. It might still be warm but at least the sun wasn't out. I hated summers in this part of Texas.

At the top of the first flight, I stopped to listen at the closed door. Sounds of some *corrido* floated up alongside the laughter of at least two women speaking in Spanish. Hmm. Maybe I shouldn't disturb them. I was a guest, after all, and was sure that they'd much rather do their thing without having me walk down in the middle of whatever they were doing. Washing up after a late supper? It was nearly ten o'clock. This was the first indication I had that Grace and her sister had actual employees other than the gardener I'd spotted earlier. I suppose it sort of made sense, though perhaps not. How did one explain the unusual nature of the guests, anyway? At least the gardener probably stayed outside and didn't have much interaction with guests.

What the hell. I opened the door.

Grace and her sister sat at a small Formica-topped table, each of them sipping on a cup of what smelled like hot tea. A thirteen-inch television sat on the kitchen counter tuned to one of the local Spanish-language stations. That's what I'd heard, not actual people, just the sounds of the *telenovela* actors. *Betty La Fea,* it looked like. I recognized it because one summer, Aunt Jane had been utterly entranced by the Mexican soap. She'd picked up a lot of Spanish. I'd been totally disinterested by the shenanigans. I didn't like American soaps either, for that matter.

"Keira." Grace sprang up, her cup clattering onto the saucer. "Is there anything—"

"No, I'm fine. We're all fine," I said. Verena had not reacted, simply sipped her tea and continued to watch her program. "I wanted a bit of fresh air," I said. "You know, outside? Out back?"

At this, Verena set her cup down and turned to me. Now both sisters were staring at me with identical odd expressions. Their eyes glinted in the kitchen light, each of them staring as if I were something out of P.T. Barnum, yet at the same time, they remained somber, no smile or any other semblance of courtesy crossed their faces. Creepy.

Once again I doubted the decision to hole up here. Sure, it would be tougher at a fancy hotel, but frankly, you throw enough money at the staff and they would ignore just about anything. I knew this. Been there, done that, partied like it was 1999—oh yeah, it kind of was. My dad had paid the very substantial bill afterward. Not that I'd done the wild party thing justice, I mean, they'd had crazy rock stars trash the place much better . . . or so the manager had told me. He'd been part of the party that night. What? He was cute.

"It's okay, right?" I asked, motioning toward the outside again. "It's safe?"

At the word "safe," Grace started, but Verena just sipped her tea, still staring at me.

"It is safe out there, right?" I repeated.

"What, oh, yes, I suppose it is." Grace waved an unsteady hand. "The door." She pointed to a screen door to the left of the sink area.

Had I interrupted something or was it the thought of my going out back that disturbed her? I frowned and stepped toward the door. "I'll just go out then."

"Wait. You'll be needing a lantern—I mean—" Grace went to the sink and scrambled in the left-hand drawer. "A flashlight? The sun's set."

"No, no, that's fine." I waved her away as she brandished a tiny plastic flashlight toward me. "I'll be okay without it."

Verena got to her feet soundlessly. "Leave her be, Sister," she said in her whispery voice. "She doesn't need the flashlight, she has her own light."

Grace's eyes looked a bit wild as she bit her lip and nodded. "Yes. Well, then."

Before I could say anything or rather, do anything I'd probably regret later, I pulled open the screen door and scampered down the three crooked concrete steps. Freedom. I was outside and away from whatever weirdness was in that bloody house. Shades of *Whatever Happened to Baby Jane* or some other offbeat sister movie. I had no idea what was going on with those two women but did *not* want to know. I had plenty of my own problems to think about.

I wandered for a bit, just happy to be outside in the quiet dark. I was still within the wards, but just getting out of that house improved my mood a great deal. I hadn't realized how much the atmosphere had affected me until now, when I wasn't in the middle of it.

The back of the inn wasn't much to look at from ground level either. The patio slab ran the width of the entire house. A set of French doors was the only access from the back. Must be from a sitting room or dining room. I couldn't see inside, the doors had heavy-duty Grecian blinds, all of them down and the room itself was dark. The only lights from the house came from upstairs, what looked to be a guest room. My guest room, actually. I must have left a light on. Yellow light spilled out from the side—the kitchen door where I'd exited.

As I listened, the sounds of the TV show floated through the air, tenuous noise at best. A few crickets chirped halfheartedly. It was still bloody hot. Nineties, maybe, instead of hundred plus. No traffic noise, no streetlights. We were in this weird patch of land, semi-attached to the bustling city, yet not really part of it. Beyond the cement slab of what could have been a very nice patio if furnished, the usual bunch of live oak, scrub, cactus and then the edge of the cemetery.

Light suddenly flooded my surroundings as the full moon came out from behind a cloud. Clouds? That was brilliant. Maybe we would get some relief. I looked up but my excitement vanished as I realized that there were only a few patchy clouds tonight, nothing near enough to rain from.

The moonlight marked a path between the trees, worn and old, but obviously kept up. Gravel with rocks marking the sides shone the way into the small graveyard. Keeping to the path, I entered the cemetery proper.

Guadalupe Ramon Quinteras, b. 1893, d. 1919 Ora pro nobis. Emilio Vasquez, b. 1822, d. 1907. Francisco Reyes Ramirez, b. 1819, d. 1844. As I read the names on the worn markers, I began to realize they had one thing in common. They were Mexican names, Spanish names, all dead at least a hundred years or more. Servants? That made the most sense. This inn was near a part of San Antonio that once housed the laborers and servants of those in the mansions in the King William district. At the far edge of the property, just beyond another stand of live oak, the moonlight glinted on glass. Must be the window of the garden shed.

"They come here to be shriven."

I started, not having heard anyone approach. The old gardener stood just behind me to my left, straw hat worn on his head, weathered skin telling tales of many years. He dressed casually, faded loose cotton chinos and an equally ancient T-shirt his only garb. Bare feet brown against the cracked gray of the dirt. He leaned against a rake, one hand clutching a gardening glove, the other sporting its match. What the hell was he doing out here in the dark?

"Who? What?" My thought process couldn't grasp what he'd said. Who was he talking about?

"Them." He waved the dangling gardening glove toward the tilting headstones. "The dead."

What the hell was the old man talking about? Had the heat parched his brains?

A low rumble sounded in the far distance. Was that thunder, finally? Were we getting rain? I tilted my head to the sky, trying to make out clouds.

The man chuckled and wiped his brow.

"*Après la sécheresse, le déluge . . .*" I muttered, modifying the famous Louis XV quote. After the drought, the deluge.

"Perhaps you mean, *après vous*?" The man turned his attention to me. "Though that noise was not thunder but a dump truck. There is a facility a few hundred yards or so over the ridge. Acoustics around here are funny sometimes."

"I'm no duc d'Anjou," I retorted, trying to grasp the idea of a gardener, a manual laborer, recognizing both the language and the mangled quotation.

"Nor is your man Madame de Pompadour," he returned drily.

I stepped back. This was not computing. Not at all. Who was this man?

As if he heard my thoughts, he pulled his straw hat off his head to reveal a tonsure and swept the hat before him in a near-formal courtly bow. "Señora, Fray Antonio de Olivares, *a su servicio*."

CHAPTER FIFTEEN

*"If there were no ministers and no priests, how long would
there be any churches?"*

—*Lemuel K. Washburn*

*W*hat the . . . ?

"You're a priest?"

Yeah, way to state the obvious, Keira.

"*The* priest," he said, "if you wish to be precise . . .
and I believe you do." He gave me an odd look, coy, yet
at the same time, quizzical as if he were trying to figure
me out. "You are meeting in my church."

Okay, was not expecting that. "Your church? You
mean the old chapel in the basement?"

The priest raked a bit of the ground. "Yes, well, once
my church. Now, abandoned."

I opened my mouth then shut it again. No point in
mentioning that I knew it was no longer consecrated. "I
rather got the impression that chapel hasn't been in use
for a very long time," I ventured.

"You are correct," he said with a small smile. "Parts
of the inn were built back in the early days when the city
was no more than a fort. One of the earliest masses was

held right here." He pointed to a marker just a few paces from where I stood. I leaned over as the stone wasn't meant to be read standing up. This wasn't a gravestone, but a block of marble, carved into a squarish three-foot-by-two-foot block and set into the ground. Ornate leaves and vines intertwined two numbers: seventeen and ninety-five, carved praying hands between them—meant to be a year, I thought. A stylized carving of some female saint or another dominated the middle of the block. At the saint's feet, the legend: *La primera misa se dijo aquí Fr. Justicio de la Reyna. 2 de Marzo de 1795. Señora, ora pro nobis.* Latin. Pray for us. I may not be great at Spanish, but I did know some Latin. Part of my recent training. Why? Because Gigi insisted I learn something of the tongue, even though it wasn't at all part of my heritage.

"Many of our people came from Spain, France, other parts of the world," she'd said. "Knowing your mother tongue, English, French, and that bastardized version—"

"Joual," I'd put in, just to mess with her.

"Is all fine, but you need to learn the basis of the Romance languages," she'd continued, insistent that I concentrate. I'd laughed, but listened.

I was now beginning to understand that three months hadn't been near enough. I'd learned some protocols, a ton of physical strength and spell moves, plus some language and history. I was still only an egg. But she'd wanted me to go, to claim my rule alongside Adam, to train on the job, as it were.

"The first something," I did my best to translate the Spanish part of the inscription. "Mass?"

"Yes. The first mass in the area was said here, on

this spot." The old man squatted, leaning on his rake, a brown spotted and wrinkled hand passing lovingly along the letters, the carved decorations. "The chapel and the Rose Inn were built a little later. Mass was held here, outside, in the sight of God and nature."

"I thought your God could see all and everything. So wouldn't indoors be just as good?"

His hand stilled. "Sometimes," he said. "Sometimes, I just prefer to be outside without impediment. I'm sure you understand."

I squatted in front of him and examined the carving. "Tonight? Yes. Fresh air is good. Though still too hot."

He reached down and picked up some dirt, rubbing it between his fingers. "This piece of land has always been barren," he said. "Back before humans settled there; before the Canary Islanders came to the fort of San Antonio de Bexar."

"Always?"

"Yes."

"Then good thing you built here," I said. "Not good for farmland."

"Perhaps." He brushed his hand against his pants and touched the carving of the saint, a fond look on his face. "We dedicated it to Our Lady," he said. *"Nuestra Señora de los Dolores."*

"Our Lady of Sorrows?" I knew that name. There was a church in another part of San Antonio called that. Used to amuse me, as they had a "fun and food fest" every year in the spring. The signs always cracked me up: *"Our Lady of Sorrows Fun & Food Fest."* Did no one else notice the irony? But then again, I knew so little of modern Catholicism, only vague recall from reading and, well, from being friends with Bea. "This church is called that, too?"

"Yes. Though the other one in town was built and named after this one."

"Can you do that?" I asked, intrigued.

"Use the same name?" He chuckled. "My little church never meant much to those with money," he said. "It was always the church of the poor, the servants. I don't suppose they cared. Nor do I think that is an issue with the Holy See. There is a church by this name in Mexico."

My initial guess was right, this cemetery had been for servants and the poor. A wisp of cloud slid past the now risen moon and I shivered. Something was off here. Why was this man, a priest, tending to a cemetery at night? Or in early afternoon, for that matter—when I'd seen him from the upstairs window.

The breeze brought the sound of crickets and cicadas to my ears, the scent of dry dust. The cloud passed and the moon once again shone on us. To me, the yard was near as bright as day, though the lines were softer, the shadows hid more. Night never held terror for me, nor did it frighten me. Nowadays, I lived in the night, slept during the day for the most part. The dark held potential, anticipation of time spent with those I loved. But for humans, it was not the same. I stood and wiped my sweaty hands on my shorts.

"So, Fray Antonio, what brings you out tonight?"

His shrewd eyes glittered in the moonlight as he looked up at me from his squatting position. His right hand still caressed the smooth stone, fingers following the carved lines of the image of Mary, the saint carving now identified. "I tend to the last resting places," he said. "Someone must . . . *I* must."

He struggled to stand, using the rake to help him.

I could almost hear his old joints creaking. I wanted to offer a hand, but something stopped me. Sure, my shields were at maximum, but skin to skin contact . . . no, not yet. "I have tended this land for a long time. I chose . . . I chose perhaps unwisely once," he said. "Thus I remain."

"Chose unwisely?" I prompted.

He stretched and put a hand to his lower back, hissing a little. "I am sorry. My back."

"Shall we go inside and sit somewhere comfortable? I'm sure we can get something cold to drink and you can rest a little. Surely your duties can wait." I couldn't imagine how long this poor man's day could be if he was still tending to the cemetery this late at night.

The moon went behind another cloud. This time, when I looked up, the sky was far less clear. Dark patches obscured both moon and stars. I tried to adjust my sight to compensate. Shadows danced in the breeze, seemed to swirl around the tombstones. Few of them were more than crude rocks hewn from limestone and other native materials, carved with no finesse. Such a difference from the cemetery at the Wild Moon, which was the resting place of the ranchers who settled the area.

Another shiver down my sweaty back. My feet began to itch as if I were standing on an ant mound. I looked down, but saw nothing but darkness. Fog? No, couldn't be, the air was too dry. We'd had no rain for weeks. Maybe just an optical illusion . . . maybe not. My skin crawled just a little, as if tiny pricks of insect feet poked it. I shivered again. *Damn it, what was that?* I'd once felt something similar, a long time ago as a child. We'd gone on a family trip, driving across country, learning of the historic places of the country we'd claimed as home. I hadn't realized then that the trip was mostly for me, to experience new people, new places, to learn. I was nine or so at the time? We'd visited so many places, so many monuments, museums, historic buildings. I'd been fascinated, only two years out from Underhill. I'd soaked it all up. Then we'd gone to Gettysburg. I'd been fine in the museum, but then we walked out on the parkland itself. Less than five minutes in, I'd started screaming, feeling the death of all those soldiers buried beneath my feet. Tucker had to carry me off the field and drive me back to our hotel. They said it took more than two hours to calm me down.

Okay, enough, I was out of here. This place may be no Gettysburg, no Culloden moor, but something happened here, something not so good and not so normal. I wasn't up to exploring it now, not by myself with a human beside me. This called for company of my own sort . . . and maybe even daylight.

"Come, let's go inside. You can get comfortable. You're obviously in pain." I used the excuse in hope that the priest would join me . . . or not, really. I wanted to talk to him. He seemed to have been there a long time, perhaps he knew enough of the history of this place that I could determine why I felt so uncomfortable. But if he preferred not to, I was fine with that, too. There had to be information elsewhere, or I could track him down in the daytime and perhaps convince him to go somewhere for a coffee.

"Pain, yes, well." He rubbed at his back again and looked toward the back door of the inn. "I'd rather not discuss this inside there."

"Why, don't you trust me?"

"It is not you that I don't trust."

"The sisters?"

"Perhaps. There is more there than meets the eye."

"I know that," I said, frustrated at his hints. "Look, let's not play around, okay? I get cranky when people start playing games with me. I'm perfectly well aware that this isn't your standard old house, old chapel, old cemetery. Just tell me what you know."

He set his hat back on his head with a pat. "Yes, answers. I know them," he said. "I will be happy to speak with you. Would you accompany me to the church?"

"But you said you didn't want to go inside?" I was now officially confused.

"Ah, well, yes, my church, the chapel," he said. "No, I didn't mean that one." He pointed behind us. "Over that small ridge, behind the stand of trees. There's a small limestone building I use as a church now. It serves its purpose. The older ladies of the neighborhood still come."

"Neighborhood?"

"It's not close, but this is the closest church where they can still hear Mass said in Latin."

"I thought the Catholic Church stopped doing that decades ago."

"They did. But I did not. It comforts my parishioners."

"I had assumed you were retired," I said, indicating his rake.

"Retired?" He snorted a bitter-sounding laugh. "No, retirement is a luxury for those who are not me. Come, we can sit, I can get you a cool drink when we get there. It's not far."

Should I? I did have my phone and no doubt Adam,

Tucker, and Niko could be there faster than one small human could do anything. But no, wait, church. *Still in use*. Damn.

"We can speak here," I began, trying to figure out how to explain when a buzz followed by Lady Gaga's "Telephone" interrupted us. I pulled my phone out of my pocket.

"Dad?" I answered, wondering why he'd be calling us now.

"Keira, we've got a problem. Minerva's missing."

CHAPTER SIXTEEN

"Never give up, never surrender."
                    —*Jason Nesmith in* Galaxy Quest

"Missing? What?" I scrambled away from the cemetery, striding toward the kitchen door of the inn. "Father, sorry, I need to—"

The old man nodded and turned to walk away.

"Father? Since when do you call me that?" My own father sounded perplexed.

"No, sorry, not you, Dad. I was talking to a priest."

"I don't think I'm going to ask," he said.

"More later," I answered. "Let me get inside so everyone can hear, hang on, okay?"

I ran up the small set of steps, absently noting that neither of the sisters was in the kitchen. With as much speed as I could, I practically flew down the stairs to the basement, silently thanking my training as I leaped over four pews that had been stacked across the bottom of the staircase.

"Crap, Keira, sorry." Tucker rose with a sheepish look. "I didn't—"

"Hush, listen." I held the phone in my palm, thumbing on the face-to-face software. "Missing, Dad? You said Gigi'd gone to do research. What makes you think she's missing?"

Gasps from Tucker and Niko. Adam made no sound, but rose to join me. The other two flanked us.

Dad shook his head. "She left me a message on my phone," he said. "Time stamp was earlier today. For some strange reason, I didn't get it until a few minutes ago."

"Cause for concern?" Adam asked.

"Yes, a lot," Dad replied. "She wanted me to call her. She said, and I quote: 'Huw, I'm going to be gone for a bit, but just thought of something. Give me a call would you?' And that's it." He scratched his head with his free hand. "I called her phone several times, getting nothing but voice mail. Called the guys, too. Same thing."

By "the guys," I knew Dad meant her two Protectors. "Why do you think she's missing? It's not as if she's never ignored a phone call," I asked.

"Something about the tone of her voice," Dad said. "Made me worry, so I used that 'find my phone' feature. We've installed it on all the phones here."

A sinking feeling permeated my body. "No, don't tell me. You found the phone, but no Gigi."

"Exactly. The phone, along with the phones of both her Protectors, were in a hotel room in downtown Vancouver. No sign of any of them. All their toiletries, their clothes, everything was still there. Duncan and I talked to the hotel staff, none of whom remember seeing her leave."

I passed the phone to Tucker and paced away from the group, my fists tight and tense as the rest of my body. What in the name of all that's brilliant was happening? Where did she go?

"There were no signs of struggle," I heard my dad saying. "I called in Gareth." Good move since Gareth was not only Rhys's son, but was stationed in Vancouver as part of the Royal Canadian Mounted Police. "He found nothing. I even tapped a few of our seers," he continued. "None of them could See her. At all."

I flew back to the group and grabbed the phone. "At all? That's impossible."

"I know. Which is why I called you. You're her heir. Maybe you can try?"

"Explain," Adam demanded. "Why is this impossible? Don't seers only see possible futures?"

"Mostly," I said, "but these seers, family seers, can *always* see our chieftain. It's a way to keep tabs, in case—"

"In case of something just like this," Tucker added. "There's a blood connection with them, literally. Seers share blood with our leader so that they can reach her in times of trouble."

"As with our bond," Adam said. "I understand. Did you do this as well?" he asked me.

"No, not as the heir," I said. "That bond would have interfered with ours, so I asked that we postpone it until Gigi stepped down—centuries from now."

"Wait, Keira, I'm getting a notification that someone's trying to call."

The screen went dark as my dad answered his other call. I bit my lip, clutching the phone as if it were a lifeline. I wanted the caller to be Gigi. Wanted her to say she'd just been shopping, had left the phone behind.

"Could she just have left the phones behind?" Niko asked, echoing my thoughts.

"Not in a million years," Tucker said.

"Not even. She might be the chieftain, our leader,

but she never, ever leaves no way to contact her," I said. A thought occurred to me. "Adam, the Batphone, is that to her normal phone?"

"I don't know." He strode over to the table and picked it up, pushing the programmed shortcut. "Worth a try."

As the first ring sounded, I grabbed onto Tucker's arm. She had to answer. That's why she didn't have her regular phone, right? Because she had the other phone?

"Keira, sorry," Dad's face came back onto my own phone. "That was your brother Duncan. He went to see one of the cousins, to see if they could help out at the hotel room by casting a location spell. Only that didn't work, either."

"Hang on, Dad," I said. "Adam's trying the Batphone."

"The what?"

"Sorry, it's a phone Gigi gave him a while back," I explained. "Programmed with speed dial to her. Like the Batphone, she always answers if the call is from this phone."

"Except for now," Adam said. "It's rung four times and went to voice mail." He spoke into the phone he was holding. "Minerva, it's Adam. No one can find you. If you get this message, please call us." He disconnected the call.

"It's not ringing her regular phone," Dad said. "I've got that one here." He waved it in front of the camera lens on his phone. "It's on and charged. I was hoping that someone would call her that could shed some light on this."

"Did you check her phone's history?" I asked. "Calls made, etcetera?"

"We did. Nothing stood out. A call from you yesterday, a few calls out to family in the past few days. One to Gideon, also yesterday."

"Dad! That call to Gideon didn't stand out?" I practically screamed at my father.

"Calm down, honey. It didn't stand out because I knew that she'd called him. She told me."

"Why?"

"Because she wanted to tell me? I don't know." Dad's voice got huffy. "I'm doing the best I can, Keira."

Argh. He'd misunderstood me. "No, Dad, sorry for yelling," I said in a much calmer tone. "I meant do you know why she called Gideon?"

"I expect to ream the boy out," he said. "She was quite unhappy with him."

"Huw, did she tell Gideon she was disinheriting him?" Adam asked.

Dad frowned. "She what? Disinherited him? When?"

"She told us she'd begun preparations to remove him from any succession," Adam said. "Keira is to be sole heir now."

Dad's face grew grim. "That's news to me. I don't like this at all. She told me what happened down there. What Gideon did. I suppose I shouldn't be surprised that she decided to cut him loose. Though . . ." His brow furrowed, he moved away from the phone's camera lens.

"Dad? Though what?"

"Keira, I need to call you back," he said as his face once more came into view. "Can you see if you can find Gideon? He's there, isn't he?"

"Here? Not with us," I said. "We've had to move off the Wild Moon. We're staying in an old place in San Antonio."

"Why?"

"Didn't Gigi tell you the details?" Did my family not bloody talk to each other? He'd just said she'd told him what happened.

"Look, honey, you know how closemouthed my great-grandmother can be," he said. "She gave me the SparkNotes version. That Gideon showed up at your Reception and claimed Challenge. Then she gave the scholars the parchment, but that was the gist of it. Nothing about you removing yourselves from the ranch. I sort of figured you'd had to put Gideon up on the property, that's how usually these things work."

"Have you had a chance to help them out yet?" I asked. "The scholars, I mean."

"A little. My experience with Faery Challenges is admittedly rather limited."

"You know of Challenges?" Adam interrupted.

"I do. I am rather old, you know." This last was said with a bit of humor. "I know our dear leader got some notion in her head to help you but she has no experience. I don't know what she was thinking."

"But you do? How? You're at least three centuries younger than she is," Tucker remarked. "Even Adam couldn't decipher all the information."

My father raised a brow. "Minerva may be older than I am, but I was her emissary to the Sidhe royals for centuries," he said. "I lived Below for a long time, wooing Branwen. While there, I made acquaintance with many much older than I."

"You did? How come you never told me?" I asked.

"It's never been that important. How did you think I knew where to find you when I came to get you?"

"I never thought about it," I said.

"Sweetheart, let me go back to work with the scholars, see what I can do. While I'm doing that, you might call—*do* you have Gideon's number?"

I had his number all right, but it had nothing to do with a phone. "No, Dad, I don't." Hadn't had it for years. When I'd left him, I made sure to delete all his contact information from the phone I'd had then.

"I'll send it to you," he said. "I think you should at least call him. See what he knows. I'll work here and see what more we can tell you about this Challenge of yours."

"Papa," Tucker began, his voice worried. "Do you think she's okay?"

"Minerva? She has to be." With that, he disconnected.

I walked over to one of the couches and sank onto the seat, letting every muscle I had relax as much as I could. "He didn't say he was sure," I said. "What if she's not? What if . . ." I took a deep breath, willing myself to calm down.

"If she's not, we will deal with it." Adam joined me on the couch and took my hands in his. "We will deal."

"I think we should fly to Vancouver," I said. "Look for her. I can go to the hotel room and see what I can find out."

"I'd be the first to agree," Tucker said, "except for one thing."

"What's that?"

"If we leave here, willingly, after Truce was declared and after we've established our temporary location, it's tantamount to abandonment. By terms of Truce, we'll have to let our claim go and Gideon wins."

"How long have you known this?" I accused. "Seriously, Tucker, I thought you'd told me everything. Did you know this?" I addressed both Adam and Niko.

Niko only shook his head.

"It's standard Truce—" Adam began.

"Standard Truce protocols, what*ever*," I said, my voice heated. "You guys have *got* to be completely in full-on disclosure mode from now on. Pretend I'm totally stupid and give it to me in simple words. I don't know Truces. I don't know Challenges. I obviously don't know what questions to ask, and now my bloody matriarch is missing somewhere and our seers can't even locate her. If she's . . . if she's dead . . ." I closed my eyes against that thought. Anger, yes, I could do anger, thought it was mostly frustration. I knew Tucker hadn't kept information from me deliberately, nor had Adam. It was simply one of those situations where they didn't know what I didn't know, and I didn't realize that I'd been missing data. Despair, however, that was an emotion I couldn't handle so well. If Gigi was truly gone, dead, passed over, that meant I was the new ruler. I couldn't be, not yet. I wasn't anywhere near ready.

Sure, I could pretend. I'd been okay with doing the ruling thing over Texas and the Southwest. That was cake. I would ease my way in with Adam's help and we'd enjoy the next several decades just learning each other, learning how to be rulers. He'd ruled a vampire tribe, but nothing of this magnitude. Gigi had promised to be there for us, to help us learn. She told me she was going to be around for a long time to come. Damn it. I wasn't ready. She had to be all right.

I voiced my concern out loud. "What if she's dead?"

"She's not dead," Tucker said, with a certainty I couldn't argue with. "You'd know it."

"I'd know?"

"You're the heir, Keira. If Gigi died, whether by choice or not, you'd feel it."

I had to take his word for it. "Okay then, I'll accept that."

"What now?" Niko asked. "If we can't go to Canada to search for her, what do we do?"

"We wait some more," Adam said. "Here, you and Tucker sit and I think the four of us need some information sharing. Tucker, I'll explain the terms of Truce if you can share what you know of the various runespells on the parchment."

CHAPTER SEVENTEEN

"The important thing is this: To be able at any moment to sacrifice what we are for what we could become."
—*Charles du Bos*

A headache beat its pounding rhythm against my brain. My eyes watered with the strain of looking at tiny imperfections in the parchment skin, at minuscule curlicues of ink. Two hours after Dad's phone call and the four of us were no better off. Sure, I understood Truce now—basically, we were stuck here for the duration. So much for my brilliant idea of moving to a hotel. We couldn't leave here (other than forays to town for supplies, but two of us must always remain on property); we couldn't go back to the ranch.

Dad had texted me, asking me to wait for his call a little later on. He thought he'd found something regarding Gigi and had some information regarding the Challenge, but he needed to consult with one more person before he got back to us.

I didn't wait well. I'd buried myself in reviewing the parchment, touching it, stroking the letters, muttering various revealing spells. Nothing. I'd balked at calling

Gideon and made the others swear to let me call him, but later. Yeah, I knew it was stupid, but talking to him right away would have been more stupid. In the mood I was in, I'd just yell. If I could calm myself, get a grip on my emotions, I could approach the call rationally. Talk to him as one person to another, keep my cool. I was going to need time to regroup, to get myself in the right frame of mind.

"Keira." Adam spoke to me with a gentleness I'd not heard from him for a while. "Come away from there, you are in pain. I can feel your headache." His cool hands rubbed my temples. "Come over to the couch and lie down for a bit, love. This isn't helping you."

I let him lead me. He sat and I lay down, my head on his lap. He stroked my forehead. I closed my eyes and concentrated on the soothing touch. My headache began to fade. I slowly let myself fade with it, dropping into sleep.

I woke, swearing, as my phone rang in my ear.

"Damn it." I grabbed for it, narrowing its location down to Adam's pants pocket.

"Sorry, love," he said. "I should've moved the phone."

I shot him a glare as I mumbled into the phone. "Dad? You find something?"

"Enough."

I sat up at the tone of his voice. I'd rarely heard my father sound so tired.

"Did you call Gideon?"

I fumbled, nearly dropping the phone. "Sorry, Dad, I didn't."

"Keira, why ever not? Damn it, girl, we're not playing games here."

I cringed, feeling about ten years old, caught doing something stupid. "I know, I'm sorry. I promise I'll call when we're done."

Dad sighed. I left the call on just audio, not really wanting to see his disappointed expression. "It's not good, hon. I had a tough time with the wording, but from what I can decipher, this is an old-style sacrificial Challenge."

"What?" *Sacrificial?* Adam's voice spoke over mine. "No, not good at all, Huw."

I put the phone on speaker and set it down onto the table. Tucker and Niko came down the stairs, each carrying a tray of food. I motioned them over.

"Huw, what's the bottom line?" Adam dropped into full business mode.

The other two set down the food trays, pulled around the armchairs, and sat, listening.

"There's a lot of history of such," Dad said. "Long established tradition for these kinds of Challenges. Your cousin means to oust you entirely, Keira. To rule in your stead, to bind all the land to him."

"All of it?" I still felt a little fuzzy from my nap. "The ranch?"

"No, I mean everything under your rule."

"How can he do that?" Adam asked. "Minerva said the Truce involved just the Wild Moon property."

"And so it does. Buried in the writing is the fact that the property at the Wild Moon stands as center, it represents all your holdings. If you can bind this land to you, then your rule is safe."

"Then how do we do this? What kind of sacrifice?"

A rustle of paper, then my dad began to quote. "Willing and unwilling meet and marry. Blood of the willing. Heart of the unwilling. Replenish and fulfill. *Rhoi a gadael yn byw. Mêr esgyrn. Gwaed ac esgyrn.*"

"Give and let live. Blood, marrow, and bone." I automatically translated the Welsh, though Adam and Tucker wouldn't need me to.

"It's very traditional," Dad said. "Shared blood given freely reawakens the land, calls the rains. You said the land was dry, barren, a drought and heat wave?"

"Yes," Adam answered. "I thought it was due to our natures, our infertility."

"Could be. Could just be a curse."

"A curse?" I asked. "But who? Adam bought the ranch slightly more than two years ago. Been living on it for nearly a year. The drought only just started a few months ago."

"It started shortly after your Change," Dad said. "When you became heir."

"And that means what exactly?"

"When you Changed, part of the magicks included tying the land to you," Dad explained. "When you pledged yourself to Adam, the magicks felt the death."

"So Gideon somehow cursed it?"

"I doubt he would have been able to do so directly," Adam said. "But Huw, if you're right, Gideon is just exploiting this fact. By claiming Challenge and tying the magicks to this, he's basically caused something similar to a curse, correct?"

"Yes, exactly. In order to break it, you must tie the land back to you by blood and bone."

Adam stood abruptly, crossing to the other side of the room. "That is an ancient curse, Huw, far more ancient than I. It's not just symbolic."

"No, I'm afraid not."

"So by sacrifice you mean, to the death?" I asked. Dad was confirming everything I'd suspected in the beginning. Death for life. Damn that black-souled bastard Gideon to eternal torment.

Three nods agreed with my assessment. Dad was silent on his end.

"This is like some sort of twisted religion. What do you want from me, Gideon?" I said to the air as I flew off the couch and began pacing. "To have me sacrifice myself like some latter-day Jesus Christ, washing away sins?" I caught the view of the former chapel's altar out of the corner of my eye. "Much good it did him in the end. He still died horribly."

"He rose again." Niko's voice, soft but strong, came from behind me. "Keira, I understand that my religious beliefs are not yours," he said. "And I know that the history of a demigod sacrificing himself for his people isn't unique to Catholicism, or even to any of the Christian sects. Tucker's taught me about Baldur's sacrifice, about the Fisher King and the other legends and myths. They had to come from somewhere."

"What's your point, Niko?" I asked, my rant deflated.

"Myth or not, parts of them are true, it seems." Niko put an arm around me and led me back to sit down. "Call him. Call Gideon. We should have done a long time ago. We should have humbled ourselves and asked him to give us the translation, to work with him to see if he could accept some sort of compromise."

"He wouldn't have done it—he won't do it," I protested. "I know him. He's getting a hard-on knowing that we couldn't easily read this. I've absolutely no doubt that this was part of his plan—to frustrate me, all of us."

"Or he wished you to call him and ask him," Adam said. "I do not know him as well as you do, but I can see that being a motive."

"As do I, Keira," Dad agreed. "I'm sorry I don't have better news, but Adam's right. Call Gideon, play nice and perhaps this can be settled without bloodshed." Without another word, he closed the connection.

"And Gigi?" I turned to Adam, searching his face.

"He may not have anything to do with her disappearance. Like us, he, too, is bound by terms of Truce. I do not know where they settled, but he and his people must be somewhere close by." Adam seemed certain.

"How come?"

"He's managed to hire someone, or convince someone to desecrate the cemetery," Adam said. "He could not have returned to Faery through that particular door, not once he agreed to Truce. So he's bound to be somewhere near, as we are."

Cemetery. I'd almost forgotten. "Not to change the subject or anything, but did you know there is a priest here?" I asked him. "I ran into him outside. He looked like the gardener at first."

"A priest?" Adam looked around the chapel room. "I'm not understanding."

I quickly ran through my odd encounter with Antonio de Olivares.

In a blur, Adam crossed the room and grabbed my arm. "That was his name? Are you sure? Describe him."

I pulled away, rubbing my arm. "Adam, what the—?"

Adam's eyes focused on me. "Apologies. Please. Describe him."

"Short, probably around five four at the most. Old. Weathered skin. Worn clothing. A straw hat. A tonsure, which I thought was weird, because isn't that for monks?"

Adam turned from me and stared up the stairs. "He was outside?"

"In the cemetery. Adam, what the hell?"

He turned back to me, his brows lowered. "It can't be," he said. "No. It's been . . ." He took my arm again. "Come, we are going outside. Niko, Tucker, remain here, please."

Tucker put down his book, and before Adam could say another word, my brother was in front of us, arms crossed. "No bloody way," he said. "I am not letting you two go gallivanting around out there without backup." He looked to Niko. "Are we?"

"No, we are not." Niko carefully placed the laptop he'd been using back on the table and joined Tucker. "Your clan chief is missing. You are the sole remaining Kelly heir. Adam is the sole heir to the Unseelie Court. If you think Tucker and I, who are your blood-bonded Protectors, are going to let you out of our sight right now . . ."

Adam gave a curt nod. "Very well. Come along."

With that, he pushed aside the four pews and bounded up the stairs. I shrugged and followed.

CHAPTER EIGHTEEN

"There are only two ways to live your life. One is as though nothing is a miracle. The other is as though everything is a miracle."

—*Albert Einstein*

Outside, the night remained still. The earlier darkness I'd felt was gone, replaced by the clear moonlight. No more clouds obscured its face. The cemetery stones all shone, as if newly scrubbed.

"Interesting," Adam said as he examined the historical marker. He stood and wiped his hands on his slacks. "I don't recall . . ." With Niko practically plastered to his side, he wandered away from the marker, toward the far end of the cemetery. "He said his church was beyond that ridge?"

"Yes," I said. "A building he's using as a chapel, in any case. Adam, what the hell are we doing up here, anyway? Do you know this priest?"

Adam didn't answer right away, instead, he crouched down to read a stone half hidden by some dried-out blooms, fancy ribbons torn and faded. Other dead bouquets encircled the marker and the plot as if someone had wanted to embrace their departed loved one by surrounding him or her with flowers. "Guadalupe Rivera de Caminante," he read. "Beloved wife." A distant look crossed his face as he brushed the top of the stone marker. "Beloved by many."

"Adam?" Niko ventured a touch to Adam's shoulder. "Are you all right?"

With a shake, Adam straightened and came to me. "I may know this priest," he said, answering my question. "But if he is who I think he is, then there are more questions than answers."

"As if that's any different," I muttered. "Where do you know him from?"

"I believe that should be 'when.'" The priest's voice came from behind us. Startled, I whirled, a hand outstretched, a protection spell at my lips. Adam grabbed my wrist.

"No, don't."

The small man, now decked out in black, his priest's collar glowing white against the starkness of the shirt, stepped forward. "Nightwalker, it's been a long time."

"It has." Adam sounded grim. I didn't take my eyes off the priest, all sorts of wrongness pinging my Spidey-Sense. "I see she is buried here." He indicated the grave he'd just been at.

"She is."

"You tend to her."

The priest bowed his head. "I must."

Adam studied the small man, who remained with head bowed, hands folded in front of him, like some penitent, some petitioner waiting for an answer from his liege. Though, that couldn't be the case. Adam was no priest's liege—that was impossible. This old man was

no vampire, either, nor fey. I would have known. Even
if in some strange way, Antonio de Olivares had been
sworn to Adam somehow as a child, a young man, when
he'd swore his vows to the Church, all other allegiances
became null and void.

"How?" Adam finally spoke.

"A curse."

"You were cursed to live?"

"I was."

Seriously? Was he truthful or just crazy? I'd never
heard of this type of curse. Before I could figure out
how to politely phrase "gee, how the hell did that work,"
Fray Antonio opened his eyes, his gaze pinning me.

"I know what you are thinking, child." The priest
addressed me. "All you have known up to now was your
world and that of Faery."

"You know of Faery." I stumbled over the words
that, until now, I'd never uttered in front of any human
other than Bea.

"He knows of many things," Adam said. "If my cal-
culations are correct, this man is more than two hundred years old."

"Wait, explain," I insisted. "Back to square one. I
need the whole story. Obviously, you two know each
other."

"Back in the olden days . . ." The priest chuckled.
"Although, I suppose that term's gone out of fashion."

"It has," Adam said. "But do go on, explain. Keira
has a right to know the entire story."

"As do we all," Niko muttered. I had to agree with
him. Hell, right now, I might settle for even part of the
story, instead of cryptic conversations between my centuries old vampire and this human man who looked to

be in his late sixties, but Adam said was more than two hundred.

"Yes, I suppose," the priest mused. He stopped speaking for a few breaths, then began again. "I wasn't a very good priest. Like many of my brethren, I caroused. I took women, took what they offered. I lived a very happy life."

"Women?" I asked. "Aren't Catholic priests supposed to be—"

"Celibate? Yes, we are. And I am. Now, at least." He shook his head. "We were so far from the Church, our own origins. So lonely in this rather rough place. So few women, so few luxuries. I was never of an order that embraced full poverty, you understand. I took my vows later in life, after . . ." A worn hand rubbed against his collar. "I fell in love. I wanted to keep her, but . . ."

"Then why didn't you marry her?" I asked. "It's been done. Men leaving the priesthood for love. To marry and raise children."

"I couldn't. I was a priest . . . *am* a priest. Though I broke my vows in the past, I could not abandon my vocation. My calling is no different whether or not I love secularly. God came first. She did not like that."

"And she was married already." Adam's words fell like an anvil. *Beloved wife*.

"Her?" I pointed to the grave. What was he trying to say? So what, he fell in love, it didn't work out. Not the first priest, nor the last, I was sure. After a moment, he continued.

"When I told her that we had to stop, that we had no future as man and wife, that I could not live as husband to her, she wouldn't accept it. She ran off, crying. Three days later, we found her body washed up on the banks of the river. She'd thrown herself in. She left behind a husband and a young daughter."

"The San Antonio River? Isn't it pretty shallow?"

"We'd had days of hard rain back then, following a severe drought. The land couldn't take the water so fast, so the river flooded."

I stared at the man, not knowing what to say. *Sorry? It sucks?*

"I went to her family to request her body, so I could give her the last rites. But to no avail. She'd told her sister of our love. Her sister told her *abuela*. The old woman practiced *Brujería*. She'd never converted to our faith."

The plot thinned. I could guess what had happened next.

"She cursed you," Adam said. "The old woman." He stepped over to the grave again.

He bowed his head. "With eternal life. My penance to live and know that I'd caused her granddaughter to commit a mortal sin; her soul to burn in Hell forever."

"A *bruja*? A witch? Was your lover one of mine?" I had to ask. Humans couldn't work magick. They tried, but only those with fey blood had the ability.

"I believe she was of mixed blood," he said. "Not Kelly by name, as the family had come from Spain, but indications are that they came from a branch of your clan."

"Indications?"

"About fifty years ago, I met your leader, Minerva Kelly."

"Here?" Adam looked startled. "You know Minerva?"

"I know many people."

"Can't be family," I told him. "Kelly blood can't mix with human blood."

"Fey, perhaps," Adam said. "Many of the local fey mixed with the incoming humans, the Spaniards as they settled here. It was a diversion."

Diversion. Shit, is *that* what he called it? No wonder we'd had so many half-bloods and mixed-bloods at our Reception. I didn't really care that much, but damn, couldn't they have at least practiced some birth control?

The priest spread his hands out, raising his gaze to meet Adam's. "Here is where I am cursed to live. Here is where I must stay. I grow older and more feeble in tiny increments."

I gasped. That was one hell of a curse—eternal life, but not eternal health. I'd not wish that on—no wait, I might actually wish that on Gideon, except I didn't want him to live. Too damn bad that he, like the rest of us Kellys, already had the near-immortality thing as part of our genetic heritage. None of us could die naturally. We could choose death, or die from beheading or exsanguination, but that was about it.

"Minerva tried to lessen the curse," he continued. "But to no avail. She succeeded only in ridding me of some of the pain of aging." He twisted a hand in front of him. "Some days it hurts less than others."

"That's evil—" I began.

"Not evil." Father Antonio came forward and took one of my hands in his. "Deserving."

"No one deserves this kind of punishment," I argued, pulling away. His skin felt of crepe, thin, broken blood vessels below chugged slowly. The stain of death was everywhere on this man, yet he still walked and talked, was solid. "No one."

"Perhaps, perhaps not," he said. "But it is my cross and I shall bear it as long as God sees fit to make it mine." He gave Adam a look that I couldn't interpret. "Unlike some of us."

I didn't respond. Held my tongue on my first instinct which was to say that I believed in no god, no ultimate power other than that of nature and biology. I used to want the pagan gods, the ones that governed my life's beliefs as a youngster. But frankly, recent events had turned me into practical thinker Keira, who believed in the power of honor and loyalty and love, not in some amorphous "being."

"I did nothing wrong," Adam said.

"You preyed on them."

"I did no such thing. They offered themselves, willingly."

The priest's eyes flashed anger. "Willingly? That is what you name it?"

"It is what it is," Adam said. "I preyed on no one. I came here for shelter and was given it."

"You took my daughter away."

CHAPTER NINETEEN

—

"For those who wish to climb the mountain of spiritual awareness, the path is selfless work."

—*Bhagavad Gita*

"Antonia was yours?" Adam strode over to the priest. "You lie."

"I can no longer tell falsehoods. Lupe and I were lovers for nearly a decade," he said. "Her husband was impotent."

"Not impotent," Adam said. "Infertile. We vampires cannot sire children. When she died, I placed Antonia in a school in Europe. She completed school and married well. She had a good life."

I sat, flat on the dusty ground. Holy crap. This entire exchange now made sense. "You, Adam, Guadalupe was *your* wife?" The other shoe dropped; *de Caminante*—her last name translated to Walker. Some Spanish women added the husband's name onto their own patronymic. Evidently, she'd been one of those.

"For a time," he said. "She was a lovely woman. I was lonely in those days. I'd wandered to America, to find whether or not I liked it enough to remain. Found the Rose Inn. Niko stayed behind to run my estate. I met Guadalupe at a dance. She liked me, I liked her. Though I knew that as a mortal human, we could only be lovers for a few years, she didn't seem to care. She came up pregnant. I knew the child couldn't be mine, but she wouldn't confess as to her other lover, so I married her to keep her from being shunned by the community. Her daughter was born and she insisted on naming her Antonia, after the parish priest, whom she said had been a comfort." He snorted a laugh. "I hadn't quite realized what kind of comfort until now. I'd assumed her lover had been one of the local soldiers."

Adam peered into the priest's face. "Before she killed herself, she told me she was having an affair. I didn't begrudge her it, how could I? When I told her that, she burst into tears and told me she was pregnant again. I'd have been willing to keep up the farce for as long as needed."

"She was pregnant?" The priest's voice was only a whisper.

"Two months along."

"Then why?"

"You told us why," Adam said, his voice hard. "She wanted you. She loved you. You could have left the church, gone somewhere else to start over. I do not blame myself for her death."

"No, nor should you." The man sighed. "This burden is my own. I carry it knowingly."

Niko muttered something I couldn't hear.

Okay, well, this had been a more than interesting night. I stood, brushed the dirt off my ass and approached both Adam and the priest. "Father . . ." I stumbled over the word, not used to formally addressing a priest.

"Call me Antonio, please."

"Antonio, then." How to phrase this? "So I get all this mea culpa of yours, but considering this woman died, when?"

"In the year of Our Lord, eighteen hundred and twenty-two. She was thirty. I was forty-two."

"Don't you think your penance has long been paid?" I asked. "Have you ever researched how to end the curse?"

He smiled, as if amused. "Countless times. Countless resources."

"And?" I prompted.

"I have found no definite answer." He shrugged as he motioned us both forward. "Only vague hints."

"So you remain here," Adam said.

"I remain. I tend the graves and the spirits." Antonio made a vague motion, indicating the cemetery. "They are restless. All except her. I bind her with flowers."

"Flowers?" I looked at the dried blooms, trying to identify them. I could feel no spells, nor had he admitted to having any magicks other than this curse of long life.

"Amaranth for immortal love, blue violet for faithfulness, lavender for devotion," he chanted, ticking the names off on his fingers. "Circled with honeysuckle for bindings of love, wound with witch hazel, a magickal spell, sprinkled with fennel for strength."

A remedy for a human. The language of flowers used to love and bind a restless spirit. It could work. The magick was in nature, not in the person. A homely solution but plausible.

"You speak of restless spirits," Adam said. "Keira spoke of the darkness that invaded here earlier, of the spirits bound within this inn."

"There is darkness here," Antonio agreed. "It is rising. Something has stirred it, has coaxed it from sleep."

"What has happened here?"

"Not just here. I feel it in the bones of the earth. A deep unrest."

A shiver ran through me. "Adam, I want to get out of here," I said. "He's right. Something's stirring and it's not good." I reached a hand out. "Antonio, come with us. The chapel seems to keep much of it out."

He shook his head with a sorrowful look. "I cannot. I can no longer enter that which was mine."

"The chapel?"

"Yes. When the old woman cursed me, she denied me the comfort of those places that are God's. I cannot set foot on consecrated ground."

"But you told me you say Mass."

"I can still act *in persona Christi*—in the person of Christ. That other place is only a building I use, nothing more," he said. "It was never consecrated by the Church nor is my small group of worshipers officially sanctioned by Rome."

Niko's choked voice interrupted. "But they believe you are still a priest—the sacraments . . ."

"I am still a priest. Yes, my position is . . . unique. I have never asked to be laicized; the Church has never dismissed me." The old man stood straighter. "At ordination, a priest is told 'You are a priest forever.' The *bruja*'s curse may restrain me, but God made me a priest. And, even a lay person can give the sacraments if there is no one of the Church available," Antonio chided. "The old women are happy to hear Mass, to take communion, to give confession. This does no harm. The Church tells us that the effect of a sacrament comes *ex opere operato*."

I furrowed my brow as I attempted a translation. "By the work done?"

He nodded. "It is the principle of the sacrament itself, not the holiness or otherwise of the person giving it. If I am wrong, then the sin is on my head, not on theirs."

"Antonio," Adam's voice was gentle. "Come with us. The chapel underground is no longer consecrated. We could not use it if it were so. Come, rest. The spirits will wait and you can do little to tend the ground now. Come sleep."

With a reluctant sigh, Antonio took my proffered hand. I winced at his touch, my nerves raw with his emotion. Guilt, grief, sorrow all tangled in the sucking blackness of despair. I gritted my teeth and led him forward.

Once inside, I made up one of the cots for him. Within minutes, he was asleep, a peaceful look on his face. I cast a simple do-not-disturb spell around him, just enough to make sure he wasn't bothered by our coming conversations.

"He can stay here as long as he likes," Adam said. "It doesn't matter that he knows what we are doing. There is little he can do to affect us."

I watched the priest sleep. "I'm sorry," I said, reaching over and placing a kiss on Adam's forehead. "I'm sorry about all of that."

He knew what I was talking about. "It was a long time ago. I regret not knowing the truth then, perhaps I could have helped."

"Or not," Niko said as he sat down next to us, a brimming mug of ice cold beer in one hand. He handed it to me and I gulped it down with pleasure.

"Thanks, where'd you get this?"

"The sisters had mugs in the freezer," Tucker said. "I appropriated them for our drinks."

"Excellent."

Before I could settle in to enjoy the wonderfully cold libation, Adam handed me my phone. "Call."

Damn it. I knew I had to. I wasn't just avoiding this because I was lazy. There was history there that none of these men knew about. When I'd come home, tail tucked between my legs, frightened out of what little wits I had left, neither Adam nor Niko had been there. Tucker had only seen the aftermath.

I girded my mental loins, then dialed. One ring. Two. Three. I took a deep breath and mentally prepared a message for his voice mail.

"Keira, darling, what on earth possesses you to call me of all people?" Gideon's smarmy smile came across in his tone as he answered. "Do you miss me?"

"Hardly," I said. "Look, Gideon, I don't care for this situation any more than you do, I'm sure, but something's come up."

"I'm sure a lot of *things* come up around those lovely men of yours," he drawled.

"Don't be more of an asshat than you normally are. We read the Challenge. We know the score. Adam and I are willing to talk terms."

"Terms?" Gideon dropped all pretense. His voice grew hard, angry. "What makes you think that there are any terms to discuss? You've interpreted the Challenge, well, bully for you. Kudos, too, since I didn't expect you to do that so quickly. But there are no terms, Keira. None. The Challenge stands as is."

I rubbed my eyes, trying to avoid catching Adam's

gaze. I didn't want to get distracted. "What do you want, Gideon? To rule? To take the land from us? That doesn't make sense to me. You could've ruled alongside Drystan, been part of the Unseelie Court, gotten your jollies there. What changed?"

"Drystan . . . my *father* . . . expected more than I was willing to give. I want it all, lover."

"Don't call me that," I snapped.

Tucker waved a hand to get my attention. "Gigi," he mouthed. I nodded that I understood.

"Gideon, I don't have any idea what Drystan offered you, but okay, fine, whatever. I'm sure Gigi would have set you up somewhere, like she did me and Adam."

"Fat chance," Gideon said. "She was as eager to kick me to the curb as my father was. Seems I'm *persona non grata* in both places."

"So you sought out the Seelie? You do remember everything that happened to me, right? What makes you think they'd take you in under their wing?"

Gideon laughed. "They did, didn't they? Put out the fatted calf and all that . . . at least, the pregnant cow."

I nearly choked at his attitude. "You call your wife a cow? I'm sure that goes over well in the bedroom."

"Oh, I've yet to bed the fair Aoife," Gideon admitted. "Drystan was right, the child is not mine in the usual ways."

"If that's so, then why would the high queen name you the child's father? As pseudo-heir?"

"I made her an offer she couldn't refuse."

"That being?"

"Nothing I wish to share with you. Though do tell my brother that sharing you is simply delicious."

Adam whirled and walked away, his lips tight against words I could nearly feel exploding from his mouth.

"Bully for you, then," I snarled. "You got the cow without even having to pay for the milk."

Gideon chuckled. "Oh, my, it's good to cross verbal swords with you again, Keira. I missed that. These Sidhe are so very . . . boring."

"Then why? And how?"

"Why? Because I wanted to. I can rule with their help. How? We bonded, Aoife and I, shared blood, as you did with my brother. Her child is now mine by virtue of our blood-bond. Blood and breath, dear cousin, she is mine by blood and breath." With that, he closed the connection.

"Blood and breath. Oh my god." I grabbed at Tucker's hand. "Adam, back when I was dating Gideon, in London—those words. Tucker, you remember what I looked like when I came back home, right?"

Tucker nodded. "You were subdued, scared."

"Yes, exactly. Gideon scared the ever-living shite from me. He'd crossed a line. That's when I ran back to Texas fast as I could. Did I ever tell you what he did?"

"Exactly? No," Tucker said. "Only that he'd gone too far."

"He wanted more power, more knowledge," I said. "He'd exhausted everything available to him, to us, as pre-Changelings. We could only use the more homely magicks—warming charms, small location spells, et cetera. That's when he decided to go another route. When he began to invoke the Dark. I went along for a little while, figuring he'd not be able to go too far, after all, our abilities were limited. But then, he did."

"Go too far?" Adam prompted as he came back to sit with me.

"Yes. Way too far. He'd somehow uncovered some old grimoire in Gigi's library. In a part of the collection off-limits to us kids. This was part of her collection that was housed in the London house, had been there for centuries."

"Wait, those books were locked up by pretty strong wards, if I recall," Tucker said. "How'd he get past them?"

"Honestly, I don't have a clue," I said. "He could've charmed his way into someone's bed, I suppose. There were plenty of adults staying there in those days."

"That's possible," Tucker said. "Several people have access to the library wards. They're mostly meant to keep out kids. What did he find?"

"Spells using blood magick," I said. "A lot of them. Not a one of them neutral. That last spell he wanted to try. He'd actually started. Had gathered all the ingredients. It was more of a ritual calling." I took a deep breath. "I just remembered. The spell he wanted to use involved blood and breath."

"Literally?" Adam took my face in his hands as if to pull the memory from me, to see what I'd seen.

"Yes, as in a sacrifice." Guess it was good to know that this particular leopard didn't change his spots.

CHAPTER TWENTY

"Your actions will follow you full circle around."
                    —Indigo Girls, "Center Stage"

"We have no more choices." Adam let me go and stood. "Between what you've told me and the desecration at our cemetery, we must go there now. If Gideon is willing to invoke sacrificial magick of his own accord, I've no doubt he has every intention of breaking Truce—or has already done so. We've been sitting here like fools as he plays his games behind our backs."

"But the terms?" I said. "If we go back onto the land . . ."

"We'll be careful." Adam turned to Tucker. "Pack up a day's worth of supplies. We'll have to hurry, but I think we should wait no longer. Keira, could you talk to Bea, see if she'll put us up? I'm sure we can sunproof some of the windows at your old place."

"On it," I said, and removed myself to the back room to make the call. I could hear the guys making plans. Finally, something to do. It was past midnight, but if we drove fast, we could make it to Bea's by three-thirty or four.

"Hello?" Bea's sleep-fuzzy voice answered.

"Bea, hon, sorry to wake you, but it's important."

"Keira? You okay? What's wrong?"

"No, nothing—well, nothing you need to worry about," I said. "I just wanted to ask if it's okay that Adam, Tucker, Niko, and I came to stay with you."

"Of course. When?" She yawned.

"Now."

"Now?" I could hear her turn on the light. "Sure, but . . ."

"*M'ija,* it's a long, long story and I'll explain when we get there, okay?"

"Fine, I guess," Bea said. "You sure everything's all right?"

"Don't fret, I promise it's all okay. We'll be there in about three hours, *sí*?"

"*Sí,* sure. You still have a key, right?"

"I do. You go back to sleep. You working in the morning?"

"Yeah, but later. Noe's taking the opening shift along with Tio and Tia."

"Excellent. See you soon." I hung up and reentered the main room. "All set with Bea. We can lightproof the windows—some duct tape, those really thick trash bags. We can do that when we get there, at least take care of the guest room windows so you two can sleep. Tucker and I can finish up the rest of the house once it's daytime and we won't be disturbing Bea."

"Good."

"May I come with you?" The quiet voice came from the far corner. Antonio. I'd forgotten about him.

"You want to come with us? Why?"

"Perhaps I can help," he said.

"With Sidhe magicks? Sorry, Antonio, I appreciate the offer," I said, "but this isn't something you need to help with."

"I would like to try. I can no longer stand by. You have shown me courtesy and compassion, traits lacking in so many. I could perhaps run errands, do things that free you to do what you do best."

He had a point. I couldn't involve Bea in this, pregnant as she was. I could perhaps call Dixxi back to help out, but she'd be better off continuing her research at the Health Science Center. Frankly, the priest could be our fetch-and-carrier without too much trouble.

"Do you drive?" I asked.

"I can. I am a man of many years, but have garnered many talents." He grinned at me.

I threw up my hands. "Fine then, join the party."

"Antonio, come, you can help me pack up," Tucker said.

As I tucked the phone back into my backpack, Adam leaned over and whispered. "That was nice of you."

"He wanted to help, let him help. I can't imagine living as he does. If helping us helps relieve his burden even one small bit, who am I to stop him?"

Adam kissed me, a brief peck on the lips. "Thank you."

"For inviting the priest?"

"No, for going along with my plan." He kissed me again. "We could be exposing ourselves to just about anything. We're breaking Truce."

I shrugged and folded a blanket. "Better than wasting our time here. Now that we know the terms of the Challenge, I have no intention of fulfilling it that way. No one is going to die for us. We'll just have to come up with something else." I tossed the blanket on the couch. "I've not forgotten that Gigi is missing," I said. "I just think that action is better than inaction. I can't find her sitting here, any more than I can do anything about the Challenge sitting here."

"I didn't think you had forgotten her. I agree, whatever happens next, at least it will be as the result of us doing something."

"It could very well be a trap." I sat on the edge of the couch, watching Niko and Antonio pack the contents of the mini-fridge into a green cooler as Tucker hauled boxes of books up the stairs, a laptop bag over each shoulder.

"That hadn't escaped me." Adam put his arms around me and laid his head atop mine. "As you said, I have no intention of going down without a fight."

"You think it will come to that?"

"A fight?" Adam stroked my hair. I closed my eyes and let myself get lost in the sensation. "I do. Part of me wonders if my brother meant this to happen."

"To lure us back to fight? Maybe." I purred as Adam's hands went to my shoulders, kneading the tense muscles. "That feels good."

He kissed the top of my head and kept up with the massage. "I wish we could do nothing but this for the rest of the night, love, but we have places to go."

"And people to see," Tucker exclaimed. "Stop with the canoodling, you two. We're loaded up and ready to go."

"Did you tell Grace or Verena?" I said, unwilling to move just yet.

"They weren't around so I left a note on the kitchen table," Tucker said. "Told them we had to leave and to feel free to charge us whatever."

"That works."

I leaned my head back onto Adam's abdomen. "Thanks, love."

He bent his head and kissed my lips. "Anytime."

"Shall we?" Tucker asked, getting impatient.

Without a word, Adam stepped back and offered me his hand. I took it as I stood and without further ado, we climbed the stairs.

"Onward through the fog," I murmured as Tucker started the engine. "I can't help but feel we're going to our doom."

"As long as it isn't Mount Doom, I can deal," Tucker laughed and turned out of the drive.

"We few, we happy few, we band of brothers." Antonio's voice came from the back of the Rover. I sat up shotgun, while Adam, Niko, and Antonio shared the back with the various bits of luggage that hadn't been lashed to the roof of the car.

"For he today that sheds his blood with me shall be my brother." Adam completed the line and took Antonio's proffered hand and shook it. I watched the interaction with a bemused smile.

"Let us all hope it does not come to that," Niko said with a grimace.

Hope. It was pretty much all we had left, except for our own unique brand of chutzpah. I prayed it would be enough.

CHAPTER TWENTY-ONE

"An open door invites callers."

—*Turkish Proverb*

After I deposited the vampires at Bea's, with Niko and Antonio covering the guest room windows, I convinced Tucker to take a quick trip out to the cemetery before dawn.

"A recce, only, bro," I pleaded. "Just a drive by. I want to see what I can feel." Feel. That was a glorious word. At three miles out from the Rose Inn, I'd felt a great weight lift and the world began to seem lighter, less oppressive. With caution, I'd released some of my shields. Bit by bit as we drew closer to Rio Seco, to our lands, I began to feel normal again. By the time we hit the main road into town, the one that led past the strip center, I'd been able to relax my shields to their usual strength. I gloried in it. It was as if—no it was *exactly* because, I had arrived home. Despite the Challenge, despite the barrenness, I felt the call of the land. Of home and hearth. I knew that we could figure something out, damn it. I just knew it.

"Okay, a quick reconnaissance only," Tucker agreed.

"No getting out of the car, no driving too close. We'll just go to the crossing and see if we can feel anything."

I jumped up and hugged my brother. Energy spiked between us as I held him tight.

"Whoa, what was that?" Bea shuffled into the living room dressed only in a pair of stretchy black pants and a sports bra. Her abundant black hair was tied back into a messy ponytail.

I laughed and twirled, giddy with delight. "Energy, Bea. Clean family blood-bonded energy."

Bea shook her head and grabbed a mug from the rack, pouring herself some coffee. I'd started a pot the moment we'd arrived. "I saw Adam in the small guest room talking on his phone," she said. "Where's Niko?"

"Lightproofing the other guest room with the priest," Tucker said. "Keira and I are going to do a quick recon visit. We'll be back inside the hour." He left the room, going down the hallway to the bedroom area. The house was small, a master bedroom with en suite bath, a couple of guest rooms. A nice size living room with eat-in kitchen. I'd lived here for nearly two years until Adam came back into my life. Then I'd given the house to Bea. She needed a place of her own.

Bea sipped her coffee with a frown. "This tastes funny." She took another sip, then put down the cup and walked over to the fridge. "Priest? Is that some sort of title for one of your family?"

"Nope," I said. "A real priest as in Roman Catholic. Long story."

She handed me her mug of coffee. "Here, I can't drink this."

I took it and savored the aroma. It was heavenly. "It's wonderful, Bea, you don't like it?"

She shook her head as she poured a glass of milk. "Stupid pregnancy hormones," she said. "I can't seem to drink coffee anymore."

"That truly sucks," I said. "But thanks for this."

She nodded and sat down at the kitchen table. "Priest, huh? You roping in all the religious types, now?"

"Just the one," I laughed. "Bea, it's so good to be here. To see you. Like old times."

"Except with two vampires, a wolf, and a priest." She gave me a milk mustache smile. "Only you, Keira."

"Yeah, well." I shrugged. "That's kind of my life anymore."

"The Reception was nice?"

"Until Gideon showed up, yeah," I said. I'd gone to her bedroom as soon as we'd arrived and given her the down 'n' dirty of the situation. She'd taken it in stride, rolled over and asked to be allowed to go back to sleep for a little while. That had been just over an hour ago. "Why did you get up?"

"I normally get up around now," she said. "Do some yoga stretches for a while, eat breakfast, then shower and go to work."

"I thought you said you didn't need to open the café?"

"I don't need to," she said, "but I do anyway. Tio and Tia are too old to be taking up my slack. I'm perfectly healthy. There's no reason to cut back my hours yet." She spread her hands on her abdomen. "I'm not even showing yet," she said. "I'll save the coddling for when I'm big as a house."

"Sounds like a plan. You feeling okay?"

"Other than the coffee? Yeah," she said. "Fine. Dixxi

said she'd come visit once a week to draw blood, weigh me, and all that jazz."

"Good." Since Bea was pregnant with a half-wer child, she couldn't go to a regular doctor. A werewolf herself—and aunt to Bea's baby—Dixxi was primarily a geneticist, but had plenty of medical knowledge and was helping Bea out.

Tucker came back into the room. "Adam's off the phone now," he said. "He told Dad where we were. Still no word on Gigi."

My bubbly mood burst. "Damn it."

Tucker nodded. "Yeah, but unfortunately, there's not much we can do. Word's out to all the Kellys, on this continent and all the others. Dad's put out an APB, basically. We'll find her."

"For the love of—Tucker, has he mobilized the entire Kelly clan? Isn't that likely to cause panic?" I loved my Dad, but he wasn't the political sort.

"Panic how? It's not as if we don't have an heir in the wings." Tucker shrugged and picked up my backpack. "We going?"

Oh bloody hell. "Where's Adam?"

"He went into the other room to get more supplies. He wants to tape up Bea's bedroom while she's not using it and then start on the living areas."

"Did you tell him we were going?"

"I did."

"He didn't like it, did he?" Which is why he was currently not in the living room. He wasn't going to try to argue me out of it. He knew better and he wasn't about to air our dirty linen in front of Bea. None of us had stated it outright, but all of us knew that Bea was to be protected. She was as much our charge, as much family as any of the people who had pledged fealty to us, who'd taken blood oath. She was mine and whatever I could do to protect her, I would.

"Not so much." Tucker's tone was wry.

Bea's eyes grew round. "Is this dangerous, Keira? Where you're going."

Crap. Neither Tucker nor I had mentioned the cemetery to her, considering that was the place where she'd nearly been raped, then killed. Nor had I mentioned that little matter of the Challenge restrictions. I'd only told her that we'd left as part of the Challenge, but not the part about possible consequences of our return.

"We'll be fine, *chica*," Tucker chucked her under the chin, like he used to do when Bea and I were both kids. "You know I'll take care of my sister."

"You'd better," Bea said into her glass of milk. "Go on then, do whatever you have to. I'll make sure the others get to bed in time."

"There's a camp bed on the porch," Tucker said. "If you like, I can bring it in here for Antonio."

Bea shook her head. "He can sleep in my room," she said. "For now, anyway. I'll be at the café until closing. We can talk about this later."

I leaned over and gave her a quick hug. "Thanks, *chica*. For everything."

"*De nada, chica*," she whispered into my hair. "Take care of yourself, okay?"

"Always."

The trip seemed shorter than usual, both of us keeping quiet on the way, as if to process everything we'd learned, everything we'd experienced over the past couple of days. Too much. Too soon. Where was Gigi? Had she done something stupid, or was she squirreled away somewhere hatching a new plot? I wouldn't put it past her. Like me, or maybe I was like her, she wasn't one to sit back and let things unfold slowly. If she could, she'd be right in the thick of it, stirring the pot with every intention of making it come out her way. She'd managed so far—her genetic games producing three possible heirs. Me, Gideon, and the late unlamented Marty. Marty, unfortunately had been somewhat of a dud, a biological sport who'd managed to inherit all sorts of recessive genes, leaving him a Kelly manqué, with not one iota of magickal ability. Then me, who'd Changed far too early, nearly dead from exsanguination as I'd brought Adam out of a coma. Turns out, near-death experience is what triggers the Change for an heir, go figure. Gideon, not to be outdone, had managed to hex himself into a coma, hoping to Change. Once he'd done so, he'd run off to Faery and found his long lost father—Drystan.

Now here we were, at opposite ends, a weird-ass face-off about to happen as if we were fulfilling some long ago prophecy. Except I didn't believe in prophecy. Even our Kelly seers knew better than that. Prophecies were usually uttered by humans who only played at having Talent. The real thing wasn't so much a prediction as a potential. No future writ in stone. No swords buried in stone either, for that matter. Just two cousins on opposite sides of what was sure to become a battle royale. I wasn't kidding myself anymore. I knew that our breaking Truce wasn't going to result in mere pesky annoyances, but in all-out war. I had to prepare, and a reconnaissance of the old cemetery was step one.

"Bloody hell," I whispered as Tucker pulled up

alongside the road that would lead us close to the small cemetery. "Can you feel it? I didn't even have to crack open a window."

Tucker nodded, his face grim.

The atmosphere above the cemetery roiled; dark shapes, darker than the night, twisted in a grotesque parody of some sort of danse macabre. The very air seemed thick and bloated.

I threw up a warding spell around the Rover and the feeling of oppression lessened a bit.

"What is that?" Tucker asked, his big hands gripping the steering wheel.

"Some of the same," I said. "The same spirits I felt in the cemetery at the Rose Inn. Only here, there are more. Way more."

"Gideon?"

"Had to be. The warespells we saw in the photos. Must have—" I fell back against the seat as something else hit my senses.

"What the fuck?" I scrabbled forward again.

Tucker's arm shot across, stopping me. "You're not opening that door."

"No, I'm not," I said. "I'm not an idiot. I just need to . . ." I pressed a palm against the glass of the passenger side window, concentrating. I could feel a different energy behind the dark shapes, something cleaner, more familiar. As I probed, the darkness thickened, the shapes melding together, more and more of them whipping faster and faster into the maw of the center. It grew, pulsing in the dark, blocking the night.

"Keira, what is that?" Tucker's voice seemed to come from far away. I ignored him.

"C'mon," I urged, "c'mon. I can feel you."

With a shudder of air and a *whoomph* of nearly silent sound, the dark shape shredded into its component pieces, all of which slowly settled down, below our sight.

Tucker grabbed my arm and tore it away from the window. "Keira? Are you all right?"

"Damnation." I sank back against the seat and put a hand over my eyes. "I'm fine. Only I don't think things are."

"What? You're not making sense." I knew that Tucker's frustration was only his worry for me.

I took my arm down and looked directly into his eyes. "The door to Faery is wide fucking open."

CHAPTER TWENTY-TWO

"Do not ask questions of fairy tales."

—*Jewish Proverb*

"Open, how?" Adam paced the small room. Tucker had turned the car around and returned to Bea's without another word. He'd been at the Faery portal with me before. He knew the dangers of the place.

"I don't know," I said. "Those shapes, the dark spirits hid the magick from me at first. It wasn't until they started to coalesce that I began to feel—"

"Coalesce?"

I kept untangling my braid. I was exhausted, wrung out. I wanted to do nothing more than to get some sleep. "Yes, coalesce. Like the many pieces wanted to create a whole."

"That does not sound good."

"It doesn't," I agreed. "But behind the dark wall, I felt the door. Which is why I had to try to find out if I was just imagining it or not." I put down my hairbrush. "Stop pacing, damn it."

Adam sat on the bed and regarded me. "It's open."

"Completely. So open that anyone could access

Faery without knowing how to. We need to set a guard, or figure out how to close the door again."

"I'm not sure I can do that."

"Well then, we just go on into Faery, find your bloody father and have him close it." I motioned for Adam to get off the bed so I could pull down the covers. "Adam, I'm bloody well beat, love. I can't think anymore. Let's get some rest, okay?" I could barely keep my eyes open. As much as my brain wanted me to take care of this now, I had to rest, to recharge.

"I don't like the idea of leaving that door open any longer than we have to."

"I set up some notice-me-not wards around the crossing," I said. "Left a voice mail at the sheriff's office that we were back, and that we'd take care of the vandalism. I don't want any of the deputies to get sick." I slid underneath the covers and laid my head on the pillow. "Come to think of it, there weren't any cars out there." I yawned. "Carlton must have given up watching the place."

"Of course." I never heard him leave the room.

"We need backup, Keira," Tucker argued over breakfast. "We have to get some help."

I shoveled a forkful of eggs into my mouth and chewed to give me time to calm down. After swallowing, I spoke as calmly as I could. "I know, Tucker. We've got two vampires that can't come with because it's broad daylight. Bea's out of the question. Who else?"

Tucker gripped his coffee mug tight. "I don't want us to be alone out there."

"I wasn't planning to do anything rash, Tucker," I said. "I just wanted to see it during the day. Bring Antonio along. He can help keep an eye out."

"I'm happy to," the priest's voice came from the living room. "I can even help bless the land again."

"See?" I finished my eggs and tossed the fork onto the plate. "C'mon, we can do this, okay?"

Tucker shook his head. "No bloody way am I going out there without Adam and Niko," he said. "I'm happy to bring the priest along when we go, but what we saw last night scared the crap out of me. Dad agrees, by the way."

"You called him?"

"Yeah, first thing when I got up. I told him about what we saw."

"What was his take?"

"That Gideon's somehow spelled the spirits angry," Tucker said. "Our family isn't attuned to the dead for nothing."

"Yeah, well, I suppose." I rose from my seat and joined Antonio in the living room. He was reading a Bible, his probably, as I didn't think Bea had one. "Anything interesting?"

He shook his head and closed the book, a finger marking his place. "It comforts me."

I didn't know what to say to that, so I ignored it. "Fine, Tucker, you win," I said. "I'll wait until dusk."

"Good. I'm going to get some groceries," he said. "Antonio, would you care to come along?"

"I will." The old man pushed against the arm of the chair, struggling to stand. After a moment, he put out a hand. "Tucker, if you wouldn't mind?"

Tucker crossed the room and held out his arm. Antonio grabbed it and hauled himself into a standing position. "It's getting a bit worse," he said with a rueful smile. "Some days better, some days bad."

"I wish there was something I could do," I said. "I'm so sorry. I can't even help you up." I'd accidentally tried to do so earlier in the day. Antonio had risen early, started coffee and fixed a mess of scrambled eggs and bacon. He'd then settled into the armchair. When I'd smelled the coffee, I'd gotten up, leaving Adam asleep. I'd brushed against Antonio and nearly fainted. He felt like death.

Had our removing him from the place he'd been cursed caused more harm than good? Perhaps. I'd offered to return him, to call him a car or something, but he'd refused. He didn't want to go back to the Rose Inn. I respected that.

"You are helping by allowing me to help, Miss Kelly. I thank you." He tucked his arm into Tucker's with a jaunty smile. "Now, let's go buy food."

I watched as the two of them left through the front door. Locking it behind them, I sank back onto the couch, once one of my favorite places to sit and contemplate the universe. I'd lived here two solitary years, entertaining myself as I supposedly watched out for Marty, my penance from Gigi for refusing to leave with the clan when they departed en masse to live in Canada. Gigi. Where was she, damn it? Why hadn't she surfaced?

With a deep breath, I began the meditation breathing she'd taught me. In, count, out. In, count, out. I let my thoughts fly through my head, latching onto none of them. Clearing my thoughts, clearing my brain. Soft sounds of breathing from the bedrooms entered my consciousness. Adam and Niko. They'd bunked together as—with day dawning—they'd run out of time lightproofing the second guest room. Tucker had slept on the living room couch. Even though it was quite long, it barely fit his six-foot-four length, especially when he slept sprawled out as he liked to. I'd protested, but then realized he needed to do this, to stand guard so to speak. I let him. We'd set up the camp bed for Antonio behind the couch.

I'd taken the other guest room and slept for hours, deep and solid. No nightmares, no dreams I could remember. I'd only woken up to the smell of breakfast somewhere around eleven-thirty or so. I could still smell the savory eggs, the rich coffee, the meaty aroma of the crisp bacon. *In, count, out. In, count, out.*

I sank deeper into my own consciousness, letting the mundane slide past, focusing on centering myself. Inside, deeper and deeper. As I settled into my trance state, I did a subconscious body and energy check. I was topped off, shields strong and steady.

I let my awareness drift out, away from my center. Gigi . . . Where are you? I focused on feeling her—her vitality, her soft scent, the smoothness of her milky skin beneath mine when she leads me in a spell. Her voice, lilting through Welsh, then back to English, then Welsh again as she speaks of our heritage, teaches me our protocols. Songs of love, laughter, and our people as she sings me lessons in the wee hours, my body weary, muscles aching from sparring. With a breath and a whisper I am re-energized, the zing of power racing through me, soothing my aches and removing the pain. She is mother, father, leader, mentor. She is Teacher. She is . . .

. . . *sitting alone in an empty room. All white walls, floors, no windows. She sits in full lotus, eyes closed against the too bright light, chest rising and falling in cadence with mine. The room is warded tight. Spells shine against the walls, the floor, chains of unseen light trap her there. She wears white on her body, a color not commonly seen as part of her wardrobe, some sort of loose tunic and leggings. She is barefoot, her hair loose, dark waves falling past her shoulders to her waist. Nothing to constrict. Nothing to bind, except the wardspells.*

"Gigi," I whisper.

Her eyelids flutter, but do not open.

The wards shimmer, shaking against my intrusion. I read the words embedded within the spells. Words meaning lock out. Meaning she is prisoner here.

I whisper again. "Where are you, Gigi?"

She begins to form a word with her lips.

The world smashed me back to reality as Tucker and Antonio entered the front door, laden with groceries. I winced and fell over, my half lotus unraveling as I hit the floor.

"Keira!" Tucker dropped the bags on the floor and ran over to me. "You okay?"

I nodded. "Yeah, sorry, a bit of a headache."

"Were you meditating on the couch?"

"Yeah, dumb idea."

"Especially since you knew we'd be back soon," he said and rescued the grocery bags. "You should go lie down for a bit more, okay?"

"Tucker," I stood in excitement. "I saw Gigi."

"What? How?"

"She was in some sort of white room," I said. "Meditating, like I was. Only the room was warded beyond the telling of it."

"It was a vision?"

I snagged a banana from the bunch on top of one of the bags. "I don't know. She heard me calling to her. I know it." I peeled the fruit and took a huge bite, chewed and swallowed. "I'm not going to say she is actually in a white room," I said. "I'm sure that was more symbolic than anything, but she's definitely behind wards."

"Did you get a sense of where?"

"Not around here." I waved my hand, banana and all.

"I didn't think she was," Tucker said. "Anything more concrete?"

"Not *around here,* around here," I tried to explain. "She's not anywhere."

Tucker's brow furrowed. "That's not possible."

"It is." Adam walked out into the living room, avoiding the windows. I'd closed all the curtains and taped them over, but it wasn't the same as blackout curtains. "I think Minerva is elsewhere. Below."

"That's it!" I grabbed him into a hug. "That's what I felt. Elsewhere. The feel of Faery. It's the Between."

"Then how do we get her out?" Tucker asked. "You don't expect to charge in there, do you? Faery isn't like here. You can't just follow a map."

"No, but we can check out the open door at the cemetery," I said. "I want to ward it and shut it so that no one can wander in there. Then we can figure out how to get to Gigi."

"Do you think that's why it's open?"

Adam and I both shook our heads. "If she went to Faery, there's no need for her to come all the way here first. She would've used the door in Vancouver."

"But that door's not open," Tucker argued. "She needed to know the spell to open it."

"I think she does," I said. "She's been there before. She's no stranger to Faery."

"Then why leave everything behind in the hotel room?"

"It's not like she can use a cell phone in Faery," I said.

Tucker crossed his arms and gave us both a stubborn look. "I'm still not buying it," he said. "This doesn't sound like her at all."

"It does if she thinks she's gone to help," I argued back. "I know what I felt."

"I felt it as well," Adam said. "It woke me. What time is it?"

"Early afternoon," I said. "Nowhere near dusk."

"Then come back to bed, love," he said. "Bea's room is on the east side of the house and the dark shades and curtains are all taped up there. It's dark enough. We'll all get some more rest before we go haring off to Never-Never-Land."

I shook my head as I followed him down the hall. "As long as there's no Captain Hook." *Or a crocodile.*

CHAPTER TWENTY-THREE

"The gods' most savage curses come upon us as answers to our own prayers, you know."
    —*Lois McMaster Bujold,* The Curse of Chalion

"**I** have what I need to re-consecrate the cemetery." Antonio stood in Tucker's shadow, waiting outside the car for us. Night had finally fallen and we'd been loading up my Land Rover.

"You can re-bless it?" Niko asked, his voice reverent. "I understood this sort of ritual to require a bishop."

"I can do this," Antonio insisted. "I may not be a bishop and I may be a sinful man, but I am—was—a good priest. I perform the sacraments. I can execute the ritual of consecration. God will not deny this." Antonio climbed into the back of the Rover, a small bag clinking against his side. I had no idea what he had in there, holy water, perhaps, some other unguents and oils. "I know what to do."

"This may get hairy," I warned as I got into the passenger seat. "The spirits we felt last night were much more active than any at the Rose Inn."

"God will be with me." With that, he closed his eyes

and began to move his lips. Prayers? Perhaps. I hoped his God was listening and that—as Antonio believed—the ritual would work.

"Niko, Adam, I think it's best if you two go atop the overhang," I said. "Niko, you know where it is. It's not part of the cemetery, so you should be fine up there. I don't know how long it will take Antonio but I don't want you to be caught on the property. Tucker, Antonio, and I will go into the cemetery proper." I'd slept several more hours, then woken up to find Tucker plying me with books and more food. I'd eaten several plates of *machacado,* tortillas and cheese, followed by a couple of apples for good measure. I was going to need as much energy as I could get.

"We'll park just beyond the gates," Tucker said. "You can get to the overhang and we'll meet you in front of La Angel."

"*El* Angel," Antonio corrected.

"Nope, local custom," I said. "We all know it's wrong, but she's been La Angel for eons."

"A statue?"

"Yes, it guards the cave entrance," I said. "The one that holds the door to Faery. Though, not literally, I don't suppose. She sits out in front of it on a stone plinth. She's modeled after 'Winged Victory.' She's been there as long as I can remember."

"Where did she come from?"

"Gigi erected her," I said.

"Yeah, back a few decades ago," Tucker said. "As a sort of a tribute to the people who once lived there."

"Ranchers," I explained to the now perplexed priest. "The cemetery was in no-man's-land, where three different ranches once intersected. Now, it's just part of the Wild Moon. We take care of it. I used to have to go there as a child and clean the graves, pull weeds, generally tend to the land. It was our chieftain's way of helping me to understand mortality."

The priest nodded his head, then closed his eyes again, soon lost in the silent whispers of his prayers. He was fingering the beads of a rosary. I watched him for a few moments, mesmerized by the repetitive movements. Then I settled back into my own seat, closed my own eyes. I needed to focus.

"Keira, we're here." Adam's gentle voice woke me. I'd fallen asleep.

"Hey," I said quietly. "Where is everyone?"

"Waiting outside the car," he said with amusement as he leaned into the open passenger door. "Didn't even faze you when we parked and got out."

I smiled and kissed him. "Thanks."

"For what?"

"For letting me sleep. For being here with us."

"Always." He kissed me back, then brushed a hand along my cheek. "We will prevail."

"With you here, yes, we will." It took all the willpower I owned not to cross my fingers. Would we? I still had my doubts, but even so, I felt we had no choice. We'd picked our battle.

I watched Adam and Niko disappear behind the hill that led to the overhang. Tucker had shouldered a rope and pickaxe, a Coleman lantern swinging from one hand. Antonio clutched his small bag, a cross in the same hand, a flashlight in the other.

I took nothing. Instead, I let my hair loose, then rebraided it tightly. If we got into a skirmish, I didn't want it flying into my face. I wore cargo shorts, a black tank top and on my feet, a heavy pair of Docs, steel toes and all. Just what all the girls were wearing these days—if they expected trouble.

Tucker was geared-out in similar attire, shorts and a T-shirt and sported his own pair of steel-toed boots. Antonio wore what I considered a "priest suit": dark pants and short-sleeved clerical shirt—the black stark and forbidding, the tiny white square of the collar as much a mark of his allegiance as the Mark my own gang wore on their bodies.

"Loaded for bear, boys?" I said, hiding my own unease in humor.

"Locked and loaded," Tucker said and came up next to me. "Let's go."

Antonio paused as we reached the small symbolic gate. Only two feet in height, the gate and its attendant short fence simply marked the property line. "I'll begin here," he said. "You two go on. I work best alone."

"Be careful," I said.

He put his bag down on the ground and pulled out a stole, kissed it and draped it over his neck as he whispered. "Restore to me, O Lord, the state of immortality which I lost through the sin of my first parents and, although unworthy to approach Thy Sacred Mysteries, may I nevertheless deserve eternal joy." He was soon lost in his own world of prayer.

I watched for a moment, then motioned to Tucker to continue forward. It was unlikely any lingering spirits would harm a priest. I hoped. To be safe, I muttered a quick warding spell, my fingers weaving the air.

"You think he needs it?" Tucker asked.

"Maybe, maybe not, but I'd rather be safe than sorry."

"Point."

Tucker and I trudged forward, weaving among the first few rows of markers.

"Do you see?" Tucker pointed with the lantern. "Someone's cleaned up in here."

"No runespells, either," I said as I examined one of the gravestones. The broken ones we'd seen in the photos Carlton had sent were somehow mended, cracks still evident, but with signs of mortar as if a stonemason had repaired the breaks. All the stones were clean, scrubbed, no signs of the sigils. I pulled out my phone and dialed Adam.

"Keira, we're just about to the overhang," Adam said. "Is there a problem?"

"Not exactly. Hang on." I used the phone to snap a few photos and sent them to him. "Someone's been here."

"Was it this way last night?"

"No idea," I said. "We didn't come any closer than the crossing. That's too far away to see the actual graveyard."

"What do you feel?"

"Nothing." I stopped walking and did an exploratory sending. "It's quiet. Too quiet."

"What do you mean, 'too quiet'?"

I squatted and placed a palm on the ground. "It's a cemetery, Adam. I should be able to feel something. Death leaves a trace. But it's like this place has been wiped clean."

"Could it be the desecration?" Tucker asked.

"No, that would have muddied the aura here, not removed it."

I stood, brushed dirt off my hands and approached

a large tombstone. Placing a hand gingerly on the top, I carefully extended my senses, down, into the ground. There, below me, two sets of remains lay side-by-side, just as the engraving advertised: *Joshua and Rebecca Johnson. Taken by their Lord into the Bosom of the Angels*. One date, 1873.

"They're still there," I said. "The remains. Only . . ." I nudged past the obvious, searching for more. "I don't feel their spirits."

"They're gone? I thought that wasn't possible." Adam's voice sounded tinny and far away, the signal fading.

"It's not," I said. "Something's happened here. Something really, really bad."

Tucker set the lantern atop another stone. "I think whatever that darkness was, it gathered the spirits last night."

"And did what with them?" I put my hands on my hips. "It's the law of conservation of energy, Tucker. Things can't just poof and vanish. They had to have gone somewhere."

"Keira's right, Tucker," Adam said. "Spirits don't just disappear. Energy that strong, to remove all traces of lingering death—"

"We would have felt it—even if we'd still been in San Antonio." I squatted in front of another tombstone. This was one of the ones I'd seen in Carlton's photos with a rune painted on it. Taking a deep breath, I reached out my right hand, fingers outstretched, still wary. A brush of flesh on stone. Nothing. A firmer touch. Still nothing.

"Keira?" Adam's voice sounded concerned.

"I'm trying something, hang on."

I shut my eyes and focused. "Give up your secrets, stone," I whispered and placed my palm flat on the place where the runes had once resided.

Flash!

I fell backward nearly three yards, to land at Tucker's feet. The skin of my palm burned. "Fuck!" I scrubbed my hand in the dirt, a reflex, nothing more.

"Keira, what is it? What's wrong?" Niko's voice overrode Adam's. "We're coming down there."

"No, wait." I stumbled to my feet with Tucker's help. He'd dropped the rope. "I'm okay, don't come down." My palm still felt as if I'd placed it atop a hot stove element. Stupid, stupid, Keira, I thought. "Adam, there are still wards, spells of a sort," I said, cradling my hand. "But they're hidden now. I touched one of the stones and got tossed ass over teakettle."

"Are you all right?" Adam demanded.

"Fine. My hand's a bit sore, but I'm fine." I muttered a quick healing spell, passing my left palm over my right. The pain subsided enough for me to think. "There seems to be another layer here," I said. "Spells hiding the runes."

"Can you tell who set the spells?"

"Didn't get a sense right away, but I'm going to try."

"That doesn't seem prudent, love."

"Prudent or not, we need to know who—or what—we're up against," I argued. "Now that I know they're here, I'll take precautions."

"Keira, anyone who can spell so thoroughly and hide them so well . . ." Adam didn't need to finish that sentence.

"I know, Adam. I promise I won't do anything foolish." That time, I did cross my fingers. "I'll call you if I find anything else."

"We're at the overhang now," he said. "We'll wait here. I can see the light from the lantern, so I'm not totally out of touch."

"Good. Thanks."

I put the phone in my back pocket. "I'm going to get closer to that stone, Tucker. Cover me."

"Cover me?"

"Just be there, okay? I need to figure out if I can recognize this magick."

"If you say so." My brother moved the lantern from its perch to another stone, this one closer. The light shone across the weathered letters. Bits of mica and other particulates glinted against the smooth carvings.

I reinforced my shields, then extended a small bit of energy around my hands. As I reached out, I whispered a warding spell followed by a show-me. A pulse of white energy pulsed about five inches out from the surface of the tombstone. "This wasn't here earlier," I muttered.

"What?" Tucker bent over me, peering at the stone. "Huh. I don't see anything, but there is . . ."

"Yeah. It's not Gideon's," I said. "Not Kelly." I concentrated, trying to define what I was feeling. Soft, yet strong, it swirled above the stone's surface as if to guard? Was it keeping something out or something in? I let it flow around my hands. This time, it didn't attack, but seemed to sniff me out, like a dog testing whether or not I was a threat. I began to taste the flavor of it—spice, yet smooth, clean—on the back of my throat. No blood went into creating this. Its tantalizing near familiarity teased me. I'd felt this before, knew this—

"Son of a bitch!" Tucker howled, his feet stomping in a crazy dance.

I fell back onto the dirt, my concentration broken. "What, what?"

"Damn it!" His hands brushed at his bare calves and thighs. As I rose, I saw them. Hundreds of them crawling up his legs. Little red segmented bodies, wave upon wave of them attacking his skin.

"Fire ants." I breathed out a spell that would move a bit of air, aiming it at his legs. Nothing happened. They marched on, swirling and swarming.

Tucker continued to yell and howl and stomp. The more he brushed at them, the more seemed to be there. He took off running toward the cemetery entrance. I followed him, yelling to Adam. "Fire ants, Tucker's infested."

CHAPTER TWENTY-FOUR

"If you beseech a blessing upon yourself, beware! lest without intent you invoke a curse upon a neighbor at the same time"

— *Mark Twain, "The War Prayer"*

We passed the priest, who barely even noticed us, deep in his own world of prayer. Tucker made it to the car first, tore open the back door and grabbed a water cooler from the floor, upending it over himself. Drowning ants sluiced off his body. I snatched a towel from the car and helped wipe them off him.

His skin reddened and puffed, tiny angry bites studded every inch of exposed flesh. I took hold of his arms, checking them both. Only a few bites there, the majority of them were on his legs. Tucker huffed, his breaths short and shallow.

"Fuck, are you allergic?" I fumbled for the first aid kit without waiting for an answer. Before I could find what I was looking for, my Viking Berserker brother's eyes fluttered closed and he fell, like a redheaded tree, thumping onto the solid packed ground. "Fuck, fuck, fuck," I muttered as I scrambled in the kit. "There, I've got it." I whipped out the EpiPen and jabbed it in Tucker's thigh. When he didn't immediately come around, I snagged a second one and gave him another dose.

Adam and Niko appeared, as if out of the wind. "What happened?"

"Help me get him up," I said. "He got stung by fire ants. A lot of them."

"He's not breathing very well," Niko said.

"I know. I gave him two doses. He's actually breathing better now."

Without warning, Tucker began to convulse in our arms. He slid back to the ground as Niko wrapped his arms around him and held his head still, forcing his jaw open. Adam took Tucker's legs, holding them down.

"Healing spell, healing spell," I muttered, mentally rifling through my repertoire. "Hold him still, please," I asked as I knelt down at Tucker's head. Calling energy, I placed my hands just above his skin, not quite touching him. "*Heal,* damn you," I whispered as I forced the spell out from my hands onto him. I made three passes, up and down, up and down, over all his limbs, his torso, his face. The welts reduced a bit and he lay still. "Turn him over, please."

Niko and Adam complied. Thank the powers that be I had two vampires with me. Tucker weighed a freaking ton. It would've been difficult for me to move him on my own. I repeated my actions on his back, once again down his legs. After a few moments, he began to stir.

"Tucker, *cariad*?" Niko bent close to Tucker's face, his hand cupping my brother's jaw.

"Hello, love," Tucker grunted. "What happened?"

"Fire ants," I said. "A huge swarm of them. I didn't know you were allergic."

Tucker's brow furrowed as he stared at me in the dim light. "I'm not."

I packed up the debris from the first aid kit into a small trash bag and stuffed it underneath one of the rear seat benches. "You're not? You sure reacted as if you were. Swollen tongue, not breathing, the whole nine. I had to jab you with two EpiPens plus a healing spell to get you to breathe."

"Let me up," he said to Niko, who, with an arm around him, helped Tucker to his feet. He wavered a moment, then steadied. "Damn it. It's like I was hit by a really big truck."

"That was the biggest swarm I've ever seen," I said. "Bigger than the one Bea got into one summer when we were camping at the lake."

"Wait, that's not . . ." Tucker turned his head to look back at the cemetery. "Fire ants build mounds in moist soil," he said. "Like lakeside. Not—"

"Not in dry, cracked dirt," I finished. "I'm going back there."

"You are not." Adam put a hand on my arm. "Keira, if you're saying that there was an infestation of insects where there should be none, then something is causing that. You've already been attacked one other time to-night, I say we table this now and regroup back at Bea's house."

Regroup? Do this all over again tomorrow? I sighed. "Okay, maybe you're right. But tomorrow, I think Tucker and I need to come out here in the daylight. As much as I want the two of you with us, daylight helps us. Harder to hide."

Adam began to protest, but I held up my hand. "I promise we'll only look and not touch. I'll take pictures of all the stones if it makes you feel better. We need to get to the bottom of this. I'm willing to take a risk."

"It does a little," Adam said, "but I'm still wary of the place. There's a subtle energy here that I feel now. It didn't seem to be there until you—"

"Rang the doorbell?" Facetious or no, I was pretty sure that's exactly what I did by touching that gravestone. "I know I probably announced our presence, but . . ."

"What's wrong?" Antonio walked toward us, his stole still draped over his shoulders. "I saw you all over here."

"Tucker got into a fire ant mound," I said. "We'll need to come back tomorrow. I need to get him home."

"Oh dear, that's terrible." Antonio peered at Tucker, his human eyes not able to see well in the dim light. "Tomorrow is fine. I've begun the process, but I can finish it later," he said. "Could we do it in the daylight? It's rather difficult . . ." He let his voice trail off, a sheepish look on his face as he realized he was addressing two vampires.

"We're actually coming back during the day," I said. "Tucker and I."

"Very well then."

CHAPTER TWENTY-FIVE

"To suffering there is a limit; to fearing, none."
                                        —*Sir Francis Bacon*

"She's not at the café," I growled. "Or at least she's not answering."

We'd arrived at Bea's in record time, Tucker shivering in the back, even with a blanket on him. I drove with Adam as shotgun while Niko tried to comfort my ailing brother. I'd managed to heal down most of the ant bites, but his body was still in shock. When we'd pulled into the drive, there was no sign of Bea's car.

"Adam, I need to go find her. The café closes at nine. She should've been back by now. It's nearly midnight."

Niko looked up from where he was coddling Tucker. "Keira, it's not a good idea. We're already down one person tonight. We don't need to make it two . . . especially you."

"You're the heir," Tucker muttered from underneath his blanket. He was ensconced on the couch, wrapped in two Hudson Bay blankets and Niko. "Under no circumstances will you go gallivanting around—"

"It's Bea," I protested.

"Call Carlton," Tucker insisted. "He can go look for her."

I slapped my own forehead and dialed a number I knew all too well.

"Larsen."

"Carlton, Keira here."

"She's at the emergency clinic," he said with no preamble.

"Bea? What's wrong, what happened?"

"That's what I'm trying to find out."

Adam sprung up at the words and began to gather my backpack and keys.

"No." Niko whispered fiercely. Adam flashed fang at his second. "No." Niko removed himself from Tucker's side to take Adam into the back hallway as I talked to Carlton.

"There was a fire," Carlton was saying. "At the café."

"Is she okay?"

"A little smoke inhalation, but she's fine," he said. "The café's pretty bad off, though." He let out a deep sigh. "Keira, I'm afraid that there's more to it."

"More how?"

"Those vandals that hit the cemetery?"

"Yeah?"

"I think they're responsible."

A million thoughts whirled through my head. "How so?"

"I saw some of the same tagging signs there earlier today," Carlton said. "Along the back and side walls. Some more down by the deli. I had one of my guys take some pictures, hoping that the more evidence I could get, the easier it will be to nail the bastards when they're finally caught. Only now . . ."

"Now what? Did the entire café burn down?" My heart sank as I considered this. Bea's Place—the café established by her long-dead parents, the place we'd practically grown up in—burned to a crisp? Sure, I could pour money at it, rebuild, but the memories . . . This couldn't be happening. But it was, the saner side of my brain insisted. *It was and it is and it's all your damned fault.*

"There's a lot of damage," Carlton admitted. "More than I would've thought for a simple grease fire."

"Grease? I thought you said vandals were responsible."

"I did. Some greasy rags were up against the back door, as if someone dropped them there when they dumped the trash." He paused a moment, then continued. "Keira, the entire strip center is damaged. Smoke and water, some fire. The deli caught some sparks and it went up pretty quickly."

I sank into a chair and buried my face in my hands as I handed the phone to Adam.

"Larsen, Walker here. Were there any other injuries?"

"What? I mean. No. Just Bea. Her aunt and uncle weren't there. Noe was, but he's okay. Is Keira okay?" Carlton's voice softened a little.

"Not particularly," Adam responded. "We'll go pick Bea up at the clinic."

"They're keeping her overnight for observation," Carlton said. "Just in case."

I grabbed Adam's arm. "No," I whispered. "No blood tests."

"Thank you, we'll be in touch." Adam ended the call and whirled. "Niko. Get out there now. Pick her up. Do whatever you need to."

Niko flew out the front door, keys already in hand.

"Do whatever he needs to?" I gave Adam a quizzical look.

Adam put the phone on the counter and came to sit with me in the armchair. I scooted over to give him room. "He will glamour whomever needs it to get Bea home. You can check her out when she gets here."

"In the meantime, I'm going to check out Tucker. He's still shaking. I don't like that."

"Nor do I." Adam rose and walked over to the couch where Tucker, swaddled in blankets as if it were winter at the South Pole instead of high summer in Central Texas, looked at him with a baleful glare.

"I hate this." My brother's voice came from below the blanket, muffled. The only part of him exposed was from his eyes to the top of his fiery red head.

"As you should." Adam reached down and placed his hand on Tucker's forehead. "His fever is rising, Keira."

"Damn it." I joined him, my own hand sliding below Adam's. Tucker's skin burned with heat. His eyes glazed over as he watched me. "I'm going to have to try something else," I said. "Adam, can you get Isabel on the phone, please? Tell her what happened and what I've done. See if she's got any suggestions."

"Will do."

I pushed Tucker over as much as I could so I could perch on the edge of the couch next to him. "Close your eyes," I said in a gentle voice. "Relax as much as you can."

He nodded and complied.

Taking deep breaths, I focused inward, calling to my energy, the part that lived deep inside, at my core. Normal healing spells never touched this, but I didn't have a choice. I'd done everything I could under usual circumstances, used every trick I'd been taught, but still, Tucker's fever raged. The ant bites had all but disappeared, healed and gone in mere minutes. I had no idea why he was still burning up. With an effort, I pulled energy out my arms, to my hands, let it swirl around me as I once again passed my palms over Tucker's body. For a brief heart-stopping moment, I couldn't feel him. My eyes flew open, only to see him still shivering in his blanket cocoon.

"Sorry, hon," I said. "I need to do this." I began unwrapping the covers, exposing as much skin as I could. He was nude underneath, having stripped down in the car, afraid of lurking ants. I couldn't help but admire his strong, tough body, defined muscles deceptively smooth underneath tanned skin. No bodybuilder physique, only that of someone born to fight, born to run wild. Run wild. An idea occurred to me. "Tucker, shift."

"Do what?" he murmured.

"Shift." I rose and pushed the low coffee table aside. "Bring the wolf. I think it will help."

With no sound, Tucker closed his eyes. His body shimmered, faded, and was still.

"Tucker?" I tentatively reached toward him. He hadn't shifted. Could he not?

"Keira, don't." Adam's warning came too late as Tucker's arm whipped out, grabbed me and pulled me to him. I landed flat atop him, my back to his chest. His right arm gripped me tight against him. A growl came from his lips. I could feel the slobber dripping against my neck, sharp fangs pressing against the skin. I struggled, but couldn't budge his iron grasp. His left hand stroked my cheek, my neck, traveled down my body, cupping my breast in some parody of a lover's touch, caressing my belly, farther, down. The growl softened as his fingers sought to slide underneath my waistband.

In a flash, Adam was there, his hands on Tucker's, ripping them aside and pulling me away. My brother snarled, his face half twisted in the shift, part wolf, part human. Saliva flecks flew as his head shook from side-to-side, fast, faster. I stumbled back against Adam, my heart in my throat, trying to gather what little wits I had left. My brother, my own brother had . . . No, stop. Don't dwell on it. Figure out how—I threw a hand out toward him.

"Subside." The freakish subharmonics of my command voice echoed, bouncing off the walls and the furniture, the very air shuddering with its strength. Tucker whimpered, convulsed and was still. Slowly, his face and teeth shifted back to normal. I fell into the armchair, my chest heaving as I tried to catch my breath.

Adam crouched next to me, running his hands over my arms, cupping my jaw, kissing my forehead. "Keira, are you hurt?"

I shook my head. "I'm fine. I'm . . ." I looked over at my peaceful brother, now fast asleep, no longer shivering. "What happened?"

"The fever affected his ability to shift," Adam said. "Isabel . . ." He motioned to the phone, now broken on the floor. "She was on the line, telling me that you shouldn't let him shift, when . . ."

"Yeah, well. Too late." I gave a weary chuckle. "Did she say anything else?"

"To put him to sleep—no, not that way," he said as I jerked my head up and glared. "He needs to sleep it off. He's weak and the fever and shivering will just make him weaker."

"Well, I guess I eventually figured that out." I sighed. "Could you phone Isabel back? She's probably going a bit bonkers right now. I don't think she has your phone number."

Adam kissed my forehead again and rose. "I will. You relax here in the chair, okay? I know it's foolish to think you'll go to bed."

"Well, yeah." I snuggled into the chair, my arms cradling my head against the side. "I'll keep an eye on him. At least, until Niko gets back with Bea. Then he can take over."

Adam glanced at the kitchen clock. "He'll be at least an hour, assuming all goes well."

"Where's Antonio?" I asked. He'd gone to use the facilities when we'd returned, but I hadn't seen him since.

"I glamoured him." Adam bent to pick up the pieces of the broken phone, pulling out the SIM card.

"You did? Why?"

"He needed to sleep. I preferred to not have him wandering around."

"You don't trust him?"

Adam shook his head, his dark hair obscuring his face. "I do not. I would not say this with Niko present, as he feels a certain reverence toward the priests of his religion, but I find that this man is too much of an enigma. His story makes sense, though I do not understand why he is so eager to help us. For all I know, he plots against us."

I yawned and shuffled my body to a more comfortable position. "Plots? I'm not sure he's gone that far," I said.

"Keira, I was married to the woman he loved. The story he told us? His version only: that he rejected her and she committed suicide. Fact is, the only truth we know is that she drowned. Did she truly kill herself and her unborn child rather than be with Antonio or with me?" Adam raised one eyebrow at me.

"Okay, you've got a point," I admitted. "But if you don't trust him, why did you agree to have him come along earlier?"

"He's the only one I know who can re-consecrate that cemetery," Adam said. "At least, he already knows about us. It would be rather awkward and perhaps dangerous to involve any outside clergy at this point."

"Yes, well." I smiled at him. "Go on, go call Isabel, love. I'll be right here."

CHAPTER TWENTY-SIX

"The antidote for fifty enemies is one friend."

—*Aristotle*

Morning came all too soon. Niko had arrived back with Bea around one-thirty and I'd promptly put her to bed, despite her protests. A few quick healing spells later, she was fine and out like a light. Niko had elected to remain with Tucker in the living room. Adam and I had shut ourselves up in the main guest room, as the priest was in the other room. I'd had a long conversation with Isabel and she'd given me a few more tricks of the trade. I'd bundled Tucker up in spells and blankets so he could sleep. She'd said sleep was the best way for him to heal now.

"I want to involve Sheriff Larsen," Adam said as we readied for bed. Odd thing doing this in the middle of the night. It was normally our peak time. We'd be up and about, Adam doing business in his office, me in mine—a new perk thanks to my being the heir. Some nights I'd skip my own lessons and paperwork and help Adam out or I'd spar with my brothers.

"Do you think that's a wise move?" I asked. "Carlton's going to ask all sorts of awkward questions—the primary one being why the hell we're not at the Wild Moon and why we're staying at Bea's. Last time I talked to him, he thought we were on vacation. He's not dumb, Adam. He's going to be suspicious."

"Keira, we're limited in our choices. The four of us came back of our own accord. I can't call in our troops, so to speak. I can't risk them, too."

I flipped the ceiling fan on high and slid under the covers. "I know that. Just as I know that what happened to Tucker tonight is likely the result of a hex or curse. I'm positive that touching that gravestone triggered it."

"It's not just that." Adam slid in next to me and shut off the bedside light. "We've broken Truce. Even if we leave the premises now, we've already crossed that line."

"Then tomorrow, we go back to the Wild Moon," I said. "In for a penny, in for the entire fortune. We'll bring Bea—"

"I don't think that's a good idea. We've already exposed her. She won't be safe with us."

He was right. Bea would be better off elsewhere. "How about we send her to Dixxi? Her condo in town is big enough for Bea, Noe, and Tio and Tia. I don't want any of them here."

"A good idea. Perhaps one of the deputies can run them into San Antonio tomorrow."

"We should—"

"Tucker's not going to be at full speed yet, and you're not going alone."

"No, you're right again. I'm sorry. I'm not thinking." I kissed his shoulder. "Promise me that you'll keep reminding me, okay? I'm not used to this—to being heir, to being the one that has to duck and cover while others take the heat. It used to be so simple."

"I'll promise that if you'll promise one thing."

"What's that?"

"You let me tell the sheriff everything. I think it's time he knew."

I pushed away and sat up. "You want to *what*?"

"We need another ally, Keira." Adam pulled me back down into his embrace. "I know," he whispered. "It goes against everything you were ever taught, but we need someone on our side here. He's not beholden to us, not bonded, but he is a friend."

I muttered a few choice words under my breath then let out a sigh. "I'll think about it, okay?"

Adam laughed. "Okay." He kissed my forehead. "I know it's not easy for you, love. You've barely had enough time to realize you are the heir, much less learn how to react as one. Let's get through tomorrow, talk to the sheriff and get Bea and her family out of the way and safe, then we'll go back home."

"To the Wild Moon."

"Yes. To the Wild Moon."

I sighed, content for now. We had a plan, albeit not much of one, but we had to move forward.

At dawn, I woke and left Adam to sleep some more. I needed to check on Tucker. As I entered the living room, I smiled. Poor Niko was contorted in the armchair, one long arm dangling over the side, his head at a weird angle. I hoped vampires didn't get cricks in their necks, or he was in for a doozy.

I crept as silently as I could to Tucker's side, wary

of being caught out again. He looked to be fast asleep, his breathing regular, normal. Good. Instead of actually touching him, I used a simple diagnostic spell, the same one I'd used on Bea last night. *Brilliant, no fever*. I turned away, ready to let him keep sleeping. Niko's hand touched mine as I passed.

"He's fine, Niko," I whispered. "No fever. Why don't you go on back to bed with Adam. I'll take watch for a while."

Niko looked over at Tucker, then unbent himself, rising from the chair. He nodded at me, leaned over and touched his lips to my brother's forehead. Without a word, he walked down the hall, disappearing around the corner. I went into the kitchen and pulled out coffee and filters, enough to make a huge pot. After getting that set up and started, I returned to the chair and curled up in it, watching my brother sleep.

When the phone rang, I started out of a light doze, leaping to get it. It was the land line.

"Hello," I said, trying to keep my voice down so as not to wake Tucker.

"It's Carlton."

"Hey."

"You weren't answering your cell phone," he said. "I tried the ranch, but no one answered there, either. So I tried to call Bea to see if she knew—"

"Yeah, my phone's busted," I said. "Sorry."

"How's Bea?"

"Good. She's sleeping." The coffee's aroma began to perk me up. I tucked the receiver into the crook of my neck and shoulder and poured myself a cup. "Were you needing something?" I asked after a moment.

"Are you staying at Bea's?" Carlton asked.

"For now, yes," I said. "I wanted to make sure she was okay."

"Keira, what's going on?"

Oh, brother. It really hadn't taken him long. Our sheriff was no dummy. He'd been in the top ten at the police academy in San Antonio. He was sharp, attentive and very, very good at his job. Only he didn't know anything about our special natures.

"What do you mean, Carlton?" I blew on my coffee as I frantically tried to buy myself a little time. Was he asking about Bea? About us being back in town? What?

"I drove by the Wild Moon last night," he said. My heart sank. Damn it. He knew we'd closed up the place. Not typical for a quick vacation. "There wasn't anyone there. The place looked abandoned. Are y'all leaving?" A note of sorrow crept into his voice. I knew by "y'all" he wasn't really wanting to know about all of us. He meant me.

"Leaving?" I gulped down more coffee. "No."

"Then why close up the ranch?"

"Personal reasons." My mouth reacted before my brain could process what I was saying. Oh, yeah, like that was going to stop him from asking questions.

"You're okay? I get the feeling you're not and you're just not saying anything." More sorrow tinged with worry.

"I'm fine." I was doing an awful lot of that lately, having to tell people I was fine. I was, mostly. Only there was a part of me that wasn't. That part stayed awake all day and all night, fretting about how we were going to get ourselves out of this mess. I'd wanted action instead of inaction, and had gotten my brother hurt—a man that I'd never seen hurt physically. Ever. Bea's café had burned down, as had the deli, and no doubt there was damage to all the shops in the strip center. Did they have fire insurance? I fervently hoped so. If not, I was going to help out financially. What good is a fortune if you can't share it? I didn't know for sure that the fire was the result of our breaking Truce, but I couldn't dismiss it. I'd either started some sort of chain reaction when I'd foolishly touched that tombstone, or the arson had just been a harbinger of the "annoyances" breaking Truce brought. Whatever it was, we were smack in the middle of it and I had no more choice but to keep moving forward and hope we could succeed. I needed to. We had to win this game of Gideon's—or battle—whichever the case may be, as well as concentrate on finding my lost clan chief.

"You don't sound fine."

"I'm just tired," I said. "I was up late with Bea."

"I think you and I need to talk," Carlton said.

"We are talking."

"No, face to face."

I sighed. "Carlton, what is that going to accomplish exactly?"

"I don't know, but I'm asking you as a favor."

"Let me think about it."

"Thank you. When you call me back, use my cell. We had to close the office because of smoke and water damage. We're taking dispatch calls out of my house."

"I will." Great. The entire strip center damaged meant the only remaining stores in Rio Seco were effectively gone. If the sheriff's office had sustained damage, then so must have the dry cleaners and the video store. Damn it. Just last week, after the deaths in the pack resulted in the wers closing the deli and moving out of Rio Seco, Jacob—an undercover Texas Ranger and werewolf helping with the investigation—had said that the center looked sad. Now fire, smoke, and water had damaged or destroyed the rest of the businesses. Perhaps Gideon was right—we had killed our village.

"Take care of yourself, okay?" With that, Carlton ended the call.

I switched off the receiver and put it back into its cradle on the kitchen counter.

I went back to the living room to curl up in a chair and sip my coffee as I watched Tucker and thought things through. Adam wanted to bring Carlton into our confidence. To out us. Did that make sense? Would that stop Carlton from worrying so much, or would that simply enmesh him in our own tangled dilemma? Bea already knew about us. She'd clued in to my family's secret early during our teen years. When the adults noticed she spent nearly all her free time at our house, they'd pretty much figured she'd become a de facto daughter and there was no need to hide anything from her. She'd learned about vampires and wer much later, but she'd accepted it. Carlton, however? There was so much baggage between us—our mutual past, the fact that I'd run away from our relationship. Now he was married, had kids . . . a family that could be endangered. As sheriff, and before that a police officer in San Antonio, he'd always been in a dangerous profession. I know he still cared for me, even though I'd broken his heart. He'd never understood exactly why I'd dumped him; I'd not been able to explain that his being human was the one thing that kept me from being able to be his true partner. Considering all this—maybe telling him *was* a good thing.

Adam could be right. If we revealed ourselves, maybe Carlton could finally get whatever closure he was missing. I suppose the only question left was: Could he handle the news that there was far more to the world than he imagined—and that the "more" was about as bizarre and weird as it got?

I dozed off as I pondered the various ramifications of coming out to Carlton, my now-empty coffee cup dangling from my fingers.

CHAPTER TWENTY-SEVEN

"A true friend is one who thinks you are a good egg even if you are half cracked."

—*Bernard Meltzer*

"I would like to try to Summon my father," Adam said as he exited the bedroom. Tucker had woken, weak, but better. He'd wanted to go to sleep in a real bed, not on the couch, so I'd helped him to the guest room where I'd woken Adam. Adam and I were now both in the living room, its curtains still drawn tight and sealed with duct tape to keep out the sun. I didn't know the exact time, but it was somewhere around midmorning.

"So you've decided to call in the troops?" I teased as I bustled about the kitchen rustling up some food for me.

Adam glared at me in mock anger. "Not the full cohort. Just one soldier. I decided that it won't hurt," he said. "My father can handle himself, besides, he may be able to help us."

"Fight whatever it is that's ganging up on us?" I asked. I found a few energy bars stashed in an upper cabinet and snagged those. Tearing the wrapper off one,

I took a big bite and chewed. "Will he come?" I asked around a mouthful of food.

"That's disgusting," Adam said.

"Sorry." I swallowed. "I'm starving. I didn't mean to speak with my mouth full."

"Not that so much as . . . that's not really food, is it?" He eyed the packets with distrust as I joined him.

"These? Energy bars. Full of protein." I tore the wrapper off a second one and practically inhaled it. My belly felt hollow. "No, they're not exactly tasty, but they are quick energy."

His brow rose as he watched me devour a third, then a fourth bar. "I'm sure there is more food. Didn't Tucker buy groceries?"

"He did, but it would take too long to cook something." I licked the wrapper of the last bar and tossed it into a small trash bin. "So, now, your father?"

Adam settled next to me on the couch, his long limbs sprawled in front of him, arms crossed behind his head. I'd not seen him this relaxed in a long time. "I believe I've figured out what I need to do," he said. "I'll need some privacy, so must wait until we return to the Wild Moon tonight."

"That, or we could take the van," I suggested.

"Tucker's van? The one with no windows on the sides?" Adam sat up.

"It's still at the ranch," I said. "I could go there now and bring it back—"

"Keira, what did I say . . ."

I patted his arm. "About going alone, yes, yes, I know. I wasn't planning to. Tucker's weak, but feeling better. We can swoop in, get the van and swoop right back out again, none the wiser."

"Magick doesn't work that way," Adam protested. "It's not like a surveillance camera that one can avoid."

"I can drive fast."

"And magick is faster. We wait until dark."

I grumbled and wiggled into a more comfortable position. Once again, I waited. *For what? To breach yet another boundary?*

"Had you given any more thought to my suggestion? That we take the sheriff into our confidence?" Adam prodded my side. I knew he was teasing me, trying to reconnect in the best way possible. We'd had no real time to ourselves lately, no real time to be alone, to make love, to reconnect. He'd barely fed, only doing so when I'd insisted. Feeding from me shouldn't be hurried, he'd protested. It was as much an act of love between a bonded pair as was sex. I'd felt the lack as much as he did. Taking blood from me wasn't a one-way street. I gained energy from him as he took it from me. We needed it to keep ourselves on an even keel. Not that a few days would hurt us, but it sure made things more difficult.

I poked him back. "I did. He called earlier, by the way. He's been by the ranch. Saw it closed up."

"Bugger."

I stared at Adam in shock. I'd never heard him use such a vulgarity. "Wow, that really threw you, didn't it?"

"I was hoping we could buy ourselves some time," he said. "Him poking around there is not a good idea. I don't want him to get hurt due to us. Nor do I wish to have all of our secrets exposed." Adam tossed me his phone. "Ring him. See if he will stop by."

"Wow, and you think that's a good idea?" I asked. "Have him come here?"

"Our territory," Adam said, "at least temporarily. He'll be safer here. If we go see him, we'd have to do it after dark, and I'd rather not wait that long."

He stood in the doorway, all six foot three of him, strong, earnest, steady, clad in the requisite polyester brown uniform that seemed to be painted on his thighs. He wore his Stetson and his Sam Browne belt as if he were born to them—which, perhaps he was. Carlton's father had been sheriff before him, running the law in Rio Seco as long as I could remember. When he'd died, Carlton returned to town and had been appointed to finish out his father's term. He'd been officially elected last fall.

Brown eyes met my own gray ones as we both stood at the door. For a moment, his gaze slid down, then up again, as if appraising me. I stood with my hand on the door frame, one foot atop another, flashing back to my youth, the days when I'd stood in a similar doorway, eagerly anticipating his arrival. I almost felt embarrassed to greet him in my cutoffs and tank top, my feet bare, my hair pulled back in a sloppy ponytail.

"You going to invite me in?"

"Sorry, yes, please." I stepped back, allowing him to pass me. I let the door shut behind me as I watched him cross the darkened living room, one hand out. "Walker." He'd seen Adam sitting there. Keen eyes, our sheriff. When the doorbell had rung, Adam had gone all over vampire, stilling in the way only the dead can. He sat in shadow, having turned off the side table lamps. The only light on in the house was the small light above the stove.

"Sheriff." Adam rose, a languid move, all predator

alert and vampire rolled into one. I rolled my eyes at him. Men. "Thank you for coming so quickly," Adam continued as he motioned to Carlton to take a seat on the couch.

"Hey, Carlton." Bea's weary voice interrupted as she entered the living room. "Is everything okay?" She sat on the couch next to Carlton, her petite body dwarfed by his.

"Yes, fine, Bea. Don't worry." Carlton took her hand and gave it a squeeze. "You feeling okay?"

She hid her yawn behind a hand. "Yeah, got a lot of sleep, thanks to Keira." She smiled in my direction. I'd taken the seat next to Adam, once again, we sat like rulers on our thrones.

"I'm afraid the building's pretty much a goner, Bea," Carlton said, his tone somber. "I'm so sorry."

Tears glittered in Bea's eyes as she pulled her hand out of Carlton's, stood a bit shakily. "I . . . I have insurance," she said in a rush and went into the kitchen. I followed.

She stood at the counter, head bowed, hands splayed on the Corian as if the countertop was the only thing holding her up. "I knew it last night," she said. "When the volunteer fire crew showed up, I knew there wasn't much left to save. I was just glad we'd gotten out okay." She sniffed and wiped a tear from her cheek. "Today, it just seems worse."

I hugged her from behind and gave her a quick peck on the back of her head. "Bea, I know. It truly sucks. I'm sorry."

She nodded. "I don't think I can go out there for a while, you know. I mean, into the living room. Carlton being here just reminds me." She turned to the cupboard and pulled out a frying pan. "I'll make some breakfast, okay?"

I let her be, knowing that she needed the distraction. "Sure, hon."

"Carlton can stay if he wants." She busied herself cracking eggs. Oh. She thought he'd come by to give her a status report. Damn. Well, I wasn't going to bother her with details right now. She needed some space.

"Your priest left early, by the way," she said. "About an hour ago."

"He did? I didn't see him."

"You were asleep in the chair. I'd come out to see if you wanted breakfast, but both you and Tucker were sound asleep. I didn't have the heart to wake you."

"Where did he go?" This was most certainly not good.

"To the Lakeside Chapel. He wanted to pray, he said. Muttered something about bitter? I wasn't really paying that much attention, though." She began to whisk the eggs.

Bitter? "Damn it, is he pissed off that we had to leave the cemetery last night?"

"I don't really know," Bea said. "He was speaking in Spanish, said something odd." Her brow furrowed as she thought. "I think I heard him whisper something along the lines of '*no me hagas beber este trago amargo.*' It means 'don't make me drink this bitter drink.' I didn't ask because he seemed rather lost in thought plus, he'd made himself some coffee, so I guess he could've been talking about that. Come to think of it, he had his rosary in one hand, not counting down the decades, but just fingering the beads."

If he didn't like the coffee, why was he drinking it?

I shrugged and leaned back against the counter next to Bea. "I guess he wanted something else, I suppose. How'd he get to the chapel?"

"I told him where it was and gave him the keys to my car."

"Your car? It wasn't here when we drove back last night, then Niko picked you up—"

"I made Niko let me drive back on my own." Her steely gaze met mine. "I had to, Keira. I can't get stuck here with no transportation. My car was fine. I'd parked it at the outside edge of the lot. Been doing that a lot lately because I want to get some more exercise. Walking is good for me." Her hand went to her belly.

"It's not as if you're not on your feet all day already," I protested.

"I'm not. Tio and Tia don't let me," she said and began to whisk again. "I need to move, to be active, but they think I need to slow down and sit. It's making me a bit insane. Good thing I parked the car so far from the building, isn't it?" Tears welled up in her eyes and she stopped talking. Her livelihood gone and here I was bitching at her about her car. Some friend I was.

I hugged her again. "Yeah, good thing." With a quick kiss to the top of her head, I left the kitchen and joined Adam and Carlton in the living room.

So far, so good. They had neither come to blows nor were they glaring daggers. Instead, they were making small talk of a sort. Carlton was talking about the weather, how hot it was, how the drought was getting a lot worse. Adam sat there with an amused smile. Carlton stopped talking as soon as I entered the room. "Keira," he nodded.

"So, did Adam tell you why we called?" I asked, plopping myself down in the armchair again.

Carlton eyed me, his face neutral. "No. We were waiting for you. Bea okay?"

I nodded. "Yeah, she just needs to adjust. She's making breakfast. Asked if you wanted to stay."

"She's . . ." Carlton took off his Stetson and scratched his head. I noticed his hair, though still cropped short, was beginning to show a lot more gray than brown. "I suppose she feels the need."

"She does. So, about this . . ." I waved a hand between Adam and I.

"In light of the recent incidents," Adam began, "Keira and I felt that it was important to take you into our confidence."

"Go on."

Adam glanced over at me. I took up the gauntlet.

"Well, Carlton, it's like this." I took a deep breath, sent up a silent plea to whatever gods were listening for courage, strength, and the ability to say this without fucking it up. "I'm not human, and Adam is a vampire."

The sound of a frying pan clattering to the kitchen tile was the only sound in the room.

CHAPTER TWENTY-EIGHT

"The Great Oz has spoken."
> —*L. Frank Baum,* The Wizard of Oz

"You're . . ." Carlton slammed his hat back on his head and stood, his lips tight and angry. "You called me over here for a prank?"

I leaped up, putting both hands on his solid arms. "Carlton, please, don't be stupid. Why on earth would I say these things if they weren't true?" I looked at him, my face as open and honest as I could make it. He had to believe me.

His brown eyes searched my face, bewilderment in his expression. "How? Keira, this is just—"

"Unbelievable, I know." Adam rose. "Perhaps this will convince you." He bared his teeth, fangs sliding out.

Carlton pulled out of my grasp, stepped back, and fell onto the couch. "How. You." He pointed at Adam, who'd retracted his fangs and returned to his chair. "How'd you do that?"

I smacked Carlton on the back of his head. "You're a smart man, Carlton Larsen. Think. Use that big brain of yours. We exist. Vampires exist. Neither of us is human."

He cringed. "Keira, are you the same?"

"As Adam? No," I said. I went back to my chair, knowing full well I'd hurt him. Not physically, but emotionally. I could see his spirit breaking as his eyes went wide. "My family is a worldwide clan of supernaturals," I explained. "Simply put, we have various Talents and abilities."

"Like what?"

"Pretty much anything you'd think of as out of the ordinary," I said. "Weather affinities, healing, shapeshifting."

"Shapeshifting." Carlton rubbed his face, removed his hat again and set it carefully down on the side table. "Are you trying to tell me you can change shape?"

"Well, not all of us can," I said. "My people only inherit one primary ability at adulthood, but in my case—"

"In her case," Tucker's voice continued my explanation. I grinned as my brother and Niko came into the room, each to stand beside us in their usual positions. Tucker looked good, well rested. "She has all our Talents. Keira is heir to our clan chieftain."

"You. Tucker? I suppose you're a part of this."

"Every last inch of me," he said. "I'm a shapeshifter. And her Protector." With an extremely amused grin, my brother glanced at me and wagged his eyebrows. I laughed and nodded my head. Without another word, Tucker quickly stripped out of his clothes and shifted into his wolf shape.

Carlton's eyes widened and his mouth worked, but no sound came out. Tucker, his tail wagging, trotted over to Carlton, put his giant paws on Carlton's lap, and nuzzled at his face. "Get off! Get off, you . . ." Carlton pushed at the wolf, but Tucker stood firm. He nuzzled Carlton's neck again, then to top off his performance, licked his cheek. With a small yip that sounded suspiciously like a wolf's version of a laugh, Tucker bounded off Carlton and returned to his clothing and shifted back.

"I . . ." Carlton wiped his cheek with the back of his hand. "What the— How?"

Bea, who'd been standing in the kitchen doorway, stifled a chuckle. She entered the room with two steaming mugs of coffee and handed me one, then sat next to Carlton on the couch and offered him the other. "Here, drink this. I know it's a lot to get used to."

"You knew?" He waved a hand in our direction. "About this?"

She nodded. "Yes."

He took a huge gulp, then focused on Bea. "You know?"

She nodded and tucked her feet under her. "I've known for years," she said. "I practically grew up at the Kelly house. I couldn't help but know."

"Are you . . . ?"

"No, I'm just human, like you." Now it was my turn to stifle a laugh. Human, yes, but carrying a half-werewolf baby. I didn't think Carlton was quite ready for absolute full disclosure. Having us be different was plenty for now.

"Bea was the only human friend that I could talk to since we were kids," I added.

Carlton gave her a slow nod. "I get that. And him? Is he a wolf, too?" Carlton indicated Niko, who stood death-still at his post.

"He is mine," Tucker said. "And he is vampire."

"Despite my 'big brain,' as you called it, I'm having a devil of a time absorbing all of this." He looked at each of the three of us. Tucker, now back next to Niko and fully dressed. Adam, sitting like a king, his posture relaxed but regal. Me, with my legs tucked up in a tailor's squat, in the chair next to Adam.

Understanding flooded his eyes as the other shoe dropped. "Keira, that's why you broke up with me."

"Yes," I said. "I liked you, Carlton. A lot. It's just that marrying humans is out of the question."

"Incompatible?"

"In many ways, yes." I wasn't going to hit him up with the long life thing. He'd had enough shocks for the day. "Look, I know this is a lot to take in, but we realized that there are some things you need to know—as sheriff. As the law."

With a quick shake of his head, Sheriff Larsen was back. He'd re-donned his mental armature as the law. I hoped it would help him digest all this new information.

Adam and I gave him the quick and dirty version, skipping over many of the more esoteric details.

"Gideon, this brother of yours," he nodded to Adam, "he's out to get you?"

"More or less," I said. "We don't know everything, but he's claimed Challenge, and we've essentially broken the Truce by coming back here to Rio Seco. I don't know if the fire at the strip center was caused by that or if it really *was* just vandalism, but I'd lay my money on the former. Bea, I'm so sorry," I said to my best friend. "You know I'll take care of you."

"What can we do to help?" Carlton asked. "My guys are just human. We're no match for you people."

"No, and it would be best if you and your deputies

stayed away from the cemetery. There may be dangers there for humans as well as for our kind. You could help us by keeping an eye out," Adam said. "We are quite restricted during the day. Niko and I must remain out of the daylight. Tucker's been injured and Keira cannot wander about on her own. I am going to attempt to Call my father; if he can join us, we have more of an ability to work this out without—"Adam's lips suddenly tightened.

"Without anyone getting hurt," I completed. I knew where he'd been going. He was going to say with as few deaths as possible, with as little war as possible. That wasn't something to share. If we did go full-out Faery war, the humans wouldn't likely be affected directly. But these tricks, these pranks could very well hurt more people. The pranks existed in the human, mortal world.

"I'm assuming you'd rather I not share the details with my deputies," Carlton said.

"If you would be so kind." Adam rose, every inch the vampire king, his hand outstretched in a gesture of conciliation. He approached Carlton, who stood and accepted the handshake. "I appreciate your assistance, Sheriff. In light of everything that's happened." Adam looked Carlton directly in the eye. "Thank you."

Carlton's gaze wavered. A blink, then a searching look in my direction as he once again donned his Stetson. "We'll be in touch." With that, he gave me a small smile, strode over to the door and exited with a quick nod of acknowledgment to both Tucker and Niko. He didn't slam it shut, which, if it had been me who'd been faced with this kind of revelation, I totally would have done.

"Well, that went better than I expected." I let my

held breath out with a whoosh. "Kudos to Carlton for tamping down the freak-out."

Bea began to giggle. "Did you see his face, *m'ija*? Priceless."

"Indeed." Adam smiled at us both. "Your sheriff is most certainly one of a kind, love."

I reached over and took his hand. "Not my sheriff," I said in a fond tone. "Not for a long time."

"No, not." Adam raised my hand and kissed it.

"I took the liberty of calling Dixxi," Tucker said as he and Niko relaxed and joined Bea on the couch. "She's on her way to pick up Bea, Noe, Tio, and Tia. She wanted to do it personally, instead of leaving it to a car service."

"She's—oh no," Bea protested. "I'm not going anywhere."

"Don't get all stubborn *Mexicana* on me, girlfriend," I said. "Bea, you could be in very serious danger. You heard what we told Carlton. We broke Truce. Deliberately. Tucker's been attacked by fire ants. You've lost the café. I don't want anything else to happen to you. There's plenty of room at Dixxi's condo. Go, the four of you can stay there and be out of this mess."

Bea's additional protests subsided. She knew I was right. She'd been through enough with me recently that it wasn't a fairy tale any longer, but real dirt, grime, and blood. I didn't want any of the blood to be hers.

"Fine. I won't argue, but only because of the baby."

"C'mon, little sister," Tucker joked. "Let's get you packed." She nodded and followed him out of the room.

"Where's Fray Antonio?" Niko asked. "He wasn't in his room when I checked earlier."

"Praying, evidently," I said. "Bea loaned him her car

so he could go to the chapel." At Niko's startled look, I explained. "No, not the one at the Rose Inn. There's a non-denominational chapel over near the marina. It's not too far from here. I expect he wanted to pray before we go back to the cemetery today."

"I expect so," Niko murmured. "When are you going back?"

"As soon as Bea gets off safely," I said. "When is Dixxi expected?"

"Very soon," Niko replied. "Tucker called her about an hour ago."

"It takes at least three hours to get here from where she is," I said.

"She was already on her way," Niko said. "She'd meant to come yesterday to check on Bea, but got caught up in some lab test or something."

"Good news. She'll take care of Bea and I'll feel a hell of a lot better."

"Adam, you still wish to Call your father?" Niko asked. "Do you think that's wise?"

"I believe it's necessary, Niko. Wise? Perhaps not."

"Not a lot of what we've done in the past few days would rank up there as 'wise,'" I said. "We're stumbling around, tripping over jinxes and traps like the Scooby Gang. Only it's real magick and not some guy in a ghost suit." As Adam made to reproach me, I continued. "No, it's not as if we could have done anything differently, other than stay at the Rose Inn with our heads buried in ancient books like so many ostriches. I'm completely sure now that Gideon meant us to be afraid of breaking Truce while he diddled about here, doing whatever it is he's doing. He's set traps, to be sure, but so far, they've not been fatal. I don't think he wants to kill anyone—yet."

"Yet?" Adam prompted.

"Yeah, I got to thinking about this while you were explaining the situation to Carlton. Gideon's at least as powerful as I am, in raw strength at least, right?"

Two heads nodded.

"I'm probably better trained, at least in the Kelly Talents. The arson was nothing but child's play, a trick I would expect from a pwca or a cluracan. It's minor—all flash and distraction—nothing of major consequence. The Challenge itself and whatever's going on with the souls of the dead, the wide-open Portal to Faery? That's the trouble. The real question is . . . who's the man behind the curtain and what is he really up to?"

CHAPTER TWENTY-NINE

"The unexamined faith is not worth having."
— D. Elton Trueblood

"**D**amn it." I toed the body gingerly. "That's the third one." Shading my eyes, I examined the ground around us, looked to the horizon. "This is so not good."

"That's an understatement." Tucker's mouth was set in a grim line. "Three deer, two cows, countless rabbits. At least one javelina. That's too many to be dying simply of thirst. Both the main watering tanks should still be close to full. We've only been gone a couple of days. They can't have dried up this quickly. Niko checked them the night before the Reception."

"Question number two is why on earth did the animals wander this far out from their regular watering holes? There's nothing here but the cemetery. This is pretty unusual." I nudged at the dead deer again. Its body had already begun to bloat in the noonday sun.

"More dark magick?" Tucker ventured.

"Probably." Great. Something else to worry about. I felt as if I was deep in the middle of a coming apocalypse or Biblical plague, though instead of the Four Horsemen, or locusts and famine, we got fire ants and actual fire.

Earlier, we'd packed Bea and her family off with Dixxi, with assurances that I'd keep both the women posted as to what was happening. Without Bea knowing it, I also had phoned Ciprian, my eldest brother and Kelly clan financial whiz, to arrange some monetary relief for Bea. She wasn't poor, but she operated her small business on a fairly tight margin and would need some cash to live for a while. I knew she would refuse a direct offer from me, but I trusted Ciprian to get it done and to override any of her objections. He could help her speed up the insurance paperwork for the café, too.

I pulled my new phone out of my back pocket. Thank goodness for Dixxi, who'd stopped by a phone store in Cedar Park on the way and picked up a new one for me. "Adam, we've got more dead livestock," I said, giving him the rundown. "I think Tucker and I should go and check the water tanks."

"If the tanks are dry, there's little you can do about it this moment, Keira." Niko's voice cut in. "We fill them with the water truck, water pumped from our well. If those troughs are empty, the well might be drying up, too. Besides, you don't know how to operate the truck."

"I can try," I said, too stubborn to give up. These were Adam's rescue animals that were dying along with the native fauna. He'd spent hundreds of thousands of dollars buying the stock from defunct ranches and giving them a home here at the Wild Moon.

"Explore the cemetery first," Adam suggested, getting back on the phone. "Then, yes, if you wish, check the north tank. It's the larger of the two. Holds more than four hundred gallons. Tucker, you know where it is?"

"I do," Tucker replied. "I'm with you, Adam. We get stuff done here, then check. The priest's all set up again, by the way. We dropped him off at the entrance a bit ago. He's doing his thing."

"He told us it wouldn't take too long today," I said. "He basically needs to say some prayers and then walk around sprinkling holy water. Once he's done, Tucker and I will go back in. See what we find. I'm not planning to poke anymore tombstones." Or anything else that smacked of magick, either. This was a low-key mission. Recon, then get the hell out.

"Good. Get in, check the door, get out," Adam agreed. "Call me as soon as you know something?"

"Will do." I ended the call and stuffed the phone back into my pocket. "It's been half an hour," I said. "Shall we at least go to the gate? Antonio said it wouldn't take him more than forty-five minutes to finish the re-consecration ritual."

Tucker nodded. "Yeah, let's go."

We trudged through what was left of the dry grass, our boots making crunching noises as we walked. So little vegetation grew out here anyway, among the cactus, mesquite, and live oak, even in lush times, there was no more than spotty ground coverage. Now, it was as if we'd entered a desert; even the cacti were wilting.

Tucker kicked at a clump of what was once a tall stand of pampas grass, now only brittle blades, broken and bent in the searing sun. "Do you think his ritual will work?"

"I beg your pardon?"

Tucker shrugged and tucked his hands into his shorts

pockets. "He has no magick. I'm not really sure how this whole consecration thing works without magick."

"Huh. I guess I never really thought about it," I said. "But you've got a point. I've not got a clue either."

"Faith." I jumped as Antonio's voice answered my brother's question.

"How do you do that?" I asked, grumpy at once again being startled by this priest.

Antonio chuckled. "Do what?"

"Walk so quietly."

"Years of practice."

"You done?" Tucker asked.

"I am," he said. "The ritual is finished. The ground is now consecrated."

"How do you know exactly?" I had to ask. Tucker's question had opened a well of doubt in me. "How can I check?"

Antonio eyed me as if I'd grown a second head. "It is done. The ritual is specific and precise. I completed my task."

"And therefore the cemetery is re-consecrated, just like that?" I snapped my fingers. "Sorry, but there's no way for me to test this theory of yours?" I wanted to know for sure. We couldn't operate on just his word for it. Not now, not when perhaps even our lives were at stake.

"Doubting Thomases, the both of you." The old man mumbled as he walked away from us. "Though, I would like to return a little later and pray some more. The souls buried here are restless. There has been an unnatural darkness on this land. I'd hoped that the prayers and holy water would rid the ground of its taint, but that does not appear to be the case." He turned to face us. "Go, do what you must to shut your Faery door, then let us leave this place for now. When you are done with this thing, I come back and offer more prayers." He looked past me, at the cemetery gate, but not focused, his gaze distant as if contemplating the universe. "All gods require offerings."

I stared at him, waiting for an explanation. When none came, I shrugged. "Whatever flips your tortilla," I said. "C'mon, Tucker. Let's get going."

We made the trek to the overhang. In the harsh glare of the afternoon sun, the cemetery looked peaceful, at rest. No sign of any malevolent energy greeted us as we approached our new, more clever way onto the grounds. Instead of taking the direct route, through the various rows of markers, Tucker and I had decided ahead of time that we were going to be a bit more cautious this time and use the overhang as our entry point. "Minimizing risks," he'd called it. "Brilliant idea," I'd corrected. Why we hadn't thought of this last night, I don't know. But then again, we'd not expected an attack . . . at least not by insects.

"Looks pretty quiet down there," I said as I hung my head over the edge. "No signs of footprints."

"Wards?" Tucker scooted up on his belly next to me. The overhang was fairly solid, though without rain, who knew just how crumbly the dirt beneath us was. I wasn't about to take any unneeded chances.

I shut my eyes and extended one hand above my head, focusing on the ground about twenty feet below us. Starting at La Angel, who still stood as proud guardian in front of the cave mouth—the cave that guarded the entrance to Faery—I felt around for any wards, any signs whatsoever. A slow hum filled the air as I worked, my energies in tune with me and with my environment. This is how it was supposed to happen, not like last night. No darkness rose, no signs of anything there other than the distinct taste of Underhill.

"The door's still open," I said quietly. "Though there does seem to be some sort of energy around it, it doesn't feel like a ward."

"Early warning system?"

I shook my head. "Not really. Leakage, maybe? From Faery? It's got the flavor of Below. Sidhe, light. No dark at all."

"Keira, I'm not sure we should go down there. What if it is some other sort of trap? Do you think you can close the door from up here?"

I opened my eyes and rolled to my back, my palm automatically shielding my eyes from the sun. "Maybe. We need to walk in a circle," I mused. "Perhaps this can be done above it as well as next to it. I mean, technically, the door is an energy barrier from the Between. It doesn't actually exist physically. I suppose it couldn't hurt to try. If it doesn't work, then we'll go to plan B."

"Plan B being we go down to the cave mouth and try there."

"Yup."

"Then shall we?"

"Let's shall."

I stood and brushed off the dirt and pieces of dry grass that had stuck to my skin. I opened the rucksack I'd brought with me and took out the newly sharpened knife. It wasn't a ritual athamé, but would do in a pinch. I'd scrubbed and cleaned it with salt and silk and water as best as possible before we'd left the house. "Tucker, could you stand about ten or twelve feet to one side, please?" My brother nodded and stepped back.

Using the knife, I cut into the dry ground, tearing through a few roots still gamely gripping tight to the parched dirt. "*Yr wyf yn cau'r drws*. I close the door." I chanted as I continued to cut the intricate pattern in a counterclockwise circle. Ogham runes, the sigils of closing that Adam had drilled me in. "*Gofynnaf i'r drws i gau.*" The knife twirled in my hand, as if I were an expert. I knew better. Once the spell had begun, it only needed me to help hold it. "*Caewch y drws*. Close door. Open to none but blood." With the final rune line drawn, I took the knife and pierced my hand, letting droplets of my blood fall onto the four cardinal points of the sigil. "Close. *Mae'r gwaed yn ei gorchmynion.*" The blood commands it. I sank to my knees as a bright pulse of energy flooded the air. I bathed in it, reveled in it. It was blood calling to blood. "Keira Kelly, daughter of Huw, bonded to Aeddan ap Drystan. My blood commands the door be shut. Only blood can open it." I wrestled with the raw power shining through me. It wasn't mine, at least, not just mine. The open door responded and combined Faery magicks poured out, a beacon of power and light, encapsulating me in its embrace. Forcing myself to focus, I grasped it, controlled it, bent it to my will.

"Close now," I commanded. "Close." With supreme effort, I forced it down, braided its strands, surrounded the door and *pulled*.

It pushed back.

A deep, nearly subsonic thrum pounded through the ground upward, slamming me back to thump against Tucker. We fell, entangled together, our bodies crashing through dirt, rocks, and dead grass, the ground itself falling with us, light and energy surrounding us.

A whoosh.

Silence.

Stillness.

A complete lack of any sensory input.

A snap of something breaking beneath me. A twig? Sharp points of pain on my back, my arm. A heavy weight of another against me.

"Ow?" My voice disappeared into the empty dark. My mouth felt swollen, mushy as if full of something and I couldn't speak clearly.

A groan. Tucker's voice. "What the hell . . . ?"

My brain sent commands. Move. Feel. Listen. I sank further into the stillness, wanting to just lie there, insensate.

With a formidable effort, I struggled against the forced ennui, compelling my hand, my arm to move. Skin brushed skin. Tucker's arm? Gods, I hoped so.

"Keira, why can't I move?"

Clarity. I needed . . . Focus, damn you, I thought. I could almost feel my brain firing signals, synapses sparking, but like a misfiring car, the sparks died, alone in the dark, never reaching their intended target.

"I don't know." My mouth formed the words, molasses slowing my tongue. I could hear. I could talk, sort of, and if I worked really hard at it, I could move parts of me. It was as if we were entangled in some sort of weird TV time loop, something out of *Doctor Who* or *Star Trek*—fuck me. Time loop. Faery is out of time. I'd been trying to close the open door.

We were caught in the Between.

CHAPTER THIRTY

"These mountain beds do not agree with me."
—from the short story "Rip Van Winkle"
by Washington Irving

I'd heard of this happening—in old legends, tales told
when I was first learning at my mother's knee . . . before she'd given up on me. Travelers caught in a doorway, a chance encounter ensnaring them for all time.
The man had accidentally fallen asleep on a Faery
mound, a door had opened at the behest of someone
wishing to exit. He'd been trapped in a bubble of time,
suspended between Above and Below until someone let
him out. They'd quickly aged him and set him free. He'd
remembered nothing of the sleep, only that he'd woken
twenty years later.

"Rip Van Winkle," I managed, the slushy words
sounding more like "wibvnkl."

"Fuck." Tucker's voice managed the crisp fricative
with no problem. Why was he able to speak so clearly
when my own contributions felt as if I had a thirty-two-
ounce jar of peanut butter clogging my mouth? "How
do we get out of here?"

I made an effort to move my mouth. "Don't know." There. That sounded better. If I focused on just speaking, I could do it more easily. "We're stuck Between."

Something brushed against my hand, grasped it. My instant reaction of fear subsided. Tucker's hand taking mine, that's all. He seemed to be able to move a little more easily than me. Why? I had no clue. The only thing that came to mind was that I had been the one reciting the incantation to close the door. He'd been an innocent bystander—yeah, well, bystander anyway. He wasn't of Sidhe blood, but was as immortal as the Sidhe, so I figured that's why he was conscious and not asleep or in a coma, like Rip Van Winkle had been. Facts? Again, no clue. I was grasping at straws, combing my memory for anything that might help. The only thing I could think of was that episode of *Torchwood* where Captain Jack's long-lost brother buried him in a grave for a thousand years. Since Jack couldn't die, he'd just be there, alive for centuries. Could that happen to us? It could, it very well could. The Between was just that—between realities. It was a place through which you passed to go into and out of Faery. It did not exist in either Faery or the mortal realm.

I took a deep mental breath. Adam. Adam and Niko knew where we were. They'd find us.

"Don't worry, sis," Tucker said, his voice gentle, soothing as his hand squeezed mine. "Adam and Niko will come for us."

"Just what I was thinking," I said, my voice breaking free of the mush, now clear and loud. "Wow, I can talk again. That's a relief."

"What do you think happened?" Tucker asked.

"To my voice? No idea."

"That, too." Tucker sounded amused. "I meant to us."

"I guess that energy wasn't just leakage from Faery. I was stupid to continue. We've stumbled into the equivalent of a spider web, caught Between."

A hand squeeze. "Not stupid, Keira. You did what had to be done."

"Stupid," I insisted. "I keep doing this, Tucker. Barging in without thinking. Figuring I can just fix things, take care of things. Instead, I keep fucking up. When am I going to go too far and get someone killed?"

"Don't beat yourself up. You tested for traps and there weren't any."

"That just means whoever set it is better at this than I am."

"See, you couldn't have known," Tucker said. I knew that tone. That was "big brother taking care of little sister" tone. "Keira, we're all muddling through this as best we can. We're fighting against things that can't be seen, against someone more twisted than Texas politics. We can only do our best. Don't beat yourself up."

"I suppose you're right," I said. "It's just that . . ."

"I know, little sis. I know. This was supposed to be a time of relaxation and fun—learning to be heir. Instead, we're up to our elbows in dark magicks."

"Aren't we though?" I heaved an internal sigh and prepared to wait. I could wait without going too far into crazy, right?

A thousand eons later—though perhaps really only minutes, a blinding flash of white light flooded us, bathed us in its radiance, then as quickly as we'd been trapped, we were standing in the midst of a room. It glowed with this light, rock walls of the natural cave gleaming. I'd been here before.

"Daffyd." I addressed my Sidhe cousin who stood across the room. He looked exactly the same as the first time I'd seen him, long silvery white hair falling back from a high forehead, down to his knees. His robes shone silver, too; his skin alabaster. "How long were we in there?" I asked.

"I do not know, my lady cousin," he said, his voice like the ringing of a silver bell, clear, yet cold. "I felt your vibrations and came directly. It was a disturbance . . ."

"A disturbance in the Force?" I joked.

Daffyd's expression did not change. He simply waited in silence until I said something he understood.

"Where have you been, Cousin?" I asked. "After we left Vancouver, where did you go?"

"Back among our people." He nodded and approached. "I went home."

"Not my people," I spat out, unable to keep the derision out of my voice. "They stopped being mine when my mother let me become little more than a slave."

"Your mother went Above." Daffyd's voice remained neutral, ignoring my outburst.

"Don't I know it." I pushed past him, finding myself in the same bland, nearly empty room in which I'd first encountered him some months ago. "Haven't redecorated have you?" Same rock chair/throne, same shiny rock walls, stalactites and stalagmites glowing in the light from Faery.

"I don't understand."

"Never mind." Thankful to be somewhere I could *move,* I immediately started to do some stretching and bending, my muscles aching in that good way they feel after being still for too long. My body felt as if I'd been bound up in swaddling for *days*. Tucker soon joined me and we both began a series of flowing movements, a habit I'd gotten into during my training. We moved singly, but in synch as we glided from our opening to the final cross hands and then closing posture. Not even needing to say a word, we changed tack and continued into the partnered pushing hands exercise for a few minutes. In no time at all, my muscles felt normal again, strong and energetic.

I put my palms together and bowed to Tucker, who mirrored my movement.

"Thanks, bro, I needed that." I felt a million times better. "Daffyd, what happened to us? Why were we caught like that?" I joined my brother, perching in the center of the immense chair in a half lotus. "Most important, how do we close this bloody door so that no unsuspecting humans get past it?"

"My apologies, Keira, it was I who set the wards." Daffyd bowed, slid into a kneeling posture in front of me and bared his neck. Okay, whoa, horsey. I suddenly got a mental picture of me in a throne, Tucker at my side and Daffyd kneeling before me like some medieval courtier waiting for his queen to grant him a boon. Then again, not so out of the ordinary for us, really. Daffyd had sworn fealty to me some months ago. Nevertheless, it still made me uncomfortable. In the context of a ritual, a Reception, yeah, I was okay enough with it, but here and now, not so much.

"Stand up, Daffyd, please." I also stood and approached my cousin. "What brought you back here?"

"I felt the door open," he said as he obeyed. "A spell, a dark one, calling on things we dare not call. I am attuned to this particular doorway."

"We?"

"The Sidhe—Seelie or Unseelie. Some spells we do not use."

Spells even Sidhe wouldn't use? That was some seriously powerful mojo. "Did you recognize the specific spell?" I asked. If he had, maybe we could figure out a way to combat it, to neutralize it.

"Not as such," he said. "I only felt the vibrations, because I lived here for a time and am attuned to this place. The underground portion of this cave can be considered a part of Faery, an odd pocket to be sure, not precisely in Faery but still beholden to it. It became a sort of home when I resided here and became imbued with a sense of myself. When I felt the spells, I hurried here as fast as I could. I was too late to prevent the door opening, but I was able to set wards to warn me should anyone attempt to enter Faery through here or tamper with the door."

A dry laugh escaped me as I recalled my spider web analogy. "Well, you're certainly prettier than Shelob."

Tucker threw back his head and laughed, the first healthy laugh I'd heard from my brother in days. "Well, I for one am glad he's not a giant spider."

Daffyd looked on in amusement, not bothering to ask us to clarify our references. He'd gotten used to our sibling banter during out trip to Canada. "I've disabled the trap wards for now," he said, "but the door remains open. It must be shut, but I was unable to do so alone. Perhaps, with your help?"

"Count me in on those not able to," I said.

"That is not good news." Daffyd's face fell, the first true emotion I'd seen from him. "An open Faery portal is more than just a door," he said. "It can Call to people. To those who can hear, can feel it. When I saw you there, trapped, I had hoped that you simply had attempted to enter Faery and had been caught. You say you tried to close the door?"

"Exactly," I said. "That's what I was trying to do when we fell through the ground."

"Fell through?"

"The overhang outside, above the cave mouth? That's where I did the spell."

Daffyd's brow furrowed. He strode over to the entrance to the sloped path that led to the large cave mouth and peered upward. "You were not behind the angel statue? Not at its level?"

Both of us shook our heads. "No, we think the cemetery has a lot of booby-traps set," Tucker said. "We thought it better to not attempt crossing the ground again."

"Odd." Daffyd raised a hand toward the opening and shut his eyes. After a moment, he turned and strode back to us, his robes whipping about his legs. "There is very dark magick out there."

"We know." I paused before continuing. "Daffyd, my cousin Gideon set runespells in the cemetery somehow. He's issued Challenge."

Daffyd's eyes glittered in the fey lights. "Challenge? Are you then under Truce?"

"We are. Until Lughnasa," I said.

"You should not be here." His voice was sharp. "My queen, it is very dangerous for you."

"Don't you think I know that?" I exploded. "Daffyd, Gideon desecrated sacred ground. He's burned down the town's main sources of revenue. I have good reason to believe he's plotting with the high queen. He's managed to marry her daughter, who is pregnant with her mother's acknowledged heir. My cousin wants this land, this door to Faery. He wants to send us packing, but I'm sure that he's got a ton of ulterior motives. At this point, we're willing to take our chances but not willing to blindly wait out the Truce period."

"He broke Truce first?"

"Maybe," I said. "If not in body, then in the spirit of Truce. He or one of his minions did the damage you feel up there." I motioned in the general direction of the cave mouth. "Marks on tombstones, vandalized graves—the type of thing humans dismiss as childish pranks. The marks were all runespells. We didn't get very far in trying to decipher them when Tucker was hurt."

"Hurt?"

"Insects."

Daffyd seemed lost in thought and wouldn't meet my gaze. Then, with an abrupt nod, he spoke. "He came to Court, your cousin. I saw him, all cock of the walk, strutting into the Great Hall. I admit to a great surprise when the queen—your aunt—received him. After a few days of courtly banter, they began to meet in her privy chamber." Daffyd fixed me with a steady look. "Her daughter was not part of these meetings."

"Do you mean that Aoife is as much a pawn as we are?" I demanded answers. "And my mother? What part does she play in this? She came with him, you know. Above. It was her hand that proffered the Challenge."

"Branwen?" If he'd been a bearded scholar, I could imagine him stroking his beard right now. "This is certainly news," he said. "Though I did not see your mother in attendance in the queen's chamber with Gideon, I also did not see her at Court. Not proof of anything,

I know. Of habit, however, she attends Court daily, as is her personal wont and right as a lesser queen. I did not remark on it then, as I was preoccupied with the arrogant stranger."

"So you don't know anything." I deflated, my sudden hope that he knew Gideon's plan flattened. "Great. So we're back to square zero now."

"At least we're not still stuck Between," Tucker said. When I shot him a murderous look, he shrugged. "Just trying to lighten things up a bit. Daffyd, any chance of you scoping out what's what?"

"Of scoping . . . you mean of spying on the high queen? You must be joking." Daffyd's voice raised in surprise and not a little bit of anger. "I cannot spy on my queen."

"Not at all." Tucker rose and approached Daffyd, his large frame towering over the slender Sidhe. Daffyd was tall, but Tucker was taller and much broader. His red hair gleamed, his expression menacing. "You swore fealty to Keira," he growled. "You owe her. You owe all of us."

"It will do no good if I were to be discovered," Daffyd said, standing strong. "Though a cat may look at a queen, a courtier interfering in a queen's business ends ill. Though your cousin is no longer at Court, there are others with whom our queen plots."

"She is not *my* queen," I muttered. "I owe allegiance to no one but my own clan chief."

"Who is missing," Tucker said. "Until she is found, Keira is in charge of our clan, as her heir. So, Daffyd, does that alter your attitude? After all, the Kelly leader is of the same rank as the Sidhe high royalty."

Daffyd stepped around my brother and approached me. "Your chief missing? I do not understand."

"Gigi . . . Minerva Kelly, chieftain of the Kelly clan is missing. She's disappeared and hasn't been reachable." I slumped against a smooth part of the wall. "Daffyd, Tucker's right. In principle, I'm head honcho right now. Since this position is the equivalent to that of the high queen—"

"Keira, your leader is far from missing. She's with Queen Angharad."

CHAPTER THIRTY-ONE

"If we still advise we shall never do."

— *Elizabeth I*

I didn't waste any time. "Okay. That's it. You're coming with us," I said and grabbed onto Daffyd's arm. "Tucker, lead the way. We'll have to take our chances crossing the cemetery."

"Where are you taking me?" Daffyd asked.

"Home with me. You've got a lot of explaining to do and I want Adam to hear all of this."

Without a word, Daffyd followed Tucker and me as we climbed up the rock pathway, through to the cave mouth. It was still light outside. No sign of the priest anywhere, though if he had truly consecrated the cemetery as he said he had, he wouldn't be able to walk the property—at least I thought so. Hopefully, he was waiting in the car.

I pulled out my phone and checked the time. Great, it was only a couple of hours after we'd begun the ritual. We'd been lucky—or Daffyd had traveled fast.

I dialed Adam the moment we reached the cave entrance. "We've found Gigi," were the first words out of my mouth.

"Found her? Where?"

"She's playing at something with Angharad," I said.

"It seems our esteemed matriarch thought she'd head them off at the pass, so to speak," Tucker interrupted, explaining nothing.

"I don't follow."

"Stupid bloody woman decided to confront the bloody Sidhe queen."

"She did what?"

"She's gone Underhill. Holed up with Angharad. Effectively, she's missing in action."

"How do you know this?"

"Tucker and I got stuck in a Sidhe trap set by Daffyd. He'd been trying to guard the open door. He showed up to get us out and just told me about Gigi."

"Damn it. I was afraid of this."

"You knew?" How could he have?

"Not knew, but guessed." Adam sounded weary. "I didn't sleep much after you left. Woke early so I could make some calls. It occurred to me that Minerva may have tried the door in Vancouver, realized she couldn't enter that way, so went somewhere else."

"Where?"

"Wales. Raine is still in London and I was able to get in contact with her. She confessed that Minerva set us up. Minerva glamoured herself so no one would recognize her, hopped the plane with Raine just after we spoke to her. She and Raine were the ones to lay a false trail for your father to find."

Bloody fucking fool of a Kelly matriarch. What in all the seven layers of my own special hells had she thought she was doing? Gigi may be a Kelly, but Angharad was a right bitch of a Sidhe who held nothing but contempt for us upstart aboveground magickal folk. In her eyes, we were lower than nothing. Not that she'd ever admit it in front of anyone who mattered. I only knew her true feelings about us because she'd never noticed me. Not once she'd decided I was less magickal than her left boot, an invisible girl, sliding through the shadows and twisted pathways of Faery, hearing so much, understanding so little until adulthood. I knew I'd suppressed most of it, memories surfacing only as I'd begun my Change to adulthood, started my transition to Kelly heir.

"Gigi planted the phones at the hotel, didn't she?"

"Seems so," Adam said. "At least, one of her Protectors did the deed, whilst Raine flew Minerva to Wales after dropping off our vampires. Raine flew back after Gigi went Underhill. Evidently, Minerva's glamour was strong enough to fool even Rhys, Ianto, and Liz—none of them noticed. They thought that the person with Raine was a copilot. Some cousin they'd not met."

"Damn that woman," I gritted out the words through teeth so tightly clenched, if I were human, I'd be buying an entire fleet of luxury cars for some orthodontist. I whirled to face the cave opening, held back the energy swirling around me, my own Texas tornado, itching to be loosed on someone, somewhere. It was probably a good thing that neither Gideon nor my mother were around.

Two hands caught me before I stormed outside.

"Keira, get a grip," Tucker said softly. "You can't just prance through the cemetery without taking precautions. We can't know for sure if the ground's safe—even if it may be consecrated again."

I stopped and took a deep breath, then spoke to

Adam. "We've got a bit of a situation, love," I said and quickly told him more about what had happened. "The door here's still open. You and Niko can get out here via the overhang, then we can all go Below. We'll go get Gigi. You and me, Tucker and Niko. Slide down, through Faery, find her. Settle this stupidity once and for all." The Four Musketeers . . . or the Four Horsemen, I thought bitterly. Though this apocalypse would be for Angharad, not the mortal world.

"And that will accomplish . . . ?" Adam sounded skeptical.

"We can confront Angharad on her own turf, three rulers against one. Find out what Gideon's truly up to and put a stop to this."

"How, Keira? Storming the castle isn't an answer so much as a declaration of—"

"War?" I whispered, realizing that my bullheaded "go now and kick some fey ass" impulse would be less than effective unless I truly planned to trip that particular wire and take the consequences. Truce, I'd break, but starting a war? I couldn't make that decision foolishly.

"All-out war," Adam agreed. "We can't afford a Faery war, Keira. We're not in the days of the Firbolg and the Tuatha Dé Danann and tiny human tribes cowering in their caves or crude huts. Billions of humans populate the Earth. Too many would die as a result of what is, after all, a simple family squabble. Our spells could not directly affect them, but we could kill the land for good. Do you wish to unleash full-on famine, drought, pestilence? That's what we could bring, if we do this."

Damn it all, he was right. The apocalypse wouldn't be confined solely to Angharad. "So what *do* we do?" I asked. "What *can* we do?"

"We wait?" Niko's voice came over the speaker. "We continue to work on our strategy, work on the Challenge and we wait."

A horrible thought occurred to me. Being trapped in Faery . . . oh holy . . . "Adam, would the same rules apply to Gigi as to humans?" I asked, my words tumbling over each other in my haste to wash that thought out of my head. No, they couldn't? We weren't human, but as magickal as any Sidhe, if not more so. Gigi was our matriarch, our leader, a couple of millennia of practice, of wielding stronger magicks than I'd ever seen Below. "Insofar as being Below, I mean. Trapped there, loads of time passing up here?"

"I do not know," Adam admitted. "Minerva, you—you're both strong, more talented than any one Sidhe, any fey in existence."

"And Gigi's beyond crafty," Tucker said. "She's at least as sly as any in Faery."

"Oh yeah, she's a right Slytherin," I snorted, feeling a little better. "But . . . it's the Seelie Queen—"

"Queen or no, Minerva is an equal if not higher ranked ruler," Niko said. "I don't pretend to know the intricacies of the Faery courts, but I did learn about intrigue at the feet of the best in Elizabeth's court. If another queen had approached her, she would cause them no harm."

Yeah, but no harm didn't mean freedom, I thought. Nor did not being the overt cause of harm preclude getting someone else to do your dirty work—a Seelie Talent. Elizabeth herself had been known to play some pretty sneaky tricks, and she wasn't even of Faery. As for not harming a fellow queen, tell that to Mary, Queen of Scots. She'd lost her head thanks to her royal cousin.

"I'd not rest easy yet, Niko," Tucker said. "Gloriana was just as ruthless and wily as any Sidhe monarch." A soft smile played across his lips as he confirmed my own thoughts.

Niko sounded startled. "You knew her majesty?"

"For a time." Tucker seemed a bit sheepish. "It was long ago and far away, and of no consequence, *cariad*. We would not have crossed paths then," he said. "I came well after the plague that nearly took you."

"Okay, well then, enough of who's stronger, who's cannier and whether or not my brother might have seen or met his future lover in sixteenth-century London," I said. "We can muddle around and wonder, or we can figure out some sort of plan. Do we try to find Gigi? Do we leave her to her own devices in Faery? For that matter, is this part of some sort of twisted subplot of Gideon's?"

"Minerva going to Faery?" Adam asked. "If I were to gamble on an answer, that was pure Minerva. She wanted to help you, help us by intervening directly with Angharad."

I leaned against the rock wall and slid to the ground. "Fuck." Could Gideon, too, be a pawn in some overarching plot of the high queen? I'd heard of stranger plots. Then again, Gideon wasn't the type to allow himself to be used, queen or not. No, whatever the underlying machinations, I'd no doubt that both Angharad and Gideon were in this as partners.

"So do we go Below?" Tucker asked. I looked up at him, Daffyd standing at his side seemingly unsure of what to do. I didn't envy my cousin, for all his Sidheness, he'd been helpful before. He'd sworn fealty to me, yet was still sworn to his own queen, as well. His deliberate siding with us could cause interminable repercussions for him Below. Unlike me, he was full Sidhe, full Seelie. Everything he was belonged to Angharad. That was the way of the Faery Folk.

"Come back to the house and let's regroup," Adam said. "You've got the priest there with you. We couldn't just leave him while we go Below, if we decide to do that. No matter the decision, we'll need to wait until dusk so Niko and I have the ability to join you."

"That's hours from now," I said. "Adam, I don't like leaving this door open, at least, not without us here to guard it. I propose that Tucker and I wait right here at the cave mouth. You two can drive over soon as it's dark."

"Is it safe for you?"

"I think so. Antonio claims he re-consecrated the place, but we've not set foot on cemetery ground yet. This part of the land—at the cave entrance—is neutral, not included in the cemetery, so neither consecrated nor spelled."

Daffyd touched Tucker's shoulder. "I could help you with the runespells whilst we wait for Aeddan," he offered. "I can feel them from here. There are many of them. Simple, if annoying."

"Unseelie?" I asked.

"Mostly Seelie," he said. "Other things woven in, though. Darker things." He looked out toward the graveyard. "It might take some time, but between us, we should be able to remove the spells."

I rubbed my face. "Adam, I think I'm going to see if I can at least get out to the car and let Antonio know what's going on. He can go back to the ranch. Then Tucker and I will stay here with Daffyd and help him defuse the trigger spells."

"Keira, you can just phone Fray Antonio," Niko suggested. "I gave him a phone."

"Good thinking. What's the number?"

"As a matter of fact," Niko continued. "Don't worry about it. I'll take care of that for you. You three just concentrate on your side of things . . . and stay safe."

"Please be careful, love," Adam said. "Both of you. Retreat if you run into anything you can't handle and phone us. We can send someone for you if need be." Now that we'd told Carlton, it would make things a lot easier if we needed his assistance. No more trying to come up with a convoluted explanation for the weird.

"Will do," I said, crossing my fingers and ending the call.

"I saw that," Tucker said. "What was with the finger crossing?"

I scrambled to my feet and tucked the phone back into my pocket. "Just being careful," I said. "What Adam considers something I can't handle and what I know I can handle could be two vastly different things. I don't want to stop if we can get this cemetery de-rigged. And Daffyd thinks we can, right?"

"That we can remove the spells? Yes." Daffyd walked to the edge of the cave. "There are many traps, many tangled charms, but it can be done." He turned to look at me. "Without involving your consort. Or yours." He bowed to Tucker, who smiled back. "I must ask, however, if you could tell me the specifics of the Challenge that was presented. A battle for land?"

"In a way, though not quite so simple. Gideon Challenges that the land is barren, dying because of us. It states that we lose the land to him if it does not claim us, acknowledge us."

"Ah." Daffyd seemed to understand the premise, at least. "Though, perhaps, I do not grasp his purpose. Why should he wish to have your land? The world Above is large, surely there are other places."

"Many places," I said. "He does this because he can. It's personal between us," I said.

"Perhaps he simply wishes to start afresh."

"No, too simple, too . . . human. One thing he's never been is that. He pities humans."

"You are of an age with him, right?" Daffyd asked.

"Months apart," I said. "Gideon's a bit older."

"I do not understand then. Why the disparity in attitude?"

"Sorry, not following."

Daffyd cocked his head, as if figuring out how to phrase the words. "You seem easy with humans. Your friendship with the woman Bea is fierce, familial. I've seen the way you treat other humans, as well. People you don't know. There doesn't seem to be any awareness that there is a difference between you and them."

"I think I understand what you're getting at," I said. "Gideon wasn't brought up much around humans. The Kelly line in the UK is a bit more old-school."

"Traditional?"

"If by tradition you mean insular, hidebound, and exclusive, then yes." I smiled up at Daffyd. "I was mainstreamed, raised as much in the human world as I was reared as a Kelly. I'm not sure of Gigi's original intentions, now that I know some of how I came to exist, but both my late cousin Marty and I became part of the community in Rio Seco. Gideon, as far as I know, remained on the Kelly estate in the UK during his child-hood. He only went to London in his early twenties—and then, to a Kelly house in town."

"Similar to the British royals. Raised in the mortal world but not of it," Daffyd stated. "They mingle, but it is limited and with severe restrictions. I understand."

I shot him a quizzical look. "You know of the current British royals?"

"I *have* watched some television," he said. "On days I could roam."

Tucker threw a casual arm around my shoulder as he explained further. "Gideon was even more isolated from the mundane world when you take into account being Talented. As kids, youngsters, especially in the modern world, we do our best to shield humans from accidental magick. That's why most of our primary homes are in the countryside. Fewer neighbors."

"For all I know, all of this was part of Gigi's master plan," I grumbled. "Mainstreaming me, isolating Gideon, half-and-half really with Marty. He went to school part-time, I think. I never really paid much attention to him when I was in school, since Marty was nearly four years my senior. Maybe she figured she'd see what we'd turn out like."

"It bloody well sounds as if Minerva experimented with all aspects of your lives," Tucker growled. "I am sorry I never saw that before. None of us had knowledge of her plan to breed heirs. Seems as though she did it with a scientific set of conditions, to see which one of you emerged the victor."

A hell of a point. I could certainly see that having been her goal. Three possible heirs via biological she-nanigans, then manipulating our environments as we developed, aged, became adults. "Oh, that's just more than I wanted to consider right now," I said. "Gigi's own version of nature vs. nurture? I hope she's happy with her little Darwinian experiment."

"Galtonian," Tucker said. "Francis Galton coined the phrase. He was influenced by Charles—"

I glared, effectively shutting him up. "Really? You want to do that now?"

He mock bowed. "My apologies, my lady."

"Okay, then," I said. "So maybe Gigi set us up—again. Old history now. Let's get on with our task, shall we?"

CHAPTER THIRTY-TWO

*"'Tis now the very witching time of night,
    When churchyards yawn, and hell itself breathes
out . . ."*
                                    —William Shakespeare, Hamlet

The sun had barely set when we finished the last of the dismantling spells. With Daffyd's help, it went quickly if not entirely without incident. Tucker had sustained at least three bad cuts. I'd suffered a blow to the head and scraped both knees and an elbow when a particularly nasty spell resulted in me being tossed like a rag doll against one of the larger funerary statues. At least there were no more plagues of insects. No ants, no locusts—though I admit I covertly watched the horizon for any unexplained, swiftly moving dark clouds. No frogs or rains or any other sort of living thing, either, though right now, a rain of anything resembling water would be welcome. I dripped with sweat, my red tank top darkened to nearly black with perspiration and dirt. Tucker had removed his T-shirt within the first hour and bound his hair back with the shirt, using it as a sort of do-rag. Daffyd, on the other hand, seemed as cool and collected as if he carried his own stasis field with him. I couldn't do any cooling charms, not even a small one as we were afraid that any magick could trigger a trap we'd not seen.

I slumped onto the floor of the cave mouth, happy in the slightly cooler temps inside. "Those last few were doozies," I said as I wiped my face with the hem of my top. "Ugh. This is totally gross. My shirt's soaked." I pulled it off and threw it to the ground, leaving me wearing my sports bra, also soaked. "I'm disgusting. And I stink."

"I think it's safe to cast a couple of spells now," Tucker said. "I'm in the same boat you are, sis."

I waved a hand and set a cooling charm along with one that helped act as a fan to move the air. Instantly, I felt better.

"Got any cleaning spells up your sleeve—oh wait, you don't have any sleeves." Tucker grinned and snapped his shirt at me. I threw a stinging hex at him.

"Ouch." He rubbed his side. "Gee, thanks, sis."

"Don't slap at me with your stinky shirt next time," I said. "And no, I don't know any personal hygiene spells. They weren't exactly included in the repertoire during my training. Gigi said we'd work on that kind of stuff later."

Tucker threw back his head and laughed. "You asked her about hygiene spells?"

"Yeah, so what? I did do a lot of physical activity," I said. "The mountains in British Columbia may be a lot cooler than here, but I still got stinky."

"Allow me." With neither a wave or incantation, nor nose wriggling nor eye blinks, we were clean. Daffyd simply smiled.

"May the light shine on you in perpetuity," I breathed, thankful to feel fresh again. Along with the charm I'd set, the atmosphere inside the cave mouth was almost pleasant. Tucker grinned and tossed his shirt back on.

"Hello, down there," Adam called.

I got to my feet, pulled on my tank and walked outside, enough so I could see up to the overhang. Two heads peeked out over the edge. "Come on down, we're all—"

With no warning except a rumbling sound, the earth itself began to move. A cloud of dust and debris showered onto my head. I stumbled, nearly fell but caught myself, keeping upright only by grabbing onto La Angel's marble robes. "Adam!" Both his and Niko's head had disappeared from view.

"We're fine."

I sighed in relief. "Tucker, Daffyd. Get out of there," I cried out as the ground continued to shake. Earthquake? We'd had one or two before, but nothing of major consequence. This area lay along the Balcones Fault and so was prone to a few shakes now and again. This, though, strong enough to shake me, to nearly knock me down—this was no minor adjustment to the fault line.

Tucker and Daffyd came running out. Tucker grabbed onto me and the statue, his strong arms holding me as still as he could. "The cave . . ." His breath was strained, rough. "Part of the wall began to collapse," he said. "Daffyd tried to go down, but—"

"The path has been obliterated," Daffyd said. "We can no longer remain here."

"Adam, meet us back at the bottom of the hill," I said. "We've got to leave."

"Will do."

The three of us ran, did our best to keep our balance as we did so. For a brief moment, I considered shifting to wolf, given that four paws were better than two human length legs when trying to maneuver on unstable ground. After a particularly vicious shake of the ground, I thought better of it. I'd have to stop, strip, and shift. That took time.

We managed to make it to the graveyard entrance without further incident. As we passed through the gate, the quake stopped, ground solid and still once more. I turned to survey the cemetery damage. Stones uprooted and falling over, a few of the smaller statues keeled to one side as if in a drunken dance. Nothing too horrible. Nothing that couldn't be fixed.

"That was . . . unexpected," Adam said as he joined us. "Daffyd." Adam acknowledged my cousin with a curt nod.

"The last time I felt a quake this intense," Tucker said, "was back fifty or more years ago . . . and that was in north Texas, not here." He bent down and pulled up some dirt and grass, letting it run through his fingers. "We're more likely to get tornadoes—"

I clapped my hand over his mouth. "Stop that. Don't tempt fate."

"I doubt fate or fault lines had anything to do with it," Adam said, his voice nearly as dry as the ground we stood on.

I looked at him, then at Niko and Tucker. Tucker shrugged. "Surely not Gideon . . . I mean, fire ants, okay, that can happen. Simple hexes and charms with some trigger spells. The fire at Bea's. But an earthquake? That's some heavy-duty earth magick. He's not capable of that. Hell, *Gigi's* not capable of that."

"Nor is my father," Adam admitted. "Is Angharad?" His piercing gaze turned on Daffyd, who met it without flinching.

"Perhaps," he said. "My queen has many Talents she has not revealed to us all. Though this . . ." He crouched and like Tucker, ran his hands through the dirt. "I feel little of her magick here," he said. "I am no expert in this matter, however."

"We need to leave this place," Niko said with a growl. "There is still a darkness here that I mistrust."

"Yes, darkness that we could not cleanse," Daffyd said as he straightened. "We rid the stones of the runespells," he said. "There were many variations on the same thing—triggers bound to warnings bound to spells to keep us away. But yet . . ."

I closed my eyes against the night and listened. No sounds of birds, rustling of animals walking through the parched grounds. Not even insects humming. The aftermath of the shaking earth? Extending my sense with care, I reached forward with my thought. The hum of cleansed magick beneath, along the ground and the stones we'd meticulously de-spelled. But there was also . . . something else. It was as if a yawning void lay underneath everything, waiting. A slumbering beast? Or simply the residue of the dark magicks used to desecrate the land and prop open the door to Faery?

"Something's still there," I said. "Daffyd's right. The cemetery is mostly safe. There's nothing but clean energy at the surface and on the tombstones, but I feel . . . it's like an oil slick or black ice hiding just below the surface." I shook my head and looked at the three men. "I'm sorry I can't be more clear, but I can't identify it."

"Booby traps upon booby traps," Niko muttered. "I

dislike these layers of magick. I do not know how to fight them. We should leave."

"We haven't shut the door yet," I said. "We can still go Below. Confront Angharad. Talk to Gigi."

"The way's blocked," Tucker said. "The pathway to the lower cave's all filled with rubble. We can move it, but it will take time."

"We won't need that," I said. "With Adam, Daffyd, and me here, the three of us can incant the doorway into existence. A good thing, though, the rubble will keep out any passersby. If they can't get into the lower cave, they won't be able to reach Faery or be trapped in the Between."

"Then I vote we go," said Tucker. "I'm tired of this faffing about. Let's go to the source. Adam?"

Adam looked at each of us in turn, his gaze searching. "This is not child's play, nor a task to be undertaken lightly," he began.

"No, but it is a task we can do," Tucker argued. "What choice remains? Every time we muck about in this hellhole of a cemetery, bad things happen. Do we keep fucking with whatever is guarding this place and get all the Biblical plagues along with an apocalypse? Don't think I hadn't noticed, Niko." He turned, his hand on Niko's shoulder. "I've studied your Bible, as I did all the legends and myths of most peoples," Tucker said. "I get the symbolism. Whoever set this up has a twisted sense of humor. We've even got the dead animals. I guess we're okay if we haven't run across a seven horned once-dead lamb."

Or the actual Apocalypse was coming, I thought. "Well, come on then. Let's go. Adam, do you think we can access the door via the overhang? I wasn't able to close it up there, but we can probably open a Way. It really is wide open."

CHAPTER THIRTY-THREE

"The line it is drawn. The curse it is cast."
  —*Bob Dylan, "The Times They Are A-Changin'"*

Once again, as we'd done in Vancouver, I found myself following Adam in a circle, walking widdershins, as he spoke cool, rolling words in the Old Language. Words I now knew more intimately, with my own magick and Talents imbuing them with strength of will. Beside me, Daffyd, hand-in-hand with me as we repeated the words, using our Sidhe powers. Niko and Tucker took our six, also with joined hands, there for comfort, protection, and love.

Round once, twice, thrice. Our steps measured and precise. The air shimmered with energy, the very molecules dancing with power and light. Step by step, the barrier between worlds thinned as we spoke the final words. Closing the circle one last time, we slid from the world Above to the one Below. Underhill and beyond ken of mortal humans. A world I'd long since forsaken, yet which remained too much a part of me even now.

The shape of a man appeared, silhouetted against

the outpouring of light. Odd, I wondered if this were what some people saw as they died on an operating room table. Bright lights, dim shapes. Could the barrier stretch at that time, allowing humans to see, if only a glimpse, into the Shining Lands? That would certainly make a great deal more sense than some amorphous heaven full of harp-wielding chubby angels and dead relatives. I always preferred the flaming sword version of angels, myself. If you equated them with the elf-warriors of my childhood, then yeah. Same thing, different Bible.

"She is waiting." The shape spoke and as we approached, formed into that of a tall blond with icy silver-gray eyes. A face I recognized only too well—he'd been my mother's sidekick/mentor/toady—I was never sure which exactly. It was due to Geraint's insistence that I'd been cast out of Faery in the first place. Huh. In retrospect, maybe I owed him one.

"Father." Daffyd bowed, the gesture from son to sire.

"Geraint." I nodded, keeping it curt and far from obeisance. Only a greeting. "She knew we were coming?"

"Of course." He turned, his green robes flowing and twisting with his movement. "Follow me."

"Once more, unto the breach . . ." I grinned and took Adam's arm. Despite the fact that I was dressed in a wrinkled pair of cargo shorts, a cotton tank top and Docs, I was going in there as a queen in my own right, Adam as king—a royal pair with our Protectors. Niko and Tucker took their usual flanking positions, Niko careful to roll up a sleeve to expose my Mark—a magickally imposed tattoo signifying my House. This Mark was part of the blood-bond I had with all my

Protectors—Niko, Tucker, Rhys, Ianto, and Liz. To the world we were entering, it was the same as livery. A silent declaration they were under my protection, as well. Any harm to them was harm to me.

As before, when we'd visited the Unseelie realm, we strode through blank corridors, the doors to other places in Faery—Seelie this time—closed to us. A direct path to the lion's den . . . or something like that. I barely remembered the high queen herself, though I was far from a stranger to her ways and her decisions. I mostly remember my mother and Geraint speaking about her and what she'd done, said, seemed to say. No different from a gossipy corporate environment or a mortal royal court and its environs, though with the added bonus of real power and the very handy ability to simply destroy your more vocal opponents—literally, not metaphorically.

Soon, we'd arrived at the entrance to the Great Hall. I remembered this place well. I'd spent my early days cringing in corners, behind tapestries, hoping to remain unnoticed. Oh yeah, the times were most definitely *a-changin'*.

Glittering throngs of Sidhe lined what I liked to refer to the red carpet, the aisle that led to the throne. Instead of a carpet of any color, the pathway was littered with flower petals and leaves. Oak and ash, exotic orchids and petals of most flowers under the sun Above covered the floor. The courtiers and their ladies fair simply stood, cups of wine or mead in hand, curious as to the identity of these visitors. The Sidhe entertained few anymore, the days of free congress long over, way before my time. As the modern world progressed, the Sidhe regressed, became smaller somehow, its world tighter and less open.

Ahead of us, she sat on a throne of wood and bone, woven together with strands of hair, cemented with tears and blood. At either side, a man: Lugh, Protector of the Realm and his son, Cúchulainn, named after the one of legend. They were her guardians, her strength and consorts. Both men were dark of hair and eye, pale of skin. They'd been the bane of my existence once, teasing me, taunting me. I let my gaze pass over them as if they were nothing more than furniture. Lugh remained steady, unmoving, but his son flinched—only a little, but I saw it. Good.

Angharad's hair flowed unbound, waves of pure gold rippling nearly to the floor. Her gown was nearly the same color as the gorgeous locks. Her face, a paragon of beauty. She was the definition of the word. I began to feel self-conscious, dirty, in my mundane clothing. My hair was the wrong color, I was attired improperly. I was nothing. I wanted to hide. A sneak peek out the corner of my eye. There, my old tapestry. The one I used to hide behind—

Adam took my hand and my mind cleared. No. I was no longer the queen's castoff, no longer the filthy urchin child with no magick. I shook off the strands of her will, ignoring her attempt to belittle me for now. I remained silent, biting my tongue against the nasty words that were forming. I wanted to curse her for making me feel that way again: soiled, worthless, filthy.

"Daughter of Branwen, you come seeking your kin." Sounds like bells wove throughout the words, her voice dancing within the music. My heart soared at its song. All I wanted to do was to please my fair lady.

Another squeeze of Adam's hand and I took a deep breath, bolstering my shields. "Stop." I gazed directly into those icy gray eyes, so similar to my own. "No tricks, Angharad. I won't stand for it." Whispered sighs of disbelief spread through the crowd behind us. I'd addressed their queen by name. "I'm not that sad little girl you once threw out with the gnawed bones of your meals. We came here to get answers, and to get my clan chief back."

"We have no time for Sidhe trickery," Adam said, his voice as cold as I'd ever heard it. "Things are happening Above, things that can be traced to only you. All of this must stop, Angharad. The human world is no longer your playground. Produce Minerva Kelly and stop your petty games."

"Games? I play no games, Aeddan son of Drystan. Your father can tell you that."

"My father does not soil his hands with the like of Seelie politics," Adam replied. "I do not know your intent, nor do I care. You've had enough fun. Where is Minerva?"

Another tinkling laugh, this one reeking of roses and rue. "Minerva is quite comfortable," she said. "We are in the midst of negotiations. I doubt that she would appreciate this interruption."

"And I doubt that we appreciate your continuing to block us," I said. "I want to see my clan chieftain. It is my right." Behind me, more twitters and whispers. I'm sure they were all absolutely fascinated with this event unfolding in front of them.

Angharad's smooth brow furrowed, her mouth grew tight. "You vex me, daughter of my sister."

"Well, aunt, the same could be said about you," I quipped.

The entire room hushed, all sound stilled as if

someone had pressed the mute button. I knew I was being impertinent, but I didn't want to play the honey-tongued political games of the Sidhe. I was crap at it and I knew it. Even Adam wasn't so hot at it anymore—as Unseelie, he'd rarely had to fence with his language. As vampire king, he no longer needed to. Verbal sparring was a Seelie game, one I never learned, nor wished to.

"You are certainly direct." Angharad rose, a flowing, liquid motion as if she had no bones. "Very well. Lugh?" Her Guardian whirled and disappeared behind a tapestry. I knew it concealed the entrance to the Queen's Chamber . . . a place I'd never actually been. The queen remained standing, but did not descend the steps from the dais to the floor. "I am sorry we must meet again under such . . . inauspicious circumstances. I welcome you, nonetheless. You are my Guests."

I heard her capitalize the word, using the ancient meaning.

"I accept . . . for now." I gave her a slow nod.

She nodded back, and the room filled with music again, the hidden players in an alcove somewhere above us. I couldn't deny the music filled my soul and my heart. Sidhe music was meant to do that. It Called to those of blood and enchanted those mortals foolish enough to try to catch a glimpse of the Fair Folk during full moons at Faery mounds. Too many mortals became ensnared, enslaved because they were too arrogant or just plain dumb.

The queen motioned to a set of chairs that appeared next to her, two of them matching hers, only less ornate and at a lower level on the dais, one in a different kind of wood and set one level between ours and hers. Ours, yes, I knew this game. I looked at Adam, who nodded. Well then, here we go, I thought. With as much élan as I could muster, I closed the distance to the dais, mounted the steps and settled into the right-hand chair. Adam, regal as ever, sat in the one to the left. He looked the part, dressed in his usual black shirt and black trousers. Me, I knew I was just playing a part that had been handed me thanks to the cruel genetics dance. Sure, I'd subsumed my anger at having been dealt this hand. I was learning to live with it, with being the heir to a clan that spanned the entire globe. Of having to play politics, learn to manage those who managed multinational conglomerates, all in the name of Kelly solidarity. But I'd not consented to this type of charade, though I'd follow through with it. I had to.

We listened politely to the musicians, Tucker and Niko silent beside us, Niko on Adam's left, Tucker to my right, both standing in guard posture.

"He is a pretty one, your vampire." Angharad leaned to Adam, her whisper more stage than *sotto voce*. "He looks rather familiar."

Adam simply returned her lascivious gaze with his own neutral one. "My thanks for the compliment, Lady."

I knew Niko was practically vibrating with humiliation and anger, though he concealed it well. Our bond let me sense some of his emotions if I didn't shield from him, and here, I'd done what I could to open up to Adam, Tucker, and Niko, while closing off to the Sidhe. I wanted to pat Niko on the arm and tell him to ignore her. She was a right bitch.

As the song came to a flourishy finish, Lugh returned, Gigi at his side. Adam and I stood as we saw her. She looked fine. No outward evidence of any injuries. She was dressed in a simple white gown, her own Mark sewn in vivid red on the right shoulder, her dark hair worn loose to her shoulders. Compared to the rest of us, she was tiny, small-boned and delicate, but she carried her power with grace and strength. No one there would underestimate her, despite her dainty appearance. Her simple hairstyle and garb outshone the fuck out of Angharad's pretentious regality. I'd seen Gigi's dress before, only once. It was a high ceremonial gown that she'd worn to the celebration of her most recent century. She'd had it sewn of Faery silk and woven with spells of protection. Smart woman, my great-great granny.

"My dear," Gigi approached us with hands outstretched. I ran down the steps and grasped her hands, pulling her into a hug.

"You okay?" I whispered.

"Fine," she whispered back. She stepped away from me and smiled at Adam, who'd joined us. "Adam, so good of you to come."

"Minerva." Adam bowed his head, a deeper bow than he'd given Angharad. "We were worried, my lady."

Gigi laughed, her own musical voice cleaner and more wholesome than that of the high queen, though until now, I'd thought it pretentious. Maybe it was something all leaders learned to do, speak volumes with a simple laugh.

"You are becoming so like me, my child," she continued, studying my face. "You've done exceptionally well."

With a sinking feeling in my heart, I knew that

she was only stating the truth. The one thing that I'd wanted to avoid was to become like Minerva Kelly, cold and passionate only about the state of the clan, willing to sacrifice anything that threatened her way of life and that of her people. *Like* her? As I recalled everything I'd done in the past few days, I knew I was becoming her.

CHAPTER THIRTY-FOUR

"Come at the king, you best not miss."
—*Omar Little,* The Wire

As I mentally swallowed that tidbit of information, I let Adam take the lead.

"Minerva. Lady," he said with a slight nod to both. "We did not only come Below to ascertain the health of the leader of our family, but to request an audience. Your majesty, if you would be so kind as to grant us a private consultation? There are matters that would best be discussed within." He motioned toward the tapestry in the doorway.

Angharad descended, silks flowing as she moved. The motion of the fabric reminded me of Grace Rose, and her own unhurried movements. Two of a kind, though one mortal and the other Faery. Fey blood left a mark, no matter how diluted.

"I grant your request, Aeddan ap Drystan. Join me, you and your ladies. We shall meet in my chamber." She floated past us, without even a backward glance. Adam, Gigi, and I followed, with Tucker and Niko falling into step behind us. One of the door guards made as if to stop Niko. I turned and gave him what Bea's Tia used to call the stink-eye. "He is my Protector. He goes where I do. They both do."

The guard simply fell back to his position.

"Huh, that worked."

Gigi chuckled. "Did you not expect it to, child? You are royalty here, no matter how much they wish to ignore it or deny it."

"Royalty," I snorted. "Fat lot of good that does me. Gigi, why—"

She shook her head. "Not now, Keira. Later."

I glanced around, seeing no one. Angharad was at least twenty paces ahead of us, but that didn't preclude her being able to hear. Well, that, and I knew the very walls—or the illusions of walls—had ears here. Anything said within the realm of the Fair Kingdom could easily come to the notice of its queen. "Very well, but you've got a ton of 'splaining to do."

"I know."

A few minutes later, we'd arrived at the end of the hall. A set of intricately carved double doors opened into a large round room. In the center, a round table, made to seat ten. The walls were of a light wooden paneling, sections of the wall sported beautifully embroidered tapestries, much grander than those in the Great Hall. A roaring fire filled the enormous fireplace opposite the doorway. Funny, I'd neither felt hot nor cold since I'd arrived Below. I remember my childhood being filled with icy walls, chill stone floors. The fire seemed to give off no heat, just light and dancing flames, moving to the beat of some unseen musician, a sprightly reel instead of a staid pavane.

With a flourish, Angharad settled into a high-backed

chair, nearly a twin in style to her elaborate throne, only this one was smaller, narrower, more suited to sitting at table. The rest of us chose chairs across from her, me directly in front, Gigi to my left, Adam to my right. Tucker next to Gigi, Niko next to Adam. Good, they weren't going to play silent guardian in here, but equal family members, which they were.

The queen took a moment to settle into her chair, an affectation, I was sure, as no one who had that innate sense of grace and fluidity could have sat with anything less than perfection. She was playing a role—one that suited her ill. No need to get all fluttery now, I thought. We all knew the kind of brazen steel backbone she had, what sort of perfectly practical sense of majesty and rule. She remained silent as she studied each of us in turn. Galadriel preparing to read hearts and mind before handing out gifts? Hardly. This was more the focused inspection of a polite antagonist.

"Cut the bullshit," I finally said. "We're here, so deal with it. You know the reason we came. I'm sure it's the same reason Minerva has been here with you. We want to rein in Gideon."

"As I said before, you are direct." Her steel-hard eyes narrowed. "He is my new heir—through the child," she said. "As such, he has the freedom to Challenge."

"Why, Angharad?" Adam lost his flowery words, but still retained his cultured tones.

"He wanted to reclaim the land. It belonged to Minerva's clan, now owned by vampire, not Kelly. The land must be fertile."

"I hate to burst your bubble," I said, "but I'm sure you already know that the land in question, the Wild Moon ranch, never belonged to my family—at least in the human sense of coin exchange and paperwork. We simply used it as hunting ground. The ranch is ours insofar as we rule the area, but I'm positive my chieftain has already told you these specifics. However, you still persist in allowing Gideon to continue with this farce. Do you want to take over Above? Rule Kelly, as well as the Seelie Court?"

She smoothed a pale hand over a strand of hair, seemingly unaffected. "I have little wish to rule Above," she said. "If Gideon wishes to do so, I will not stand in his way. The Challenge is valid and you must prove your claim in order to remain."

I couldn't believe this. We'd come here and all she could say was "so sorry, it sucks to be you"? I turned my head to catch Gigi's eye.

"Now you know why I've been here so long," Gigi said with a rueful smile. "We've been dancing this same *pas de deux* since I arrived."

"I have no intention of changing my position," Angharad informed us. "You may argue, cajole, and beg all you wish. I gave Gideon free rein to deal with his affairs Above as he sees fit. Your coming here will not alter that."

"If we can't alter the terms," Tucker put in, "then would you perhaps tell us how we keep Gideon from harming any more of our people or our property? The Challenge is not yet failed on our side, nor proved on his, yet he continues to beleaguer us with petty and not-so-petty runespells and traps."

One of Angharad's perfectly formed brows rose in a delicate arch. "Traps?"

"He placed a series of warding and trigger spells on an old cemetery," I explained. "Tucker was nearly bitten

to death by ants and a fire destroyed our town's center."
I was being a bit vague here, but I didn't know how to
explain a retail strip center to a Faery queen . . . not
that she'd actually care. Gigi suppressed an outcry. Her
hand gripped my thigh, initially, she'd just rested it on
there, no doubt to show solidarity, but now, her fingers
dug into muscle. I slid my own hand under the table
and pried her hand loose. I'd forgotten she didn't know
about any of this.

"Of what use would either of those things be to my
son," Angharad asked. "A cemetery? This is a place of
the dead, correct?"

Okay, then, I guess I was going to have to step back
to the grade one version. I hadn't realized she wouldn't
know the term. "Yes, it is a sacred place where mortals bury and revere their dead. Cemeteries, no matter
where they exist physically, are considered to be taboo,
off limits. Gideon's little games resulted in the place being desecrated, vandalized."

"My son did that?" She relaxed her posture a little, just enough to make her seem—not more human,
but less of an automaton. Was she pleased at what
Gideon—her "son"—had done or was she perturbed?
I couldn't tell from her lack of expression.

"We believe so," Adam said.

Angharad bared her lovely teeth. "You do not
know?"

"We are under Truce," Adam explained. "The local
law sent us pictures of the sigils. I recognized some of
them."

"Truce? You have broken Truce and yet you come
here to ask to have me interfere with a legitimate Challenge?" Her eyes fired sparks now, anger in every line of

her body. That moment of slight relaxation vanished, as if only a wisp of a dream. "Be wary, Aeddan, Prince. Even you must obey Sidhe laws."

"We broke nothing that was not already broken," Niko's hard voice answered the queen. He'd sat there so quietly, almost too quiet. With every fiber of his vampire self, Niko hated the Sidhe. They had come in the night and stolen his only friend, long ago, when he was a young boy in an orphan's home. That Adam, one of the dreaded Dark Ones, had later become vampire and saved Niko's life went a long way to repairing his grief, though he'd never forgotten his child self's terror. "Whether Gideon, whom you now call 'son,' was himself there in body, he deliberately and with malice destroyed part of the land that he wishes to claim within Challenge," Niko continued, his own demeanor as fiery as that of the queen's. "Truce is not just pretty words meant to be danced around with guile and cunning. It is a binding law, broken by spirit as well as flesh. Gideon broke Truce first. Therefore, we, bonded to Kelly and Walker, were within our fair rights to return to our land to mend what was damaged."

I sat back in both shock and no small measure of glee. I had to fight the wide-ass grin that wanted to plaster itself across my startled face. Niko, the arrogant puppy turned Protector now Champion—with words instead of sword, but Champion nonetheless. Adam lowered his gaze, his face, too, twitching in a smile. Gigi hid nothing, her own face beaming as she regarded Niko. Tucker, ditto. White teeth flashed a proud grin.

"You speak well for a Nightwalker, young Nicholas," Angharad said. "I will grant you the truth of your statement. Since this land of the dead is part of the claimed land, it indeed falls within the Truce and as such, breaks it. Truce is no longer in effect." Her words rang, echoing throughout the room, the wood and stone itself vibrating in response. Her magick surrounded us and sealed the proclamation. At last, I thought, as I let my muscles relax.

"So now what?" I ventured, my tone more friendly than before. "Do we get to go back home?"

Angharad exchanged a look with Gigi, her eyes shuttered. Gigi gave a barely perceptible nod. I cocked my head and looked at my great-great-grandmother, who ignored me. "Now, you may return to your home," the queen finally said. "However, this does not negate the initial Challenge. That remains, but you may stay at your heart's home."

So this was it? We get to go back to the ranch, but if we still couldn't prove our claim in whatever fashion required by the Challenge, we'd have to leave? This wasn't right. "Ang . . . Lady," I said. "I'm afraid I don't quite understand. Gideon broke Truce and that's it. We ignore it and still go on with this Challenge?"

"The rites of Challenge are even more ancient than I, Keira Kelly," Angharad intoned. "I can no more prevent a Challenge that has begun than I can animate clay into life."

"So Truce was nothing more than a way to get us away from home?" I was trying to be calm here, to not sound like a whiny child. "What purpose does that serve?"

"Truce is a method by which both parties remain on neutral territory," she answered. "You have the advantage now, of residing on the land. Though that is no guarantee of your winning the Challenge. The claim must result from the land. It must recognize you and yours. The magick will know when that occurs."

"So no more waiting until Lughnasa?"

"No. If you can claim it now, then so be it." She stood. "Now, go. Return to your home. You have wearied me."

With a languid wave of an elegant hand, light flashed, an actinic glare that blinded me. In the next breath, we were standing in front of the Wild Moon gate.

CHAPTER THIRTY-FIVE

"Là où il y a le désespoir, que je mette l'espérance."
(Where there is despair, let me sow hope.)
                                        —*Prayer of St. Francis*

Home. We were finally home. Yet. Wait.
        "Where's Gigi?" No sign of our petite matriarch. Just me, Adam, Tucker, and Niko.

I strode down the entrance road, Adam beside me, as I dialed.

"What are you doing?" Adam asked.

"Calling that son-of-a-royal-bitch," I muttered, listening to the rings on the other end. Four rings, then switch to voice mail. Instead of leaving a message, I ended the call. "She kept Gigi, Adam. I can't bloody well phone a Faery queen, but I can call Gideon and have him deliver a message to his new 'mother.'" I stuffed the phone into my pocket. "He didn't answer."

"I see that." Adam's voice was soothing and calm. "Keira, having seen Minerva, she didn't look as if she were a prisoner," he reminded me. "Perhaps she wished to stay."

"Or maybe, Angharad magicked her back to the

enclave." Tucker supplied a guess. "I'll phone there. Let's get to Adam's house, though before we call. I'd rather do it indoors, not in the open."

Was he afraid of something? "You expecting a problem?"

"Not expecting," he said. "Just being cautious. Truce may be over, but that doesn't preclude Gideon from playing more tricks."

"Quite the opposite, I would think," Niko piped up. "Now that Truce is null and void, what's to stop him from overtly attacking?"

"Fuck." We hurried down the road, past the Inn and down to the small cul-de-sac where Adam's house sat, undisturbed and looking just like we left it, so few days ago. We hurried inside, shutting the door. I threw up a few warn-me spells, along with some extra wards and shields, just in case. "There's still some food in the deep freeze," I said to Tucker. "Could you round us up some steaks or something? We can broil them. I think there's a loaf of two of bread in there, too."

"Sure thing." Niko and Tucker disappeared into the kitchen and I flopped onto the couch, every bone and muscle in my body aching.

"I hurt all over," I said as Adam picked up my feet, then set them on his lap as he sat down.

He undid the laces on my Docs, and pulled them off, along with my socks. "Foot rub?"

I nodded. "Yes, please."

We sat that way for a little while, him massaging my feet while I tried to relax and not think about everything that had just happened. I could hear Tucker and Niko canoodling a little in the kitchen. Before I reminded Tucker to call the enclave, I'd give them some time. We'd all gone through so much. We needed to reconnect, feed the bond, as it were.

I woke to the smell of something that wasn't steak. Garlic, cheese, something else. Adam was no longer on the couch, but he and Niko sat at the small dining table. Tucker was just exiting the kitchen with a serving platter. Pizza, that's what it was.

"No steak," I mumbled as I got up and joined them.

"We figured it would take too long to defrost and cook," Tucker said as he served me a piece of the extra large pie. "This is one of those gourmet ones you like."

I chomped down on the steaming hot slice with a grin. "Thanks," I mumbled. "'S good."

Tucker smiled back at me. "You're welcome. I talked to Dad, by the way."

My mouth was full so I gave him a quizzical look.

"Gigi's not at the enclave, but a message did arrive from her," he continued. "Seems Drystan sent up a messenger via the door in Vancouver."

"My father seems to be meeting with Angharad and Minerva now," Adam said.

"Your father?" I managed to swallow the pizza so I could talk. "Seriously?"

"Evidently so," he said. "The message didn't say much more than that the three of them were meeting to discuss long-term plans and to not worry."

I sat back in my seat and took a big gulp from the water glass that Tucker put in front of me. "Thanks, bro." Why couldn't I help but think this was not a good thing? "The three top leaders of the three major supernatural clans in a summit meeting? Look how well the last one turned out."

"It got me you," Adam said, unhelpfully.

"It also got Gideon."

"Well, true. Though perhaps he may soon be in our past."

"Why do you say that?" I asked. "We still have to prove our claim to be able to stay here and keep the Wild Moon. And we still don't know how to do that."

"No, but since we are no longer under Truce, I've put out a Call."

"Call?"

"To our kith and kin. Everyone who is blooded to us or beholden to us in any way."

"And you did this why, exactly?"

"Because more heads are better than the four of us," Tucker added. "Eat up, there's another pizza in the oven."

I quickly grabbed the last slice of the one on the table as my brother got up to retrieve the second pizza. Good thing he knew my ability to eat. Even though Niko and Adam didn't particularly care for pizza and these days, preferred getting their food the old-fashioned way, I'd halfway expected to have to share with them. "More brains will be a good thing," I said.

"I also phoned Antonio," Niko said. "Told him where we were and gave him the gate code. He should be here shortly."

"Was he at Bea's? What time is it anyway?" I turned to look at the clock on the fireplace mantel in the living room but from where I sat, I couldn't see it.

"Believe it or not, it's barely nine-thirty," Adam said.

"The same day?" I held out my glass to Tucker who refilled it. "Or is it tomorrow?" Or even later?

"The same day," Adam said. "We not only lost no

time in Faery, but came back to about five minutes after we left."

"That's rather handy," I said. "So what now?"

"I've called John and his family to return," Adam said. "They'll be here within a couple of hours—seems our other Protectors anticipated trouble—either that or just wanted to flout our authority."

"What do you mean?"

"Remember I said I'd spoken with Raine?"

I nodded around a last bite of pizza.

"Soon as we'd ended our conversation, she told Liz and the twins. They convinced her to head back along with all our vampires. They arrived in Vancouver and are just now finishing up in customs. Your dad and other family are meeting them in town. Once they've refueled, it's only a matter of a few hours' flight here."

I wiped my mouth with my napkin and grinned. "I love them, my brothers and sister-in-law. Remind me to tell them that." I almost wriggled in my glee. My family coming home again. Vancouver and the enclave may be another home, but this place here in Texas, this was my heart home, at least for now.

Adam smiled. "I will. In the meantime, Niko and Tucker are going to go out and check the water tanks, see if we can fill them. If the well's dry, we'll have to make some calls, get some emergency backup water."

"What are you and I going to do?"

Adam's mouth slid into a grin, the spark of humor that had been missing now returned. Sure, we still had a Challenge to face, but we were home, on our own turf. "I, for one, am going to take a shower. Care to join me?"

"Do you even have to ask?" I rose and took his hand. "See you later, boys." I waved as Adam and I descended the stairs to our bedroom.

"Where's the priest?" I asked as I exited the bedroom some hours later, seeing no sign of the old man. "You know, this is getting rather annoying. He keeps disappearing. I wanted to ask him some questions."

"He wanted to go to the library," Tucker said from his lazy position on the couch. He was reading a book, Niko lying down with his head in Tucker's lap. "It's too late tonight but I sent him over to the Inn library. He asked if he could go there and just come back here later. I think he'd rather not be a bother and not get in our way."

"Now that he's done his job?" I shrugged and braided my hair. "Not a bad idea. One less person to worry about. Adam, what do you think?"

Adam emerged, fully dressed but for his shoes. I loved him in bare feet. "Does he still have his phone?"

"Yes, I made sure that he has all our numbers, including Carlton's."

"Good. Then he's better off," I said. "Any sign of arrivals?"

Niko nodded from his supine position. "A few water sprites from across the lake. They're hanging out at the swimming hole," he said. "We filled that up when we got water to the tanks. North one was bone dry, but the well was fine. Filled up the tank and the swimming hole, and made sure there's enough feed and water for the stock in both sections. We also received nymphs, some dryads, and a few were-deer from up north."

"Three phone messages from the wolf tribes west of

us," Tucker said, "and a smattering of texts from a few other groups. They're all coming."

"You two were busy," I said as I ensconced myself in one of the plush armchairs.

"As were you," Niko teased.

I popped a spare elastic hair band at him. He snatched it out of the air and threw it back at me. I batted it away, laughing. "You know, I feel much . . . I don't know, lighter?" I leaned back and relaxed. "Maybe being at home is the difference. It's not as dark here, not oppressive."

"Though there is still something," Tucker said, his tone sobering. "When we were on the grounds, taking care of the water, I know I felt a presence."

"Daffyd, perhaps?" I asked. "He disappeared when we were in Faery. Maybe he's come back to help?"

Tucker shook his head and put his book down on the end table. "No, it was dark. Daffyd shines, as do most Sidhe, even Unseelie. This was kind of a lack of light."

"Like that underlying scummy feeling at the cemetery," I mused. "Felt like a layer of dirty oil, or something equally as disgusting."

"Yeah, a feeling more than anything physical," Tucker agreed.

I sighed. "Well, I suppose we'll have to figure that out, too, unless it's all part and parcel of the Challenge and claim," I said. "Could just be the way the land is responding to the drought and we're just more in tune with it than normal."

Adam crossed the room to sit at my feet. "That is a possibility, indeed."

A soft tingling sensation swept across my bare arms.

I'd dressed once more in a tank top and shorts—new ones—but had foregone shoes for the moment. "Someone's approaching," I said.

Adam nodded and rose, his movements as fluid as Angharad's had been. "I felt the wards."

"It's Carlton," I added, puzzled. "What brings him out here? Surely he's not answering the Call."

"Wouldn't that be a trip," Tucker laughed. "If all along, Carlton Larsen had fey blood."

I tossed a cushion at him and he caught it. "That's something I know isn't true."

"I'll just go see to the door, shall I?" Niko rose and crossed the room, opening the front door before anyone could knock. "Please, come in, Sheriff." Niko swung the door wide open and stepped aside. "We've been expecting you."

Carlton, for once in casual wear, entered, looking a bit taken aback. His hand went up to remove the hat he wasn't wearing.

"Mr. . . ." he started to address Niko, but paused.

"Marlowe," Niko supplied. "Nicholas Marlowe. I'm called Niko."

"Right." Carlton gave a brusque nod. "Keira. Walker. Tucker." He acknowledged us, and without further ado, came in and sat in the other armchair. Niko shut the door and came back to the couch.

"What brings you here tonight, Sheriff?" Adam said, leaning against my legs.

Carlton looked as if he were embarrassed by something. Interrupting us at home, maybe? We did paint a pretty picture of domesticity, I thought. Tucker and Niko lounging together on the couch, comfortable as long-marrieds, yet with the awareness of a nearly new relationship with every glance and touch. I found my-self playing with Adam's hair, something I did out of habit, as I loved running my hands through its silky smoothness. His hair was nearly longer than mine.

"I got a call earlier tonight about some funky lights over at the north end of your property," Carlton said. "I wasn't in town, but I hurried back to check it out. When I got there, the place was dead quiet. Cleaned up there, did you?"

"Yes." Adam didn't elaborate. "I am sorry you had to come this far on what turned out to be a wild goose chase," he said. "My apologies, Sheriff."

"No apology, needed," Carlton said. "I told you I'd keep an eye out, and I will. So y'all back home now for good?"

"I hope so." I stopped playing with Adam's hair. "Carlton, we're still under Challenge and if we can't prove the land belongs to us, we'll end up having to leave."

He seemed to ponder this, his brown eyes never leaving my face. He cleared his throat. "What can I do to help?"

"You can be careful," Adam said. "This is not something you can be a part of, Sheriff."

"But I want to help." Stubborn cop. Almost as stubborn as my vampire . . . or me.

"I know you do," I said, keeping my voice gentle. "And we appreciate it, truly, but it's not a matter of us allowing you or not. You actually can't. It's, well . . . it's a blood thing."

CHAPTER THIRTY-SIX

"We cannot destroy kindred: our chains stretch a little sometimes, but they never break."
—*Marquise de Sévigné*

He started, his fingers curling as if he missed having his Stetson as a prop. It had been a long time since I'd seen him in anything but regulation brown and brown. Now, he was wearing worn Levis and a button-down shirt in pale blue, sleeves meticulously rolled up halfway on his forearm. He still wore the same old Lucchese boots, a present from his father when he'd graduated the police academy. Larsen Senior had saved up for years to afford them. Carlton looked really good, happier than the last few times I'd seen him. Maybe his marriage was finally settling down after last year's separation.

"You don't mean actual blood, do you?" Carlton sounded appalled that he'd voiced those words. "No ritual sacrifices or anything like that?"

"Carlton, please," I said. "That's crap and you know it."

"I know nothing of the sort," he said. "Last year,

you told me those dead Sitka deer we found over by the lake weren't a result of any cult, yet here, we've got two blood-drinkers and well, you two." He pointed to Tucker and me. "Why should I believe anything you've fed me before?"

I closed my eyes and counted to ten. I couldn't lose my temper. He was hurting. I'd as much betrayed him as if I'd gone and gotten pregnant by someone else when we were dating.

"There are many legends that are truth, Sheriff," Adam said as he rose to his knees, "but Keira was not lying nor being disingenuous. We do not perform blood rituals, nor animal sacrifices. My people and I live a quiet life and prefer it that way."

"You don't drink blood?"

"Not without permission." Adam's gaze remained steady, but not challenging. Though he was no longer sitting, he remained in a position lower than that of Carlton, a subtle, yet effective piece of body language. Niko and Tucker, however, perched on the edge of the couch, ready to intervene should this become more than a confrontation of words.

Carlton seemed to digest the words slowly, methodically, just as he did most things. When the penny finally clinked into place, he flushed bright red and he dropped his eyes. "Sorry," he mumbled. "I'm . . . I really put my foot in it, didn't I?"

I laughed, the tension broken. "Yeah, well, it's not as if there's a manual, is there?"

He smiled and raised his head. "No, Keira, there's never been a manual where you're concerned."

In that instant, I saw the young man he once was, naïve, eager, and so very loving and kind. I mourned his loss at the same time that I said a silent prayer of thanks for having broken off our relationship when I did, instead of stringing him along. It had been rough, we'd said many hurtful things to each other, but in the end, I'd done the right thing. We could have never continued. He'd wanted forever, along with white picket fences and a gaggle of kids. I couldn't even give him a decade, nor children.

The distant hum of a motor interrupted our conversation.

"A plane." Adam stood and went to the window. "Niko, get the lights, would you? Tucker, do you mind?"

Niko ran to the back of the house to switch on the runway lights. A set of controls were here, and one in the main Inn. A nice perk, thanks to my dear great-great-granny, who'd supplied the ranch with all sorts of amenities while I'd been in Canada training.

"That should be the cavalry arriving now," I said with a smile.

"Cavalry?" Carlton stood. "You expecting company?"

"Only family," I said. "You don't have to leave on their account. Since you know what's going on, it might be a good idea for you to stay and take part."

"In what? Some sort of family summit?" Carlton joked, his demeanor once again friendly.

"Precisely," Adam said absently. "Sheriff, do stay if you wish. Though I'd advise you to perhaps keep your skepticism in check. Not everyone is as easygoing as we are."

Carlton shook his head. "Easygoing? Are you sure you want me to meet these other people?"

I laughed. "Don't let him scare you," I said. "It's

likely to be a bit tense, but I'll tell them to lay off and leave you alone."

"You?"

"Carlton, I know it's tough to really understand, but I truly am their liege. With my leader off on a, well, having her own political summit meeting, I'm in charge. They'll do what I tell them."

"No shit?"

"No shit. Come on, let's meet the family." With that, I skipped outside, Niko having graciously opened the door and left it open. Tucker and Niko were already on the porch. Adam and I exited one after the other, walking over to stand at the head of the short set of steps. Carlton wandered out, still shaking his head. He walked over to Tucker, who was at my left and propped a foot up on the lower porch rail.

A large group approached, entering from the darkness beyond into the lighted semicircle near the house, chattering among themselves. Their excitement bounded beyond them like a puppy, eager and anxious to please, to be petted. Bouncing happy energy of family together—Kelly, vampire, a few fey thrown in for good measure. I looked at Adam, who had a serene smile on his face, the father welcoming home his children. Two dark heads separated from the pack and ran ahead, joined by a bright redhead, all three bounding up the stairs. They nodded and then stood behind and beside us. Rhys and Ianto on either side, one step down, Liz to my direct left, her hand quickly grasping mine and squeezing. The rest of our Protectors, home at last.

The small dark man in front reached the bottom step and stopped, his face beaming as he knelt. The rest followed suit, all smiling.

"Welcome," Adam said. "Welcome home. We are so pleased you came."

My father held out his hands as Adam swept down the stairs to take them. "My son, my liege. I pledge to you all that is Kelly blood. All our resources and abilities are yours." Oops. I was supposed to be down there. I hurried down the steps and took one of my father's hands. "My daughter. We are yours to command."

"Dad. All of you," I raised my voice to be heard. "Do you give this gift freely?"

Dozens of voices responded. "We do."

I sighed in happiness. "We, your lieges, thank you." I held out my right wrist to Adam, who took it and, fangs bared, bit me, bringing blood. I turned my wrist over and let a few drops fall onto the ground. "By heart and blood, we accept your generous gift." A collective cheer morphed into a grand round of applause.

I mock curtseyed and hauled my father into an enormous hug. Behind me, I could hear Carlton's surprised exclamation. "She really meant it, didn't she?"

Tucker laughed. "She did. Welcome to the madhouse."

CHAPTER THIRTY-SEVEN

"Más vale onza de sangre que libra de amistad."
(Better an ounce of blood than a pound of friendship.)
— Spanish Proverb

Grace Rose fluttered around the large table we'd set up in the main dining room at the main inn. John, the day manager and his family had returned along with all the vampire staff and within the hour, things were back to almost normal at the Wild Moon. The chef, a longtime employee of Adam's, was in the kitchen with his staff, doing his best to whip up some semblance of meals for the nearly three dozen people that had arrived and needed to eat something other than blood or small prey. A midnight brunch, courtesy of Le Cordon Bleu–trained staff. A few of my brothers had gone hunting— all six of them were now here, as were my aunts, Jane and Isabel, who'd set up in one of the guest houses. Grace and Verena had arrived by car not twenty minutes after the plane touched down. When I'd asked how they knew to come, Verena had simply stared at me and smiled her vacant smile. "We were Called."

"Grace, sit the hell down, you're distracting me."

Ciprian, my eldest brother, tossed his pencil down and ran a hand through his silver gray locks. He charmed his hair that color so he could make financial deals for the family. No one ever trusted a young whippersnapper, he'd said often, so he'd chosen to look older. "If you don't have anything to contribute, why don't you go to the kitchen and see if Henri needs any help serving."

"Certainly." She slid away, her mind on who knew what. At the Rose Inn, I'd thought Verena to be the spacey one and Grace to be at least somewhat grounded in the modern world. Here, though, it was as if they'd switched roles. Verena, though still a bit looney tunes, held her own in the discussion, while Grace did little more than wander about aimlessly.

My brother stabbed a finger at the Challenge parchment, which we'd rolled out onto the table and fixed down with clear tape. "That there. The passage that talks about Truce and consequences, I don't think you've seen the last of the problems."

"What makes you say that?" I asked. "Angharad herself spoke Truce to be dissolved. I felt the magick."

"She may have," Ciprian said in his precise, dusty way, "but this magick has already been set in motion. She didn't mention that, did she?"

"No." My blood was beginning to boil again. "She said nothing of the sort. In fact, she said very little of use to us at all. We were whisked out of there faster than I could ask anything else."

"I'm sure that was her intention," Tucker said. "She's still got far too many schemes up her silky sleeve."

"I'll take Faery Follies for $500 with a side of 'duh,' Alex," I said to the room at large. "Dad, you're the only one in this room that knows her at all. You spent time in

Faery courting." I didn't even want to say my mother's name. She was dead to me.

"She's *The* Seelie, Keira, as Minerva is The Kelly—all the tricks and powers combine in her to make her the quintessential Seelie Sidhe." He stood and walked around a bit. I'd gotten my habit of pacing from him. "She's like the ultimate Trickster. She does what she does how she does it. Just when you think she's going to do one thing, she starts to do another, then goes right back to thing one. I'm sorry, but knowing her only makes it more complicated."

"If I may," Antonio spoke in a quiet tone.

I nodded. "Go ahead." Though what a Catholic priest could tell me of the Faery, I had no idea. We'd exhausted all our combined knowledge, even calling in each of the various vampires who lived on the ranch, some of them centuries old, to see what they could contribute. We'd gotten very little. Carlton had gone home, promising to be back in the morning. He'd walked out starry-eyed and rather lost.

"Short of actual battle, there seems to be little you can do to force the land to honor your claim," he began.

"We know that already," I said, trying to keep the frustration out of my voice.

"Yes, we do. However, have you considered real battle?"

Adam stood. "As a last resort only, Antonio. I've no taste for that sort of bloodshed. I've seen far too many wars to wish to begin another one."

"Then I'm afraid that you must find a way for the land to accept something else in return." Antonio brushed his hand over a particular passage that had eluded most of us. Vague words talking about blood and sharing and giving. We'd done that. I gave of my own blood, as had Adam, Tucker, and Niko, speaking ritual words of binding to ourselves and to the land. With each drop, we'd felt something, a shimmery shudder of acceptance, but nothing concrete. All of us agreed that it hadn't been enough.

A buzz in my pocket startled me. I reached for the phone as I stepped away from the discussion. Carlton's number lit up the small screen.

"Hey, what's up?"

"Hey." His voice sounded tired and defeated. "Keira."

"Yes?" Crap. How bad was it? And was it? He'd left not that long ago. Barely a couple of hours. "What is it, Carlton?"

"Flu. Ten cases. Both my . . . kids." His voice broke. "High fevers, chills. Their mother is with them in the ER in Boerne now. The Coupes were both admitted, as were Lenny and Angie from the video store. At least five more cases reported from Austin and a half dozen in Fredericksburg. Could this be . . ." He didn't finish his question. He didn't have to.

"I don't know," I said, utterly truthfully. "There's no way to tell."

"Doctors haven't seen this strain before, they're saying."

"God, Carlton, I'm so sorry. I'll send someone, okay? Boerne, you said?" I could have Isabel go there, pose as a specialist from the UK. She'd done it once or twice before that I knew of. She could tell if they were magicked or if this truly was simply an unfortunate strain of summer flu.

"Yeah, sure. I'd appreciate it. There's one other

thing." Carlton paused. "Hang on a sec, would you?" He must have put his hand over the phone speaker, though I could hear him talking to a doctor.

"Adam," I frantically waved. "Have Isabel go over to the hospital in Boerne. There's some sort of fast-acting flu. Both of Carlton's kids are in the ER."

He nodded and excused himself from the room. Ciprian looked over at me and I held up a hand, signaling him to hold on.

"Sorry about that, Keira," Carlton said. "That was the doctor. Both kids are spiking high fevers. I told him you were sending over a specialist. Told him it was someone who happened to be visiting you. He is coming, isn't he?"

"She," I said. "My aunt Isabel. You remember her, right? She's one of our best healers."

A soft sigh escaped him. It almost sounded like a sob. "Thank you."

"Wait, Carlton, you said there was something else?"

"Yeah, I'm sorry. On the way to the hospital, I saw a number of dead cattle, deer, other animals at the side of the road. I don't think my wife noticed, she was in the back with the kids."

"Just dead?"

"Mostly. A few looked like something had been taking big bites, but that could be carrion eaters. I thought you needed to know."

"Thanks. You take care, okay. If you need anything at all, tell Isabel. She'll deal." Adam walked into the room and gave me the high sign. "She's on her way now, Carlton. Hang in there, yeah?"

"I will, thanks."

"He's in bad shape," Adam said as he joined me. I thumbed off the phone.

"Yeah, barely holding it together. Kids are both spiking high fevers. Adam, he saw a bunch of dead livestock on the roadside on his way into Boerne from here. What do you think's happening?"

"I looked, and there before me was a pale horse. Its rider was named Death, and Hades was following close behind him. They were given power over a fourth of the earth to kill by sword, famine and plague, and by the wild beasts of the earth." Antonio intoned the words as if he were preaching a sermon.

"What the—" I faced the elderly priest. "Revelations? You've *got* to be kidding me."

"You mentioned it before. Pestilence, death, earthquake. These are all signs of the end."

"*Your* end," I muttered. "Antonio, legends from your Church teachings mean little to me or mine. I can't argue with you that we've seen these things, but I know the cause. It would so be like Gideon to use these types of events to make people afraid."

"They are not precisely of my Church," he said. "There are many who believe this and I have come to do so also. I have had many years to read, to listen to others speak. Though I am of the One True Church, my mind has been opened."

I wasn't sure what he was referring to—my practical knowledge of various types of Christianity was fairly shallow. Niko saw us and rushed over, his face full of concern. I was sure I was projecting confusion, uncertainty. And not a small amount of anxiety.

"We Catholics don't believe in an apocalypse," Niko explained. "End-times theology is a Protestant fundamentalist belief. Gideon's traps and tricks don't really gibe with that, either, but . . ." Niko gave me a hesitant shrug.

Oh well, wonderful. The cursed Catholic priest had been spending his time watching the fire-and-brimstone screamers on TV and believed their insane rhetoric? I rubbed at my forehead. "Antonio, what Gideon's done is simply use old tricks to frighten people."

The priest glared. "The result will be the same. Apocalypse. The Four Horsemen have arrived. The seals have broken—did you not say the door to Hell would not close? The only thing left is rivers of blood and a willing sacrifice given in love to appease the angry Lord. The Lamb is coming."

"Door to Hell?" What on earth was he on about?

"The door to the world below."

"The door to Faery is open," I said. "Though I admit my life was pretty much hellish when I was there, Faery is no more Hell than is driving in Houston during rush hour." I looked for a way out of this mess. Had Antonio flipped what was left of his lid? I knew living that long of a life in ever-increasing pain had to take some sort of toll. Was his brain affected, too? I studied his face, stared into his eyes. No. Not the eyes of a madman, but someone absolutely convinced in his faith—no matter how oddly frankensteined out of his own Church's teachings and those of others.

"Come with me, Father." Niko took Antonio by the shoulders. "Let's go rest, all right?" With no protest, the old man let Niko lead him away.

"What was that about?" Tucker asked. I looked over to the table. Most of the people there were still talking, arguing the same bloody points over and over again.

"He's expecting the second coming," I said, weary of the whole thing.

"Really?"

"Without a doubt," I said. "Trumpets and everything. He said the door to Hell was open and that we'd begun to see the signs that the Horsemen were riding."

"Who's to say he's not right?"

"You've got to be kidding me."

Tucker began to laugh, but stopped, sobering in an instant. "Crap, Keira, take away all the religious symbolism and mumbo-jumbo . . ."

"What?"

"He's not altogether wrong. We've been worried about the door to Faery being open in case someone accidentally went into Faery, right? What if we've been going about this backwards? What if Gideon opened the door to let someone . . . or a lot of someones out?"

"Fuck me. The door to Hell isn't far off the mark." Nor would it be untrue to call it Pandora's box or anyone of those mythological stories where someone opens something they shouldn't and unleashes . . . Faery. All of it to the world Above. Pandemonium and yes, apocalypse. I sank into a nearby chair. The priest wasn't insane after all.

CHAPTER THIRTY-EIGHT

"Funny thing about black and white: You mix it together and you get gray. And it doesn't matter how much white you try and put back in, you're never gonna get anything but gray."
—Lilah, "Habeas Corpses" (Angel: the Series, 4–8)

"We call him out," I insisted. "Gideon and his minions. A showdown, if you will. We've got our own army now." Adam, Niko, Tucker, and I were arguing our point to the rest of the gang. By now, most of the vampires had retired for the day. Isabel had returned, reporting that Carlton's children and the rest of the flu victims were resting comfortably. She'd been able to help, surreptitiously healing in the guise of examining the sick. Moments ago, she'd gone to her guest house to join Jane and sleep.

Me, sleep? What the heck for? Tucker and I had scrambled to dig out the books we'd brought back with us from the Rose Inn. We'd left them at Bea's, but some kind soul had thought we might need them so sometime earlier that evening, the books had all arrived and boxes piled against the wall of the dining room. The only people left to discuss this with us were my father, Ciprian, and the representative for the Snake clan, a group of lesser fey that watched over the local fauna—at least the ones that slithered instead of walked on four legs.

I shoved the open book underneath Ciprian's face. "There, see. The Four Horsemen and all that rot. I don't think Gideon's any more a scholar of this than I am—hell, his understanding of it is probably less than mine. But you've got to admit, on the surface and for someone who is no expert, this wave upon wave of drought, fire, illness, and general misfortune could be the rallying point for some fundie freak. Gideon's no fool—I can't dismiss the idea that he's playing as many games as he can. He *expects* this to end up in full-out war. I say we bring the war to him. We've got tooth and claw on our side. Gideon has only magick. I've got plenty of that, as do the rest of you."

"If we do this, Keira, there's no turning back." Ciprian read over the passage I'd highlighted. I knew what it said. Stuff about the number of the beast, slaughter, famine, pestilence, conquest . . . all the same things Antonio had quoted. "I'll give him one thing, the boy is clever. He's done just enough to raise questions and make people wonder. After all, some of these preachers had little else to point to when screeching their sermons about Hurricane Katrina and the AIDS epidemic being God's punishments. All of this stuff coming within weeks—now days—is plenty of grist for that mill."

"Too clever by far," Adam said. "Using enough symbology to frighten those who fear the end of the world and recall half-remembered Biblical passages. Truly heinous. This is no longer a simple fight of one-upmanship, if it ever was. I believe Keira and Tucker are correct. Gideon is planning to distract us with these plagues, whilst Calling forth the Dark Fae and all other sorts of mischief."

"Dark Fae?" Niko's voice quavered just a little.

"Fey who live in the darkness," Adam explained. "They are more wild magick than anything else. They thrive on chaos and confusion."

"We cannot unleash Faery on the mortal world." The ringing tones of my mother preceded her entrance by a millisecond.

"Branwen." I watched her glide into the room, decked out in true Sidhe finery, a misty light green tunic flowing over a solid white dress. Her hair was caught up in an intricate set of braids wound with pearls.

"Going to a party or is that what the well-dressed Sidhe wears to a war room?" I didn't bother keeping the sarcasm out of my voice. How dare she waltz in here?

"War? It has come to that, then?" She stopped several feet short of me.

"Perhaps. Why are you here?"

"May I approach?" She opened her arms, palm upward, and bowed her head. Okay, wow. What was this?

"Come." Adam spoke before I could get my own voice back.

With a smooth glide, my mother took a step forward, then sank to one knee, bowing even further. "I came to offer myself," she said.

"We accept your gift," Adam intoned. Me? I was still beyond the capability of coherent speech.

Branwen stood, tucking her hands together in front of her. "I must offer my humblest apologies to my daughter, and to her husband."

"Go on," I said.

"I believed that your cousin wanted to right things," she explained. "To unite Faery and to claim our rightful place in the world. We've been fading, Keira. Fading quickly." She looked directly at me. "I'm sure my queen neglected to tell you that when you visited."

"You were there?"

"I was. Did you not wonder why so many closed doors in a place that once rang with the laughter of tens of thousands?"

Truth? Not really. I'd blocked so much out of my head from those times, I only remembered my misery and my dank hidey-holes. The glitter and glare of the Faery throng was no more a part of my life than was shopping at the Galleria with the *Real Housewives* of wherever. I shook my head in answer to her question.

"There are too few of us left. We close doors to hide just how few." She walked over to the table and laid her hand on the parchment. "When Gideon gave me this to give to you, I took him at his word. I was wrong." She looked at me. "I came back up after I'd spoken with my queen, with Minerva, and with the high king of the Unseelie Court. They continue to discuss long-term strategy. They do not see what is in front of their eyes. Your land, it is no longer barriered, nor boundaried by spell. Gideon removed the boundaries as part of the Challenge, yet did not perform the required ritual to bind the land to whomever wins the claim."

"What does that mean?"

"That the magick no longer is constrained to Challenge outcome," Adam said. "We weren't going down the wrong path after all. What we've done should have bound the land to us." He slammed a hand against the hard wood of a chair. "That's why nothing was working."

Branwen nodded. "Gideon has put a Geas on the land."

"How could he do that?" I protested. "Geas is placed on a person, not a place."

"It is a curse, nonetheless," Branwen continued. "The land is encumbered."

I was sure she didn't mean that in the modern day real estate sense, yet, oddly, the current legal definition probably evolved from this more traditional magickal one. Instead of having property title tied down by legal issues, this land had spells achieving the same effect. Too bloody good, Gideon. Too bloody good. I had to applaud his efforts, even though I hated what he'd done.

"You are too easily led by others, Branwen," Adam remarked. "First, you allow your initial championship of your own daughter, in whom you sense magick, to be overruled by those with silkier tongues. Now, when given a chance to reconnect with her, you support someone who dips into the Darkness to achieve his questionable goals."

"I only ever wished for peace and comfort," she protested. "Since childhood, I was but a pawn in my queen's long game. I was given to Huw Kelly to produce a child. I did so. I could not fight for her. It was a losing battle. Instead, I let her father raise her."

"You're her mother."

"I am a horrible mother. I never wanted a child. I was forced."

I gasped, and turned to look at my father, who started at her words. He began to speak, but my mother continued.

"He did not force me to lie with him, Keira," Branwen interjected before Dad could say anything. "My

queen coerced me to become pregnant, to remain with
Huw until you were born. I wished none of these machinations."

Machinations. Machiavellian ones. Gigi. "It all falls
back to Gigi and her cronies, doesn't it?" I said. "Playing games with my generation, hoping for what? Power?
As if they didn't have enough already." The words were
bitter in my mouth.

"Minerva needs to be here to help," Adam said. "If
Gideon is calling up the Darkness, wanting the barri-
ers to fall between Faery and Above, he's totally out of
control. He'll do nothing more than unleash Chaos."

"Chaos and all her sisters," Tucker muttered. "Has
the Darkness spread Below?"

Branwen nodded. "It has begun," she said. "Slowly,
inexorably, it has infested us. We fade now even more
rapidly."

"I'm reluctant to go back to the cave door," I said.
"That cemetery is riddled with Dark. It was dormant
when we were there earlier, but there's no guarantee that
it stayed that way. Especially with everything Carlton's
told me. It sounds like something's been let loose, or is
at least seeping out. We need to drag Gigi out of there
whether she wants to come or not. She can help, then
go back to have her summit with Angharad when we've
put this matter to rest. For that matter, the other two
might as well be a part of this—Angharad and Drystan,
I mean."

"You'd Summon the three highest?" Adam asked
with an amused drawl.

"In a New York minute," I stated. "Their crap got us
into this, they can bloody well come help out and put
the Dark back where it belongs."

"We could walk Between," Branwen suggested. "It's not as easy as using an established portal, but can be done."

I turned to Adam. "We're going to need more than just Branwen's magick to pull us all through," I said. "You used it before, when the Millers took Niko. Think you can do it again?"

Adam looked surprised. "I don't know," he said. "Niko was in danger. I believe the only way I was able to do it before was because of our blood tie. My anger overrode my sense and I just—" He shrugged. "I didn't stop to think about it. I simply did it."

"You maneuvered Between?" Branwen asked. "That's a pure Faery ability. It should be lost to you, Aeddan."

"Needs must, I suppose."

"It should be physically impossible," she insisted.

"So should I," I said, my words bitter. "There is never supposed to be more than one heir. That has been the case for the entire history of our clan. Why can't Adam be able to use some ability in crisis mode? It's been known to happen in humans, a rush of adrenaline—"

"But this is fey ability," Branwen protested. "He died, faded, then woke as vampire."

I turned this suggestion around in my brain. If she was right, if Adam's Sidhe abilities should not exist, then there is no way he could have done what he did. No way he could've taken me and Tucker with him through the Between to Niko's side. How had it happened?

"Many things have happened that shouldn't have," Niko said. "Perhaps Adam's blood exchange with Keira awakened some of the dormant Sidhe within him. Necessity pulled the power to him."

"So not dead, only sleeping?" I asked, letting the sarcasm through. "He's not a Monty Python parrot."

"No, but he is a Sidhe prince," Branwen argued. "He is Drystan's heir to the throne of the Unseelie Court. I believe yon vampire is correct. Aeddan, have you tried a Summoning?" She waved a dismissive hand in the air. "Not to the lesser fey, but to true Sidhe."

"I have not," Adam said, a thoughtful look on his face. "I'd meant to . . ."

Branwen nodded. "Do it. It is one of the most basic of our skills—"

"Yet requires a great deal of power," I finished her thought. "Adam, we have nothing to lose at this point. Try it."

Adam took a deep breath and let it out slowly. "I will try it. But not here. Keira, with me?"

I jumped off the table and followed him.

Within minutes, we were in the privacy of our bedroom. "Are we doing what I think we're doing?"

"Exactly."

CHAPTER THIRTY-NINE

*"I love you as certain dark things are to be loved, in se-
cret, between the shadow and the soul."*
                            —Pablo Neruda, *"Sonnet XVII"*

He tore off his clothing. I did the same.
        I groaned as he slid atop me, my skin already
slick with sweat from our short time outside in the heat.
His own skin seemed to burn as it touched mine. I licked
at his collarbone, then bit down, teeth scraping skin,
breaking it, bringing blood. He gasped, and rolled us
over, his hands grasping my arms. I straddled his groin,
my knees gripping his sides as we bit, licked, kissed.
This was no leisurely lovemaking, but a joining to raise
power, to Call and Summon. Could we do it? I forced
aside my doubts and let myself sink into the sensations,
pushing worry and thought and plans away, focusing
only on this. This before me now.

Power surged between us as once again, I plun-
dered his mouth, taking, wanting, needing, connecting.
Adam's palms slid down my back, cupped my ass as
he lifted me, then speared me on his cock. I threw my
head back, letting the feelings wash over me. I reached

a hand back between us to caress his sac, my other hand reaching forward to slide across his chest. His own hands came up, his thumbs brushing my nipples ever so lightly. I growled and he returned it, sounds of our union, of the power within us meshing, combining. The hunger rose inside me, meeting his. It crashed, burned, merged. Pulsed with light and darkness, joining us. Blood called to blood. Dark, powerful, needful. Adam raised his torso, one arm around me to press me to him as I rocked atop him. I turned my head to the side, baring my neck. With another growl of want, he sank his fangs deep, brought the blood pounding to the surface. Take. Want. Have. I rode the waves of pleasure and power, the energy surging between us, binding us, sealing together.

With a cry, I came again, as Adam did, his body shuddering. He threw his head back and together, we threw the Call out into the air. I collapsed against him and we both fell to the bed, sated, sore, and depleted as the magick flew out from our bodies, resonating in the air.

A few moments later, I started to giggle, tried to suppress it, and failed. It became full-out laughter.

Adam stroked my hair, most of which had escaped the braid. "You all right?"

"I think you broke me," I said through the laughter. "I can't bloody move."

He chuckled. "If it's any consolation, neither can I."

"That was . . ." I sighed in contentment, the laughter subsiding. "Yeah."

"Indeed."

"Um. Adam? Keira?" Liz's voice floated down the stairwell. "We've got company."

"They sent you?" I chuckled as I imagined my six brothers arguing who'd get to come interrupt us. "They figure we wouldn't attack you?"

She laughed. "Something like that. You'd best get dressed and come up. Gigi's here."

"It worked, huh?"

"Oh yes," she said. "Drystan and Angharad are here along with her. Boy, is that one a bloody piece of work."

I sank back onto the pillow. All of them. Shitebloody-tastic. I burst out into laughter again. We'd managed to Summon the three most powerful leaders of the super-natural community . . . by fucking.

"There's a faction of the fey who wish to be a legitimate part of the world of man," Drystan was explaining when Adam and I entered the dining room. Someone had cleaned the place up, removing all the detritus from hours of meetings, and had pulled together more tables and chairs. At one end of the room, our thrones stood on their dais. Adam raised a brow and looked at Rhys, who was grinning. Great, my brother, the next Martha Stewart.

Drystan nodded at the both of us and continued. "They are full of ennui and wanting more challenges than they get Underhill. These are not high fey. The lower ones, mostly—sprites, dryads, nymphs, satyrs, pucks. They enjoy causing a bit of trouble as sport. Gideon has bestirred the Dark Fae, as well."

"I'd say this was more than a bit of trouble, wouldn't you, Father?" Adam and I walked over to the main table and sat in the two chairs Rhys indicated. Not thrones, but he'd pulled Adam's comfy office chair out and a second one from Niko's office. The large table was round, like the one we'd sat at in Faery, but as with that one, this table had a distinct head. Screw Arthur and his knights, round tables didn't automatically mean equality for all. This show? *We* were running it. They were on our turf now.

Angharad sat in one of the regular dining chairs, looking as if something—or everything—smelled putrid. Her body was stiff, unmoving, her back not even touching the back of the chair. As a contrast, Gigi, still dressed as we'd last seen her, lounged next to her, clearly in her element. One of her Protectors stood behind her, his face relaxed and cheerful. His liege was back and as far as he was concerned, all was right with the world. Her other Protector stood at the main entrance to the room, staring forward in silence, but also radiating glee.

"Welcome," I said with a happy grin. "I bid you welcome." I tried to hide my glee at the fact that the Summoning had bloody well worked. Adam's Sidhe Talent *was* still there. Branwen had been right. The lady in question sat in a chair to the left of her queen. I nodded to her. Later, when this was over, we were going to make amends.

"These fey, Father, are they behind the problems we've had?"

"I believe so," he said. "Gideon doesn't seem to be the sort to stick his own neck out if he can have someone else do it for him."

"Hear, hear." Rhys clapped. I shot him a dirty look and he subsided. He was standing behind us, along with the other four, Ianto, Liz, Tucker, and Niko. Let's see, five Protectors. Gigi had one of hers. Drystan—none, though it could be said that ours extended to him by courtesy. Angharad. None. I didn't begrudge Rhys his joy one bit. Finally, we were the ones in charge.

"My grandson is no risk taker," Gigi agreed.

Drystan nodded. "He's enlisted several factions of Dark Fae, some others from even your side of the fence, Angharad." Angharad continued her impression of a statue. "He means to raise a bloody army."

"Take over the world, yes, we figured that out," I said. "Thing is, what do we do about it? The land is still tainted with the Darkness he Called, and we have been unable to lay claim even using all the rituals we knew of and some we tried for the hell of it."

"There are fewer of us daily," Drystan admitted. "Your mother told me she'd revealed the same about the Seelie Court to you earlier."

"Yes, go on."

He made an uncertain motion. "That's just it. You Summoned us. At this point, you—and Aeddan, I presume—hold the power. We must do your bidding."

Another whispered "hear, hear" from Rhys made me duck my head to hide my shit-eating grin.

"You will fight with us?" Adam asked.

"If need be," Drystan replied. "We will do everything in our power to avoid a fight, however."

"The High King of the Unseelie Court afraid of a fight?" Angharad's languid drawl cut in. "Surprise, surprise."

Drystan bristled. "I have never been afraid of fighting, Lady. Sometimes avoidance is the simplest and best answer. What would fighting my son do? Cause more bloodshed, more death? Is this why we came Above? To doom our people to one last battle before they fade completely? Those so-called glory days are long since gone from this world and from ours. We are not those people anymore."

Bully for Drystan.

"You avoid the true matter, as always," Angharad spat back. "You talk around and around, but never speak of the one thing that would solve this unequivocally."

Drystan shot her a murderous look. Gigi straightened from her relaxed pose and took hold of his shoulder before he could rise from his chair. "Settle down," Gigi commanded. "This petty bickering continues to get us nowhere."

"Nor will it change," Angharad said, addressing Gigi. "You and the king wish to remain in the dark, hiding from the truth." She laughed a bitter, broken sound. "Such an irony, this. The Unseelie speaking nothing, the Kelly hiding, and the Seelie Queen willing to speak plain and without guile." She turned her attention to me. "Do you wish to know the truth, child? It is far from pretty or even difficult. It is unrelenting and formidable in its brutality."

I gripped the arm of my chair. This was the Sidhe High Queen. A woman for whom a walk in the park could mean walking across the bodies of her enemies. Seelie were cold, calculating, and known to have little emotion in judgment, but brilliant in battle and politics. They were the Vulcans of the Sidhe world, all logic and practicality with a veneer of sugar and spice to make the bitter medicine taste nicer as they slipped the poison in. For her to refer to something as "brutal" turned my blood to ice.

"Explain." Adam's voice sounded harsh in my ear. I snuck a peek at his face. It was set, his brows lowered, his eyes shuttered. I took his hand. His own hand quivered underneath mine. He was holding something back, some strong emotion.

"I helped Gideon write this." Angharad flicked the corner of the parchment, which was still spread out on the tabletop. "He adjusted the wording before he delivered it you. Originally, this called for a fairly standard proving—which you have already attempted. Your attempts failed not because the land rejects you, but because the under layer of spells used now requires more."

"And what is *more*?" I asked, dreading her answer.

She looked at me, her eyes the dark gray of battleship hulls. "It is no longer a blood gift, but a full sacrifice, Keira Kelly. Someone who is blood-tied, bonded to you, part of your life must give freely of his or her life, out of love."

Shouts of "no" rang throughout the room as the heretofore silent bystanders reacted to the news. I blanched, the blood leaving my face. My head swam, dizzy with the knowledge, with her confirmation, that what we'd feared was true. No more playing around with what-ifs or possibilities—the only answer was one I was unwilling to accept.

"We ask no one to die for us," Adam said, biting the words out. "What are the consequences if we do not fulfill the Geas?"

Angharad fell back, her posture now relaxed. "The land will die. The drought will continue, other plagues of weather, insects, illness. The livestock will continue to fail as will the crops. People will fall ill. One by one, the families will leave and the land becomes barren—cursed for eternity. By avoiding the death of one, you bring the death of many." She studied her hand, as if not affected by this news.

"It truly is a curse." Adam's grim voice echoed in the stillness following this pronouncement. "*We* are cursed." He stood, whirled in place, strode over to the door, then back to me, face full of anger and resentment. "Blast this land, these people. We can sacrifice no one."

I closed my eyes against the whirlwind of emotions, tears streaming down my cheeks. How could I ignore this? These people were ours, as much as the fey, the others of my kind were. They might be humans, but this community, this town was more my home than any other physical place. I grew to adulthood here, was part of the community. This was not just a random location, with people I didn't know. At the same time, could I allow a sacrifice? Could I be cold enough to stand by and watch as someone I loved died on my behalf? I couldn't think. Couldn't make the impossible choice. "I've . . . I need some air."

Without looking anyone in the eye, I pushed my chair back and left the room.

Tucker made as if to follow me, but a murmur from Adam stopped him.

CHAPTER FORTY

"Tout le sang qui coule rouge." (*All blood is red.*)
—*Eugene Bullard*

I stormed out of the Inn, practically running as I reached the main courtyard in front of it. I sank onto a bench near the night-blooming garden. Night. It was still night. We'd spent how long inside having sex? Then how long arguing? It had seemed like days but was probably only an hour total. I shook my head, dashing tears out of my eyes with my fist. It didn't matter. Nothing bloody mattered except Gideon and his stupid, stupid Challenge. There was no way we could ask anyone to do this for us. To die on our behalf? Was I willing to do it myself? Could I bring myself to do it? Maybe. If Adam were right there, nearby. He could turn me, make me vampire. I never thought that was possible before. I'd thought all vampires came from humans, but that turned out to be a wrong assumption. He'd kept his powers, too, or at least recovered them. Could I still be the Kelly heir if I were the walking dead?

Who the hell cared, anyway? I didn't. If being the Kelly heir meant I had to deal with these sorts of decisions, then I was abdicating the position right now. Gigi could go play genetics with someone else and get herself a new guinea pig/beck and call girl, because I'd had enough. I stood. It was time to run.

I changed the moment I exited the ranch gates. Wolf would be a preferred shape. I could run as wolf and not tire. Not think so much. I didn't even think about disrobing before I shifted. My clothes tore as the wolf took over. I ran.

Faster and faster, I ran away from the Inn, from the ranch, from the knowledge that the only answer was no answer but one I was not prepared to give.

As I reached the cemetery gate, I saw a small fire and a tent pitched near La Angel. Cautious, I crept closer, wondering who on Earth had come out here.

The tent flap opened, and Antonio appeared. "Welcome, Keira," he said, a smile crossing his face as he exited. "Come, join me."

I changed back to human. "How did you . . . ?"

He handed me a pair of stretchy yoga type pants and a T-shirt. "Yours?" I asked as I put them on.

"Yes."

The shirt was a bit tight, but would work. The pants were too loose and reached only to mid-calf on me, like a pair of capris. No matter, I was clothed and felt more myself.

"After I spoke with you earlier, I decided to come camp here," he said. "To guard the place."

"Guarding? From whom?"

"Whomever means harm." He motioned to his campsite. A couple of folding camp chairs sat outside. "Come."

I accepted his invitation, my weariness finally washing over me. I lowered myself into the chair.

"But how can you be here?" I asked. "On holy ground? You re-consecrated the cemetery earlier, didn't you?"

"I had, but the ground has reverted, the cemetery is desecrate again. I was hoping I could figure out how to re-consecrate it," Antonio said. "Reading, researching. Praying." His eyes were steady on mine. "Would you pray with me, Keira Kelly? I can offer you little but what I have is valuable."

"And that is?"

"I can hear your confession."

The bitter laugh was mine. "Confession is good for no soul, priest. It's only for laying your own guilt and shame on others. A false hope."

The old man laid his lined hand on top of mine. "It is sharing a burden, Keira. A sharing of misery. Sharing sorrow halves it. Sharing joy, multiplies."

"There is no joy in my choices, priest," I said, words like bullets of pain. "Nothing I can share."

"Try me." The old priest swept some branches and dirt aside and seated himself at the base of what was left of the Angel. His dark eyes shone in the darkness, catching the dim light of his lantern.

I looked into those eyes, old, knowing. A human who had lived longer and with more sorrow and pain than any of his brethren. He'd seen countless die. Seen countless suffer through lives of poverty in his small parish. Now here he was among those that cannot die, yet he could never be one of us. He could come to wherever we ended up, away from this bitter, dying land, live among others of long life. But he'd always be different, always an outsider, mortal, dying in millimeters, his body eventually fading into nothing but knots of pain and suffering. His hand twitched, knuckles swollen with arthritis. He spread his fingers as best he could, regarding them.

"You see more than others," he said. "My hands began hurting some months ago." He rubbed them together, wincing. "Even modern medicines don't help. I believe that was part of the curse."

Curse. Why curses? I sank down beside him and took his hands in my own and concentrated. A small warming charm enveloped our hands. Too hot for me to bear normally, but it seemed to soothe him.

"Thank you."

I nodded and let him go. "You're welcome."

"Do you know what you are going to do?"

I shook my head and buried my face in my hands. "No," I whispered.

"You are a good person, Keira Kelly," he said. "Sit here for a few moments, let the power of the Lord help you decide. I will continue my rounds."

He took his time standing. I could almost feel the aches in his joints, his muscles. I looked up at him through my tears. "You think that there is an answer then?"

"There is always an answer, child. Just not necessarily the one we want." He nodded and walked away, lantern swinging shadows and light around him.

I sat another few minutes, wishing he were right. There's a certain comfort in his kind of faith, in letting a higher power take your worries, your woes and letting go. But he couldn't understand. In this situation, I was the higher power. For all intents and purposes, I was the one making the final decision. I stood and patted the Angel's wings, glad we'd restored her to her former glory. "Watch over him," I whispered. "He is a good man."

I let him go, on his quest to wander the night. I needed some answers.

I removed my clothes and shifted again, this time, carrying the clothing in my mouth. The night remained silent as I loped back to the ranch.

CHAPTER FORTY-ONE

". . . Tho' Nature, red in tooth and claw; With ravine, shriek'd against his creed . . ."

—*Alfred, Lord Tennyson*

The sound of a footstep made me look up. "Hey," I said. Instead of entering the Inn, I'd chosen to sit outside, on the same bench as before.

Adam motioned to the bench. "May I join you?"

"Always."

He sat, close, but not touching, as if he were afraid to set me off again. I inched closer so our thighs were touching. He put an arm around my waist and I laid my head on his shoulder.

"You were gone a while," he said. "I've been waiting."

"I went to the cemetery."

"You have different clothing on."

I nodded. "Yeah. I changed, forgetting to strip first. When I got to the cemetery, I found Antonio. He had some clothes. Did you know that crazy priest took a tent out there and is camping on-site? He wants to guard the place." I told Adam what we'd discussed. "I can't let it happen, Adam."

"I know." He kissed the side of my head. "I've no intention of asking this of anyone, either."

"They're all waiting for us?"

"Yes."

"I suppose we should go back inside."

"In a bit."

We sat there quiet in the dark, undisturbed for at least twenty minutes. I allowed myself to soak in the nearness of the one person who truly understood me. He had no choice, really. We were bonded, by blood, by breath, by love. I hadn't planned this, not so early in my life. I'd be thirty-eight in a few weeks. In my clan's reckoning, I was still a child. Normally, Change didn't happen until your fifties. But I had to be the special case, because I was the heir, winner of the random gene pool drawing. Only in my case, the randomness had been cut by the sharp knife of Minerva Kelly's manipulations.

"I still want to fight the bloody bastard," I said. "Find him, wound him, and force him to remove the Geas."

"That might work." Adam's tone clearly said "you're cute thinking that it would be so easy, but I still love you."

"There's plan B."

"And that is?"

I filled him in on my idea about my becoming vampire.

For several extremely long seconds, he said nothing, his entire body stilling. Crap. Had I pissed him off that much? I'd only ever known him to do this stillness thing when in the throes of an anger so deep, he had to control it lest he hurt someone. I cringed, not wanting to look at his face.

His hand began to stroke my hair as he relaxed. "My love, you do have a unique way of finding solutions."

I sat up. "You're not angry?"

"Not in the least." He chuckled and kissed me. "I'm not saying it's the best plan, but it might just work. I doubt that my brother would have considered such a selfless offer."

"A very stupid offer if you ask me." The taunt came from our right. We leaped up, both of us in a semi-crouch, defenses rising.

"Did you think it would be that easy?" Gideon strolled up the pathway, grinning. He wore black, a simple tee and slacks. His hair, once nearly as long as Adam's, hugged his scalp, shorn close. Preparing for battle?

"New 'do?" I said.

"Don't you think it suits me?" He preened, a hand running down his side, and onto his thigh. "I was going for a more metropolitan look."

"How did you—" I spat the words. He should not have been able to access the land. I'd warded it when we'd returned home.

"Breach the wards without you knowing?" He waved a hand. "You Called, my dear cousin. Despite our little . . . differences . . . I am still family."

"You're no family of mine, Gideon Kelly."

"Get off my land," Adam growled. "You trespass."

"It is not your land yet, Nightwalker, your human paperwork means little to the magick. Don't you feel it?" Gideon whirled like a giddy schoolchild. "It sings."

Beneath me, a thrum of energy, foul, bitter, oily, shook the ground as if it were trying to break through its prison walls. "When the land rejects you fully, I shall release them."

"To what end, Gideon?" Behind me, the scatter of running feet as our Protectors approached. Our bond had kicked in, alerting them to our danger. That they'd not sensed Gideon earlier was probably due to the same magick that had allowed him to cross the wards.

"To win." He threw up his hands and cast something in my direction that I didn't recognize. I ducked, only to hear the air sizzle with a fire shield. It surrounded us, burning nothing but clear air. We were stuck there until it vanished, or until I could figure out how to remove it. Adam, me, Tucker, Niko. The others clamored outside the shield.

"Go after him," Rhys yelled. "Bloody wanker!"

"No, don't!" I yelled back. "Every one of you stay put," I said. "He's dangerous and powerful. I don't want anyone to get hurt. We can't just—" The fire vanished. Gigi stood there, wiping her hands together.

"Go," she urged. "We'll hold the fort here."

"Hold the . . ." Then the noise hit us. Screams and cries from behind a storage shed. Flashes of light, green, red, orange through the windows as spells were cast and countered inside the Inn.

"How many?" Adam asked.

"Enough." Gigi turned to leave, then paused. "The four of you go, quickly. He's gone to the cemetery to begin his final spellcasting. I wish I could send more but we'll need everyone to fight here."

"He can't do that," I protested. "He has to wait for the full moon. For Lughnasa."

"He lied." Gigi pointed upward. "It's the dark of the moon. He will use that to his advantage." She whirled and ran in the direction of the shed. Vampires streamed from the nearby cottages, fangs bared.

We ran toward the gate, toward the van that was parked just inside. Small two-legged creatures bit and clawed at my legs as I passed them. I threw out stings and burn hexes, just enough to make them go away. I couldn't stop to finish them off, couldn't waste the energy.

Tucker, whose long legs soon outdistanced mine, pulled open the van door and fumbled under the mat for the keys. We did this out here, on our ranch, left keys in the common vehicles. A gremlin or pixie danced on the roof of the van, its big eyes bulging as it laughed. He held the keys in his hand. With a smirk, he tossed them in his mouth and ate them.

"Never mind," I yelled. "We can run."

Adam grabbed my hand and pulled at me. "Keira, stop. Take Tucker's hand. Niko, come." In an instant, I understood. We held on tight to each other and Adam muttered the syllables. With a rush, we slid Between, glimpses of Faery light now dimmed flew by us as Adam concentrated. I lent him what power I could, boosting our speed. With a pop, we came back into the mortal world less than a hundred yards from our target—the cemetery gate. He'd done it. Needs must.

"Niko and I will go to the overhang," Adam said. "You and Tucker can go in the front."

I headed for the main gate. I needed to warn the priest, to get him out of there—if he wasn't already dead. "Tucker, cover me, yeah? That bloody priest is camping out here."

"What the bloody blazes is he doing here?"

"Guarding it, he said. Wolf now?"

"Yes."

We pulled off our clothing and shifted, picking up

the discarded clothes in our teeth. We were on the same wavelength. Normally, I couldn't care less, but I did *not* want to face Gideon naked. We slinked closer to the tent. Antonio's fire was out, a tendril of woodsy smoke curling into the sky. Damn it. Was he taken? Was he hurt or killed?

I shifted back and pulled on the shirt and pants. "Tucker," I whispered. "Stay wolf for now. Go left. See if you can find the priest. I'll check to the right. If you find him and he's alive, get him the hell out of here."

The furry head nodded in understanding and slid left, behind a tombstone, keeping to the shadows. The final sliver of the moon still hung in the sky. Gigi was wrong, it wasn't the full dark of the moon yet, but just barely not. It was plenty for me to see by, though.

I crouched and crawled my way around the perimeter, trying to sense anything out of the ordinary. Beneath me, the Darkness roiled, hungry, anxious to escape its prison. Where was Gideon? I couldn't reach out to feel him, as I didn't want him to find me first. For all intents and purposes, I was practically blind and deaf. I couldn't use the senses I'd been born to use—the Talents drilled into me by Gigi, by my trainer, my aunts. Seeking, sounding, finding, all perfectly honed and great things to have, but each carried with it a signature energy trace. He'd know I was here.

A metaphysical thump sounded, its vibration cutting through me like a sonic boom. I fell onto a patch of burrs, biting my lip against the yell that wanted to break free. Fuck. What the hell was that? Then I knew. The door to Faery had slammed shut. That wasn't Gideon who'd done that. He wanted the door open so he could have his Darkness, his Dark Fae join him. I silently cheered whoever had had the *cojones* to attempt that maneuver.

My knee burned as I tried to crouch again. Damn it. I must have scraped it against stone, not even noticing. I cast a small healing spell, then froze, listening to hear if anyone reacted. When I heard only silence, I began to move again, this time, more carefully. I'd gotten all of three feet when I heard his voice.

"Looking for me, dear Cousin?"

CHAPTER FORTY-TWO

"When you look into an abyss, the abyss also looks into you."

—*Friedrich Nietzsche*

I rolled and ducked, tossing a binding spell in his direction. I still hoped that we could capture him, force him to undo the magick that bound this place to a sacrifice.

"Too easy, my dear." He taunted me from behind a tombstone. "I expected that."

"Expect this, bastard." I rose, and using both hands sent a ball of mage fire forward. It sparked, slid across the face of the large stone he'd ducked behind and splattered uselessly onto the dry grass. I didn't worry about the fire spreading, mage fire only ate flesh, not vegetation. Our own special version of napalm.

Behind me, a commotion. I ducked again, scooting away from my current position. Three vampires ran by, pursuing a couple of sharp-toothed pixies. I'd laugh, but the situation was far too serious for humor. Maybe later. If we survived this.

A flash blasted my eyes as a spell flew by me. I

blinked, glad he'd missed me, but then Darkness wrapped around me like a cocoon. I couldn't see, hear. My shouts stopped short, the sound cut off by the roiling Darkness. It smothered me in its density, shutting down too many of my senses. I dropped, crouching as low as I could, hoping to minimize myself as a target. I felt heat as something else whizzed by me. I rolled to my right and scuttled backward as soon as I faced upward.

"Dissipate, damn you," I whispered, struggling to remember the right word, the right spell to counter the blinding. *"Claro."* As it shredded, I tore the blinding spell away from my face and tossed it aside like so much dirt.

I sprang to my feet, hands out throwing defensive shield spells as I took stock of the situation. Two vampires down to my left. A small brown fey hung on the back of one of Gideon's fighters, long claws and teeth tearing skin, long tongue lapping up the free-flowing blood. At least three red-clad bodies sprawled behind him. Where had these people all come from? Had the fight at the Inn spilled out here, or were there more soldiers? I hoped it was the former.

Where the hell was Gideon?

Tucker's Berserker roar from behind startled me into another defensive roll. I recovered as quickly as I could, frantically trying to see if my brother needed help. Long arms swung wildly, an axe clutched in each hand. Tucker's face and hands were stained red with other people's blood, his braids dark and wet with it. An axe crunched bone as it met the slim neck of a dark elf—one of Gideon's Dark Fae, I wagered. *Good for you, Tucker,* I thought. Good for you.

"Keira, duck." I flattened as a silver knife flew

through the air, thudding into a nearby live oak. A hand reached down.

"Andrea. Didn't know you'd come." I straightened my shirt and brushed off some grass and twigs. "Enjoying the fight?"

A fierce grin appeared on her face. She was skinny, but taut with muscle, blond hair slicked back into a tight ponytail. "I got at least five of them before I got through the gate," she said. Wait. Gate. Vampires. Cemetery. Oh, yeah. No longer consecrated. It was getting hard to keep up.

"Where are Adam and Niko? I sent them to the overhang, but I don't know if they made it there."

She nodded, her eyes searching, keeping vigilant. "Yes, they are there. Adam meant to shut the door to Faery, to keep more of these creatures from coming out."

"So he's the one who did that?"

"He was able to close it?" She grabbed my arm and pulled us to one side, ducking behind a small statue of a young angel. "How do you know?"

"I felt it," I said. "The door slammed shut."

"Good. That Sidhe queen went up there with him."

"Angharad?"

"Yes, I believe that was her name," Andrea said. "Tall blond bitch with an attitude?"

I laughed. "That's her, all right."

Andrea pulled the silver knife out of the tree trunk with little effort, even though it was buried halfway to its hilt, at least four inches. "This will come in handy."

"It's silver." Vampires were allergic to silver.

She shrugged. "The handle isn't. There are a few things crawling around that dislike silver as much as we do."

"Then go for it." I prepared to continue my journey toward La Angel and I hoped, Gideon. "You seen my cousin?"

"The raving lunatic megalomaniac? He's around somewhere."

Oh, I was liking her more and more. We'd never gotten to know each other before she'd left the ranch to run security at Adam's estate in Great Britain. I was looking forward to a few girl chats with someone as deadly as I could be. Liz was great, but she was a pilot by trade and had few fighting skills. I could already see Andrea and I bonding over sparring sessions, us against my brothers. That would be a right treat.

"That's the one," I began to say when her hands pushed me and I stumbled over a low tombstone, my arms flailing. A silver blade, flat and deadly sliced through the air. With horror, I watched as it continued its arc, through flesh, sinew, and bone, to exit the other side of Andrea's thin neck. She fell, lifeless. Without a coherent thought, I pushed mage fire through my hands. It sparked and hit the Fae square in the face. His flesh dripped and sizzled as the fire ate its way inside, flesh falling in fiery gobbets to the ground. I watched in grim satisfaction.

"Die you bloody bastard," I whispered. Andrea's pale hair, gory with blood, was the last thing I saw as I slipped away intent on finding my final prey.

I had a hunch that Gideon was at the cave, doing whatever he could to reopen the door. The sounds of fighting were beginning to diminish, which must mean that only a few of his extra special brand of nasties had made it out before my guys and the Wicked Bitch of the Seelie Court had slammed the door against the rest. I stifled my anger over Andrea's death and kept moving, trying to hear Gideon's voice. Raving lunatic megalomaniacs weren't ever too quiet in the movies I watched. They liked to gloat. Maybe there was an Evil Overlord Handbook or something, like a football playbook. I could imagine it now: Tonight, we're running the Shotgun Split End Cross Halfback Draw, followed by an off-tackle Rant and Rave for good measure.

Sure enough, I heard the noise before I saw him. He was at the base of La Angel, three dead Dark Fae at his feet. He paced forward and backward, then would stop, turn to the cave mouth and fling his hands forward, muttering another spell. I watched, ready for action, but too amused to do anything about it. After several tries in various languages, he screamed, "Why won't you bloody open?"

"Try saying '*Mellon*,'" I called as I stood up and revealed myself. Oh, sarcasm, what a lovely, lovely weapon. I knew he'd read *Lord of the Rings* and would get the reference. I also knew it would piss him off.

With a growl, he whirled, a bolt of the same blinding spell arcing out from his fingertips. This time, though, I was ready. I dropped and rolled to the right, coming back up into a crouch behind the tombstone of one Josiah Bartlet.

"You bitch," Gideon snapped. "What did you do to the door?"

"I did nothing," I called from behind my hiding place. "It wasn't me."

"Then who the—"

"I believe you're looking for me." The drawling voice made me cheer inside. "*Son*. Or should I say, *former* son."

I leaped up to see Angharad standing like some goddess of destiny at the mouth of the cave, hair and dress as tidy as if she'd stepped out of her boudoir.

"*You* shut it? Why?" Gideon demanded. "We were working together. You've named me de facto heir until the child is born."

"No longer. When I agreed to your proposition, there was no mention of you placing a curse on this land, of subverting Challenge by encumbering it. You have broken not only Truce, but trust, Gideon son of Raven. You are riven from my family. You may no longer claim blood ties to the Seelie Sidhe."

"Your daughter is pregnant with a child you bound to me. A blood-bond you created. We did the ceremony."

Angharad laughed. "You truly believe that I would blood-tie my own flesh-and-blood to someone without his proving? There was no true bond since there is no child. A glamour only."

I stifled my instinct to laugh in Gideon's face—the player played. He'd been so intent on strutting his stuff as Big Man on Campus, he'd missed what should've become obvious to anyone of magick after more than a few days in Aoife's company—that the pregnancy was simply a spell to trick the mind. I'd only seen her for less than an hour, but I bet I'd have figured it out given enough face time with her.

"You lied!" Gideon's face looked like he was about to explode in an apoplectic fit. Me? I was sitting on a tombstone enjoying the show. Hells, all I needed was a tub of buttered popcorn, some greasy nachos, and a Big Gulp. Above on the overhang—balcony seats!—Adam and Niko watched, both of them as amused as I was.

" You failed *my* Challenge, my test, Gideon, Raven's

child." With this pronouncement, Angharad waved a hand and muttered a few words. In a flash, she slid out of sight into the Between.

Before I could begin my own gloating, Gideon threw up a hand and cast a flashbang. Caught off guard, I dove for the ground, but wasn't fast enough. My ears rang and eyes watered. I rolled, scrambled and rolled again, trying to keep moving in case he came for me. I couldn't hear, damn it. I let my eyes shut, tears streaming down my face. Trying to focus on my other senses, I *Reached,* trying to establish a perimeter of safety as I shielded. I couldn't throw any spells, in case I hit Adam or Niko. Minutes passed. Nothing happened, other than I sat there, waiting for the aftereffects to die down enough so I could maneuver.

When the ringing finally started to fade, I heard Adam's voice calling. "Keira, you all right? Gideon's gone."

I raised a hand above my head and waved it. "Fine. I'm fine," I said, my voice sounding in echoes in my own head. "I'm here."

"Stay still," Adam said. "There's no sign of any more of Gideon's fighters. You should be safe there."

That was good news. Though the fact Gideon had gone disturbed me.

Long minutes later I was finally able to blink the last of the tears out of my eyes. My hearing had returned to nearly normal. I stood, trying to get my bearings. La Angel was to my upper right. I made my way there.

Adam and Niko were arguing in quiet whispers.

"What is it? What's wrong?"

"I think we need to try to get the door open," Adam said. "We believe Gideon's gone Below to loose the Dark Fae into Seelie territory bypassing Above alto-

gether and letting them Between. He's after Angharad.
If he defeats her—"

For a swift moment, I hesitated, my instinct to let them
fight their battle in Faery and stay there, but I knew that
couldn't happen. If Gideon won, by whatever chance,
he'd be able to open the doors now shut. Her death would
mean the spells chaining them would vanish and he could
allow the Darkness free reign over the world.

"He's also got Minerva and Drystan," Niko supplied. "Adam didn't want to worry you."

"What the hell happened?" I asked. "I was out of
commission for about what, ten minutes?"

"More," Adam said. "A lot more. All this opening
and closing of the door and magickal activity seems to
have created pockets of unstable time. It seems to be
passing at different rates in different parts of the cemetery. We're mostly out of it up on the overhang, but we
noticed the anomalies as soon as we got up here. We'd
hoped to get a better sense of the action, to figure what
to do next when we saw you three."

I dropped my head and kicked at a rock, swearing
under my breath. Great. Fan-bloody-tastic. "So Gideon
snatched Gigi and your father?"

"More like swept them along as he slid Between,"
Adam said. "They'd just shown up when he slid out.
At the last possible second, he grasped their hands and
pulled them along with him. It happened too fast to get
to them."

"Do we know for sure he's Below?"

"The fact that he was yelling something about 'getting that bloody queen' leads me to believe so." Adam
shook his head. "I'm afraid if we don't open the door,
we may not be able to find him in Faery."

"Why not?"

"Going there through a door makes things more stable," Adam replied. "Trying to use pathways in the Between is fine if your goal is just to get to Faery and you have deep knowledge of navigating its Ways. I've long since lost that knowledge. We could be lost in there for years, trying to find a familiar place."

"In that case, I guess I have to open a door."

CHAPTER FORTY-THREE

"Then the king and all Israel with him offered sacrifices before the Lord."

—*1 Kings 8:62*

The mouth of the cave yawned wide and empty. Beyond it, if I concentrated, I could feel the energies of the door chained tightly to itself as if literal links of steel bound it. Part of me wanted to just throw all my energy at it, to see if I could burst the chains. Sure, I'd probably end up letting the rest of the Darkness and Chaos through. No doubt they, and it, were panting at the other side of that door waiting for their master to defeat Angharad. I sighed and focused, trying to see the spells the queen had used to create the bindings.

And if I figured out how to remove them? Could I do what Adam asked? Open Pandora's box and let it all out? Gideon might just win then, despite our having soundly routed his forces. Then again, if I didn't, we could lose Gigi and Drystan. Gideon's power was strong, fueled by the dark energies he'd allowed inside. He might simply incarcerate the two of them while he went looking for Angharad to take his anger out on her, but he might also decide he didn't need them any longer and kill them. It wasn't easy to kill a Sidhe king or the Kelly clan chief, but there were ways, and Gideon, no doubt, could put his hands on a number of those ways.

Hell of a choice I had, wasn't it?

I slammed my hand against the rough stone. "Damn him forever," I yelled into the impenetrable darkness within the cave. "Damn him, damn him, damn—FUCK!" I'd sliced open the side of my hand. I shook it and brought it to my mouth to ease the pain. The moonlight was enough to let me see the damage. Moonlight? No longer the dark of the moon, but now nearly half full! More of that pesky time imbalance. Great. Had I been in here nearly two weeks now? Were Adam and Niko frantic with worry?

I sucked at the wound. It wasn't horribly deep, but deep enough to draw blood. I was going to need to do a healing spell. I was pretty shite at it when it came to doing it on myself especially after tonight's battle, but this was a small enough cut. I shook my hand, trying to remove some of the blood so I could see the edges of the torn skin. Drops flung every which way, on the rock, on the ground. As the drops hit the parched dirt, the ground beneath me seemed to tremble, just a little, like a wee shrug.

"What was that?" I spoke out loud, my words swallowed by the night. I waited a moment, and nothing else happened. Surely my blood on the ground wouldn't—I squeezed the wound which had already begun to close and forced a few more drops of blood on the ground. Plop. Plop. They lay there in the dirt, shining. Nothing. Okay, then I must have imagined—

Another shudder, this time stronger, underneath my

feet. I dropped to one knee and placed my uninjured hand on the ground, palm flat to the dirt. The movement wasn't originating here. That much I could tell. I shut my eyes and concentrated, letting shields lower and my energy pour outward. I had to be careful, had to make sure that whatever was causing this didn't actually touch me, just in case it was some manifestation of the Darkness. I slid awareness just under the surface of the soil. "Find it," I whispered. My energy sang, pulsing in place as if sniffing out its prey. A moment later, it sped away, toward the center of the cemetery. I kept hold of it as I stood, worried that someone had inadvertently run into something he couldn't handle. The night remained silent as I exited the cave. No signs of any more fighting. With Gideon vanished, his minions had scattered. A few bodies still lay on the ground. Some his. A few ours. I peered up at the sky. I was back in normal time . . . or what seemed normal to me. The final, nearly transparent sliver of the moon hung among the stars, winking in and out of what could only be rain clouds gathering. Rain. Blessed be. Something had gone right tonight if we were getting rain.

Should I shift? I could scent things better as wolf. Yet, if I did, what if I came across something I had to fight with magick? I couldn't cast spells in animal form. At least, I didn't think so. Deciding against shifting, I followed the energy path. It shone for me, a silvery ribbon pulsing in the moonlight, as if made of the moon's own light, faint, but steady. I followed its path, extending my shields around me, strengthening my protection.

"Keira?" A soft voice called. Adam.

"I'm OK," I called back. I knew that Niko was probably chomping at the bit, his Protector instincts on overdrive, but I ruthlessly tamped down emotion. I didn't want either of them to join me just yet. Not until I knew what I faced.

The night was quiet as I carefully walked the path. No night insects calling, no breeze rustling the dead leaves. The path wandered a bit, as if following some-one's stride, not exactly straight, but more or less in the same direction. Where was it leading? This wasn't ex-actly a large place. The gate came into view, the light path veering to the right just before it. Was that Anto-nio? Had he made it away safely or had he hid during the battle? I didn't want to call out. If the priest had stayed and somehow survived, any lingering physical manifestation of the Darkness might hear me and find him first. I couldn't put him at risk.

The shining ribbon curved once more, between two gravestones, back again toward the rear of the ceme-tery, back in the direction I'd just come from, toward the Angel. I could see her some dozen yards or so in front of me, the edges of her wings faintly lit by the moon. A shadow passed in front of her. My heart thud-ded in my chest. I stopped, tried to focus my vision. A light wavered in front of the statue. Antonio again? Had he come to pray in the aftermath?

I saw that the path of my energy led directly to the clearing in front of the statue. I ran then, leaping over gravestones, over piles of dead leaves and grass. I let my unconscious take over as I wove through the tangled brush and undergrowth. Before I reached the clearing, I smelled it.

Blood. Fresh, liquid, and lots of it.

One last leap over a mutilated body and up a small rise and I froze.

Antonio knelt in front of La Angel, facing her, both arms held out a little to the side, a rosary dangling from his right hand. Blood dripped from his fingers, pooling on the ground. He'd set the lantern at the feet of the statue. She looked as if she were alive, illuminated by the dancing light. A breeze had sprung up, making even the shadows dance.

Soft words carried in the no longer still air. *"Ave Maria, gratia plena; Dominus tecum: benedicta tu in mulieribus, et benedictus fructus ventris tui Iesus. Sancta Maria, Mater Dei ora pro nobis peccatoribus, nunc et in hora mortis nostrae. Ave Maria, gratia plena; Dominus tecum: benedicta tu in mulieribus, et benedictus fructus ventris tui Iesus. Sancta Maria, Mater Dei ora pro nobis peccatoribus, nunc et in hora mortis nostrae."*

Over and over again he repeated the Latin prayer, the Hail Mary prayer, his voice weaker with every repetition.

"Antonio?" My feet wouldn't move, couldn't move. It was as if he'd cast a ward against me. How? I tried to move again, putting my whole energy into it. Nothing. My feet stuck to the ground, locked in place as if encased in concrete.

The priest's voice faltered. *"In hora mortis . . ."* He shuddered, a weak movement, and attempted to speak again. *"In hora mortis . . ."* At the hour of our death. Why?

"Why?" I screamed at him. "Why this?" My words fell flat, as if the wards he'd somehow raised blocked sound, as well as people. "Why are you doing this?" I struggled against the invisible glue that held me in place. C'mon, Keira Kelly. You are the heir. You have more power than this. Sweat beaded on my brow and trickled into my eyes as my muscles strained. The ground shivered and shook again, as if another earthquake was beginning. The blood scent grew stronger, permeated the air around me. I growled in frustration and sank to my knees, palms flat on the earth. "Let me through," I commanded in a whisper. "Let me—"

A bark and growl from behind me. I turned and fell to a sitting position.

Tucker leaped to my side and shifted back to human. He knelt next to me and took me into his arms. "Keira." He kept whispering my name over and over again, face buried in my hair. "I thought—" He stopped, his body tense as strung wire. "What?"

"Antonio," I said, slumping against my brother's chest. "He's . . ." I didn't finish, not needing to.

"He chose to be the sacrifice." Tucker's voice sounded awed. "Why?"

I pushed him away, needed to see this through. Needing to watch. The priest's body swayed as if pushed by the wind, which had increased. The wards fell.

"He's fading," I said, trying to scramble to my feet. "I want to—"

"No, you can't." Tucker put his arm around my waist. "He has to finish this. Don't make this worth nothing."

A soft cry from the priest, then the words again. The same prayer.

"I know." I sank back against Tucker, letting him take some of the weight from me. "I know."

"The cemetery is re-consecrated," Tucker said quietly. "Adam and Niko couldn't enter. They saw him from the overhang and tried to jump down, but he'd already managed to re-consecrate the ground."

I nodded and wiped my face of the tears that now flowed without interruption. "I didn't ask him to do this."

"I know." Tucker's arm tightened around my waist.

A noise from above made me look up. Adam and Niko stood atop the overhang once more. "We can't come down," Adam said softly. "He's completing the ritual. We wished to honor his choice."

I nodded, focusing only on the priest. I vaguely saw Adam and Niko bowing their heads, as if standing vigil. Niko's hands were folded, his lips moving in prayer. Of the four of us, he was the only one originally human, raised as a Christian. He was still a believer.

Time ticked slowly, minutes stretching into forever as I watched the life draining from the small old man. He'd lived several human life-spans, alone, outside of society, caring for a church no one attended. A part-fey human—someone like me, like Adam—had cursed him, caused him to live this unnatural life, yet he still had the humanity to do this—give his life, give his blood to save me from having to condemn others. He took the choice from me, took my burden and gave himself. I couldn't understand this. Couldn't know how he'd made this decision. But I knew that for the rest of my many, many centuries, I'd never forget him.

Thunder sounded in the distance. I looked up. Clouds scudded across the sky, hiding the moon. I realized that the wetness I was feeling on my face was no longer just my tears. It had begun to rain.

Fray Antonio slumped to one side. I pulled away from Tucker and rushed forward.

"Father," I said as I gently scooped an arm under his shoulders and held him up.

He smiled, his eyes fluttering closed. "It is raining."

"It is," I said, inanely.

One breath. Then a second. "All is well, then?"

I had to strain to hear him. "Yes."

"Good." His eyes opened and he stared into mine. "You must care for them all now," he said. "It is up to you."

I nodded. "I will."

He closed his eyes again. "I am at peace."

With a rattling breath, he was gone.

CHAPTER FORTY-FOUR

"The past cannot be cured."

—*Elizabeth I*

Before I could wipe away my tears, I heard him.

"So you think you figured it out, dear cousin." Gideon's smarmy voice made me clench my fists tighter.

"Did I not?" I tossed the words to him as casually as I could, considering the fact that I was standing in the rain, facing my once lover, now enemy.

Gideon laughed, a shrill mad sound. He'd lost it. Power slid to madness as he cackled. What was next, lunatic ranting? He threw his hands out, shrieking a spell.

I fell, rolling instinctively, then back on my feet with a shield spell surrounding me. My hands splashed bloody water as I extended my arms, whispering the mage fire out of my body. It sizzled away from me in direct line toward Gideon. A blink and he was gone, hiding behind some sort of dis-illusion, a notice-me-not stronger than I'd ever seen. I crouched behind a tombstone to *Listen*. There, to my right and forward about two dozen paces. I closed my eyes and focused, calling forth more magick. A quick toss over the stone and I rolled to my left, behind another marker.

"Bitch!" Gideon yelled. I felt the magick slice open his flesh. Arm perhaps? Too bad, nothing fatal. "You think you've won? You think the land belongs to you now? I was once able to open the door to Faery. I will do it again."

A flash to my right. Another spell gone awry. He still didn't know where exactly I was. Damn it, where was my cavalry, anyway? Though my vampires couldn't cross the newly consecrated ground, Tucker most certainly could. Maybe he was sneaking in under wolf guise. Gideon might could shapeshift since he theoretically had all the Talents, as I did, but he didn't grow up in a house full of them. I had, and I'd learned from the best.

"Still silent, my former love?" Gideon continued to taunt me. "Did you not understand the meaning of the Challenge? Was it too difficult for you?"

I ignored him. His voice hadn't moved, which meant he hadn't. Not much with the battle strategy this one.

Suddenly, I felt a presence behind me "Thanks, bro," I whispered.

"Not a problem." The quiet voice came from behind me. I turned my head to nod. There he was, crouched at the stone behind me, still in human form. He'd not spoken loud enough for Gideon to hear him over his own ranting.

I nodded and turned back toward Gideon. He really had lost it.

"Come on out, Keira," he said. "This is no fun without you. I want to show you. To show you how I've won."

"Not biting, Cousin," I yelled past a rumble of thunder. "You want to talk, then talk."

Another twisted laugh. Tucker slid next to me, now fully nude. "Want me to shift?"

I shook my head. "Not yet. I'm not sure what he's up to."

"The priest wasn't enough," Gideon ranted. "You think he fulfilled the Geas? Oh yes, he brought the rain, well, goody for him." Sounds of splashing made me peek around the left side of the stone. Nope, Gideon was just kicking water, but not moving anywhere closer.

"What the—?" Tucker whispered.

I shrugged. "He's gone batshit haywire full-on McRanty pants crazy."

"Don't be whispering about me, dear Keira," Gideon said. "I can hear you. Is that your darling brother with you? Too bad the dead men can't leave their perch now, but no, the priest took care of that. Funny, isn't it. He gave up his life for you, yet his sacrifice only blocked the ability for your vampires to rejoin you. What will they do when I kill you, Keira, what then?"

With no warning, Gideon's face appeared over the tombstone. I shrieked and rolled left, tossing a flashbang at him. After counting to five, I opened my eyes. "Tucker? Where are you?" I couldn't see him. The rain was heavier now, with flashes of lightning punctuating the rolling growl of thunder. A bark from my far right. I scrambled in a zigzag toward him, trying to avoid Gideon, who was blind and deaf from the flashbang, but yet throwing out curses and spells. In too little time he turned his head in my direction. Damn it, he'd tossed my spell as if it were no more than a Fourth of July sparkler.

"The land requires more lives," Gideon said. "Not just the life of someone who gave themselves willingly, that was a possibility I'd planned for." He cackled. "Don't you want to hear? Don't you want to understand?"

I pushed the wet hair from my face and stood figuring that if he was talking like this, he'd not be saying spells. "Okay, I'll bite," I said. "What in the name of all the hells are you talking about?"

"Hell, well, yes, it is Hell, isn't it?" He vanished into the cave mouth.

Tucker slinked around the right, positioning himself nearer to the entrance. If Gideon emerged, he might could jump him. I motioned to him to get ready, as I sensed—"No, wait!" I cried as Gideon appeared, this time dragging Gigi with him, and behind her, Drystan. Both were bound with some sort of chain. I could see the glimmer of magick on each link. He'd captured them and somehow dragged the both of them back through the Between to here.

"What the—?" I stepped back, nearly tripping over a tombstone.

"Did you not wonder why all the wardspells?" Gideon sneered. "I had a sprite paint them. She'd never bound to you or to me, but she wanted to be mine. I promised her she could. Our dear matriarch went Below, to confront my dear mama-in-law. My father did the same. At that point it was too easy."

"You don't think I didn't know that? After all, Angharad ended up disowning you, you idiot. Let them go and I'll be lenient." Okay, so I was totally full of shit right there, but I had no idea what to do. I wasn't fluent in mediator speak.

Gideon laughed and shoved Gigi and Drystan in front of him. Crazy like a fox indeed. He wasn't taking any chances now. If I let loose spells, I could very well injure them instead of Gideon. Tucker backed away, as well. Nothing he could do at this point without risking the others. "Angharad is a wicked queen, but not so stupid as to hold these two hostage. Oh no. I bespelled her when I found her. She never saw it coming."

I caught my breath. He what? How? How could Gideon Kelly have power over a high queen more than two millennia old? Sure, I figured they'd battle, but honestly, I never imagined him being able to take Angharad on and win.

"She's gone now," he said. "I forced her out Above. Captured her spirit and ate it."

Tucker stumbled, now in human form. I caught his gaze. We were up shit creek without even a boat, much less a paddle. I'd heard of spirit eaters, in legend, in song. They were fearsome creatures, a long-dead Talent bred out of Kelly. The last one had finally crossed over more than twelve centuries past. They could literally suck the life right out of you, taking your power, your anima, everything that made you, you. Had Gigi's insane breeding experiment given rise to a Talent long since lost?

Gigi's face grew hard as she listened to Gideon. I couldn't catch her eye. She was too caught up in my cousin's speech.

"Drystan was easier to catch," Gideon said. "He still wanted to talk to me. Imagine that."

"Gideon . . ."

"What, dear Cousin? Did you want to talk to me now?"

I wiped the rain from my face again, a fruitless task. "Why?"

"Why? You ask me that?" He forced Gigi and Drystan to sit on one of the boulders. "You who were mistreated in the Seelie Court, then forced Above, to live with Huw and those six dogs? You lived with *humans,* Keira," he said, making the word "human" sounds like "maggot" or "disease." They twisted you. You're less now. You could have stayed with me. Done this together with me. Been my queen."

"Done what? Kill? I'm not that sort of girl," I said. Though I kind of was. I'd killed before, not that long ago, and had little remorse. Not out of desire to win something, but yes, in revenge. In self-defense.

Gideon huffed a laugh. "Yes, well, not a discussion I wish to get into now. I think it's time to finish my job."

"And that would be?"

"The land will be mine, all of it, when I release the bonds on these two."

"How so?"

"The chains are life bonds," he said, his face shining with the light of zealotry. "Angharad helped me bespell them, thinking she was going to form alliance with me through her daughter. She thought the chains were for you and Adam."

I gripped the stone tight, ignoring the rough pain as it scraped my palms. I couldn't toss a spell, however much I wanted to. Any spell near those charmed bonds and both Gigi and Drystan, immortals though they may be, could die. Their life energies, which were tied up in those chains, would simply disintegrate if any random magick as much as touched one link.

"So now what, Gideon?" I asked. "You kill them and

then what?" I kept him talking as Tucker slid behind me, low to the ground. Maybe, just maybe, if we worked it right . . .

"Then I shall rule. All lands beholden to them will come to me."

"And me?" I challenged.

Gigi's head raised at this, her eyes focused and flashing. She was trying to communicate something to me, only I didn't have a clue. I couldn't split my attention, couldn't afford to take my eyes off Gideon. Her gaze cut to him, then to me. She nodded her head. All I could do was to go with my gut here and hope she could follow my lead.

Gideon's eyes narrowed as he studied me. "You, my dear, I save for last. It will be a pleasure to see your own life's blood nourishing this once parched dirt." He motioned to the ground below him. "You will join the priest in death."

"I'm not the only heir left alive," I said. "Despite your well-laid plan. If Drystan dies, then Adam becomes King of the Unseelie Court. You're plain shit out of luck, Cousin."

"Bring it on," Gideon growled. "Once I take their energy, your man will be no match for me. He will die the true death, as will any blood-bonded to you." He ran a hand through his sopping hair. "There's a spell for that, don'tcha know?"

I sprang, another flashbang again at my fingertips, both hands casting at Gideon's face as I sent a silent plea to the powers that be to help me avoid the chains. At my movement, Gigi pulled Drystan with her to the side of the boulder and onto the ground behind it.

CHAPTER FORTY-FIVE

"Better to burn out, than to fade away . . ."
    —Neil Young, "Hey Hey, My My (Into the Black)"

"**O**ne," I called as I ran forward, letting my magick tell me where I was. "Two, Three." I was counting on my great-great-granny to hold onto my insane cousin long enough for me to get there and to keep her eyes shut while I was counting.

On "ten," I jumped. Gigi's feet pushed out, catching Gideon's calves. As he stumbled, I snagged him, wrapping my arms around his arms and torso while binding him with my own version of a rope charm. "Bind tight now," I whispered as the vine-like rope twisted around my cousin's arms, hands, legs, neck. "Bind especially tight." I let him go and watched as the rope slid across Gideon's face, forcing his mouth open, digging into his tongue. I looked only long enough to know he couldn't get free. Then I went to help Gigi and Drystan.

"There's nothing you can do to help us," Gigi said as Tucker joined me and we both hauled them to a sitting position back on the boulder. Drystan remained silent, all the spark gone out of him. Their chains twinkled in the rain like little faery lights.

"What do you mean?" I asked. "We've neutralized him. He'll take these off. I know it. He's a coward at heart."

Strangled sounds came from said coward. I didn't even bother to turn around.

"Ah, dear child," Gigi said with a wan smile. "I was foolish with that one. These chains cannot be broken, not even by him."

"Wait, are you telling me—?"

Drystan's broken voice tore my attention from Gigi. "My son was all too thorough, child. He created this spell so that anyone breaking the chains, even him, would end with the same result. The one breaking the chain would sap our spirits. We shall die."

"No," I said. "No and no and no. You are still alive. There is still a chance."

With a soft whoosh, two bodies joined us, having leaped from above. Adam and Niko.

Tears were in Adam's eyes as he cupped his father's face in his palm. "I regret this, Father. More than I can say."

Drystan nodded. "You will be a good king, my son."

"Wait just a fucking minute," I demanded. "No giving up allowed. I did not go through all of this to give the fuck up. And how the hell are you and your sidekick here able to be on this ground anyway? It's consecrated again."

Adam stroked his father's hair and looked at me. "Running water," he said. "Water breaks magick. At least temporarily insulates us."

"Then water can very well break the magick of this—"

"No, Keira, dearling," Gigi interrupted. "This isn't earth magick that enslaves us. It's Dark spirit magick."

"Then what do you suggest we do?" I asked. "I can't. I just can't." With tears flowing down my cheeks, I embraced my great-great-grandmother. "No," I whispered.

"No worries, pet," she said in a bright voice. "You will be a good queen."

"Queen?"

"Adam will inherit his father's throne," she said. "Nice that he's rediscovered his magick, isn't it?"

I sobbed and held onto her. "Tell me you didn't set all this up."

She chuckled, her voice growing weaker. "The battle? Gideon's insanity? No. Even I'm not that good."

"Son." Drystan croaked the word. "Rule well. Teach them to survive in this new day. This modern world."

"You want me to bring them Above?" Did he?

Drystan nodded. "It is time we learned to live here as well as Below. Isolating ourselves only leads to . . ." He coughed and choked.

"Don't speak," Adam said and wiped the spittle from Drystan's mouth. "I understand."

"Let them mingle with the mortals. Learn to be a part of the world you know. Too many died tonight."

I stared at him. We'd lost a few, sure, but I wouldn't count that as too many, unless he meant even one life.

"Most of the Seelie Court died in battle," Gigi said, taking up where Drystan left off. "My grandson was ruthless. He lured them Between, used his power to drink their spirits."

"That's why he was so powerful. But, Gigi, I don't get it. Why was I able to take him down?"

"For that, you must thank the priest," she replied.

"His sacrifice was not in vain. He was able to make this ground sacred once again, to cleanse it of Darkness. Gideon's power lay in the Darkness he'd consumed. It left him."

"And he lost his mind." I saw it now. My cousin had banked on ingesting enough spirits, enough souls to fuel him, to bolster his core power to a point where he could best us all. It would have been a win for him had it not been for Antonio, a broken man, who only wanted to die in peace. I hoped he'd found that. That he'd made it to his heaven to be reunited with his lost love. Sure, I knew that most Catholics believe that suicide was a mortal sin and that both Antonio and Guadalupe were now burning in eternal hellfire. But I didn't care. I didn't believe in Hell. Hell was here, right now, right in front of me as I watched the woman who was my mentor and guide, and yes, often the bane of my existence, fade away in front of me, choosing death so I could live. A few gurgles reminded me that Gideon still drew breath. I ignored the sounds, knowing that eventually, there would be no more.

"I only now began to really know you," I said to Gigi. "We would've been quite the pair, wouldn't we?"

"Yes," she whispered. "I regret having so little time to train you, child." With a kiss to my cheek, she stood and *pushed*. Her arms flew out to her side, as did Drystan's, breaking their bonds. Without another word, they faded into the rain. The empty chains fell to the ground. I stood a moment, watching as Gigi's spirit shimmered forth. She smiled at me and I knew what I had to do. After all, I'd trained for this. Trained to be an Escort. I took her hands and closed my eyes, concentrating. In less than the time it took to count to twenty, it was done. I'd opened the Veil. She walked through, her eyes sparking. I sobbed as it closed. She had very much taught me well. This had been my first task with the Family. I'd learned to escort those who'd tired of living and wanted to move on. I didn't know what was on the other side. All I knew was how to open that particular door and how to be there to help them across. I'd never expected to have to do it for her.

Adam and I clung to each other as the rain continued to drench us. A moment later, a soft vibration worked its way up, inside of me. Energy filled me as I sobbed in Adam's arms, his own energy thrumming in time with mine. I knew this magick, this power. It was hers, Gigi's. I could feel Drystan's essence filling Adam. Those bloody, bloody rulers. By dying, they offered themselves to us. Made their energy part of us.

Tucker and Niko held each other next to Adam and me; the four of us supporting each other in our grief.

Behind me, the strangulated gasps stopped as the rope vines continued their work. Eventually, the noises stopped. So did the vines.

CHAPTER FORTY-SIX

"Let the rain kiss you. Let the rain beat upon your head with silver liquid drops. Let the rain sing you a lullaby."
—Langston Hughes

Three days of rain replenished the hopes of the Rio Seco, the dry river dry no more as the much needed water filled cisterns, wells, and watering tanks all throughout the county. Nearly all the flu victims were now at home recovering and no new cases had been reported in the last forty-eight hours. At the Wild Moon, the party hadn't stopped in more than forty-eight hours. Kelly, fey, and vampire alike rocked twenty-four seven, as food, wine, and all sorts of liquors flowed as abundantly as the rain—a wake and remembrance for Minerva, the Kelly of Clan Kelly. For Drystan, high king of the Unseelie Sidhe. By the morning of the third day, the downpour had gentled into a soft, misty fog. Not enough sunlight to fry my vampires if they wanted to go outside—and they did, the lot of them. Dancing, singing, carousing, celebrating life. Everyone partied.

"We need to go," I said as I rolled over in bed and looked at my sated and very pleased husband.

He grinned and brought a lock of my hair to his mouth and kissed it. The day after the battle, he'd asked Jane to cut his own long mane. I'd laughed and left him to it. When I'd returned, he'd sported a cropped cut. I almost hadn't recognized him. He looked amazing, not that he'd slacked in that department before. Niko and Tucker had followed suit. I'd shaken my head and accepted it. What else could I do? I recognized it for what it was, a symbolic shearing off of the past. We had to mainstream soon, bring together all our worlds now that Adam and I had inherited the rule of Kelly and the Unseelie Court. I'd not cut my own hair yet, oddly reluctant to let it go. I was doing it later today, though. After we completed our final task. After it was all done. I wanted to bury the priest. To give him his last official rites as a human. Then, I'd be done with the past, ready to move forward into the future.

A knock on the door. "It's me," Tucker announced and entered without waiting for us to say anything. We'd all grown closer since that night. Now, we knew with a simple mental ping where each of us was and what he or she was doing. Niko and Tucker knew when not to bother us and we knew the same about them. It certainly made things easier.

He bounded inside and hopped on the bed next to Adam, propping his head on his hand. "We're nearly ready," he said. "I figured I'd come get you guys, otherwise, we'd have to wait all night."

"Bea and Dixxi get off okay?"

"Yup. They'll be in New York for the week. Ciprian said their paperwork would be ready by the time we're ready to go."

"Good." We'd made a decision that night, after we'd

all gone home, after telling the others what happened, and after comforting everyone who was still alive. We'd come out way ahead there, too. Seems that most of Gideon's followers had very little knowledge of the world Above. Kellys and vampires held the upper hand easily, dispatching all the enemies with only one loss— the commercial stoves in the kitchen. Somehow, they'd blown up. A spell gone awry or something. In any case, that was a small price to pay. I'd told Niko and Adam about Andrea's death on the way back to the ranch. We'd cried for hours, the four of us together, then had fallen asleep in mine and Adam's bed, exhausted and needing to be near each other. We'd not woken up until the party was into its second day.

Now, the four of us headed back to the cemetery. I drove my Rover instead of Tucker's van with the blackout windows. We didn't need it because of the overcast skies. I'd not bothered to check the forecast because I could now tell the weather at least fifty times more accurately than the most sophisticated equipment. This misty day would remain so through at least sundown, plenty of time for us to do what we needed to do.

The door to Faery remained spelled shut and I intended to keep it that way. It's what Gigi wanted. I knew, because when she'd died, she'd sent every bit of her energy into me. That was the true secret of the Kelly clan chief. Each of them passed along their knowledge and their energy to their successor. I now knew what she'd felt about me, the overwhelming pride, the sheer joy in seeing me grow. She'd been harsh, because she'd been afraid. Afraid that Angharad would learn of my abilities, and come to claim me for herself. That would have never happened, but she'd had no way of knowing for sure.

Tonight, after the sun went down, we'd leave this place for good. The plane was already fueled up and waiting on our runway. John and his family had left this morning on a commercial flight to prepare the manor for our arrival. This time, we weren't coming back. We signed over the ranch to Carlton Larsen. He didn't know that yet. The paperwork wouldn't arrive on his desk until we were long gone. I loved Texas. Loved this ranch and this town and the people in it. But home was were my heart was and that meant Adam and my blood family. Ciprian had arranged for passports for Bea and Dixxi under some sort of rush process. They were going to England with us, sponsored by us as family members. I didn't ask questions. I just took my brother's word that the fix was on. The rest of us all had UK citizenship, so this wasn't a problem. Dixxi could set up her genetics lab and work with some of the best scientists on the planet. Bea could have her wer baby in peace. Tio and Tia had elected to retire south, to Corpus Christi, instead of joining Bea in England. Noe, her young nephew, wanted to remain in Texas, staying with a distant cousin so he could finish college.

I liked it when all my plans fell into place. We'd fought and won, with minimal losses . . . though my heart broke every time a new memory of Gigi's flashed into my conscious. She'd been nearly two thousand years old. I couldn't mourn her short life, nor could I mourn the loss of knowledge that hadn't actually been lost. Instead, I toasted the memory of one of the most enigmatic and infuriating women I'd ever known.

I drove right up to the cemetery gate and the four of

us entered. Enough water still flowed along the ground to allow Adam and Niko to come inside. The place looked as if nothing had ever happened.

"Who?" I whispered aloud as I looked in all directions.

Every tombstone was once again in its place. Every statue whole and standing tall. No sign of bodies, blood, nor debris. Not a whisper of Darkness disturbed the peace, only fresh flowers on each and every single grave indicated that anyone had been there at all. A sprig of rosemary—for remembrance, a voice whispered in my head—and a single white flower, six-petaled with a pointy tip on each petal and a dark center.

"Star-of-Bethlehem," Niko said. "For hope."

I nodded. "Nice. But who did this?"

"Some brownies." Daffyd walked toward us, having exited the cave mouth. "They wanted to help. To make amends for their kin."

"They had nothing to do with the destruction," I said. "They had no need."

"No, but they did have a right," Daffyd answered as he stepped through the stillness.

"They did have a right," I agreed. "And you? What brings you back here? The door is still closed."

"It is," he confirmed. "Once again, though, I put a warding on it. This time, to tell me if you were near."

I laughed. "Well, here we are, dear Cousin."

"Yes. And with two vampires during the day. Did things change that much? I admit, I know little of your kind, but it was my understanding that the day was anathema. They are on sacred ground, as well."

"Only the sun," Adam said. "There is little sunlight today." He held out a hand. The soft moisture collected in his palm. "The earth is happy and the running water allows us to be here for a time."

Daffyd smiled. "I am glad you all came," he said. "I wanted to let you know that we took the liberty of removing the body of Antonio, the man of his god."

"You did? Why? We came here to collect him, so he could be buried properly."

"He has been taken to a proper resting place," Daffyd assured me. "We wish to keep him with us, lying in state, as a remembrance."

I was taken aback by his statement. "Remembrance of what?"

"What true selflessness is. He sacrificed himself so that you did not have to make that choice. That is true trust and faith."

I took Daffyd's hand. "He was not the only one. Thank you, Cousin."

"Daffyd, might I ask . . . what happened to Aoife?" I looked at Adam in surprise. I'd totally forgotten about Angharad's daughter.

"She elected to retire to another part of Faery with her attendants. You do realize she was never with child."

"Yes. Her mother told us so," I said.

"Then you also know that your mother, Branwen, left with Aoife, as well."

"She did? Then who rules?" And here I'd thought everything was sussed out in the Seelie Court. They'd had plenty of heirs. Aoife, followed by Branwen, followed by . . . oh, holy hells bells. I opened my mouth but no words came out.

"Yes, cousin," Daffyd said. "You are next in line for the throne." He kneeled, his robes spreading onto the muddy ground. "Welcome, Cousin. Welcome, my queen."

Adam shook his head. "To think I thought this was all over."

"Bloody unlikely," I snapped. Why hadn't I realized that? True, I'd not known that Aoife would keep to her intent and exempt herself from ruling, especially now that Gideon and her mother were both dead, but Branwen? I guess she really didn't want to play politics. I sighed. "What does this mean for me now, Daffyd?"

"For now, nothing," he said. "If you'll give me leave to handle things for a short time, you can continue with your plans up here. Once you get settled in your new home, then come Below. We can plan then."

"Very well," Adam said. "Thank you. We'll be in England by morning and will settle at my estate in Wiltshire."

"Most excellent!" Daffyd's face lit up. "There is a door very close to you then."

"Yes, I know." Adam smiled. "At Stonehenge."

Stonehenge? Oh, that's just bloody wonderful.

"Then perhaps we shall see each other shortly after all," Daffyd said.

"Perhaps so." Adam nodded.

"May I then wish you a blessed and fruitful marriage," he said. "I was not able to attend your Reception and your joining."

"My thanks," I said after I'd wrapped my head around the fact that we were going to live near Stonehenge. Yeah, like that wasn't a hotbed of supernatural power or anything. Adam hadn't told me, but to be fair, if I'd stopped to think for more than two minutes, I would have put two and two together and come up with ancient stone monument. I mean, where else would a vampire build an estate?

"May your union be also blessed with many children," Daffyd continued.

"That's not exactly possible," I laughed. "Vampires can't make babies." My aunt Jane had used that line on me once, begging me to come home and make wee babies for the good of the Clan lines. I'd balked. Thank goodness.

Daffyd's eyes narrowed. "Surely that is a fallacy," he said. "The reason Gideon took up with Aoife in the first place was that he was deathly afraid that you and Adam would procreate, and result in Minerva and Drystan giving the rule to you both."

"It is magick that powers me, Daffyd," Adam explained. "I have no viable seed. I have a heart which does not beat unless I will it to."

"No," Daffyd insisted. "You've returned to yourself. You are whole again. I can feel it."

Was he right? I'd not noticed but then again, I'd noticed little but sleep, eat, sleep these last couple of days. We'd talked in bed this morning, but had done little else. Sure, he had Sidhe magick, but . . . we'd even shared blood, and he'd fed as per usual. He'd needed to feed, had felt hollow, he'd said.

"Adam, if I may." He nodded and I placed my palm against his chest. He wore cotton today, in deference to the wet weather. The soft material slid against my skin. I focused deeper. First, only the familiar flavor, the taste/scent/feel of the same man I'd shared a bed and so much else with over the past nine months. Then there it was, a flutter, vague as a butterfly's wings or the breath of a flower petal as it touched your skin. Deep within, his energy had changed. No longer just the deep musky spice and vanilla scent of the vampire part of him, I also sensed the green, the living energy of the Sidhe. As I discovered it, so did he. Nowhere near as strong as my own heartbeat, but there nonetheless.

"What happened?" His voice was barely audible as he placed his palm over mine and followed my awareness inside.

"A resurrection of sorts," Daffyd said. "The living part of you is now blended with the other."

"What does that mean?" Adam sounded bewildered. "I can feel it. Something different, but I'm still not truly alive."

"I do not know," Daffyd admitted. "You are the first vampire I know that began life as Sidhe. You are no doubt the first vampire that has merged his two natures."

Adam blinked against tears that threatened to fall. I pulled him close and whispered, "It's always something, isn't it? At least life won't get boring."

He grinned and kissed me. "No, I don't suppose it will."

The End

For in that sleep of death what dreams may come,
When we have shuffled off this mortal coil,
Must give us pause. There's the respect
That makes calamity of so long life.

—William Shakespeare
Hamlet, Act 3, Scene 1

Fantasy.
Temptation.
Adventure.

Visit PocketAfterDark.com, an all-new website just for Urban Fantasy and Romance Readers!

- Exclusive access to the hottest urban fantasy and romance titles!

- Read and share reviews on the latest books!

- Live chats with your favorite romance authors!

- Vote in online polls!

 www.PocketAfterDark.com

26119

EVIL DOESN'T STAND A CHANCE

Bestselling Urban Fantasy from Pocket Books!